Make time for friends.
Make time for Debbie Macomber.

DEBBIE MACOMBER

Summertime Dreams

DEBBIE MACOMBER

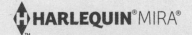

HARLEQUIN®MIRA®

Harlequin MIRA is a registered trademark of Harlequin Enterprises Limited, used under licence.

First Published in Great Britain 2016
By Harlequin Mira, an imprint of HarperCollins*Publishers*
1 London Bridge Street, London, SE1 9GF

© 2016 Harlequin Books S.A.

ISBN 978-1-848-45446-0

The publisher acknowledges the copyright holder of the individual works as follows:
A Little Bit Country © 1990 Debbie Macomber
The Bachelor Prince © 1994 Debbie Macomber

0716

Our policy is to use papers that are natural, renewable and recyclable products and made from wood grown in sustainable forests. The logging and manufacturing processes conform to the legal environmental regulations of the country of origin.

Printed and bound by
CPI Group (UK) Ltd, Croydon, CR0 4YY

A Little Bit Country

As always, to my wonderful husband and children, who fill my life with laughter and love. Special thanks to Nicole Jordan for a hundred different things, but mostly for believing in me.

One

"Help! Fire!" Rorie Campbell cried as she leaped out of the small foreign car. Smoke billowed from beneath the hood, rising like a burnt offering to a disgruntled god. Rorie ran across the road, and a black-and-white cow ambled through the pasture toward her, stopping at the split-rail fence. Soulful brown eyes studied her, as if the cow wondered what all the commotion was about.

"It's not even my car," Rorie said, pointing in the direction of the vehicle. "All of a sudden smoke started coming out."

The cow regarded her blankly, chewing its cud, then returned lazily to the shade of a huge oak tree.

"I think it's on fire. Dan's going to kill me for this," Rorie muttered as she watched the uninterested animal saunter away. "I don't know what to do." There was no water in sight and even if there had been, Rorie didn't have any way of hauling it to the car. She was so desperate, she was talking to a cow—and she'd almost expected the creature to advise her.

"Howdy."

Rorie whirled around to discover a man astride a chestnut stallion. Silhouetted against the warm afternoon sun, he looked like an apparition smiling down at her from the side of the hill opposite Dan's car.

"Hello." Rorie's faith in a benign destiny increased tenfold in that moment. "Boy, am I glad to see another human being." She'd been on this road for the past two hours and hadn't encountered another car in either direction.

"What seems to be the problem?" Leather creaked as the man swung out of the saddle with an ease that bespoke years of experience.

"I...I don't know," Rorie said, flapping her hands in frustration. "Everything was going just great when all of a sudden the car started smoking like crazy."

"That's steam."

"Steam! You mean the car isn't on fire?"

The man flipped the reins over his horse's head and walked toward the hood of the sports car. It was then that Rorie realized the man wasn't a man at all, but a boy. Sixteen, or possibly a little older. Not that Rorie was particular. She was just grateful someone had stopped. "A friend of mine insisted I drive his MGB up to Seattle." She sighed. "I should've known that if anything went wrong, I'd be at a total loss about what to do. I should've known..."

The boy whipped a large blue-starred hankie from the hip pocket of his faded jeans and used it to protect his hand while he raised the hood of her car. The instant he did, a great white cloud of steam swirled up like mist from a graveyard in a horror movie.

"I...thought I'd take the scenic route," Rorie explained, frantically waving her hand in front of her face to dispel the vapor. "The man at the gas station a hundred miles back said this is beautiful country. He said I'd miss some of the best scenery in Oregon if I stuck to the freeway." Rorie knew she was chattering, but she'd never experienced this type of situation before or felt quite so helpless.

"It's not only the best scenery in the state, it tops the whole country, if you ask me," the boy murmured absently while he examined several black hoses beneath the raised hood.

Rorie looked at her watch and moaned. If she wasn't in Seattle before six, she'd lose her hotel reservation. This vacation wasn't starting out well—not at all. And she'd had such high expectations for the next two weeks.

"I think you've got a leak in your water pump," the teenager stated, sounding as though he knew what he was talking about. "But it's hard to tell with all that fancy stuff they got in these foreign cars. Clay can tell you for sure."

"Clay?"

"My brother."

"Is he a mechanic?" Rorie's hopes soared.

"He's done his share of working on cars, but he's not a mechanic."

Rorie gnawed on her lower lip as her spirits plummeted again. Her first concern was getting to a phone. She'd make the necessary arrangements to have the car repaired and then call the hotel to ask if they'd hold her room. Depending on how close she was to the nearest town, Rorie figured it would take an hour for a tow truck to arrive and then another for it to get her car to a garage. Once there, the repairs shouldn't take too long. Just how hard could it be to fix a water pump?

"How far is it to a phone?"

The young man grinned and pointed toward his horse. "Just over that ridge…"

Rorie relaxed. At least that part wasn't going to be much of a problem.

"…about ten miles," he finished.

"Ten miles?" Rorie leaned her weight against the side of the car. This was the last time she'd ever take the scenic route and the last time she'd ever let Dan talk her into borrowing his car!

"Don't worry, you won't have to walk. Venture can handle both of us. You don't look like you weigh much."

"Venture?" Rorie was beginning to feel like an echo.

"My horse."

Rorie's gaze shifted to the stallion, who had lowered his head to sample the tall hillside grass. Now that she had a chance to study him, she realized what an extraordinarily large animal he was. Rorie hadn't been on the back of a horse since she was a child. Somehow, the experience of riding a pony in a slow circle with a bunch of other six-year-olds didn't lend her much confidence now.

"You…you want me to ride double with you?" She was wearing a summer dress and mounting a horse might prove…interesting. She eyed the stallion, wondering how she could manage to climb into the saddle and still maintain her dignity.

"You wearing a dress and all could make that difficult." The boy rubbed the side of his jaw, frowning doubtfully.

"I could wait here until someone else comes along," she offered.

He used his index finger to set his snap-brim hat further back on his head. "You might do that," he drawled, "but it could be another day or so—if you're lucky."

"Oh, dear!"

"I suppose I could head back to the house and grab the pickup," he suggested.

It sounded like a stroke of genius to Rorie. "Would you? Listen, I'd be more than happy to pay you for your time."

He gave her an odd look. "Why would you want to do that? I'm only doing the neighborly thing."

Rorie smiled at him. She'd lived in San Francisco most of her life. She loved everything about the City by the Bay, but she couldn't have named the couple in the apartment next door had her life depended on it. People in the city kept to themselves.

"By the way," he said, wiping his hands with the bright blue handkerchief, "the name's Skip. Skip Franklin."

Rorie eagerly shook his hand, overwhelmingly grateful that he'd happened along when he did. "Rorie Campbell."

"Pleased to meet you, ma'am."

"Me too, Skip."

The teenager grinned. "Now you stay right here and I'll be back before you know it." He paused, apparently considering something else. "You'll be all right by yourself, won't you?"

"Oh, sure, don't worry about me." She braced her feet wide apart and held up her hands in the classic karate position. "I can take care of myself. I've had three self-defence lessons."

Skip chuckled, ambled toward Venture and swung up into the saddle. Within minutes he'd disappeared over the ridge.

Rorie watched him until he was out of sight, then walked over to the grassy hillside and sat down, arranging her dress carefully around her knees. The cow she'd been conversing with earlier glanced in her direction and Rorie felt obliged to explain. "He's gone for help," she called out. "Said it was the neighborly thing to do."

The animal mooed loudly.

Rorie smiled. "I thought so, too."

An hour passed, and it seemed the longest of Rorie's life. With the sun out in full force now, she felt as if she was wilting more by the minute. Just when she began to suspect that Skip Franklin had been a figment of her overwrought imagination, she heard a loud chugging sound. She leaped to her feet and, shading her eyes with her hand, looked down the road. It was Skip, sitting on a huge piece of farm equipment, heading straight toward her.

Rorie gulped. Her gallant rescuer had come to get her on a tractor!

Skip removed his hat and waved it. Even from this distance, she could see his grin.

Rorie feebly returned the gesture, but her smile felt brittle. Of the two modes of transportation, she would have preferred the stallion. Good grief, there was only one seat on the tractor. Where exactly did Skip plan for her to sit? On the engine?

Once he'd reached the car, he parked the tractor directly

in front of it. "Clay said we should tow the car to our place instead of leaving it on the road. You don't mind, do you?"

"Whatever he thinks is best."

"He'll be along any minute," Skip explained, jumping down from his perch. He used a hook and chain to connect the sports car to the tractor. "Clay had a couple of things he needed to do first."

Rorie nodded, grateful her options weren't so limited after all.

A few minutes later, she heard the sound of another vehicle. This time it was a late-model truck in critical need of a paint job. Rust showed through on the left front fender, which had been badly dented.

"That's Clay now," Skip announced, nodding toward the winding road.

Rorie busied herself brushing bits of grass from the skirt of her dress. When she'd finished, she looked up to see a tall muscular man sliding from the driver's side of the pickup. He was dressed in jeans and a denim shirt, and his hat was pulled low over his forehead, shading his eyes. Rorie's breath caught in her throat as she noticed his grace of movement—a thoroughly masculine grace. Something about Clay Franklin grabbed her imagination. He embodied everything she'd ever linked with the idea of an outdoorsman, a man's man. She could imagine him taming a wilderness or forging an empire. In his clearly defined features she sensed a strength that reminded her of the land itself. The spellbinding quality of his steel-gray eyes drew her own and held them for a long moment. His nose had a slight curve, as though it had been broken once. He smiled, and a tingling sensation Rorie couldn't explain skittered down her spine.

His eyes still looked straight into hers and his hands rested on his lean hips. "Looks as if you've got yourself into a predicament here." His voice was low, husky—and slightly amused.

His words seemed to wrap themselves around Rorie's throat, choking off any intelligent reply. Her lips parted, but to her embarrassment nothing came out.

Clay smiled and the fine lines that fanned out from the corners of his eyes crinkled appealingly.

"Skip thinks it might be the water pump," she said, pointing at the MGB. The words came out weak and rusty and Rorie felt even more foolish. She'd never had a man affect her this way. He wasn't really even handsome. Not like Dan Rogers. No, Clay wasn't the least bit like Dan, who was urbane and polished—and very proud of his little MGB.

"From the sounds of it, Skip's probably right." Clay walked over to the car, which his brother had connected to the tractor. He twisted the same black hose Skip had earlier and shook his head. Next he checked to see that the bumper of Dan's car was securely fastened to the chain. He nodded, lightly slapping his brother's back in approval. "Nice work."

Skip beamed under his praise.

"I assume you're interested in finding a phone. There's one at the house you're welcome to use," Clay said, looking at Rorie.

"Thank you." Her heart pounded in her ears and her stomach felt queasy. This reaction was so unusual for her. Normally she was a calm, levelheaded twenty-four-year-old, not a flighty teenager who didn't know how to act when an attractive male happened to glance in her direction.

Clay walked around to the passenger side of the pickup and held open the door. He waited for Rorie, then gave her his hand to help her climb inside. The simple action touched her; it had been a long time since anyone had shown her such unselfconscious courtesy.

Then Clay walked to the driver's side and hoisted himself in. He started the engine, which roared to life immediately, and shifted gears.

"I apologize for any inconvenience I've caused you," Rorie said stiffly, after several moments of silence.

"It's no problem," Clay murmured, concentrating on his driving, doing just the speed limit and not a fraction more.

They'd been driving for about ten minutes when Clay turned off the road and through a huge log archway with ELK RUN lettered across the top. Lush green pastures flanked the private road, and several horses were grazing calmly in one of them. Rorie knew next to nothing about horse breeds, but whatever these were revealed a grace and beauty that was apparent even to her untrained eye.

The next thing Rorie noticed was the large two-story house with a wide wraparound veranda on which a white wicker swing swayed gently. Budding rosebushes lined the meandering brick walkway.

"It's beautiful," she said softly. Rorie would have expected something like this in the bluegrass hills of Kentucky, not on the back roads of Oregon.

Clay made no comment.

He drove past the house and around the back toward the largest stable Rorie had ever seen. The sprawling wood structure must have had room for thirty or more horses.

"You raise horses?" she said.

A smile moved through his eyes like distant light. "That's one way of putting it. Elk Run is a stud farm."

"Quarter horses?"

That was the only breed that came to mind.

"No. American Saddlebreds."

"I don't think I've ever heard of them before."

"Probably not," Clay said, not unkindly.

He parked the truck, helped Rorie down and led her toward the back of the house.

"Mary," he called, holding the screen door for Rorie to precede him into the large country kitchen. She was met with the smell of cinnamon and apples. The delectable aroma came from a freshly baked pie, cooling on the counter. A black Labrador retriever slept on a braided rug. He raised his head and thumped his tail gently when Clay stepped over to him and bent down to scratch the dog's ears. "This is Blue."

"Hi, Blue," Rorie said, realizing the dog had probably been a childhood pet. He looked well advanced in years.

"Mary doesn't seem to be around."

"Mary's your wife?"

"Housekeeper," Clay informed her. "I'm not married."

That small piece of information gladdened Rorie's heart and she instantly felt foolish. Okay, so she was attracted to this man with eyes as gray as a San Francisco sky, but that didn't change a thing. If her plans went according to schedule, she'd be in and out of his life within hours.

"Mary's probably upstairs," Clay said when the housekeeper didn't answer. "There's a phone on the wall." He pointed to the other side of the kitchen.

While Rorie retrieved her AT&T card from her eelskin wallet, Clay crossed to the refrigerator and took out a brightly colored ceramic pitcher.

"Iced tea?" he asked.

"Please." Her throat felt parched. She had to swallow several times before she could make her call.

As she spoke on the phone, Clay took two tall glasses from a cupboard and half filled them with ice cubes. He poured in the tea, then added thin slices of lemon.

Rorie finished her conversation and walked over to the table. Sitting opposite Clay, she reached for the drink he'd prepared. "That was my hotel in Seattle. They won't be able to hold the room past six."

"I'm sure there'll be space in another," he said confidently.

Rorie nodded, although she thought that was unlikely. She was on her way to a writers' conference, one for which she'd paid a hefty fee, and she hated to miss one minute of it. Every hotel in the city was said to be filled.

"I'll call the garage in Nightingale for you," Clay offered.

"Is that close by?"

"About five miles down the road."

Rorie was relieved. She'd never heard of Nightingale and was grateful to learn it had a garage. After all, the place was barely large enough to rate a mention on the road map.

"Old Joe's been working on cars most of his life. He'll do a good job for you."

Rorie nodded again, not knowing how else to respond.

Clay quickly strode to the phone, punched out the number and talked for a few minutes. He was frowning when he replaced the receiver. Rorie wanted to question him, but before she could, he grabbed an impossibly thin phone book and dialed a second number. His frown was deeper by the time he'd completed the call.

"I've got more bad news for you."

"Oh?" Rorie's heart had planted itself somewhere between her chest and her throat. She didn't like the way Clay was frowning, or the concern she heard in his voice. "What's wrong now?"

"Old Joe's gone fishing and isn't expected back this month. The mechanic in Riversdale, which is about sixty miles south of here, says that if it is your pump it'll take at least four days to ship a replacement."

Two

"Four days!" Rorie felt the color drain from her face. "But that's impossible! I can't possibly wait that long."

"Seems to me," Clay said in his smooth drawl, "you don't have much choice. George tells me he could have the water pump within a day if you weren't driving a foreign job."

"Surely there's someone else I could call."

Clay seemed to mull that over; then he shrugged. "Go ahead and give it a try if you like, but it isn't going to do you any good. If the shop in Riversdale can't get the part until Saturday, what makes you think someone else can do it any faster?"

Clay's calm acceptance of the situation infuriated Rorie. If she stayed here four days, in the middle of nowhere, she'd completely miss the writers' conference, which she'd been planning to attend for months. She'd scheduled her entire vacation around it. She'd made arrangements to travel to Victoria on British Columbia's

Vancouver Island after the conference and on the way home take a leisurely trip down the coast.

Clay handed her the phone book, and feeling defeated Rorie thumbed through the brief yellow pages until she came to the section headed Automobile Repair. Only a handful were listed and none of them promised quick service, she noted.

"Yes, well," she muttered, expelling her breath, "there doesn't seem to be any other option." Discouraged, she set the directory back on the counter. "You and your brother have been most helpful and I want you to know how much I appreciate everything you've done. Now if you could recommend a hotel in...what was the name of the town again?"

"Nightingale."

"Right," she said, with a wobbly smile, which was the best she could do at the moment. "Actually, anyplace that's clean will be fine."

Clay rubbed the side of his jaw. "I'm afraid that's going to present another problem."

"Now what? Has the manager gone fishing with Old Joe?" Rorie did her best to keep the sarcasm out of her voice, but it was difficult. Obviously the people in the community of...Nightingale didn't take their responsibilities too seriously. If they were on the job when someone happened to need them, it was probably by coincidence.

"A fishing trip isn't the problem this time," Clay explained, his expression thoughtful. "Nightingale doesn't have a hotel."

"What?" Rorie exploded. "No hotel...but there must be."

"We don't get much traffic through here. People usually stick to the freeway."

If he was implying that *she* should have done so, Rorie couldn't have agreed with him more. She might have seen some lovely scenery, but look where this little side trip had taken her! Her entire vacation was about to be ruined. She slowly released her breath, trying hard to maintain her composure, which was cracking more with every passing minute.

"What about Riversdale? Surely they have a hotel?"

Clay nodded. "They do. It's a real nice one, but I suspect it's full."

"Full? I thought you just told me people don't often take this route."

"Tourists don't."

"Then how could the hotel possibly be full?"

"The Jerome family."

"I beg your pardon?"

"The Jerome family is having a big reunion. People are coming from all over the country. Jed was telling me the other day that a cousin of his is driving out from Boston. The overflow will more than likely fill up Riversdale's only hotel."

One phone call confirmed Clay's suspicion.

"Terrific," Rorie murmured, her hand still on the receiver. The way things were beginning to look, she'd end up sleeping on a park bench—if Nightingale even had a park.

The back door opened and Skip wandered in, obviously pleased about something. He poured himself a glass of iced tea and leaned against the counter, glancing from Rorie to Clay and then back again.

"What's happening?" he asked, when no one volunteered any information.

"Nothing much," Rorie said. "Getting the water pump for my car is going to take four days and it seems the only hotel within a sixty-mile radius is booked full for the next two weeks and—"

"That's no problem. You can stay here," Skip inserted quickly, his blue eyes flashing with eagerness. "We'd love to have you, wouldn't we, Clay?"

Rorie spoke before the elder Franklin had an opportunity to answer. "No, really, I appreciate the offer, but I can't inconvenience you any more than I already have."

"She wouldn't be an inconvenience, would she?" Once more Skip directed the question to his older brother. "Tell her she wouldn't, Clay."

"I can't stay here," she returned, without giving Clay the chance to echo his brother's invitation. She didn't know these people. And, more important, they didn't know her and Rorie refused to impose on them further.

Clay gazed into her eyes and a slow smile turned up the edges of his mouth. "It's up to you, Rorie. You're welcome on Elk Run if you want to stay."

"But you've done so much. I really couldn't—"

"There's plenty of room," Skip announced ardently.

Those baby-blue eyes of his would melt the strongest resolve, Rorie mused.

"There's three bedrooms upstairs that are sitting empty. And you wouldn't need to worry about staying with two bachelors, because Mary's here—she has a cottage across the way."

It seemed inconceivable to Rorie that this family would take her in just like that. But, given her options, her arguments for refusing their offer were weak, to say the least. "You don't even know me."

"We know all we need to, don't we, Clay?" Skip glanced at his older brother, seeking his support.

"You're welcome to stay here, if you like," Clay repeated, his gaze continuing to hold Rorie's.

Again she was struck by the compelling quality of this man. He had a stubborn jaw and she doubted there were many confrontations where he walked away a loser. She'd always prided herself on her ability to read people. And her instincts told her firmly that Clay Franklin could be trusted. She sensed he was scrupulously honest, utterly dependable—and she already knew he was generous to a fault.

"I'd be most grateful," she said, swallowing a surge of tears at the Franklins' uncomplicated kindness to a complete stranger. "But, please, let me do something to make up for all the trouble I've caused you."

"It's no trouble," Skip said, looking as if he wanted to jump up and click his heels in jubilation.

Clay frowned as he watched his younger brother.

"Really," Rorie stressed. "If there's anything I can do, I'd be more than happy to lend a hand."

"Do you know anything about computers?"

"A little," she said. "We use them at the library."

"You're a librarian?"

Rorie nodded and brushed a stray dark curl from her

forehead. "I specialize in children's literature." Someday she hoped to have her own work published. That had been her reason for attending the conference in Seattle. Three of the top children's authors in the country were slated to speak. "If you have a computer system, I'd be happy to do whatever I can..."

"Clay bought a new one last winter," Skip informed her proudly. "He has a program that records horse breeding and pedigrees up to the fourth and fifth generation."

A heavyset woman Rorie assumed was the housekeeper entered the kitchen, hauling a mop and bucket. She inspected Rorie with a measuring glance and seemed to find her lacking. She grumbled something about city girls as she sidled past Skip.

"Didn't know you'd decided to hold a convention right in the middle of my kitchen."

"Mary," Clay said, "this is Rorie Campbell, from San Francisco. Her car broke down, so she'll be staying with us for the next few days. Could you see that a bed is made up for her?"

The older woman's wide face broke into a network of frown lines.

"Oh, please, I can do that myself," Rorie said quickly.

Mary nodded. "Sheets are in the closet at the top of the stairs."

"Rorie is our guest." Clay didn't raise his voice, but his displeasure was evident in every syllable.

Mary shrugged, muttering, "I got my own things to do. If the girl claims she can make a bed, then let her."

Rorie couldn't contain her smile.

"You want to invite some city slicker to stay, then fine,

but I got more important matters to attend to before I make up a bed for her." With that, Mary marched out of the kitchen.

"Mary's like family," Skip explained. "It's just her way to be sassy. She doesn't mean anything by it."

"I'm sure she doesn't," Rorie said, smiling so Clay and Skip would know she wasn't offended. She gathered that the Franklins' housekeeper didn't hold a high opinion of anyone from the city and briefly wondered why.

"I'll get your suitcase from the car," Skip said, heading for the door.

Clay finished his drink and set the glass on the counter. "I've got to get back to work," he told her, pausing for a moment before he added, "You won't be bored by yourself, will you?"

"Not at all. Don't worry about me."

Clay nodded. "Dinner's at six."

"I'll be ready."

Rorie picked up the empty glasses and put them by the sink. While she waited for Skip to carry in her luggage, she phoned Dan. Unfortunately he was in a meeting and couldn't be reached, so she left a message, explaining that she'd been delayed and would call again. She felt strangely reluctant to give him the Franklins' phone number, but decided there was no reason not to do so. She also decided not to examine that feeling too closely.

Skip had returned by the time she'd hung up. "Clay says you can have Mom and Dad's old room," the teenager announced on his way through the door. He hauled her large suitcase in one hand and her flight bag was slung over his shoulder. "Their room's at the other end of the house. They were killed in an accident five years ago."

"But—"

"Their room's got the best view."

"Skip, really, any bedroom will do... I don't want your parents' room."

"But that's the one Clay wants for you." He bounded up the curving stairway with the energy reserved for the young.

Rorie followed him more slowly. She slid her hand along the polished banister and glanced into the living room. A large natural-rock fireplace dominated one wall. The furniture was built of solid oak, made comfortable with thick chintz-covered cushions. Several braided rugs were placed here and there on the polished wood floor. A piano with well-worn ivory keys stood to one side. The collection of family photographs displayed on top of it immediately caught her eye. She recognized a much younger Clay in what had to be his high-school graduation photo. The largest picture in an ornate brass frame was of a middle-aged couple, obviously Clay and Skip's parents.

Skip paused at the top of the stairway and looked over his shoulder. "My grandfather built this house more than fifty years ago."

"It's magnificent."

"We think so," he admitted, eyes shining with pride.

The master bedroom, which was at the end of the hallway, opened onto a balcony that presented an un-obstructed panorama of the entire valley. Rolling green pastures stretched as far as the eye could see. Rorie felt instantly drawn to this unfamiliar rural beauty. She drew a deep breath, and the thought flashed through her mind that it must be comforting to wake up to this serene landscape day after day.

"Everyone loves it here," Skip said from behind her.

"I can understand why."

"Well, I suppose I should get back to work," he said regretfully, setting her suitcases on the double bed. A colorful quilt lay folded at its foot.

Rorie turned toward him, smiling. "Thank you, Skip. I hate to think what would've happened to me if you hadn't come along when you did."

He blushed and started backing out of the room, taking small steps as though he was loath to leave her. "I'll see you at dinner, okay?"

Rorie smiled again. "I'll look forward to it."

"Bye for now." He raised his right hand in a farewell gesture, then whirled around and dashed down the hallway. She could hear his feet pounding on the stairs.

It took Rorie only a few minutes to hang her things in the bare closet. When she'd finished, she went back to the kitchen, where Mary was busy peeling potatoes at the stainless steel sink.

"I'd like to help, if I could."

"Fine," the housekeeper answered gruffly. She took another potato peeler out of a nearby drawer, slapping it down on the counter. "I suppose that's your fancy sports car in the yard."

"The water pump has to be replaced...I think," Rorie answered, not bothering to mention that the MGB wasn't actually hers.

"Humph," was Mary's only response.

Rorie sighed and reached for a large potato. "The mechanic in Riversdale said it would take until Saturday to get a replacement part."

For the second time, Mary answered her with a gruff-sounding *humph*. "If then! Saturday or next Thursday or a month from now, it's all the same to George. Fact is, you could end up staying here all summer."

Three

Mary's words echoed in Rorie's head as she joined Clay and Skip at the dinner table that evening. She stood just inside the dining room, dressed in a summer skirt and a cotton-knit cream-colored sweater, and announced, "I can't stay any longer than four days."

Clay regarded her blankly. "I have no intention of holding you prisoner, Rorie."

"I know, but Mary told me that if I'm counting on George what's-his-name to fix the MG, I could end up spending the summer here. I've got to get back to San Francisco—I have a job there." She realized how nonsensical her little speech sounded, as if that last bit about having a job explained everything.

"If you want, I'll keep after George to make sure he doesn't forget about it."

"Please." Rorie felt a little better for having spoken her mind.

"And the Greyhound bus comes through on Mondays,"

Skip said reassuringly. "If you had to, you could take that back to California and return later for your friend's car."

"The bus," she repeated. "I *could* take the bus." As it was, the first half of her vacation was ruined, but it'd be nice to salvage what she could of the rest.

Both men were seated, but as Rorie approached the table Skip rose noisily to his feet, rushed around to the opposite side and pulled out a chair for her.

"Thank you," she said, smiling up at him. His dark hair was wet and slicked down close to his head. He'd changed out of his work clothes and into what appeared to be his Sunday best—a dress shirt, tie and pearl-gray slacks. With a good deal of ceremony, he pushed in her chair. As he leaned toward her, it was all Rorie could do to keep from grimacing at the overpowering scent of his spicy aftershave. He must have drenched himself in the stuff.

Clay's gaze seemed to tug at hers and when Rorie glanced in his direction, she saw that he was doing his utmost not to laugh. He clearly found his brother's antics amusing, though he took pains not to hurt Skip's feelings, but Rorie wasn't sure how she should react. Skip was only in his teens, and she didn't want to encourage any romantic fantasies he might have.

"I hope you're hungry," Skip said, once he'd reclaimed his chair. "Mary puts on a good feed."

"I'm starved," Rorie admitted, eyeing the numerous serving dishes spread out on the table.

Clay handed her a large platter of fried chicken. That was followed by mashed potatoes, gravy, rolls, fresh green beans, a mixed green salad, milk and a variety of preserves. By the time they'd finished passing around the food, there wasn't any space left on Rorie's oversize plate.

"Don't forget to leave room for dessert," Clay commented, again with that slow, easy drawl of his. Here Skip was practically doing cartwheels to attract her attention and all Clay needed to do was look at her and she became light-headed. Rorie couldn't understand it. From the moment Clay Franklin had stepped down from his pickup, she hadn't been the same.

"After dinner I thought I'd take you up to the stable and introduce you to King Genius," Skip said, waving a chicken leg.

"I'd be happy to meet him."

"Once you do, you'll feel like you did when you stood on the balcony in the big bedroom and looked at the valley."

Obviously this King wasn't a foreman, as Rorie had first assumed. More than likely, he was one of the horses she'd seen earlier grazing on the pasture in front of the house.

"I don't think it would be a good idea to take Rorie around Hercules," Clay warned his younger brother.

"Of course not." But it looked as if Skip wanted to argue.

"Who's Hercules?"

"Clay's stallion," Skip explained. "He has a tendency to act up if Clay isn't around."

Rorie could only guess what "act up" meant, but even if Skip didn't intend to heed Clay's advice, she gladly would. Other than that pony ride when she was six, Rorie hadn't been near a horse. One thing was certain; she planned to steer a wide path around the creature, no matter how much Skip encouraged her. The largest pet she'd ever owned had been a guinea pig.

"When Hercules first came to Elk Run, the man who brought him said he was mean-spirited and untrainable. He wanted him destroyed, but Clay insisted on working with the stallion."

"Now he's your own personal horse?" Rorie asked Clay.

He nodded. "We've got an understanding."

"But it's only between them," Skip added. "Hercules doesn't like anyone else getting close."

"He doesn't have anything to worry about as far as I'm concerned," Rorie was quick to assure both brothers. "I'll give him as much space as he needs."

Clay grinned, and once again she felt her heart turn over. This strange affinity with Clay was affirmed in the look he gave her. Unexpected thoughts of Dan Rogers sprang to mind. Dan was a divorced stockbroker she'd been seeing steadily for the past few months. Rorie enjoyed Dan's company and had recently come to believe she was falling in love with him. Now she knew differently. She couldn't be this powerfully drawn to Clay Franklin if Dan was anything more than a good friend. One of the reasons Rorie had decided on this vacation was to test her feelings for Dan. Two days out of San Francisco, and she had her answer.

Deliberately Rorie pulled her gaze from Clay, wanting to attribute everything she was experiencing to the clean scent of country air.

Skip's deep blue eyes sparkled with pride as he started to tell Rorie about Elk Run's other champion horses. "But you'll love the King best. He was the five-gaited world champion four years running. Clay put him out to stud four years ago. National Show Horses are commanding top dollar and we've produced three of the best. King's the sire, naturally."

"Do all the horses I saw in the pasture belong to you?"

"We board several," Skip answered. "Some of the others are brought here from around the country for Clay to break and train."

"You break horses?" She couldn't conceal her sudden alarm. The image of Clay sitting on a wild bronco that bucked and heaved in a furious effort to unseat him did funny things to Rorie's stomach.

"Breaking horses isn't exactly the way Hollywood pictures show it," Clay explained.

Rorie was about to ask him more when Skip planted his elbows on the table and leaned forward. Once again Rorie was assaulted by the overpowering scent of his aftershave. She did her best to smile, but if he remained in that position much longer, her eyes would start watering. Already she could feel a sneeze tickling her nose.

"How old are you, Rorie?" he asked.

The question was so unexpected that she was too surprised to answer immediately. Then she said, "Twenty-four."

"And you live in San Francisco. Is your family there, too?"

"No. My parents moved to Arizona and my brother's going to school back east."

"And you're not engaged or anything?"

As Rorie shook her head, Clay shot his brother an exasperated look. "Are you interviewing Rorie for the *Independent?*"

"No. I was just curious."

"She's too old for you, little brother."

"I don't know about that," Skip returned fervently. "I've always liked my women more mature. Besides, Rorie's kind of cute."

"Kind of?"

Skip shrugged. "You know what I mean. She doesn't act like a city girl…much."

Rorie's eyes flew from one brother to the next. They were talking as if she wasn't even in the room, and that annoyed her—especially since she was the main topic of conversation.

Unaware of her reaction, Skip helped himself to another roll. "Actually, I thought she might be closer to twenty. With some women it's hard to tell."

"I'll take that as a compliment," Rorie muttered to no one in particular.

"My apologies, Rorie," Clay said contritely. "We were being rude."

She took time buttering her biscuit. "Apology accepted."

"How old do you think I am?" Skip asked her, his eyes wide and hopeful.

It was Rorie's nature to be kind, and besides, Skip had saved her from an unknown fate. "Twenty," she answered with barely a pause.

The younger Franklin straightened and sent his brother a smirk. "I was seventeen last week."

"That surprises me," Rorie continued, setting aside her

butter knife and swallowing a smile. "I could've sworn
you were much older."

Looking even more pleased with himself, Skip cleared
his throat. "Lots of girls think that."

"Don't I remember you telling me you're helping Luke
Rivers tonight?" Clay reminded his brother.

Skip's face fell. "I guess I did."

"If Rorie doesn't mind, I'll introduce her to King."

Clay's offer appeared to surprise Skip, and Rorie studied the boy, a little worried now about causing problems
between the two brothers. Nor did she want to disappoint
Skip, who had offered first.

"But I thought…" Skip began, then swallowed. "You
want to take Rorie?"

Clay's eyes narrowed, and when he spoke, his voice
was cool. "That's what I just said. Is there a problem?"

"No…of course not." Skip stuffed half a biscuit in his
mouth and shook his head vigorously. After a moment
of chewing, he said, "Clay will show you around the stable." His words were measured and even, but his gaze
held his brother's.

"I heard," Rorie said gently. She could only speculate on what was going on between them, but obviously
something was amiss. There'd been more than a hint of
surprise in Skip's eyes at Clay's offer. She noticed that
the younger Franklin seemed angry. Because his vanity
was bruised? Rorie supposed so. "I could wait until tomorrow if you want, Skip," she suggested.

"No, that's all right," he answered, lowering his eyes.
"Clay can do it, since that's what he seems to want."

When they finished the meal, Rorie cleared the table,

but Mary refused to let her help with cleaning up the kitchen.

"You'd just be in the way," she grumbled, though her eyes weren't unfriendly. "Besides, I heard the boys were showing you the barn."

"I'll do the dishes tomorrow night then."

Mary murmured a response, then asked brusquely, "How was the apple pie?"

"Absolutely delicious."

A satisfied smile touched the edges of the woman's mouth. "Good. I did things a little differently this time, and I was just wondering."

Clay led Rorie out the back door and across the yard toward the barn. The minute Rorie walked through the enormous double doors she felt she'd entered another world. The wonderful smells of leather and liniments and saddle soap mingled with the fragrance of fresh hay and the pungent odor of the horses themselves. Rorie found it surprisingly pleasant. Flashes of bright color from halters and blankets captured her attention, as did the gleam of steel bits against the far wall.

"King's over here," Clay said, guiding her with a firm hand beneath her elbow.

When Clay opened the top of the stall door, the most magnificent creature Rorie had ever seen turned to face them. He was a deep chestnut color, so sleek and powerful it took her breath away. This splendid horse seemed to know he was royalty. He regarded Rorie with a keen eye, as though he expected her to show him the proper respect and curtsy. For a wild moment, Rorie was tempted to do exactly that.

"I brought a young lady for you to impress," Clay told the stallion.

King took a couple of steps back and pawed the ground.

"He really is something," Rorie whispered, once she'd found her voice. "Did you raise him from a colt?"

Clay nodded.

Rorie was about to ask him more when they heard frantic whinnying from the other side of the aisle.

Clay looked almost apologetic. "If you haven't already guessed, that's Hercules. He doesn't like being ignored." He walked to the stall opposite King's and opened the upper half of the door. Instantly the black stallion stuck his head out and complained about the lack of attention in a loud snort, which brought an involuntary smile to Rorie's mouth. "I was bringing Rorie over to meet you, too, so don't get your nose out of joint," Clay chastised.

"Hi," Rorie said, and raised her right hand in a stiff greeting. It amused her that Clay talked to his animals as if he honestly expected them to understand his remarks and join in the conversation. But then who was she to criticize? Only a few hours earlier, she'd been conversing with a cow.

"You don't need to be frightened of him," Clay told her when she stood, unmoving, a good distance from the stall. Taking into consideration what Skip had mentioned earlier about the moody stallion, Rorie decided to stay where she was.

Clay ran his hand down the side of Hercules's neck, and his touch seemed to appease the stallion's obviously delicate ego.

Looking around her, Rorie was impressed by the size of the barn. "How many stalls are there altogether?"

"Thirty-six regular and four foaling. But this is only a small part of Elk Run." He led her outside to a large arena and pointed at a building on the opposite side. "My office is over there, if you'd like to see it."

Rorie nodded, and they crossed to the office. Clay opened the door for her. Inside, the first thing she noticed was the collection of championship ribbons and photographs displayed on the walls. A large trophy case was filled with a variety of awards. When he saw her interest in the computer, Clay explained the system he'd had installed and how it would aid him in the future.

"This looks pretty straightforward," Rorie told him.

"I've been meaning to hire a high-school kid to enter the data for me so I can get started, but I haven't got around to it yet."

Rorie sorted through the file folders. There were only a few hours of work and her typing skills were good. "There's no need to pay anyone. If I'm going to be imposing on your hospitality, the least I can do is enter this into the computer for you."

"Rorie, that isn't necessary. I don't want you to spend your time stuck here in the office doing all that tedious typing."

"It'll give me something productive to do instead of fretting over how long it's taking to get the MG repaired."

He glanced at her, his expression concerned. "All right, if you insist, but it really isn't necessary, you know."

"I do insist." Rorie clasped her hands behind her back and decided to change the subject. "What's that?" she asked, gesturing toward a large room off the office. Floor-to-ceiling windows looked out over the arena.

"The observation room."

"So you can have your own private shows?"

"In a manner of speaking. Would you like to go down there?"

"Oh, yes!"

Inside the arena, Rorie saw that it was much bigger than it had appeared from above. They'd been walking around for several minutes when Clay checked his watch and frowned. "I hate to cut this short, but I've got a meeting in town. Normally I wouldn't leave company."

"Oh, please," she said hurriedly, "don't worry about it. I mean, it's not as though I was expected or anything. I hardly consider myself company."

Still Clay seemed regretful. "I'll walk you back to the house."

He left in the pickup a couple of minutes later. The place was quiet; Mary had apparently finished in the kitchen and retired to her own quarters, a cottage not far from the main house. Skip, who had returned from helping his friend, was busy talking on the phone. He smiled when he saw Rorie, without interrupting his conversation.

Rorie moved into the living room and idly picked up a magazine, leafing through it. Restless and bored, she read a heated article on the pros and cons of a new medication used for equine worming, although she couldn't have described what it said.

When Skip was finished on the phone, he suggested they play cribbage. Not until after ten did Rorie realize she was unconsciously waiting for Clay's return. But she wasn't quite sure why.

Skip yawned rather pointedly and Rorie took the hint.

"I suppose I should think about heading up to bed," she said, putting down the deck of playing cards.

"Yeah, it seems to be that time," he answered, yawning again.

"I didn't intend to keep you up so late."

"Oh, that's no problem. It's just that we start our days early around here. But you sleep in. We don't expect you to get up before the sun just because we do."

By Rorie's rough calculation, getting up before the sun meant Clay and Skip started their workday between four-thirty and five in the morning.

Skip must have read the look in her eyes, because he chuckled and said, "You get used to it."

Rorie followed him up the stairs, and they said their good-nights. But even after a warm bath, she couldn't sleep. Wearing her flower-sprigged cotton pajamas, she sat on the bed with the light still on and thought about how different everything was from what she'd planned. She was supposed to be in Seattle now, at a cocktail party arranged for the first night of the conference; she'd hoped to talk to several of the authors there. But she'd missed that, and the likelihood of attending even one workshop was dim. Instead she'd made an unscheduled detour onto a stud farm and stumbled upon a handsome rancher.

She grinned. Things could be worse. Much worse.

An hour later, Rorie heard a noise outside, behind the house. Clay must be home. She smiled, oddly pleased that he was back. Yawning, she reached for the lamp on the bedside table and turned it off.

The discordant noise came again.

Rorie frowned. This time, whatever was making the racket didn't sound the least bit like a pickup truck parking, or anything else she could readily identify. The dog was barking intermittently.

Grabbing her housecoat from the foot of the bed and tucking her feet into fuzzy slippers, Rorie went downstairs to investigate.

As she stood in the kitchen, she could tell that the clamor was coming from the barn. A problem with the horses?

Not knowing what else to do, she scrambled up the stairs and hurried from room to room until she found Skip's bedroom.

The teenager lay sprawled across his bed, snoring loudly.

"Skip," she cried, "something's wrong with the horses!"

He continued to snore.

"Skip," she cried, louder this time. "Wake up!"

He remained deep in sleep.

"Skip, please, oh, please, wake up!" Rorie pleaded, shaking him so hard he'd probably have bruises in the morning. "I'm from the city. Remember? I don't know what to do."

The thumps and bangs coming from the barn were growing fiercer and Blue's barking more frantic. Perhaps there was a fire. Oh, dear Lord, she prayed, not that. Rorie raced halfway down the stairs, paused and then reversed her direction.

"Skip," she yelled. "Skip!" Rorie heard the panic in her own voice. "Someone's got to do something!"

No one else seemed to think so.

Nearly frantic now, Rorie dashed back down the stairs and across the yard. Trembling, she entered the barn. A lone electric light shone from the ceiling, dimly illuminating the area.

Several of the stalls' upper doors were open and Rorie could sense the horses becoming increasingly restless. Walking on tiptoe, she moved slowly toward the source of the noise, somewhere in the middle of the stable. The horses were curious and their cries brought Rorie's heart straight to her throat.

"Nice horsey, nice horsey," she repeated soothingly over and over until she reached the stall those unearthly sounds were coming from.

The upper half of the door was open and Rorie flattened herself against it before daring to peek inside. She saw a speckled gray mare, head thrown back and teeth bared, neighing loudly, ceaselessly. Rorie quickly jerked away and resumed her position against the outside of the door. She didn't know much about horses, but she knew this one was in dire trouble.

Running out of the stable, Rorie picked up the hem of her robe and sprinted toward the house. She'd find a way to wake Skip or die trying.

She was breathless by the time she got to the yard. That was when she saw Clay's battered blue truck.

"Clay," she screamed, halting in the middle of the moonlit yard. "Oh, Clay."

He was at her side instantly, his hands roughly gripping her shoulders. "Rorie, what is it?"

She was so glad to see him, she hugged his waist and only just resisted bursting into tears. Her shoulders were heaving and her voice shook uncontrollably. "There's trouble in the barn...."

Four

Clay ran toward the barn with Rorie right behind him. He paused to flip a switch, flooding the interior with bright light.

The gray mare in the center stall continued to neigh and thrash around. Rorie found it astonishing that the walls had remained intact. The noise of the animal's pain echoed through the stable, reflected by the rising anxiety of the other horses.

Clay took one look at the mare and released a low groan, then muttered something under his breath.

"What's wrong?" Rorie cried.

"It seems Star Bright is about to become a mother."

"But why isn't she in one of the foaling stalls?"

"Because two different vets palpated her and said she wasn't in foal."

"But..."

"She's already had six foals and her stomach's so stretched she looks pregnant even when she isn't." Clay opened the stall door and entered. Rorie's hand flew to her heart. Good grief, he could get killed in there!

"What do you want me to do?" she said.

Clay shook his head. "This is no place for you. Get back to the house and stay there." His brow furrowed, every line a testament to his hard, outdoor life.

"But shouldn't I be phoning a vet?"

"It's too late for that."

"Boiling water—I could get that for you." She wanted to help; she just had no idea how.

"Boiling water?" he repeated. "What the hell would I need that for?"

"I don't know," she confessed with a shrug, "but they always seem to need it in the movies."

Clay gave an exasperated sigh. "Rorie, please, just go to the house."

She made it all the way to the barn door, then abruptly turned back. If anyone had asked why she felt it so necessary to remain with Clay, she wouldn't have been able to answer. But something kept her there, something far stronger than the threat of Clay's temper.

She marched to the center stall, her head and shoulders held stiff and straight. She stood with her feet braced, prepared for an argument.

"Clay," she said, "I'm not leaving."

"Listen, Rorie, you're a city girl. This isn't going to be pretty."

"I'm a woman, too. The sight of a little blood isn't enough to make me faint."

Clay was doing his best to calm the frightened mare,

but without much success. The tension in the air seemed to crackle like static electricity.

"I haven't got time to argue with you," he said through clenched teeth.

"Good."

Star Bright heaved her neck backward and gave a deep groan that seemed to reverberate in the stall like the boom of a cannon.

"Poor little mother," Rorie whispered in a soothing voice. Led by instinct, she carefully unlatched the stall door and slipped inside.

Clay sent her a look hot enough to peel paint. "Get out of here before you get hurt." His voice was low and urgent.

Star Bright reacted to his tension immediately, jerking about, her body twitching convulsively. One of her hooves caught Clay in the forearm and, almost immediately, blood seeped through his sleeve. Rorie bit her lip to suppress a cry of alarm, but if Clay felt any pain he didn't show it.

"Hold her head," Clay said sharply.

Somehow Rorie found the courage to do as he asked. Star Bright groaned once more and her pleading eyes looked directly into Rorie's, seeming to beg for help. The mare's lips pulled back from her teeth as she flailed her head to and fro, shaking Rorie in the process.

"Whoa, girl," Rorie said softly, gaining control. "It's painful, isn't it, but soon you'll have a beautiful baby to show off to the world."

"Foal," Clay corrected from behind the mare.

"A beautiful foal." Rorie stroked the sweat-dampened

neck, doing what she could to reassure the frightened horse.

"Keep talking to her," Clay whispered.

Rorie kept up a running dialogue for several tense minutes, but there was only so much she could find to say on such short acquaintance. When she ran out of ideas, she started to sing in a soft, lilting voice. She began with lullabies her mother had once sung to her, then followed those with a few childhood ditties. Her singing lasted only minutes, but Rorie's lungs felt close to collapse.

Suddenly the mare's water broke. Clay wasn't saying much, but he began to work quickly, although she couldn't see what he was doing. Star Bright tossed her neck in the final throes of birth and Rorie watched, fascinated, as two hooves and front legs emerged, followed by a white nose.

The mare lifted her head, eager to see. Clay tugged gently, and within seconds, the foal was free. Rorie's heart pounded like a locomotive struggling up a steep hill as Clay's strong hands completed the task.

"A filly," he announced, a smile lighting his face. He reached for a rag and wiped his hands and arms.

Star Bright turned her head to view her offspring. "See?" Rorie told the mare, her eyes moist with relief. "Didn't I tell you it would all be worth it?"

The mare nickered. Her newborn filly was gray, like her mother, and finely marked with white streaks on her nose, mane and tail. Rorie was touched to her very soul by the sight. Tears blurred her vision and ran down her flushed cheeks. She blotted them with her sleeve so Clay couldn't see them, and silently chided herself for being such a sentimental fool.

It was almost another hour before they left Star Bright's stall. The mare, who stood guard over her long-legged baby, seemed content and utterly pleased with herself. As they prepared to leave, Rorie whispered in her ear.

"What was that all about?" Clay wanted to know, latching the stall door.

"I just told her she'd done a good job."

"That she did," Clay whispered. A moment later, he added, "And so did you, Rorie. I was grateful for your help."

Once more tears sprang to her eyes. She responded with a nod, unable to trust her voice. Her heart was racing with exhilaration. She couldn't remember a time she'd felt more excited. It was well past midnight, but she'd never felt less sleepy.

"Rorie?" He was staring at her, his eyes bright with concern.

She owed him an explanation, although she couldn't fully explain this sudden burst of emotion. "It was so... beautiful." She brushed the hair from her face and smiled up at him, hoping he wouldn't think she was just a foolish city girl. She wasn't sure why it mattered, but she doubted that any man had seen her looking worse, although Rorie was well aware that she didn't possess a classic beauty. She was usually referred to as cute, with her slightly turned-up nose and dark brown eyes.

"I understand." He walked to the sink against the barn's opposite wall and busily washed his hands, then splashed water on his face. When he'd finished, Rorie handed him a towel hanging on a nearby hook.

"Thanks."

"I don't know how to describe it," she said, after a fruit-less effort to find the words to explain all the feeling that had surged up inside her.

"It's the same for me every time I witness a birth," Clay told her. He looked at her then and gently touched her face, letting his finger glide along her jaw. All the world went still as his eyes caressed hers. There was a primitive wonder in the experience of birth, a wonder that struck deep within the soul. For the first time, Rorie understood this. And sharing it with Clay seemed to intensify the at-traction she already felt for him. During that brief time in the stall, just before Star Bright delivered her foal, Rorie had felt closer to Clay than she ever had to any other man. It was as though her heart had taken flight and joined his in a moment of sheer challenge and joy. That was a silly romantic thought, she realized. But it seemed so incred-ible to her that she could feel anything this strong for a man she'd known for mere hours.

"I've got a name for her," Clay said, hanging up the towel. "What do you think of Nightsong?"

"Nightsong," Rorie repeated softly. "I like it."

"In honor of the woman who sang to her mother."

Rorie nodded as emotion clogged her throat. "Does this mean I did all right for a city slicker?"

"You did more than all right."

"Thanks for not sending me away... I probably would've gone if you'd insisted."

They left the barn, and Clay draped his arm across her shoulders as though he'd been doing it for years. Rorie was grateful for his touch because, somehow, it helped ground the unfamiliar feelings and sensations.

As they strolled across the yard, she noticed that the sky was filled with a thousand glittering stars, brighter than any she'd ever seen in the city. She paused midstep to gaze up at them.

Clay's quiet voice didn't dispel the serenity. "It's a lovely night, isn't it?"

Rorie wanted to hold on to each exquisite minute and make it last a lifetime. A nod was all she could manage as she reminded herself that this time with Clay was about to end. They would walk into the house and Clay would probably thank her again. Then she'd climb the stairs to her room and that would be all there was.

"How about some coffee?" he asked once they'd entered the kitchen. Blue left his rug and wandered over to Clay. "The way I feel now, it would be a waste of time to go to bed."

"Me, too." Rorie leaped at the suggestion, pleased that he wanted to delay their parting, too. And when she did return to her room, she knew the adrenaline in her system would make sleep impossible, anyway.

Clay was reaching up for the canister of coffee, when Rorie suddenly noticed the bloodstain on his sleeve and remembered Star Bright's kick.

"Clay, you need to take care of that cut."

From the surprised way he glanced at his arm, she guessed that he, too, had forgotten about the injury. "Yes, I suppose I should." Then he calmly returned to his task.

"Let me clean it for you," Rorie offered, joining him at the kitchen counter.

"If you like." He led her into the bathroom down the hall and took a variety of medical supplies from the cabinet above the sink. "Do you want to do it here or in the kitchen?"

"Here is fine."

Clay sat on the edge of the bath and unfastened the cuff, then rolled back his sleeve.

"Oh, Clay," Rorie whispered when she saw the angry torn flesh just above his elbow. Gently her fingers tested the edges, wondering if he needed stitches. He winced slightly at her probing fingers.

"Sorry."

"Just put some antiseptic on it and it'll be all right."

"But this is really deep—you should probably have a doctor look at it."

"Rorie, I'm as tough as old leather. This kind of thing happens all the time. I'll recover."

"I don't doubt that," she said primly.

"Then put on a bandage and be done with it."

"But—"

"I've been injured often enough to know when a cut needs a doctor's attention."

She hesitated, then conceded that he was probably right. She filled the sink with warm tap water and took care to clean the wound thoroughly. All the while, Rorie was conscious of Clay's eyes moving over her face, solemnly perusing the chin-length, dark brown hair and the big dark eyes that—judging by a glance in the mirror—still displayed a hint of vulnerability. She was tall, almost five-eight, her figure willowy. But if Clay found anything attractive about her, he didn't mention it. Her throat muscles squeezed shut, and, although she was grateful for the silence between them, it confused her.

"You missed your vocation," he told her as she rinsed the bloody cloth. "You should've been a nurse."

"I toyed with the idea when I was ten, but decided I liked books better."

His shoulders were tense, Rorie noted, and she tried to be as gentle as possible. A muscle leaped in his jaw.

"Am I...hurting you?"

"No," he answered, his voice curt.

After that, he was an excellent patient. He didn't complain when she dabbed on the antiseptic, although she was sure it must have stung like crazy. He cooperated when she wrapped the gauze around his arm, lifting and lowering it when she asked him to. The silence continued as she secured the bandage with adhesive tape. Rorie had the feeling that he wanted to escape the close confines of the bathroom as quickly as possible.

"I hope that stays."

He stood up and flexed his elbow a couple of times. "It's fine. You do good work."

"I'm glad you think so."

"The coffee's probably ready by now." He spoke quickly, as if eager to be gone.

She sighed. "I could use a cup."

She put the medical supplies neatly back inside the cabinet, while Clay returned to the kitchen. Rorie could smell the freshly made coffee even before she entered the room.

He was leaning against the counter, sipping a cup of the fragrant coffee, waiting for her.

"It's been quite a night, hasn't it?" she murmured, adding cream and sugar to the mug he'd poured for her.

A certain tension hung in the air, and Rorie couldn't

explain or understand it. Only ten minutes earlier, they'd walked across the yard, spellbound by the stars, and Clay had laid his arm across her shoulders. He'd smiled down on her so tenderly. Now he looked as if he couldn't wait to get away from her.

"Have I done anything wrong?" she asked outright.

"Rorie, no." He set his mug aside and gripped her shoulders with both hands. "There's something so intimate and...earthy in what we shared." His eyes were intense, strangely darker. "Wanting you this way isn't right."

Rorie felt a tremor work through him as he lifted his hands to her face. His callused thumbs lightly caressed her cheeks.

"I feel like I've known you all my life," he whispered hoarsely, his expression uncertain.

"It's...been the same for me, from the moment you stepped out of the truck."

Clay smiled, and Rorie thought her knees would melt. She put her coffee down and as soon as she did Clay eased her into his arms, his hands on her shoulders. Her heart stopped, then jolted back to frenzied life.

"I'm going to kiss you...."

He made the statement almost a question. "Yes," she whispered, letting him know she'd welcome his touch. Her stomach fluttered as he slowly lowered his mouth to hers.

Rorie had never wanted a man's kiss more. His moist lips glided over hers in a series of gentle explorations. He drew her closer until their bodies were pressed tight.

"Oh, Rorie," he breathed, dragging his mouth from hers. "You taste so good...I was afraid of that." His mouth found the pulse in her throat and lingered there.

"This afternoon I thought I'd cry when the car broke down and now...now I'm glad...so glad," she said.

He kissed her again, nibbling on her lower lip, gently drawing it between his teeth. Rorie could hardly breathe, her heart was pounding so hard. She slumped against him, delighting in the rise and fall of his broad chest. His hands moved down her back with slow restraint, but paused when he reached the curve of her hips.

He tensed. "I think we should say goodnight."

A protest sprang to her lips, but before she could voice it, Clay said, "Now."

She looked at him, dazed. The last thing she wanted to do was leave him. "What about my coffee?"

"That was just an excuse and we both know it."

Rorie said nothing.

The silence between them seemed to throb for endless minutes.

"Good night, Clay," she finally whispered. She broke away, but his hand caught her fingers, and with a groan he pulled her back into his arms.

"What the hell," he muttered fiercely, "sending you upstairs isn't going to help. Nothing's going to change."

His words brought confusion, but Rorie didn't question him, didn't want to. What she longed for was the warmth and security she'd discovered in his arms.

"Come on," he whispered, after he'd kissed her once more. He led her through the living room and outside to the porch, where the swing moved gently in the night breeze.

Rorie sat beside him and he wrapped his arm around

her. She nestled her head against his shoulder, savoring these precious moments.

"I'll never forget this night."

"Neither will I," Clay promised, kissing her again.

Rorie awoke when the sun settled on her face and refused to leave her alone. Keeping her eyes closed, she smiled contentedly, basking in the memory of her night with Clay. They'd sat on the swing and talked for hours. Talked and kissed and laughed and touched...

Sitting up, Rorie raised her hands high above her head and stretched, arching her spine. She looked at her watch on the nightstand and was shocked to see that it was after eleven. By the time she'd climbed the stairs for bed the sky had been dappled with faint shreds of light. She suspected Clay hadn't even bothered to sleep.

Tossing aside the blankets, Rorie slid to the floor, anxious to shower and dress. Anxious to see him again. Fifteen minutes later, she was on her way down the stairs.

Mary, who was dusting in the living room, nodded when she saw Rorie. Then the housekeeper resumed her task, but not before she'd muttered something about how city folks were prone to sleeping their lives away.

"Good morning, Mary," Rorie greeted her cheerfully.

"'Mornin'."

"Where is everyone?"

"Where they ought to be this time of day. Working."

"Yes, I know, but where?"

"Outside."

Rorie had trouble hiding her smile.

"I heard about you helping last night," Mary added gruffly. "Seems you did all right for a city girl."

"Thank you, Mary. You don't do half bad for a country girl, either."

The housekeeper seemed uncomfortable with the praise, despite the lightness of Rorie's tone. "I suppose you want me to cook you some fancy breakfast."

"Good heavens, no, you're busy. I'll just make myself some toast."

"That's hardly enough to fill a growing girl," Mary complained.

"It'll suit me fine."

Once her toast was ready, Rorie carried it outside. If she couldn't find Clay, she wanted to check on Nightsong.

"Rorie."

She turned to discover Skip walking toward her, in animated conversation with a blonde. His girlfriend, she guessed. He waved and Rorie returned the gesture, smiling. The sun was glorious and the day held marvelous promise.

"I didn't think you were ever going to wake up," Skip said.

"I'm sorry—I don't usually sleep this late."

"Clay told me how you helped him deliver Star Bright's filly. You could've knocked me over with a feather when I heard."

Rorie nodded, her heart warming with the memory. "Well, I tried to get you up. It would've been easier to wake a dead man than to get you out of bed last night."

Skip looked slightly embarrassed. "Sorry about that, but I generally don't wake up too easily once I'm asleep."

As he spoke, he slipped his arm around the blonde girl's shoulders. "Rorie, I want you to meet Kate Logan."

"Hello, Kate." Rorie held out a hand and Kate shook it politely.

"Hello, Rorie," she said. "Clay and Skip told me about your car troubles. I hope everything turns out all right for you."

"I'm sure it will. Do you live around here?" Rorie already knew she was going to like her. At a closer glance, she saw that Kate was older than she'd first assumed. Maybe her own age, which gave credence to Skip's comment about liking older, more mature women.

"I don't live far," Kate said. "The Circle L is down the road, only a few miles from here."

"She's going to be living *with* us in the near future," Skip put in, gazing fondly at Kate.

The young woman's cheeks reddened and she smiled shyly.

"Oh?" Skip couldn't possibly mean he planned to marry her, Rorie thought. Good heavens, he was still in high school.

He must have seen Rorie's puzzled frown, and hurried to explain. "Not me," he said with a short laugh. "Kate is Clay's fiancée."

Five

"You and Clay are...engaged," Rorie murmured as shock waves coursed through her blood. They stopped with a thud at her heart and spread out in ripples of dismay.

Somehow Rorie managed a smile, her outward composure unbroken. She was even able to offer her congratulations. To all appearances, nothing was wrong. No one would've known that those few simple words had destroyed a night she'd planned to treasure all her life.

"I hope you and Clay will be very happy," Rorie said—and she meant it. She'd just been introduced to Kate Logan, but already Rorie knew that this sweet, friendly woman was exactly the kind of wife a man like Clay would need.

"Skip's rushing things a little," Kate pointed out, but the glint of love in her eyes contradicted her words. "Clay hasn't even given me an engagement ring yet."

"But you and Clay have been talking about getting

married, haven't you?" Skip pressed. "And you're crazy about him."

Kate blushed prettily. "I've loved Clay from the time I was in fifth grade. I wrote his name all over my books. Of course, Clay wouldn't have anything to do with me, not when he was a big important high-schooler and I was just the pesky little girl next door. It took a while for him to notice me—like ten years." She gave a small laugh. "We've been dating steadily for the past two."

"But you and Clay *are* going to get married, right?" Skip continued, clearly wanting to prove his point.

"Eventually, but we haven't set a date, although I'm sure it'll be soon," Kate answered, casting a sharp look at Rorie.

The tightness that had gripped Rorie's throat eased and she struggled to keep her smile intact. It was impossible not to like Kate, but that didn't lessen the ache in Rorie's heart.

"The wedding's inevitable," Skip said offhandedly, "so I wasn't exaggerating when I said you were Clay's fiancée, now was I?"

Kate smiled. "I suppose not. We love each other, and have for years. We're just waiting for the right time." Her eyes held Rorie's, assessing her, but she didn't seem worried about competition.

Rorie supposed she should be pleased about that, at least.

"I was taking Kate over to see Nightsong," Skip explained to Rorie.

"I actually came to Elk Run to meet you," the other woman said. "Clay stopped by last night and told me about your car. I felt terrible for you. Your whole vacation's been ruined. You must be awfully upset."

"These things happen," Rorie said with a shrug. "Being upset isn't going to ship that part any faster. All I can do is accept the facts."

Kate nodded sympathetically. "Skip was about to show me the filly. You'll come with us, won't you?"

Rorie nodded, unable to excuse herself without sounding rude. If there'd been a way, she would have retreated, wanting only to lick her wounds in private. Instead, hoping she sounded more enthusiastic than she felt, she mumbled, "I was headed in that direction myself."

Skip led the way to the barn, which was alive with activity. Clay had explained that Elk Run employed five men full-time, none of whom lived on the premises. Two men mucking out stalls paused when Skip and the women entered the building. Skip introduced Rorie and they touched the tips of their hats in greeting.

"I don't understand Clay," Skip said as they approached the mare's stall. "When we bought Star Bright a few years back, all Clay could do was complain about that silly name. He even talked about getting her registration changed."

"Star Bright's a perfectly good name," Kate insisted, her sunny blue eyes intent on the newborn foal.

Nightsong was standing now on knobby, skinny legs that threatened to buckle, greedily feasting from her mother.

"Oh, she really is lovely, isn't she?" Kate whispered.

Rorie hadn't been able to stop looking at the filly from the moment they'd reached the stall. Finished with her breakfast, Nightsong gazed around, fascinated by everything she surveyed. She returned Rorie's look, not vacantly, but as though she recognized the woman who'd been there at her birth.

Rorie couldn't even identify all the emotions she suddenly felt. Some of these feelings were so new she couldn't put a name to them, but they gripped her heart and squeezed tight.

"What I can't understand," Skip muttered, "is why Clay would go and call her Nightsong when he hates the name Star Bright. It doesn't sound like anything he'd ever come up with on his own, yet he says he did."

"I know," Kate agreed, "but I'm glad, because the name suits her." She sighed. "Clay's always been so practical when it comes to names for his horses, but Nightsong has such a romantic flavor, don't you think?"

Skip chuckled. "You know what Clay thinks about romance, and that makes it even more confusing. But Nightsong she is, and she's bound to bring us a pretty penny in a year or two. Her father was a Polish Arabian, and with Star Bright's bloodlines Nightsong will command big bucks as a National Show Horse."

"Skip." Clay's curt voice interrupted them. He strode from the arena leading a bay mare. The horse's coat gleamed with sweat, turning its color the shade of an oak leaf in autumn. One of the stablemen approached to take the reins. Then Clay removed his hat, wiping his brow with his forearm, and Rorie noticed the now-grimy bandage she'd applied last night. No, this morning.

She stared hungrily at his sun-bronzed face, a face that revealed more than a hint of impatience. The lines around his mouth were etched deep with poorly disguised regrets. Rorie recognized them, even if the others didn't.

Clay stopped short when he saw Kate, his eyes narrowing.

"'Morning, Kate."

"Hello, Clay."

Then his gaze moved, slowly and reluctantly, to Rorie. The remorse she'd already sensed in him seemed unmistakable.

"I hope you slept well," was all he said to her.

"Fine." She detected a tautness along his jaw line and decided he was probably concerned that she'd say or do something to embarrass him in front of his fiancée. Rorie wouldn't, but not because she was worried about him. Her sense of fair play wouldn't allow her to hurt Kate, who so obviously adored this man.

"We're just admiring Nightsong," Kate explained, her expression tender as she smiled up at him.

"I can't understand why you'd name her that," Skip said, his mouth twitching with barely suppressed laughter. "You always pick names like Brutus and Firepower, but Nightsong? I think you're going soft on us." Considering himself particularly funny, Skip chuckled and added, "I suppose that's what love does to a man."

Kate's lashes brushed against the high arch of her cheek and she smiled, her pleasure so keen it was like a physical touch.

"Didn't I ask you to water the horses several hours ago?" Clay asked in a tone that could have chipped rock.

"Yes, but—"

"Then kindly see to it. The farrier will be here any minute."

The humor left Skip's eyes; he was clearly upset by Clay's anger. He looked from his brother to the two women and then back at Clay again. Hot color rose into his neck and invaded his face. "All right," he muttered. "Excuse me for living." Then he stormed out of the barn, slapping his hat against his thigh in an outburst of anger.

Kate waited until Skip was out of the barn. "Clay, what's wrong?"

"He should've done what I told him long before now. Those horses in the pasture are thirsty because of his neglect."

"I'm the one you should be angry with, not Skip." Kate's voice was contrite. "I should never have stopped in without calling first, but I...wanted to meet Rorie."

"You've only been here a few minutes," Clay insisted, his anger in check now. "Skip had plenty of time to complete his chores before you arrived."

Rorie tossed invisible daggers at Clay, annoyed with him for taking his irritation out on his younger brother. Skip had introduced her to Clay's fiancée. *That* was what really bothered him if he'd been willing to admit it— which he clearly wasn't.

"We came here to see Nightsong," Kate said again. "I'm glad you named her that, no matter what Skip thinks." She wrapped her arm around his waist, and rested her head against his broad chest. "He was just teasing you and you know how he loves to do that."

Clay gave her an absent smile, but his gaze settled with disturbing ease on Rorie. She met his eyes boldly, denying the emotions churning furiously inside her. The plea for patience and understanding he sent her was so obvious that Rorie wondered how anyone seeing it wouldn't know what was happening.

As though she'd suddenly remembered something, Kate dropped her arm and glanced hurriedly at her watch. She groaned. "I promised Dad I'd meet him for lunch today. He's getting together with the other Town Council members in one of those horribly boring meetings. He needs me as an excuse to get away." She stopped abruptly, a chagrined expression on her face. "I guess that tells you how informal everything is in Nightingale, doesn't it, Rorie?"

"The town seems to be doing very well." She didn't know if that was true or not, but it sounded polite.

"He just hates these things, but he likes the prestige of being a Council member—something I tease him about."

"I'll walk you to your car," Clay offered.

"Oh, there's no need. You're busy. Besides, I wanted to talk to Rorie and arrange to meet her tomorrow and show her around town. I certainly hope you remembered to invite her to the Grange dance tomorrow night. I'm sure Luke would be willing to escort her."

"Oh, I couldn't possibly intrude," Rorie blurted.

"Nonsense, you'd be more than welcome. And don't worry about having the right kind of clothes for a square dance, either, because I've got more outfits than I know what to do with. We're about the same size," Kate said, eyeing her. "Perhaps you're a little taller, but not so much that you couldn't wear my skirts."

Rorie smiled blandly, realizing it wouldn't do any good

to decline the invitation. But good heavens, square dancing? Her?

"Knowing you and Skip," Kate chastised Clay, "poor Rorie will be stuck on Elk Run for the next four days bored out of her mind. The least I can do is see that she's entertained."

"That's thoughtful of you," Rorie said. The sooner she got back on the road, the safer her heart would be, and if Kate Logan was willing to help her kill time, then all the better.

"I thought I'd give you a tour of our little town in the morning," Kate went on. "It's small, but the people are friendly."

"I'd love to see Nightingale."

"Clay." The brusque voice of a farmhand interrupted them. "Could you come here a minute?"

Clay turned to the man and nodded. "I have to find out what Don needs," he said quietly. As he met Rorie's eyes, a speculative look flashed into his own.

She nearly flinched, wondering what emotion her face had betrayed. From the minute Clay had walked into the barn, she'd been careful to school her expression, not wanting him to read anything into her words or actions. She'd tried to look cool and unconcerned, as if the night they'd shared had never happened.

"You two will have to excuse me." Weary amusement turned up the corners of his mouth and Rorie realized he'd readily seen through her guise.

"Of course," Kate said. "I'll see you later, sweetheart."

Clay nodded abruptly and departed with firm purposeful strides.

Kate started walking toward the yard. Rorie followed, eager to escape the barn and all the memories associated with it.

"Clay told us you're a librarian," Kate said when she reached the Ford parked in the curving driveway. "If you want, I can take you to our library. We built a new one last year and we're rather proud of it. I know it's small compared to where you probably work, but I think you'll like what we've done."

"I'd love to see it." Libraries were often the heart of a community, and if the citizens of Nightingale had seen fit to upgrade theirs, it was apparent they shared Rorie's love of books.

"I'll pick you up around ten tomorrow, if that's convenient?"

"That'd be fine."

"Plan on spending the afternoon with me and we'll meet Clay and Skip at the dance later."

Rorie agreed, although her enthusiasm was decidedly low. The last thing she wanted was to be at some social event with Clay. Never mind how Dan would tease her if he ever discovered she'd spent part of her vacation square dancing with the folks at the Grange.

"Bye for now," Kate said.

"Bye," Rorie murmured, waving. She stood in the yard until Kate's car was out of sight. Not sure what else to do, she wandered back into the house, where Mary was busy with preparations for lunch.

"Can I help?" she asked.

In response, Mary scurried to a drawer and once again handed her a peeler. Rorie started carefully whittling away at a firm red apple she'd scooped from a large bowlful of them.

"I don't suppose you know anything about cooking?" Mary demanded, pointing her own peeler at Rorie.

"I've managed to keep from starving for the last few years," she retorted idly.

The merest hint of amusement flashed into the older woman's weathered face. "If I was judging your talents in the kitchen on looks alone, I think you'd starve a man to death within a week."

Despite her glum spirits, Rorie laughed. "If you're telling me you think I'm thin, watch out, Mary, because I'm likely to throw my arms around your neck and kiss you."

The other woman threw her a grin. Several peaceful minutes passed while they peeled apple after apple.

"I got a call from my sister," Mary said hesitantly, her eyes darting to Rorie, then back to her task. "She's coming to Riversdale and wants to know if I can drive over and see her. She's only going to be in Oregon one day."

This was the most Mary had said to Rorie since her arrival. It pleased her that the older woman was lowering her guard and extending a friendly hand.

"I'd like to visit with my sister."

"I certainly think you should." It took Rorie another minute to figure out where Mary was heading with this meandering conversation. Then suddenly she understood. "Oh, you're looking for someone to do the cooking while you're away."

Mary shrugged as if it didn't concern her one way or the other. "Just for the evening meal, two nights from now. I could manage lunch for the hands before I leave. It's supper I'm worried about. There's only Clay and Skip who need to be fed—the other men go home in the evenings."

"Well, relax, because I'm sure I can manage one dinner without killing off the menfolk."

"You're sure?"

Mary was so completely serious that Rorie laughed outright. "Since my abilities do seem to worry you, how would you feel if I invited Kate Logan over to help?"

Mary nodded and sighed. "I'd rest easier."

Rorie stayed in the kitchen until the lunch dishes had been put away. Mary thanked her for helping, then went home to watch her daily soap operas.

Feeling a little lost, Rorie wandered outside and into the stable. Since Clay had already shown her the computer, she decided to spend the afternoon working in his office. The area was deserted, which went some distance toward reassuring her—but then, she'd assumed it would be. From what she'd observed, a stud farm was a busy place and Clay was bound to be occupied elsewhere. That suited Rorie just fine. She hoped to avoid him as much as possible. In three days she'd be out of his life, leaving hardly a trace, and that was the way she wanted it.

Rorie sat typing in data for about an hour before her neck and shoulders began to cramp. She paused, flexing her muscles, then rotated her head to relieve the building tightness.

"How long have you been here?"

The rough male voice behind her startled Rorie. Her hand flew to her heart and she expelled a shaky breath. "Clay! You frightened me."

"How long?" he repeated.

"An hour or so." She glanced at her watch and nodded.

Clay advanced a step toward her, his mouth a thin line of impatience. "I suppose you're looking for an apology."

Rorie didn't answer. She'd learned not to expect anything from him.

"I'll tell you right now that you're not going to get one," he finished gruffly.

Six

"You don't owe me anything, Clay," Rorie said, struggling to make her voice light. Clay looked driven to the limits of exhaustion. Dark shadows had formed beneath his eyes and fatigue lines fanned out from their corners. His shoulders sagged slightly, as if the weight he carried was more than he could bear. He studied her wearily, then turned away, stalking to the other side of the office. His shoulders heaved as he drew in a shuddering breath.

"I know I should feel some regrets, but God help me, Rorie, I don't."

"Clay, listen..."

He turned to face her then, and drove his fingers into his hair with such force Rorie winced. "I'd like to explain about Kate and me."

"No." Under no circumstances did Rorie want to listen to his explanations or excuses. She didn't have a lot of room to be judgmental herself. She had, after all, been dating a man steadily for the past few months. "Don't. Please don't say anything. It isn't necessary."

He ignored her request. "Kate and I have known each other all our lives."

"Clay, stop." She pushed out the chair and stood up, wanting only to escape.

"For the last two years, it's been understood by everyone around us that Kate and I would eventually get married. I didn't even question the right or wrong of it, just calmly accepted the fact. A man needs someone to share his life."

"Kate will make you a wonderful wife," she said, feeling both disillusioned and indignant, but she refused to let him know how much his indiscretion had hurt her. "If you owe anyone an apology, it's Kate, not me."

His responding frown was brooding and dark. "I know." He drew his fingers across his eyes, and she could feel his exhaustion. "The last thing in the world I want is to hurt Kate."

"Then don't."

He stared at her, and Rorie made herself send him a smile, although she feared it was more flippant than reassuring. "There's no reason for Kate to find out. What good would it do? She'd only end up feeling betrayed. Last night was a tiny impropriety and best forgotten, don't you agree?" Walking seemed to help, and Rorie paced the office, her fingers brushing the stack of books and papers on his cluttered desk.

"I don't know what's best anymore," Clay admitted quietly.

"I do," Rorie said with unwavering confidence, still

struggling to make light of the incident. "Think about it, Clay. We were alone together for hours—we shared something beautiful with Star Bright and…her foal. And we shared a few stolen kisses under the stars. If anything's to blame, it's the moonlight. We're strangers, Clay. You don't know me and I don't know you." Afraid to look him directly in the eye, Rorie lowered her gaze and waited, breathless, for his next words.

"So it was the moonlight?" His voice was hoarse and painfully raw.

"Of course," she lied. "What else could it have been?"

"Yes, what else could it have been?" he echoed, then turned and walked out of the office.

It suddenly seemed as though the room's light had dimmed. Rorie felt so weak, she sank into the chair, shocked by how deeply the encounter had disturbed her.

Typing proved to be a distraction and Rorie left the office a couple of hours later with a feeling of accomplishment. She'd been able to enter several time-consuming pages of data into the computer. The routine work was a relief because it meant she had no time to think.

The kitchen smelled of roasting beef and simmering apple crisp when Rorie let herself in the back door. It was an oddly pleasant combination of scents. Mary was nowhere to be seen.

While she thought of it, Rorie reached for the telephone book and called the number listed for the garage in Riversdale.

"Hello," she said when a gruff male voice answered. "This is Rorie Campbell…the woman with the broken water pump. The one in Nightingale."

"Yeah, Miss Campbell, what can I do for you?"

"I just wanted to be sure there wasn't any problem in ordering the part. I don't know if Clay...Mr. Franklin told you, but I'm more or less stuck here until the car's repaired. I'd like to get back on the road as soon as possible—I'm sure you understand."

"Lady, I can't make that pump come any faster than what it already is."

"Well, I just wanted to check that you'd been able to order one."

"It's on its way, at least that's what the guy in Los Angeles told me. They're shipping it by overnight freight to Portland. I've arranged for a man to pick it up the following day, but it's going to take him some time to get it to me."

"But that's only three days."

"You called too late yesterday for me to phone the order in. Lady, there's only so much I can do."

"I know. I'm sorry if I sound impatient."

"The whole world's impatient. Listen, I'll call you the minute it arrives."

She sighed. "Thanks, I'd appreciate it."

"Clay got your car here without a hitch, so don't worry about that—he saved you a bundle on towing charges. Shipping costs and long-distance phone bills are going to be plenty high, though."

Rorie hadn't even noticed that Dan's shiny sports car wasn't in the yard where Skip had originally left it. "So you'll be calling me within the next day or two?" she asked, trying to hide the anxiety in her voice. And trying not to consider the state of her finances, already depleted by this disastrous vacation.

"Right. I'll call as soon as it comes in."

"Thank you. I appreciate it," she said again.

"No problem," the mechanic muttered, obviously eager to end their conversation.

When the call was finished, Rorie toyed with the idea of phoning Dan next. She'd been half expecting to hear from him, since she'd left the Franklins' number with his secretary the day before. He hadn't phoned her back. But there was nothing new to tell him, so she decided not to call a second time.

Hesitantly Rorie replaced the telephone receiver, pleased that everything was under control—everything except her heart.

Dinner that evening was a strained affair. If it hadn't been for Skip, who seemed oblivious to the tension between her and Clay, Rorie didn't think she could have endured it. Clay hardly said a word throughout the meal. But Skip seemed more than eager to carry the conversation and Rorie did her best to lighten the mood, wondering all the time whether Clay saw through her facade.

"While you're here, Rorie," Skip said with a sudden burst of enthusiasm, "you should learn how to ride."

"No, thank you," she said pointedly, holding up her hand, as though fending off the suggestion. An introduction to King and Hercules was as far as she was willing to go.

"Rain Magic would suit you nicely."

"Rain Magic?"

"That's a silly name Kate thought up, and Clay went along with it," Skip explained. "He's gentle, but smart— the gelding I mean, not Clay." The younger Franklin laughed heartily at his own attempt at humor.

Clay smiled, but Rorie wasn't fooled; he hadn't been amused by the joke, nor, she suspected, was he pleased by the reference to Kate.

"No, thanks, Skip," she said, hoping to bring the subject to a close. "I'm really not interested." There, that said it plainly enough.

"Are you afraid?"

"A little," she admitted truthfully. "I prefer my horses on a merry-go-around. I'm a city girl, remember?"

"But even girls from San Francisco have been known to climb on the back of a horse. It'll be good for you, Rorie. Trust me—it's time to broaden your horizons."

"Thanks, but no thanks," she told him, emphasizing her point by biting down on a crisp carrot stick with a loud crunch.

"Rorie, I insist. You aren't going to get hurt—I wouldn't let that happen, and Rain Magic is as gentle as they come. In fact—" he wiggled his eyebrows up and down "—if you want, we can ride double until you feel more secure."

Rorie laughed. "Skip, honestly."

"All right, you can ride alone, and I'll lead you around in a circle. For as long as you want."

Rorie shook her head and, amused at the mental picture that scenario presented, laughed again.

"Leave it," Clay said with sudden sharpness. "If Rorie doesn't want to ride, drop it, okay?"

Skip's shocked gaze flew from Rorie to his brother. "I was just having fun, Clay."

His older brother gripped his water goblet so hard Rorie thought the glass might shatter. "Enough is enough. She said she wasn't interested and that should be the end of it."

The astounded look left Skip's features, but his eyes narrowed and he stiffened his shoulders in a display of righteous indignation. "What's with you, Clay?" he shouted. "You've been acting like a wounded bear all day, growling at everyone. Who made *you* king of the universe all of a sudden?"

"If you'll excuse me, I'll bring in the apple crisp," Rorie said, and hurriedly rose to her feet, not wanting to be caught in the cross fire between the two brothers. Whatever they had to say wasn't meant for her ears.

The exchange that followed ended quickly, Rorie noted gratefully from inside the kitchen. Their voices were raised and then there was a hush followed by laughter. Rorie relaxed and picked up the dessert, carrying it into the dining room along with a carton of vanilla ice cream.

"I apologize, Rorie," Clay said soberly when she re-entered the room. "Skip's right, I've been cross and unreasonable all day. I hope my sour mood hasn't ruined your dinner."

"Of course not," she murmured, giving him a smile.

Clay stood up to serve the dessert, spooning generous helpings of apple crisp and ice cream into each bowl.

Skip chattered aimlessly, commenting on one subject and then bouncing to another without any logical connection, his thoughts darting this way and that.

"What time are you going over to Kate's tonight?" he casually asked Clay.

"I won't be. She's got some meeting with the women's group from the Grange. They're decorating for the dance tomorrow night."

"Now that you mention it, I seem to remember Kate saying something about being busy tonight." Without a pause he turned to Rorie. "You'll be coming, I hope. The Grange is putting on a square dance—the biggest one of the year, and they usually do it up good."

"Kate already invited me. I'll be going with her," Rorie explained, although she hadn't the slightest idea how to square dance. Generally she enjoyed dancing, although she hadn't gone for several months because Dan wasn't keen on it.

"You could drive there with us if you wanted," Skip offered. "I'd kinda like to walk in there with you on my arm. You'd cause quite a stir with the men, especially Luke Rivers—he's the foreman at the Logan place. Most girls go all goo-goo-eyed over him."

Clay's spoon clanged loudly against the side of his glass dish and he murmured an apology.

"I'm sorry, Skip," Rorie said gently. "I told Kate I'd drive over with her."

"Darn," Skip muttered.

The meal was completed in silence. Once, when Rorie happened to glance up, her eyes met Clay's. Her heart felt as though it might hammer its way out of her chest. She was oppressively aware of the chemistry between them. It simmered in Rorie's veins and she could tell that Clay felt everything she did. Throughout dinner, she'd been all too conscious of the swift stolen glances Clay had sent in her direction. She'd sent a few of her own, though she'd tried hard not to. But it was impossible to be in the same room with this man and not react to him.

A thousand times in the next couple of hours, Rorie told herself that everything would be fine as soon as she could leave. Life would return to normal then.

When the dishes were finished, Skip challenged her to a game of cribbage, and grateful for the escape Rorie accepted. Skip sat with his back to his brother, and every time Rorie played her hand, she found her eyes wandering across the room to where Clay sat reading. To all outward appearances, he was relaxed and comfortable, but she knew he felt as tense as she did. She knew he was equally aware of the electricity that sparked between them.

Rorie's fingers shook as she counted out her cards.

"Fifteen eight," Skip corrected. "You forgot two points."

Her eyes fell to the extra ten, and she blinked. "I guess I did."

Skip heaved a sigh. "I don't think your mind's on the game tonight."

"I guess not," she admitted wryly. "If you'll excuse me, I think I'll go up to bed." She threw him an apologetic smile and reached for her coffee cup. Skip was right; her mind hadn't been on the game at all. Instead, her thoughts had been on a man who owed his loyalties to another woman—a woman whose roots were intricately bound with his. A woman Rorie had liked and respected from the moment they met.

Feeling depressed, she bade the two men good-night

and carried her cup to the kitchen. Dutifully, she rinsed it out and set it beside the sink, but when she turned around Clay was standing in the doorway, blocking her exit.

"Where's Skip?" she asked a little breathlessly. Heat seemed to throb between them and she retreated a step in a futile effort to escape.

"He went upstairs."

She blinked and faked a yawn. "I was headed in that direction myself."

Clay buried one hand in his jeans pocket. "Do you know what happened tonight at dinner?"

Not finding her voice, Rorie shook her head.

"I was jealous," he said from between clenched teeth. "You were laughing and joking with Skip and I wanted it to be *me* your eyes were shining for. Me. No one else." He stopped abruptly and shook his head. "Jealous of a seventeen-year-old boy...I can't believe it myself."

Seven

Rorie decided to wear a dress for her outing with Kate Logan. Although she rose early, both Skip and Clay had eaten breakfast and left the house by the time she came downstairs. Which was just as well, Rorie thought.

Mary stood at the stove, frying chunks of beef for a luncheon stew. "I spoke to Clay about your cooking dinner later this week. He says that'll be fine if you're still around, but the way he sees it, you'll be on your way in a day or two."

Rorie poured herself a cup of coffee. "I'll be happy to do it if I'm here. Otherwise, I'm sure Kate Logan would be more than pleased."

Mary turned to face her, mouth open as if to comment. Instead her eyes widened in appreciation. "My, my, you look pretty enough to hog-tie a man's heart."

"Thank you, Mary," Rorie answered, grinning.

"I suppose you got yourself a sweetheart back there in

San Francisco?" she asked, watching her closely. "A pretty girl like you is bound to attract plenty of men."

Rorie paused to think about her answer. She briefly considered mentioning Dan, but decided against it. She'd planned this separation to gain a perspective on their relationship. And within hours of arriving at Elk Run, Rorie had found her answer. Dan would always be a special friend—but nothing more.

"The question shouldn't require a week's thought," Mary grumbled, stirring the large pot of simmering beef.

"Sorry...I was mulling something over."

"Then there is someone?"

She shook her head. "No."

The answer didn't seem to please Mary, because she frowned. "When did you say that fancy car of yours was going to be fixed?"

The abrupt question caught Rorie by surprise. Mary was openly concerned about the attraction between her and Clay. The housekeeper, who probably knew Clay as well as anyone did, clearly wasn't blind to what had been happening—and just as clearly didn't like it.

"The mechanic in Riversdale said it should be finished the day after tomorrow if all goes well."

"Good!" Mary proclaimed with a fierce nod, then turned back to her stew.

Rorie couldn't help smiling at the older woman's astuteness. Mary was telling her that the sooner she was off Elk Run the better for everyone concerned. Rorie had to agree.

Kate Logan arrived promptly at ten. She wore tight-fitting jeans, red checkered western shirt and a white silk scarf knotted at her throat. Her long honey-colored hair was woven into thick braids that fell over her shoulders. At first glance, Kate looked closer to sixteen than the twenty-four Rorie knew her to be.

Kate greeted her with a warm smile. "Rorie, there wasn't any need to wear something so nice. I should've told you to dress casually."

Rorie's shoulders slumped. "I brought along more dresses than jeans. Am I overdressed? I could change," she said hesitantly.

"Oh, no, you look lovely…" But for the first time, Kate seemed worried. The doubt that played across her features would have been amusing if Rorie hadn't already been suffering from such a potent bout of guilt. It was all too obvious that Kate viewed Rorie as a threat.

If Clay Franklin had chosen that moment to walk into the kitchen, Rorie would've called him every foul name she could think of. She was furious with him for doing this to her—and to Kate.

"I wear a lot of dresses because of my job at the library," Rorie rushed to explain. "I also date quite a bit. I've been seeing someone—Dan Rogers—for a while now. In fact, it's his car I was driving."

"You're dating someone special?" Kate asked, sounding relieved.

"Yes, Dan and I've been going out for several months."

Mary coughed noisily and sent Rorie an accusing glare; Rorie ignored her. "Shouldn't we be leaving?"

"Oh, sure, any time you're ready." When they were outside, Kate turned to face Rorie. Looking uncomfortable, she slipped her hands into the back pockets of her

jeans. "I've embarrassed you and I'm sorry. I didn't mean
to imply that I didn't trust you and Clay."

"There's no need for an apology. I'm sure I wouldn't
react any differently if Clay was *my* fiancé."

Kate shook her head. "But I feel as if I *should* apologize. I'm not going to be the kind of wife Clay wants if
I can't trust him around a pretty girl once in a while."

Had the earth cracked open just then, Rorie would
gladly have fallen in. That had to be preferable to looking
at Kate and feeling the things she did about Clay Franklin.

"Don't have any worries about me," she said, dismissing the issue as nonchalantly as she could. "I'll be out of
everyone's hair in a day or two."

"Oh, Rorie, please, I don't want you to rush off because I had a silly attack of jealousy. Now I feel terrible."

"Don't, please. I have to leave…I want to leave. My vacation's on hold until I can get my car repaired and there's
so much I'd planned to see and do." She dug in her bag
for a brochure. "Have you ever been up to Victoria on
Vancouver Island?"

"Once, but I was only five, too young to remember
much of anything," Kate told her, scanning the pamphlet.
"This does sound like fun. Maybe this is where Clay and
I should have our honeymoon."

"It'd be perfect for that," Rorie murmured. Her heart
constricted with a sudden flash of pain, but she ruthlessly
forced down her emotions, praying Kate hadn't noticed.
"I'm looking forward to visiting Canada. By the way,
Mary's driving to Riversdale to visit her sister later in the
week. She's asked me to take charge of cooking dinner

if I'm still here. Would you like to help? We could have a good time and really get to know each other."

"Oh, that would be great." Kate slipped her arm around Rorie's waist and gave her an enthusiastic squeeze. "Thank you, Rorie. I know you're trying to reassure me, and I appreciate it."

That had been exactly Rorie's intent.

"It probably sounds selfish," Kate continued, "but I'm glad your car broke down when it did. Without any difficulty at all, I can see us becoming the best of friends."

Rorie could, too, but that only added to her growing sense of uneasiness.

Nightingale was a sleepy kind of town. Businesses lined both sides of Main Street, with a beauty shop, an insurance agency, Nellie's Café and a service station on one side, a grocery store, pharmacy and five-and-dime on the other. Rorie had the impression that things happened in their own time in Nightingale, Oregon. Few places could have been more unlike San Francisco, where people always seemed to be rushing. Here, no one seemed to feel any need to hurry. It was as though this town, with its population of fifteen hundred, existed in a time warp. Rorie found the relaxed pace unexpectedly pleasant.

"The library is across from the high school on Maple Street," Kate explained as she parked her Ford on Main. "That way, students have easy access."

Rorie climbed out of the car, automatically pressing down the door lock.

"You don't have to do that here. There hasn't been a vehicle stolen in…oh, at least twenty years."

Rorie's eyes must have revealed her surprise, because Kate went on, "Actually, we had trouble passing our last bond issue for a new patrol car. People couldn't see the need since there hasn't been a felony committed in over two years. About the worst thing that goes on is when Harry Ackerman gets drunk. That happens once or twice a year and he's arrested for disturbing the peace." She grinned sheepishly. "He sings old love songs to Nellie at the top of his lungs in front of the café. They were apparently sweet on each other a long time back. Nellie married someone else and Harry never got over the loss of his one true love."

Looping the strap of her bag over her shoulder, Rorie looked around the quiet streets.

"The fire and police station are in the same building," Kate pointed out next. "And there's a really nice restaurant on Oak. If you want, we could have lunch there."

"Only if you let me treat."

"I wouldn't hear of it," Kate said with a shake of her head that sent her braids flying. "You're my guest."

Rorie decided not to argue, asking another question instead. "Where do the ranchers get their supplies?" It seemed to her that type of store would do a thriving business, yet she hadn't seen one.

"At Garner's Feed and Supply. It's on the outskirts of town—I'll take you past on the way out. In fact, we should take a driving tour so you can see a little more of Nightingale. Main Street is only a small part of it."

By the time Kate and Rorie walked over to Maple and the library, Rorie's head was swimming with the names of all the people Kate had insisted on introducing. It seemed everyone had heard about her car problems and was eager to talk to her. Several mentioned the Grange dance that night and said they'd be looking for her there.

"You're really going to be impressed with the library," Kate promised as they walked the two streets over to Maple. "Dad and the others worked hard to get the levy passed so we could build it. People here tend to be tight-fisted. Dad says they squeeze a nickel so hard, the buffalo belches."

Rorie laughed outright at that.

The library was the largest building in town, a sprawling one-story structure with lots of windows. The hours were posted on the double glass doors, and Rorie noted that the library wouldn't open until the middle of the afternoon, still several hours away.

"It doesn't seem to be open," she said, disappointed.

"Oh, don't worry, I've got a key. All the volunteers do." Kate rummaged in her bag and took out a large key ring. She opened the door, pushing it wide for Rorie to enter first.

"Mrs. Halldorfson retired last year, a month after the building was finished," Kate told her, flipping on the lights, "and the town's budget wouldn't stretch to hire a new full-time librarian. So a number of parents and teachers are taking turns volunteering. We've got a workable schedule, unless someone goes on vacation, which, I hate to admit, has been happening all summer."

"You don't have a full-time librarian?" Rorie couldn't disguise her astonishment. "Why go to all the trouble and expense of building a modern facility if you can't afford a librarian?"

"You'll have to ask Town Council that," Kate returned, shrugging. "It doesn't make much sense, does it? But you see, Mrs. Halldorfson was only part-time and the Council seems to think that's what her replacement should be."

"That doesn't make sense, either."

"Especially when you consider that the new library is twice the size of the old one."

Rorie had to bite her tongue to keep from saying more. But she was appalled at the waste, the missed opportunities.

"We've been advertising for months for a part-time librarian, but so far we haven't found anyone interested. Not that I blame them—one look at the size of the job and no one wants to tackle it alone."

"A library is more than a place to check books in and out," Rorie said, gesturing dramatically. Her voice rose despite herself. This was an issue close to her heart, and polite silence was practically impossible. "A library can be the heart of a community. It can be a place for classes, community services, all kinds of things. Don't non-profit organizations use it for meetings?"

"I'm afraid not," Kate answered. "Everyone gets together at Nellie's when there's any kind of meeting. Nellie serves great pies," she added, as though that explained everything.

Realizing that she'd climbed onto her soapbox, Rorie dropped her hands and shrugged. "It's a very nice building, Kate, and you have every reason to be proud. I didn't mean to sound so righteous."

"But you're absolutely correct," Kate said thoughtfully. "We're not using the library to its full potential, are we?

Volunteers can only do so much. As it is, the library's only open three afternoons a week." She sighed expressively. "To be honest, I think Dad and the other members of the Town Council are expecting Mrs. Halldorfson to come back in the fall, but that's unfair to her. She's served the community for over twenty years. She deserves to retire in peace without being blackmailed into coming back because we can't find a replacement."

"Well, I hope you find someone soon."

"I hope so, too," Kate murmured.

They ate a leisurely lunch, and as she'd promised, Kate gave Rorie a tour of the town. After showing her several churches, the elementary school where she taught second grade and some of the nicer homes on the hill, Kate ended the tour on the outskirts of town near Garner's Feed and Supply.

"Luke's here," Kate said, easing into the parking place next to a dusty pickup truck.

"Luke?"

"Our foreman. I don't know what Dad would do without him. He runs the ranch and has for years—ever since I was in high school. Dad's retirement age now, and he's more than willing to let Luke take charge."

Kate got out of the car and leaned against the front fender, crossing her arms over her chest. Rorie joined her.

"He'll be out in a minute," Kate said.

True to her word, a tall, deeply tanned man appeared with a sack of grain slung over his shoulder. His eyes were so dark they gleamed like onyx, taking in everything around him, but revealing little of his own thoughts.

His strong square chin was balanced by a high intelligent brow. He was lean and muscular and strikingly handsome.

"Need any help, stranger?" Kate asked with a laugh.

"You offering?"

"Nope."

Luke chuckled. "That's what I figured. You wouldn't want to ruin those pretty nails of yours now, would you?"

"I didn't stop by to be insulted by you," Kate chastised, clearly enjoying the exchange. "I wanted you to meet Rorie Campbell—she's the one Clay was telling us about the other night, whose car broke down."

"I remember." For the first time the foreman's gaze left Kate. He tossed the sack of grain into the back of the truck and used his teeth to tug his glove free from his right hand. Then he presented his long callused fingers to Rorie. "Pleased to meet you, ma'am."

"The pleasure's mine." Rorie remembered where she'd heard the name. Skip had mentioned Luke Rivers when he'd told her about the Grange square dance. He'd said something about all the girls being attracted to the foreman. Rorie could understand why.

They exchanged a brief handshake before Luke's attention slid back to Kate. His eyes softened perceptibly.

"Luke's like a brother to me," Kate said fondly.

He frowned at that, but didn't comment.

"We're going to let you escort us to the dance tonight," she informed him.

"What about Clay?"

"Oh, he'll meet us there. I thought the three of us could go over together."

Rorie wasn't fooled. Kate was setting her up with Luke,

who didn't look any too pleased at having his evening arranged for him.

"Kate, listen," she began, "I'd really rather skip the dance tonight. I've never done any square dancing in my life—"

"That doesn't matter," Kate interrupted. "Luke will be glad to show you. Won't you, Luke?"

"Sure," he mumbled, with the enthusiasm of a man offered the choice between hanging and a firing squad.

"Honestly, Luke!" Kate gave an embarrassed laugh.

"Listen," Rorie said quickly. "It's obvious Luke has his own plans for tonight. I don't want to intrude—"

He surprised her by turning toward her, his eyes searching hers. "I'd be happy to escort you, Rorie."

"I'm likely to step all over your toes…I really think I should sit the whole thing out."

"Nonsense," Kate cried. "Luke won't let you do that and neither will I!"

"We'll enjoy ourselves," the foreman said. "Leave everything to me."

Rorie nodded reluctantly.

A moment of awkward silence fell over the trio. "Well, I suppose I should get Rorie back to Circle L and see about finding her a dress," Kate said, smiling. She playfully tossed her car keys in the air and caught them deftly.

Luke tipped his hat when they both returned to the car. Rorie didn't mention his name until they were back on the road.

"Luke really is attractive, isn't he?" she asked, closely watching Kate.

The other woman nodded eagerly. "It surprises me that

he's not married. There are plenty of girls around Nightingale who'd be more than willing, believe me. At every
Grange dance, the ladies flirt with him like crazy. I love
to tease him about it—he really hates that. But I wish
Luke *would* get married—I don't like the idea of him living his life alone. It's time he thought about settling down
and starting a family. He was thirty last month, but when
I said something about it, he nearly bit my head off."

Rorie nibbled on her lower lip. She inhaled a deep
breath and released it slowly. Her guess was that Luke
Rivers had his heart set on someone special, and that
someone was engaged to another man. God help him,
Rorie thought. She knew exactly how he felt.

The music was already playing by the time Luke, Kate
and Rorie arrived at the Grange Hall in Luke's ten-year-
old four-door sedan. Rorie tried to force some enthusiasm for this outing, but had little success. She hadn't
exchanged more than a few words with the foreman during the entire drive. He, apparently, didn't like this ar-
ranged-date business any better than she did. But they
were stuck with each other, and Rorie at least was determined to make the best of it.

They entered the hall and were greeted by the cheery
voice of the male caller:

Rope the cow, brand the calf
Swing your sweetheart, once and a half...

Rorie hadn't known what to expect, but she was surprised by the smooth-stepping, smartly dressed dancers
who twirled around the floor following the caller's di-

rections. She felt more daunted than ever by the evening ahead of her. And to worsen matters, Kate had insisted Rorie borrow one of her outfits. Although Rorie liked the bright blue colors, she felt awkward and self-conscious in the billowing skirts.

The Grange itself was bigger than Rorie had anticipated. On the stage stood the caller and several fiddlers. Refreshment tables lined one wall and the polished dance floor was so crowded Rorie wondered how anyone could move without bumping into others. The entire meeting hall was alive with energy and music, and despite herself, she felt her mood lift. Her toes started tapping out rhythms almost of their own accord. Given time, she'd be out there, too, joining the vibrant, laughing dancers. It was unavoidable, anyway. She knew Kate wouldn't allow her to sit sedately in the background and watch. Neither would Clay and Skip, who'd just arrived.

"Oh, my feet are moving already." Kate was squirming with eagerness. Clay smiled indulgently, tucked his arm around her waist and the two of them stepped onto the dance floor. He glanced back once at Rorie, before a circle of eight opened up to admit them.

"Shall we?" Luke asked, eyeing the dance floor.

He didn't sound too enthusiastic and Rorie didn't blame him. "Would it be all right if we sat out the first couple of dances?" she asked. "I'd like to get more into the swing of things."

"No problem."

Luke looked almost grateful for the respite, which didn't lend Rorie much confidence. No doubt he assumed this city slicker was going to make a fool of herself and of him—and she probably would. When he escorted her to the row of chairs, Rorie made the mistake of sitting down. Instantly her skirts leaped up into her face. Embarrassed, she pushed them down, then tucked the material under her thighs in an effort to tame the layers of stiff petticoats.

"Hello, Luke." A pretty blonde with sparkling blue eyes sauntered over. "I didn't know if you'd show tonight or not. Glad you did."

"Beth Hammond, this is Rorie Campbell."

Rorie nodded. "It's nice to meet you, Beth."

"Oh, I heard about you at the drugstore yesterday. You're the gal with the broken-down sports car, aren't you?"

"That's me." By now it shouldn't have surprised Rorie that everyone knew about her troubles.

"I hope everything turns out okay."

"Thanks." Although Beth was speaking to Rorie, her eyes didn't leave Luke. It was patently obvious that she expected an invitation to dance.

"Luke, why don't you dance with Beth?" Rorie suggested. "That way I'll gather a few pointers from watching the two of you."

"What a good idea," Beth chirped eagerly. "We'll stay on the outskirts of the crowd so you can see how it's done. Be sure and listen to Charlie—he's the caller. Then you'll see what each step is."

Rorie nodded agreeably.

Luke gave Rorie a long sober look. "You're sure?"

"Positive."

All join hands, circle right around
Stop in place at your hometown...

Studying the dancers, Rorie quickly picked up the terms *do se do, allemande left* and *allemande right* and a number of others, which she struggled to keep track of. By the end of the dance, her foot was tapping out the lively beat of the fiddlers' music and a smile formed as she listened to the perfectly rhyming words.

"Rorie," Skip said, suddenly standing in front of her. "May I have the pleasure of this dance?"

"I...I don't think I'm ready yet."

"Nonsense." Without listening to her protest, he grabbed her hand and hauled her to her feet.

"Skip, I'll embarrass you," she protested in a low whisper. "I've never done this before."

"You've got to start sometime." He tucked his arm around her waist and led her close to the stage.

"We got a newcomer, Charlie," Skip called out, "so make this one simple."

Charlie gave Skip a thumbs-up and reached for the microphone. "We'll go a bit slower this time," Charlie announced to his happy audience. "Miss Rorie Campbell from San Francisco has joined us and it's her first time on the floor."

Rorie wanted to curl up and die as a hundred faces turned to stare at her. But the dancers were shouting and cheering their welcome and Rorie shyly raised her hand, smiling into the crowd.

Getting through that first series of steps was the most difficult, but soon Rorie was in the middle of the floor, stepping and twirling—and laughing. Something she'd always assumed to be a silly, outdated activity turned out to be great fun.

By the time Skip led her back to her chair, she was breathless. "Want some punch?" he asked. Rorie nodded eagerly. Her throat felt parched.

When Skip left her, Luke Rivers appeared at her side. "You did just great," he said sincerely.

"For a city girl, you mean," she teased.

"As good as anyone."

"Thanks."

"I suspect I owe you an apology, Rorie."

"Because you didn't want to make a fool of yourself with me on the dance floor?" she asked with a light laugh. "That's understandable. Kate and Clay practically threw me in your lap. I'm sure you had other plans for tonight, and I'm sorry for your sake that we got stuck with each other."

Luke grinned. "Trust me, I've had plenty of envious looks from around the room. Any of a dozen different men would be more than happy to be 'stuck' with you."

That went a long way toward boosting her ego. She would have commented, but Skip came back just then carrying a paper cup filled with bright pink punch. A teenage girl was beside him, clutching his free arm and smiling dreamily up at him.

"I'm going to dance with Caroline now, okay?" he said to Rorie.

"That's fine," she answered, smiling, "and thank you for braving the dance floor with me." Skip blushed as he slipped an arm around Caroline's waist and hurried her off.

"You game?" Luke nodded toward the dancing couples.

Rorie didn't hesitate. She swallowed the punch in three giant gulps, and gave him her hand. Together they moved onto the crowded floor.

By the end of the third set of dances, Rorie had twirled around with so many different partners, she lost track of them. She'd caught sight of Clay only once, and when he saw her he waved. Returning the gesture, she promptly missed her footing and nearly fell into her partner's waiting arms. The tall sheriff's deputy was all too happy to have her throw herself at him and told her as much, to Rorie's embarrassment.

Although it was only ten o'clock, Rorie was exhausted and so warm the perspiration ran in rivulets down her face and neck. She had to escape. Several times, she'd tried to sit out a dance, but no one would listen to her excuses.

In an effort to catch her breath and cool down, Rorie took advantage of a break between sets to wander outside. The night air was refreshing. Quite a few other people had apparently had the same idea; the field that served as a car park was crowded with groups and strolling couples.

As she made her way through the dimly lit field, she saw a handful of men passing around a flask of whiskey and entertaining each other with off-color jokes. She steered a wide circle around them and headed toward Luke's parked car, deciding it was far enough away to discourage anyone from following her. In her eagerness to escape, she nearly stumbled over a couple locked in a passionate embrace against the side of a pickup.

Rorie mumbled an apology when the pair glanced up at her, irritation written all over their young faces. Good grief, she'd only wanted a few minutes alone in order to get a breath of fresh air—she hadn't expected to walk through an obstacle course!

When she finally arrived at Luke Rivers's car, she leaned on the fender and slowly inhaled the clean country air. All her assumptions about this evening had been wrong. She'd been so sure she'd feel lonely and bored and out of place. And she'd felt none of those things. If she were to tell Dan about the Grange dance, he'd laugh at the idea of having such a grand time with a bunch of what he'd refer to as "country bumpkins." The thought annoyed her. These were good, friendly, fun-loving people. They'd taken her under their wing, expressed their welcome without reserve, and now they were showing her an uncomplicated lifestyle that had more appeal than Rorie would have believed possible.

"I thought I'd find you out here."

Rorie's whole body tensed as she recognized the voice of the man who'd joined her.

"Hello, Clay."

Eight

Rorie injected a cheerful note into her voice. She turned around, half expecting Kate to be with him. The two had been inseparable from the minute Clay had arrived. It was just as well that Kate was around, since her presence prevented Clay and Rorie from giving in to any temptation.

Clay's hands settled on her shoulders and Rorie flinched involuntarily at his touch. With noticeable regret, Clay dropped his hands.

"Are you having a good time?" he asked.

She nodded. "I didn't think I would, which tells you how prejudiced I've been about country life, but I've been pleasantly surprised."

"I'm glad." His hands clenched briefly at his sides, then he flexed his fingers a couple of times. "I would've danced with you myself, but—"

She stopped him abruptly. "Clay, no. Don't explain… it isn't necessary. I understand."

His eyes held hers with such tenderness that she had

to look away. The magical quality was in the air again—Rorie could feel it as forcefully as if the stars had spelled it out across the heavens.

"I don't think you do understand, Rorie," Clay said, "but it doesn't matter. You'll be gone in a couple of days and both our lives will go back to the way they were meant to be."

Rorie agreed with a quick nod. It was too tempting, standing in the moonlight with Clay. Much too tempting. The memory of another night in which they'd stood and gazed at the stars returned with powerful intensity. Rorie realized that even talking to each other, alone like this, was dangerous.

"Won't Kate be looking for you?" she asked carefully.

"No. Luke Rivers is dancing with her."

For a moment she closed her eyes, not daring to look up at Clay. "I guess I'll be going inside now. I just came out to catch my breath and cool down a little."

"Dance with me first—here in the moonlight."

A protest rose within her, but the instant Clay slid his arms around her waist, Rorie felt herself give in. Kate would have him the rest of her life, but Rorie only had these few hours. Almost against her will, her hands found his shoulders, slipping around his neck with an ease that brought a sigh of pleasure to her lips. Being held by Clay shouldn't feel this good.

"Oh, Rorie," he moaned as she settled into his embrace.

They fitted together as if they'd been created for each other. His chin touched the top of her head and he caressed her hair with his jaw.

"This is a mistake," Rorie murmured, closing her eyes, savoring the warm, secure feel of his arms.

"I know…"

But neither seemed willing to release the other.

His mouth grazed her temple and he kissed her there. "God help me, Rorie, what am I going to do? I haven't been able to stop thinking about you. I can't sleep, I hardly eat…" His voice was raw, almost savage.

"Oh, please," she said with a soft cry. "We can't…we mustn't even talk like this." His gray eyes smouldered above hers, and their breaths merged as his mouth hovered so close to her own.

"I vowed I wouldn't touch you again."

Rorie looked away. She'd made the same promise to herself. But it wasn't in her to deny him now, although her mind searched frantically for the words to convince him how wrong they were to risk hurting Kate—and each other.

His hands drifted up from her shoulders, his fingertips skimming the sides of her neck, trailing over her cheeks and through the softness of her hair. He placed his index finger over her lips, gently stroking them apart.

Rorie moaned. She moistened her lips with the tip of her tongue. Clay's left hand dug into her shoulders as her tongue caressed the length of his finger, drawing it into her mouth and sucking it gently. She needed him so much in that moment, she could have wept.

"Just this once…for these few minutes," he pleaded, "let me pretend you're mine." His hands cupped her face and slowly brought her mouth to his, smothering her whimper of part welcome, part protest.

A long series of kisses followed. Deep, relentless, searching kisses that sent her heart soaring. Kisses that only made the coming loneliness more painful. A sob swelled within her and tears burned her eyes as she twisted away and tore her mouth from his.

"No," she cried, covering her face with her hands and turning her back to him. "Please, Clay. We shouldn't be doing this."

He was silent for so long that Rorie suspected he'd left her. She inhaled a deep, calming breath and dropped her hands limply to her sides.

"It would be so easy to love you, Rorie."

"No," she whispered, shaking her head vigorously as she faced him again. "I'm not the right person for you—it's too late for that. You've got Kate." She couldn't keep the pain out of her voice. Anything between them was hopeless, futile. Within a day or two her car would be repaired and she'd vanish from his life as suddenly as she'd appeared.

Clay fell silent, his shoulders stiff and resolute as he stood silhouetted against the light of the Grange Hall. His face was masked by shadows and Rorie couldn't read his thoughts. He drew in a harsh breath.

"You're right, Rorie. We can't allow this...attraction between us to get out of hand. I promise you, by all I hold dear, that I won't kiss you again."

"I'll...do my part, too," she assured him, feeling better now that they'd made this agreement.

His hand reached for hers and clasped it warmly. "Come on, I'll walk you back to the hall. We're going to be all right. We'll do what we have to do."

Clay's tone told her he meant it. Relieved, Rorie silently made the same promise to herself.

Rorie slept late the next morning, later than she would have thought possible. Mary was busy with lunch preparations by the time she made her way downstairs.

"Did you enjoy yourself last night?" Mary immediately asked.

In response, Rorie curtsyed and danced a few steps with an imaginary partner, clapping her hands.

Mary tried to hide a smile at Rorie's antics. "Oh, get away with you now. All I was looking for was a yes or a no."

"I had a great time."

"It was nothing like those city hotspots, I'll wager."

"You're right about that," Rorie told her, pouring herself a cup of coffee.

"You seeing Kate today?"

Rorie shook her head and popped a piece of bread in the toaster. "She's got a doctor's appointment this morning and a teachers' meeting this afternoon. She's going to stop by later if she has a chance, but if not I'll be seeing her for sure tomorrow." Rorie intended to spend as much time as she could with Clay's fiancée. She genuinely enjoyed her company, and being with her served two useful purposes. It helped keep Rorie occupied, and it prevented her from being alone with Clay.

"What are you going to do today, then?" Mary asked, frowning.

Rorie laughed. "Don't worry. Whatever it is, I promise to stay out of your way."

The housekeeper gave a snort of amusement—or was it relief?

"Actually, I thought I'd finish putting the data Clay needs for his pedigree-research program into the computer. There isn't much left and I should be done by this afternoon."

"So if someone comes looking for you, that's where you'll be?"

"That's where I'll be," Rorie echoed. She didn't know who would "come looking for her," as Mary put it. The housekeeper made it sound as though a posse was due to arrive any minute demanding to know where the Franklin men were hiding Rorie Campbell.

Taking her coffee cup with her, Rorie walked across the yard and into the barn. Once more, she was impressed with all the activity that went on there. She'd come to know several of the men by their first names and returned their greetings with a smile and a wave.

As before, she found the office empty. She set down her cup while she turned on the computer and collected Clay's data. She'd just started to type it in when she heard someone enter the room. Pausing, she twisted around.

"Rorie."

"Clay."

They were awkward with each other now. Almost afraid.

"I didn't realize you were here."

She stood abruptly. "I'll leave…"

"No. I came up to get something. I'll be gone in a minute."

She nodded and sat back down. "Okay."

He walked briskly to his desk and sifted through the untidy stacks of paper. His gaze didn't waver from the task, but his jaw was tight, his teeth clenched. Impatience marked his every move. "Kate told me you're involved with a man in San Francisco. I...didn't know."

"I'm not exactly involved with him—at least not in the way you're implying. His name is Dan Rogers, and we've been seeing each other for about six months. He's divorced. The MG is his."

Clay's mouth thinned, but he still didn't look at her. "Are you in love with him?"

"No."

Lowering his head, Clay rubbed his hand over his eyes. "I had no right to ask you that. None. Forgive me, Rorie." Then, clutching his papers, he stalked out of the office without a backward glance.

Rorie was so shaken by the encounter that when she went back to her typing, she made three mistakes in a row and had to stop to regain her composure.

When the phone rang, she ignored it, knowing Mary or one of the men would answer it. Soon afterward, she heard running footsteps behind her and swivelled around in the chair.

A breathless Skip bolted into the room. Shoulders heaving, he pointed in the direction of the telephone. "It's for you," he panted.

"Me?" It could only be Dan.

He nodded several times, his hand braced theatrically against his heart.

She picked up the extension. "Hello," she said, her fingers closing tightly around the receiver. "This is Rorie Campbell."

"Miss Campbell," came the unmistakable voice of George, the mechanic in Riversdale, "let me put it to you like this. I've got good news and bad news."

"Now what?" she cried, pushing her hair off her forehead with an impatient hand. She had to get out of Elk Run.

"My man picked up the water pump for your car in Portland just like we planned."

"Good."

George sighed heavily. "There's a minor problem, though."

"Minor?" she repeated hopefully.

"Well, not that minor actually."

"Oh, great... Listen, George, I'd prefer not to play guessing games with you. Just tell me what happened and how long it's going to be before I can get out of here."

"I'm sorry, Miss Campbell, but they shipped the wrong part. It'll be two, possibly three more days."

Nine

"What's the matter?" Skip asked when Rorie indignantly replaced the receiver.

She crossed her arms over her chest and breathed deeply, battling down the angry frustration that boiled inside her. The problem wasn't George's fault, or Skip's, or Kate's, or anyone else's.

"Rorie?" Skip asked again.

"They shipped the wrong part for the car," she said flatly. "I'm going to be stuck here for another two or possibly three days."

Skip didn't look the least bit perturbed at this information. "Gee, Rorie, that's not so terrible. We like having you around—and you like it here, don't you?"

"Yes, but..." How could she explain that her reservations had nothing to do with their company, the farm or even with country life? She couldn't very well blurt out that she was falling in love with his brother, that she had to escape before she ruined their lives.

"But what?" Skip asked.

"My vacation."

"I know you had other plans, but you can relax and enjoy yourself here just as well, can't you?"

She didn't attempt to answer him, but closed her eyes and nodded, faintly.

"Well, listen, I've got to get back to work. Do you need me for anything?"

She shook her head. When the office door closed, Rorie sat down in front of the computer again and poised her fingers over the keyboard. She sat like that, unmoving, for several minutes as her thoughts churned. What was she going to do? Every time she came near Clay the attraction was so strong that trying to ignore it was like swimming upstream. Rorie had planned on leaving Elk Run the following day. Now she was trapped here for God only knew how much longer.

She got up suddenly and started pacing the office floor. Dan hadn't called her, either. She might have vanished from the face of the earth as far as he was concerned. The stupid car was his, after all, and the least he could do was make some effort to find out what had happened. Rorie knew she wasn't being entirely reasonable, but she was caught up in the momentum of her anger and frustration.

Impulsively she snatched up the telephone receiver, had the operator charge the call to her San Francisco number and dialed Dan's office.

"Rorie, thank God you phoned," Dan said.

The worry in his voice appeased her a little. "The least you could've done was call me back," she fumed.

"I tried. My secretary apparently wrote down the wrong

number. I've been waiting all this time for you to call me again. Why didn't you? What on earth is going on?"

She told him in detail, from the stalled car to her recent conversation with the mechanic. She didn't tell him about Clay Franklin and the way he made her feel.

"Rorie, baby, I'm so sorry."

She nodded mutely, close to tears. If she wasn't so dangerously close to falling in love with Clay, none of this would seem such a disaster.

The silence lengthened while Dan apparently mulled things over. "Shall I come and get you?" he finally asked.

"With what?" she asked with surprising calm. "My car? You were the one who convinced me it would never make this trip. Besides, how would you get the MG back?"

"I'd figured something out. Listen, I can't let you sit around in some backwoods farm town. I'll borrow a car or rent one." He hesitated, then expelled his breath in a short burst of impatience. "Damn, forget that. I can't come."

"You can't?"

"I've got a meeting tomorrow afternoon. It's important—I can't miss it. I'm sorry, Rorie, I really am, but there's nothing I can do."

"Don't worry about it," she said, defeat causing her voice to dip slightly. "I understand." In a crazy kind of way she did. Dan was a rising stockbroker, so career moves were critical to him, more important than rescuing Rorie, the woman he claimed to love... Somehow Rorie couldn't picture Clay making the same decision. In her heart she knew Clay would come for her the second she asked.

They spoke for a few more minutes before Rorie ended

the conversation. She felt trapped, as though the walls were closing in around her. So far she and Clay had managed to disguise their feelings, but they wouldn't be able to keep it up much longer before someone guessed. Kate wasn't blind, and neither was Mary.

"Rorie?" Clay called her name as he burst into the office. "What happened? Skip told me you were all upset—something about the car? What is it?"

"George called." She whirled around and pointed toward the phone. "The water pump arrived just like it was supposed to—but it's the wrong one."

Clay dropped his gaze, then removed his hat and wiped his forehead. "I'm sorry."

"I am, too, but that doesn't help, does it?" The conversation with Dan hadn't improved matters, and taking her frustration out on Clay wasn't going to change anything, either. "I'm stuck here, and this is the last place on earth I want to be."

"Do you think I like it any better?" he challenged.

Rorie blinked wildly at the tears that burned for release.

"I wish to God your car had broken down a hundred miles from Elk Run," he said. "Before you bombarded your way into my home, my life was set. I knew what I wanted, where I was headed. In the course of a few days you've upended my whole world."

Emotion clogged Rorie's throat at the unfairness of his accusations. She hadn't asked for the MGB to break down where it had. The minute she could, she planned to get out of his life and back to her own.

No, she decided, they couldn't wait that long—it was

much too painful for them both. She had to leave now. "I'll pack my things and be gone before evening."

"Just where do you plan to go?"

Rorie didn't know. "Somewhere...anywhere." She had to leave for his sake, as well as hers.

"Go back inside the house, Rorie, before I say or do something else I'll regret. You're right—we can't be in the same room together. At least not alone."

She started to walk past him, eyes downcast, her heart heavy with misery. Unexpectedly his hand shot out and caught her fingers, stopping her.

"I didn't mean what I said." His voice rasped, warm and hoarse. "None of it. Forgive me, Rorie."

Her heart raced when his hand touched hers. It took all the restraint Rorie could muster, which at the moment wasn't much, to resist throwing herself into his arms and holding on for the rest of her life.

"Forgive me, too," she whispered.

"Forgive you?" he asked, incredulous. "No, Rorie. I'll thank God every day of my life for having met you." With that, he released her fingers, slowly, reluctantly. "Go now, before I make an even bigger fool of myself."

Rorie ran from the office as though a raging fire were licking at her heels, threatening to consume her.

And in a way, it was.

For two days, Rorie managed to stay completely out of his way. They saw each other only briefly and always in the company of others. Rorie was sure they gave Academy Award performances every time they were together.

They laughed and teased and joked and the only one who seemed to suspect things weren't quite right was Mary.

Rorie was grateful the housekeeper didn't question her, but the looks she gave Rorie were frowningly thoughtful.

Three days after the Grange dance, Mary's sister arrived in Riversdale. Revealing more excitement than Rorie had seen in their acquaintance, Mary fussed with her hair and dress, and as soon as she'd finished the lunch dishes she was off.

Putting on Mary's well-worn apron, Rorie looped the long strands around her waist twice and set to work. Kate joined her mid-afternoon, carrying a large bag of ingredients for the dessert she was going to prepare.

"I've been cooking from the moment Mary left," Rorie told Kate, pushing the damp hair from her forehead as she stirred wine into a simmering sauce. Rorie intended to dazzle Clay and Skip with her one speciality—seafood fettuccine. She hadn't admitted to Mary how limited her repertoire of dishes was, although the housekeeper had repeatedly quizzed her about what she planned to make for dinner. Rorie had insisted it was a surprise. She'd decided that this rich and tasty dish stood a good chance of impressing the Franklin men.

"And I'm making Clay his favorite dessert—homemade lemon meringue pie." Kate reached for the grocery bag on the kitchen counter and six bright yellow lemons rolled out.

Rorie was impressed. The one and only time she'd tried to bake a lemon pie, she'd used a pudding mix. Apparently, Kate took the homemade part seriously.

"Whatever you're cooking smells wonderful," Kate

said, stepping over to the stove. Crab, large succulent shrimp and small bite-sized pieces of sole were waiting in the refrigerator, to be added to the sauce just before the dish was served.

Kate was busy whipping up a pie crust when the phone rang several minutes later. She glanced anxiously at the wall, her fingers sticky with flour and lard.

Rorie looked over at her. "Do you suppose I should answer that?"

"You'd better. Clay usually relies on Mary to catch the phone for him."

Rorie lifted the receiver before the next peal. "Elk Run."

"That Miss Campbell?"

Rorie immediately recognized the voice of the mechanic from Riversdale. "Yes, this is Rorie Campbell."

"Remember I promised I'd call you when the part arrived? Well, it's here, all safe and sound, so you can stop fretting. Just came in a few minutes ago—haven't even had a chance to take it out of the box. Thought you'd want to know."

"It's the right one this time?"

"Here, I'll check it now... Yup, this is it."

Rorie wasn't sure what she felt. Relief, yes, but regret, too. "Thank you. Thank you very much."

"It's a little late for me to be starting the job this afternoon. My son's playing a Little League game and I promised him I'd be there. I'll get to this first thing in the morning and should be finished before noon. Give me a call before you head over here and I'll make sure everything's running the way it should."

"Yes, I'll do that. Thanks again." Slowly Rorie replaced the receiver. She leaned against the wall sighing deeply. At Kate's questioning gaze, she smiled weakly and explained, "That was the mechanic. The water pump for my car arrived and he's going to be working on it first thing in the morning."

"Rorie, that's great."

"I think so, too." She did—and she didn't. Part of her longed to flee Elk Run, and another part of her realized that no matter how far she traveled, no matter how many years passed, she'd never forget these days with Clay Franklin.

"Then tonight's going to be your last evening here," Kate murmured. "Selfish as it sounds, I really hate the thought of you leaving."

"We can keep in touch."

"Oh, yes, I'd like that. I'll send you a wedding invitation."

That reminder was the last thing Rorie needed. But once she was on the road again, she could start forgetting, she told herself grimly.

"Since this is going to be your last night, we should make it special," Kate announced brightly. "We're going to use the best china and set out the crystal wineglasses."

Rorie laughed, imagining Mary's face when she heard about it.

Even as she spoke, Kate was walking toward the dining-room china cabinet. In a few minutes, she'd set the table, cooked the sauce for the pie and poured it into the cooling pie shell that sat on the counter. The woman was a marvel!

Rorie was busy adding the final touches to the fettuccine when Clay and Skip came in through the back door.

"When's dinner?" Skip wanted to know. "I'm starved."

"Soon." Rorie tested the boiling noodles to be sure
they'd cooked all the way through but weren't overdone.

"Upstairs with the both of you," Kate said, shooing
them out of the kitchen. "I want you to change into something nice."

"We're supposed to dress up for dinner?" Skip complained. He'd obviously recovered from any need to
impress her with his sartorial elegance, Rorie noted, remembering that he'd worn his Sunday best that first night.
"We already washed—what more do you want?"

"For you to change your clothes. We're having a cel-
ebration tonight."

"We are?" The boy looked from Kate to Rorie and
then back again.

"That's right," Kate continued, undaunted by his lack
of enthusiasm. "And when we're through with dinner,
there's going to be a farewell party for Rorie. We're going
to send her off country-style."

"Rorie's leaving?" Skip sounded shocked. "But she
just got here."

"The repair shop from Riversdale called. Her car will
be finished tomorrow and she'll be on her way."

Clay's eyes burned into Rorie's. She tried to avoid looking at him, but when she did chance to meet his gaze,
she could feel his distress. His jaw went rigid, and his
mouth tightened as though he was bracing himself against
Kate's words.

"Now hurry up, you two. Dinner's nearly ready," Kate

said with a laugh. "Rorie's been cooking her heart out all afternoon."

Both men disappeared and Rorie set out the fresh green salad she'd made earlier, along with the seven-grain dinner rolls she'd warmed in the oven.

Once everyone was seated at the table and waiting, Rorie ceremonially carried in the platter of fettuccine, thick with seafood. She'd spent at least ten minutes arranging it to look as attractive as possible.

"Whatever it is smells good," Skip called out as she entered the dining room. "I'm so hungry I could eat a horse."

"Funny, Skip, very funny," Kate said.

Rorie set the serving dish in the middle of the table and stepped back, anticipating their praise.

Skip raised himself halfway out of his seat as he glared at her masterpiece. "That's it?" His voice was filled with disappointment.

Rorie blinked, uncertain how she should respond.

"You've been cooking all afternoon and you mean to tell me that's everything?"

"It's seafood fettuccine," she explained.

"It just looks like a bunch of noodles to me."

Ten

"I'll have another piece of lemon pie," Skip said, eagerly extending his plate.

"If you're still hungry, Skip," Clay remarked casually, "there are a few dinner rolls left."

Skip's gaze darted to the small wicker basket and he wrinkled his nose. "No, thanks. Too many seeds in those things. I got one caught in my tooth earlier and spent five minutes trying to suck it out."

Rorie did her best to smile.

Skip must have noticed how miserable she was because he added, "The salad was real good though. What kind of dressing was that?"

"Vinaigrette."

"Really? It tasted fruity."

"It was raspberry flavored."

Skip's eyes widened. "I've never heard of that kind of vinegar. Did you buy it here in Nightingale?"

"Not exactly. I got the ingredients while Kate and I were out the other day and mixed it up last night."

"*That* tasted real good." Which was Skip's less-than-subtle method of telling her nothing else had. He'd barely touched the main course. Clay had made a show of asking for seconds, but Rorie was all too aware that his display of enthusiasm had been an effort to salve her injured ego.

Rorie wasn't fooled—no one had enjoyed her special dinner. Even old Blue had turned his nose up at it when she'd offered him a taste of the leftovers.

Clay and Skip did hard physical work; they didn't sit in an office all day like Dan and the other men she knew. She should have realized that Clay and his brother required a more substantial meal than noodles swimming in a creamy sauce. Rorie wished she'd discussed her menu with either Mary or Kate. A tiny voice inside her suggested that Kate might have said something to warn her...

"Anyone else for more pie?" Kate was asking.

Clay nodded and cast a guilty glance in Rorie's direction. "I could go for a second piece myself."

"The pie was delicious," Rorie told Kate, meaning it. She was willing to admit Kate's dessert had been the highlight of the meal.

"Kate's one of the best cooks in the entire country," Skip announced, licking the back of his fork. "Her lemon pie won a blue ribbon at the county fair last year." He leaned forward, planting his elbows on the table. "She's got a barbecue sauce so tangy and good that when she cooks up spareribs I just can't stop eating 'em." His face fell as though he was thinking about those ribs now and would have gladly traded all of Rorie's fancy city food for a plateful.

"I'd like the fettuccine recipe if you'd give it to me," Kate told Rorie, obviously attempting to change the subject and spare Rorie's feelings. Perhaps she felt a little guilty, too, for not giving her any helpful suggestions.

Skip stared at Kate as if she'd volunteered to muck out the stalls.

"I'll write it down before I leave."

"Since Rorie and Kate put so much time and effort into the meal, I think Skip and I could be convinced to do our part and wash the dishes."

"We could?" Skip protested.

"It's the least we can do," Clay returned flatly, frowning at his younger brother.

Rorie was all too aware of Clay's ploy. He wanted to get into the kitchen so they could find something else to eat without being conspicuous about it. Something plain and basic, no doubt, like roast-beef sandwiches.

"Listen, you guys," Rorie said brightly. "I'm sorry about dinner. I can see everyone's still hungry. You're all going out of your way to reassure me, but it isn't necessary."

"I don't know what you're talking about, Rorie. Dinner was excellent," Clay said, patting his stomach.

Rorie nearly laughed out loud. "Why don't we call for a pizza?" she said, pleased with her solution. "I bungled dinner, so that's the least I can do to make it up to you."

Three faces stared at her blankly.

"Rorie," Clay said gently. "The closest pizza parlour is thirty miles from here."

"Oh."

Undeterred, Skip leaped to his feet. "No problem... You phone in the order and I'll go get it."

Empty pizza boxes littered the living-room floor, along with several abandoned soft-drink cans.

Skip lay on his back staring up at the ceiling. "Anyone for a little music?" he asked lazily.

"Sure." Kate got to her feet and sat down at the piano. As her nimble fingers ran over the keyboard, the rich sounds echoed against the walls. "Some Lee Greenwood?"

"All *right,*" Skip called out with a yell, punching his fist into the air. He thrust two fingers in his mouth and gave a shrill whistle.

"Who?" Rorie asked once the commotion had died down.

"He's a country singer," Clay explained. Blue ambled to his side, settling down at his feet. Clay gently stroked his back.

"I guess I haven't heard of him," Rorie murmured.

Once more she discovered three pairs of eyes studying her curiously.

"What about Johnny Cash?" Kate suggested next. "You probably know who he is."

"Oh, sure." Rorie looped her arms over her bent knees and lowered her voice to a gravelly pitch. "I hear that train a comin'."

Skip let loose with another whistle and Rorie laughed at his boisterous antics. Clay left the room; he returned a moment later with a guitar, then seated himself on the floor again, beside Blue. Skip crawled across the braided rug in the center of the room and retrieved a harmonica from the mantel. Soon Kate and the two men were making their own brand of music—country songs, from the traditional to the more recent. Rorie didn't know a single one, but she clapped her hands and tapped her foot to the lively beat.

"Sing for Rorie," Skip shouted to Clay and Kate. "Let's show her what she's been missing."

Clay's rich baritone joined Kate's lilting soprano, and Rorie's hands and feet stopped moving. Her eyes darted from one to the other in openmouthed wonder at the beautiful harmony of their two voices, male and female. It was as though they'd been singing together all their lives. She realized they probably had.

When they finished, Rorie blinked back tears, too dumbfounded for a moment to speak. "That was wonderful," she told them and her voice caught with emotion.

"Kate and Clay sing duets at church all the time," Skip explained. "They're good, aren't they?"

Rorie nodded, gazing at the two of them. Clay and Kate were right for each other—they belonged together, and once she was gone they would blend their lives as beautifully as they had their voices. Rorie happened to catch Kate's eye. The other woman slipped her arms around Clay's waist and rested her head against his shoulder, laying claim to this man and silently letting Rorie know it. Rorie couldn't blame Kate. In like circumstances she would have done the same.

"Do you sing, Rorie?" Kate asked, leaving Clay and sliding onto the piano bench.

"A little, and I play some piano." Actually her own singing voice wasn't half bad. She'd participated in several singing groups while she was in high school and had taken five years of piano lessons.

"Please sing something for us." Rorie recognized a hint of challenge in the words.

"Okay." She replaced Kate at the piano seat and started out with a little satirical ditty she remembered from her college days. Skip hooted as she knew he would at the clever words, and all three rewarded her with a round of applause.

"Play some more," Kate encouraged. "It's nice to have someone else do the playing for a change." She sat next to Clay on the floor, once again resting her head against his shoulder. If it hadn't been for the guitar in his hands, Rorie knew he would've placed his arm around her and drawn her even closer. It would have been the natural thing to do.

"I don't know the songs you usually sing, though." Rorie was more than a little reluctant now. She'd never heard of this Greenwood person they seemed to like so well.

"Play what you know," Kate said, "and we'll join in."

After a few seconds' thought, Rorie nodded. "This is a song by Billy Joel. I'm sure you've heard of him—his songs are more rock than country, but I think you'll recognize the music." Rorie was only a few measures into the ballad before she realized that Kate, Clay and Skip had never heard this song.

She stopped playing. "What about Whitney Houston?" Skip repeated the name a couple of times before his eyes lit up with recognition. "Hasn't she done Coke commercials?"

"Right," Rorie said, laughing. "She's had several big hits."

Kate slowly shook her head. "Sorry, I don't think I can remember the words to her songs."

"Barbra Streisand?"

"I thought she was an actress," Skip said with a puzzled frown. "You mean she sings, too?"

Reluctantly Rorie rose from the piano seat. "Kate, you'll have to take over. It seems you three are a whole lot country and I'm a little bit rock and roll."

"We'll make you into a country girl yet!" Skip insisted, sliding the harmonica across his mouth with an ease Rorie envied.

Clay glanced at his watch. "We aren't going to be able to convert Rorie within the next twelve hours."

A gloom settled over them as Kate took Rorie's place at the piano.

"Are you sure we can't talk you into staying a few extra days?" Skip asked. "We're just getting to know each other."

Rorie shook her head, more determined than ever to leave as soon as she could.

"It would be a shame for you to miss the county fair next weekend. Maybe you could stop here on your way back through Oregon, after your trip to Canada," Kate added. "Clay and I are singing, and we're scheduled for the square dance competition, too."

"Yeah," Skip cried. "And we've got pig races planned again this year."

"Pig races?" Rorie echoed faintly.

"I know it sounds silly, but it's really fun. We take the ten fastest pigs in the area and let them race toward a bowl of Oreos. No joke—cookies! Everyone bets on who'll win and we all have a lot of fun." Skip's eyes shone with eagerness. "Please think about it, anyway, Rorie."

"Mary's entering her apple pie again," Clay put in. "She's been after that blue ribbon for six years."

A hundred reasons to fade out of their lives flew across Rorie's mind like particles of dust in the wind. And yet the offer was tempting. She tried, unsuccessfully, to read Clay's eyes, her own filled with a silent appeal. This was a decision she needed help making. But Clay wasn't helping. The thought of never seeing him again was like pouring salt onto an open wound; still, it was a reality she'd have to face sooner or later.

So Rorie volunteered the only excuse she could come up with at the moment. "I don't have the time. I'm sorry, but I'd be cutting it too close to get back to San Francisco for work Monday morning."

"Not if you canceled part of your trip to Canada and came back on Friday," Skip pointed out. "You didn't think you'd have a good time at the square dance, either, but you did, remember?"

It wasn't a matter of having a good time. So much more was involved...though the pig races actually sounded like fun. The very idea of such an activity would have astounded her only a week before, Rorie reflected. She could just imagine what Dan would say.

"Rorie?" Skip pressed. "What do you think?"

"I...I don't know."

"The county fair is about as good as it gets around Nightingale."

"I don't want to impose on your hospitality again." Clay still wasn't giving her any help with this decision.

"But having you stay with us isn't a problem," Skip insisted. "As long as you promise to stay out of the kitchen, you're welcome to stick around all summer. Isn't that right, Clay?"

His hesitation was so slight that Rorie doubted anyone else had noticed it. "Naturally Rorie's welcome to visit us any time she wants."

"If staying with these two drives you crazy," Kate inserted, "you could stay at my house. In fact, I'd love it if you did."

Rorie dropped her gaze, fearing what she might see in Clay's eyes. She sensed his indecision as she struggled with her own. She had to leave. Yet she wanted to stay....

"I think I should take the rest of my vacation in Victoria," she finally told them.

"I know you're worried about getting back in time for work, but Skip's right. If you left Victoria one day early, then you could be here for the fair," Kate suggested again, but her offer didn't sound as sincere as it had earlier.

"Rorie said she doesn't have the time," Clay said after an awkward silence. "I think we should respect her decision."

"You sound as if you don't want her to come back," Skip accused.

"No," Clay murmured, his eyes meeting hers. "I want her here, but Rorie should try to salvage some of the vacation she planned. She has to do what she think's best."

Rorie could feel his eyes moving over her hair and her face in loving appraisal. She tensed and prayed that Kate and Skip weren't aware of it.

During the next hour, Skip tried repeatedly to convince Rorie to visit on her way back or even to stay until the fair. As far as Skip could see, there wasn't much reason to go to Canada now, anyway. But Rorie resisted. Walking away from Clay once was going to be painful enough. Rorie didn't know if she could do it twice.

Skip was yawning by the time they decided to call an end to the evening. With little more than a mumbled goodnight, he hurried up the stairs, abandoning the others.

Rorie and Kate took a few extra minutes to straighten the living room, while Clay drove his pickup around to the front of the house. "I'd better burn the evidence before Mary sees these pizza boxes," Rorie joked. "She'll have my hide once she hears about dinner."

Kate laughed good-naturedly as she collected her belongings. When they heard Clay's truck, she put down her bags and ran to Rorie. "You'll call me before you leave tomorrow?"

Rorie nodded and hugged her back.

"If something happens and you change your mind about the fair, please know that you're welcome to stay with me and Dad—we'd enjoy the company."

"Thank you, Kate."

The house felt empty and silent once Kate had left with Clay. Rorie knew it would be useless to go upstairs and try to sleep. Instead she went out to the front porch, where she'd sat in the swing with Clay that first night. She sank down on the steps, one arm wrapped around a post, and gazed upward. The skies were glittered with the light of countless stars—stars that shone with a clarity and brightness one couldn't see in the city.

Clay belonged to this land, this farm, this small town. Rorie was a city girl to the marrow of her bones. This evening had proved the hopelessness of any dream that she and Clay might have of finding happiness together. There was his commitment to Kate. And there was the fact that he and Rorie were too different, their tastes too dissimilar. She certainly couldn't picture him making a life away from Elk Run.

Clay had accepted the hopelessness of it, too. That was the reason he agreed she should travel to Canada. This evening Rorie had sensed a desperation in him that rivaled her own.

It was a night filled with insights. Sitting under the heavens, she was beginning to understand some important things about life. For perhaps the first time, she'd fallen in love. During the past six days she'd tried to deny what she was feeling, but on the eve of her departure it seemed silly to lie to herself any longer. Rorie couldn't believe something like this had actually happened to her. Meeting someone and falling in love with him in the space of a few days was an experience reserved for novels and movies. This wasn't like her normal sane, sensible self at all. Rorie had always thought she was too levelheaded to fall so easily in love.

Until she met Clay Franklin.

On the wings of one soul-searching realization came another. Love wasn't what she'd expected. She'd assumed it meant a strong sensual passion that overwhelmed the lovers and left them powerless before it. But in the past few days, she'd learned that love marked the soul as well as the body.

Clay would forever be a part of her. Since that first night when Nightsong was born, her heart had never felt more alive. Yet within a few hours she would walk away from the man she loved and consider herself blessed to have shared these days with him.

A tear rolled down the side of her face, surprising her. This wasn't a time for sadness, but joy. She'd discovered a deep inner strength she hadn't known she possessed. She wiped the moisture away and rested her head against the post, her eyes fixed on the heavens.

The footsteps behind Rorie didn't startle her. She'd known Clay would come to her this one last time.

Eleven

Clay draped his arm over Rorie's shoulders and joined her in gazing up at the sky. Neither spoke for several minutes, as though they feared words would destroy the tranquil mood. Rorie stared, transfixed by the glittering display. Like her love for this man, the stars would remain forever distant, unattainable, but certain and unchanging.

A ragged sigh escaped her lips. "All my life I've believed that everything that befalls us has a purpose."

"I've always thought that, too," Clay whispered.

"Everything in life is deliberate."

"Our final hours together you're going to become philosophical?" He rested his chin on her head, gently ruffling her hair. "Are you sad, Rorie?"

"Oh, no," she denied quickly. "I can't be...I feel strange, but I don't know if I can find the words to explain it. I'm leaving tomorrow and I realize we'll probably never see each other again. I have no regrets—not a single one—and yet I think my heart is breaking."

His hand tightened on her shoulder in silent protest as if he found the idea of relinquishing her more than he could bear.

"We can't defy reality," she told him. "Nothing's going to change in the next few hours. The water pump on the car will be replaced, and I'll go back to my life. The way you'll go back to yours."

"I have this gut feeling there's going to be a hole the size of the Grand Canyon in mine the minute you drive away." He dropped his arm and moved away from her. His eyes held a weary sadness, but Rorie found an acceptance there, too.

"I'm an uncomplicated man," he said evenly. "I'm probably nothing like the sophisticated man you're dating in San Francisco."

Her thoughts flew to Dan, so cosmopolitan and…superficial, and she recognized the truth in Clay's words. The two men were poles apart. Dan's interests revolved around his career and his car, but he was genuinely kind, and it was that quality that had attracted Rorie.

"Elk Run's given me a good deal of satisfaction over the years. My life's work is here and, God willing, some day my son will carry on the breeding programs I've started. Everything I've ever dreamed of has always been within my grasp." He paused, holding in a long sigh and releasing it slowly. "And then you came," he whispered, and a brief smile crossed his lips, "and, within a matter of days, I'm reeling from the effects. Suddenly I'm left doubting what's really important in my life."

Rorie lowered her eyes. "Who'd have believed a silly

water pump would be responsible for all this wretched soul-searching?"

"I've always been the type of man who's known what he wants, but you make me feel like a schoolboy no older than Skip. I don't know what to do anymore, Rorie. In a few hours, you'll be leaving and part of me says if you do, I'll regret it the rest of my life."

"I can't stay." Their little dinner party had shown her how different their worlds actually were. She wouldn't fit into his life and he'd be an alien in hers. But Kate... Kate belonged to his world.

Clay rubbed his hands across his eyes and harshly drew in a breath. "I know you feel you should leave, but that doesn't mean I have to like it."

"The pull to stay is there for me, too," she whispered.

"And it's tearing both of us apart."

Rorie shook her head. "Don't you see? So much good has come out of meeting you, Clay." Her voice was strong. She had to make him understand that she'd always be grateful for the things he'd taught her. "In some ways I grew up tonight. I feel I'm doing what's right for both of us, although it's more painful than anything I've ever known."

He looked at her with such undisguised love that she ached.

"Let me hold you once more," he said softly. "Give me that, at least."

Rorie shook her head. "I can't... I'm sorry, Clay, but this is how it has to be with us. I'm so weak where you're concerned. I couldn't bear to let you touch me now and then leave tomorrow."

His eyes drifted shut as he yielded to her wisdom. "I don't know that I could, either."

They were only a few feet apart, but it seemed vast worlds stood between them.

"More than anything I want you to remember me fondly, without any bitterness," Rorie told him, discovering as she spoke the words how much she meant them.

Clay nodded. "Be happy, Rorie, for my sake."

Rorie realized that contentment would be a long time coming without this man in her life, but she would find it eventually. She prayed that he'd marry Kate the way he'd planned. The other woman was the perfect wife for him—unlike herself. A thread of agony twisted around Rorie's heart.

She turned to leave him, afraid she'd dissolve into tears if she remained much longer. "Goodbye, Clay."

"Goodbye, Rorie."

She rushed past him and hurried up the stairs.

The following morning, both Clay and Skip had left the house by the time Rorie entered the kitchen.

"Good morning, Mary," she said with a note of false cheer in her voice. "How did the visit with your sister go?"

"Fine."

Rorie stepped around the housekeeper to reach the coffeepot and poured herself a cup. A plume of steam rose enticingly to her nostrils and she took a tentative sip.

"I found those pizza boxes you were trying so hard to hide from me," Mary grumbled as she wiped her hands on her apron. "You fed these good men restaurant pizza?"

Unable to stop herself, Rorie chuckled at the housekeeper's indignation. "Guilty as charged. Mary, you should've known better than to leave their fate in my evil hands."

"Near as I can figure, the closest pizza parlour is a half-hour away. Did you drive over and get it yourself or did you send Skip?"

"Actually he volunteered," she admitted reluctantly. "Dinner didn't exactly turn out the way I'd hoped."

The housekeeper snickered. "I should've guessed. You city slickers don't know nothing about serving up a decent meal to your menfolk."

Rorie gave a hefty sigh of agreement. "The only thing for me to do is stay on another couple of months and have you teach me." As she expected, the housekeeper opened her mouth to protest. "Unfortunately," Rorie continued, cutting Mary off before she could launch into her arguments, "I'm hoping to be gone by this afternoon."

Mary's response was a surprise. The older woman's expression grew troubled and intense.

"I suspected you'd be going soon enough," she said in a tight voice, pulling out a chair. She sat down heavily and brushed wisps of gray hair from her forehead. Her weathered face was thoughtful. "It's for the best, you know."

"I knew you'd be glad to get rid of me."

Mary shrugged. "It's other reasons that make it right for you to leave. You know what I'm talking about, even if you don't want to admit it to me. As a person you tend to grow on folks. Like I said before, for a city girl, you ain't half bad."

Rorie took a banana from the fruit bowl in the center of the table. "For a stud farm, stuck out here in the middle of nowhere, this place isn't half bad, either," she said, trying to lighten the mood, which had taken an unexpected turn toward the serious. "The people are friendly and the apple pie's been exceptional."

Mary ignored the compliment on her pie. "By people, I suppose you're referring to Clay. You're going to miss him, aren't you, girl?"

The banana found its way back into the bowl and with it went her cheerful facade. "Yes. I'll miss Clay."

The older woman's frown deepened. "From the things I've been noticing, he's going to be yearning for you, as well. But it's for the best," she said again. "For the best."

Rorie nodded and her voice wavered. "Yes...but it isn't easy."

The housekeeper gave her a lopsided smile as she gently patted Rorie's hand. "I know that, too, but you're doing the right thing. You'll forget him soon enough."

A strong protest rose in her breast, closing off her throat. She wouldn't forget Clay. Ever. How could she forget the man who had so unselfishly taught her such valuable lessons about life and love? Lessons about herself.

"Kate Logan's the right woman for Clay," Mary said abruptly.

Those few words cut Rorie to the quick. Hearing another person voice the truth made it almost unbearably painful.

"I...hope they're very happy."

"Kate loves him. She has from the time she was knee-high to a June bug. And there's something you don't know. Years back, when Clay was in college, he fell in love with a girl from Seattle. She'd been born and raised in the city.

Clay loved her, wanted to marry her, even brought her to Elk Run to meet the family. She stayed a couple of days, and the whole time, she was as restless as water on a hot skillet. Apparently she had words with Clay because the next thing I knew, she'd packed her bags and headed home. Clay never said much about her after that, but she hurt him bad. It wasn't until Kate got home from college that Clay thought seriously about marriage again."

Mary's story explained a lot about Clay.

"Now, I know I'm just an old woman who likes her soaps and Saturday-night bingo. Most folks don't think I've got a lick of sense, and that's all right. What others choose to assume don't bother me much." She paused, and shook her head. "But Kate Logan's about the kindest, dearest person this town has ever seen. People like her—they can't help themselves. She's always got a kind word and there's no one in this world she's too good for. She cares about the people in this community. Those kids she teaches over at the grade school love her like nothing you've ever seen. And she loves them. When it came to building that fancy library, it was Kate who worked so hard convincing folks they'd be doing what was best for Nightingale by voting for that bond issue."

Rorie kept her face averted. She didn't need Mary to tell her Kate was a good person; she'd seen the evidence of it herself.

"What most folks don't know is that Kate's seen plenty of pain in her own life. She watched her mother die a slow death from cancer. Took care of her most of the time herself, nursing Nora when she should've been off at college having fun like other nineteen-year-olds. Her family needed her and she was there. Kate gave old man Logan a reason to go on living when Nora passed away. She still lives with him, and it's long past time for her to be a carefree adult on her own. Kate's a good person clean through." Mary hesitated, then drew in a solemn breath. "Now, you may think I'm nothing but a meddling old fool. But I'm saying it's a good thing you're leaving Elk Run before you break that girl's heart. She's got a chance now for some happiness, and God knows she deserves it. If she loses Clay, I can tell you it'd break her heart. She's too good to have that happen to her over some fancy city girl who's only passing through."

Rorie winced at the way Mary described her.

"I'm a plain talker," Mary said on the end of an abrupt laugh. "Always have been, always will be. Knowing Clay—and I do, as well as his mother did, God rest her soul—he'll pine for you awhile, but eventually everything will fall back into place. The way it was before you arrived."

Tears stung Rorie's eyes. She felt miserable as it was, and Mary wasn't helping. She'd already assured the housekeeper she was leaving, but Mary apparently wanted to be damn sure she didn't change her mind. The woman didn't understand...but then again, maybe she did.

"Have you ever been in love, Mary?"

"Once," came the curt reply. "Hurt so much the first time I never chanced it again."

"Are you sorry you lived your life alone now?" That was what Rorie saw for herself. Oh, she knew she was being melodramatic and over-emotional, but she couldn't imagine loving any man as much as she did Clay.

Mary lifted one shoulder in a shrug. "Some days I have plenty of regrets, but then on others it ain't so bad. I'd like to have had a child, but God saw to it that I was around when Clay and Skip needed someone.... That made up for what I missed."

"They consider you family."

"Yeah, I suppose they do." Mary pushed out her chair and stood up. "Well, I better get back to work. Those men expect a decent lunch. I imagine they're near starved after the dinner you fed them last night."

Despite her heartache, Rorie smiled and finished her coffee. "And I'd better get upstairs and pack the rest of my things. The mechanic said my car would be ready around noon."

On her way to the bedroom, Rorie paused at the framed photograph of Clay's parents that sat on the piano. She'd passed it a number of times and had given it little more than a fleeting glance. Now it suddenly demanded her attention, and she stopped in front of it.

A tremor went through her hand as she lightly ran her finger along the brass frame. Clay's mother smiled serenely into the camera, her gray eyes so like her son's that Rorie felt a knot in her stomach. Those same eyes seemed to reach across eternity and call out to Rorie, plead with her. Rorie's own eyes narrowed, certain her imagination was playing havoc with her troubled mind. She focused her attention on the woman's hair. That, too, was the same dark shade as Clay's, brushed away from her face in a carefully styled chignon. Clay had never mentioned his parents to her, not once, but studying the photograph Rorie knew intuitively that he'd shared a close relationship with his mother. Blue wandered out from the kitchen and stood at Rorie's side as though offering consolation. Grateful, she bent down to pet him.

Looking back at the photograph, Rorie noted that Skip resembled his father, with the same dancing blue eyes that revealed more than a hint of devilry.

Rorie continued to study both parents, but it was Clay's mother who captured her attention over and over again.

The phone ringing in the distance startled her, and her wrist was shaking when she set the picture back on the piano.

"Phone's for you," Mary shouted from the kitchen.

Rorie assumed it was George at the repair shop in Riversdale; she'd been waiting all morning to hear from him.

"Hello," she said, her fingers closing tightly around the receiver. Her biggest fear was that something had happened to delay her departure a second time.

"Miss Campbell," said the mechanic, "everything's fine. I got that part in and working for you without a hitch."

"Thank God," she murmured. Her hold on the telephone receiver relaxed, a little.

"I've got a man I could spare if you'd like to have your car delivered to Elk Run. But you've got to understand fifty miles is a fair distance and I'm afraid I'll have to charge you extra for it."

"That's fine," Rorie said eagerly, not even bothering to ask the amount. "How soon can he be here?"

Twelve

"So you're really going," Skip said as he picked up Rorie's bags. "Somehow I figured I might've talked you into staying on for the county fair."

"You seem intent on bringing me to ruin, Skip Franklin. I'm afraid I'd bet all my hard-earned cash on those pig races you were telling me about," Rorie teased. Standing in the middle of the master bedroom, she surveyed it to be sure she hadn't forgotten anything.

A pang of wistfulness settled over her as she slowly looked around. Not for the first time, Rorie felt the love and warmth emanating from these brightly papered walls. Lazily, almost lovingly, she ran her fingertips along the top of the dresser, letting her hand linger there a moment, unwilling to pull herself away. This bedroom represented so much of what she was leaving behind. It was difficult to walk away.

Skip stood in the doorway impatiently waiting for her.

"Kate phoned and said she's coming over. She wants to say goodbye."

"I'll be happy to see her one last time." Rorie wished Skip would leave so she could delay her parting with this room a little longer. Until now, Rorie hadn't realized how much sleeping in Clay's parents' room had meant to her. Her appreciation had come too late.

"Mary's packing a lunch for you," Skip announced with a wry chuckle, "and knowing Mary, it'll be enough to last you a week."

Rorie smiled and reluctantly followed him down the stairs. As Skip had claimed, the housekeeper had prepared two large bags, which sat waiting on the kitchen table.

"Might as well take those with you, too," Mary muttered gruffly. "I hate the thought of you eating restaurant food. This, at least, will stick to your ribs."

"Goodbye, Mary," Rorie said softly, touched by the housekeeper's thoughtfulness. On impulse she hugged the older woman. "Thank you for everything—including our talk this morning." The impromptu embrace surprised Rorie as much as it obviously did Mary.

"You drive careful now, you hear?" the housekeeper responded, squeezing Rorie tightly and patting her back several times.

"I will, I promise."

"A letter now and again wouldn't be amiss."

"All right," Rorie agreed, and used her sleeve to blot tears from the corners of her eyes. These people had touched her in so many ways. Leaving them was even more difficult than she'd imagined.

The housekeeper rubbed the heel of her hand over her

right eye. "Time for you to get on the road. What are you doing standing in the kitchen chitchatting with me?" she asked brusquely.

"I'm going, I'm going." Mary's gruff voice didn't fool Rorie. The housekeeper's exterior might be a little crusty, and her tongue a bit surly, but she didn't succeed in disguising a generous, loving heart.

"I don't know where Clay is," Skip complained after he'd loaded the luggage into the MG's trunk. "I thought he'd want to see you before you left. I wonder where he got off to."

"I'm…sure he's got better things to do than say good-bye to me."

"No way," Skip said, frowning. "I'm going to see if I can find him."

Rorie's first reaction was to stop Skip, then she quickly decided against it. If she made too much of a fuss, Skip might suspect something. She understood what had prompted Clay to stay away from the house all morning, and in truth she was grateful. Leaving Elk Run was hard enough without prolonging the agony in lengthy farewells.

Skip hesitated, kicking at the dirt with the pointed toe of his cowboy boot. "You two didn't have a fight or anything, did you?"

"No. What makes you ask?"

Skip shrugged. "Well… It's just that every time I walked into a room with the two of you, I could feel something. If it wasn't for Kate, I'd think my big brother was interested in you."

"I'm sure you're imagining things."

"I suppose so," Skip said with a nod, dismissing the

notion. "Ever since you got here, though, Clay's been acting weird."

"How do you mean?"

"Sort of cranky."

"My unexpected arrival added to his problems, don't you think?" In so many ways it was the truth, and she felt guilty about that. The responsibilities for the farm and for raising Skip were sobering enough; he didn't need her there to wreak havoc with his personal life.

"You weren't any problem," Skip answered sharply. "In fact, having you around was fun. The only trouble is you didn't stay long enough."

"Thank you, Skip." Once again she felt her throat clog with tears. She was touched by his sweet, simple hospitality and reminded of how much she'd miss him.

"I still kinda wish you were going to stay for the fair," he mumbled. "You'd have a good time, I guarantee it. We may not have all the fancy entertainment you do in San Francisco, but when we do a county fair, we do it big."

"I'm sure it'll be great fun."

Skip braced his foot against the bumper of the faded blue pickup, apparently forgetting his earlier decision to seek out Clay, which was just as well.

"You don't like the country much, do you, Rorie?"

"Oh, but I do," she said. "It's a different way of life, though. Here on Elk Run, I feel like a duck in a pond full of swans."

Skip laughed. "I suppose folks there in the big city don't think much of the country."

"No one has time to think," Rorie said with a small laugh.

"That doesn't make any sense. Everyone's got thoughts."

Rorie nodded, not knowing how to explain something so complex. When Skip had spent some time in the city, he'd figure out what she meant.

"The one thing I've noticed more than anything is how quiet it is here," she said pensively, looking around, burning into her memory each detail of the farmhouse and the yard.

"I like the quiet. Some places, the noise is so bad I worry about ear damage," Skip said.

"I imagine if I lived here, I'd grow accustomed to the silence, too. But to be honest, I hadn't realized how much I enjoy the sounds of the city. There's something invigorating about the clang of the trolley cars or the foghorn on the Bay early in the morning."

Skip frowned and shook his head. "You honestly like all that racket?"

Rorie nodded. "It's more than that. The city's exciting. I hadn't really known how much living there meant to me before coming to Elk Run." Rorie wasn't sure how to describe the aroma of freshly baked sourdough bread, or the perfumed scent of budding rosebushes in Golden Gate Park, to someone who'd never experienced them. Country life had its appeal, she couldn't deny that, but she belonged to the city. At least, that was what she told herself over and over again.

"Ah," Skip said, and his foot dropped from the bumper with a thud, "here's Clay now."

Rorie tensed, clasping her hands in front of her. Clay's lengthy strides quickly diminished the distance between the barn and the yard. Each stride was filled with purpose, as though he longed to get this polite farewell over with.

Rorie straightened and walked toward him. "I'll be leaving in a couple of minutes," she said softly.

"Kate's coming to say goodbye," Skip added.

Rorie noted how Clay's eyes didn't quite meet her own. He seemed to focus instead on the car behind her. They'd already said everything there was to say and this final parting only compounded the pain.

"Saying thank you seems so inadequate," Rorie told him in a voice that wasn't entirely steady. "I've appreciated your hospitality more than you'll ever know." Hesitantly she held out her hand to him.

Clay's hard fingers curled around her own, his touch light and impersonal. Rorie swallowed hard, unable to hold back the emotion churning so violently inside her.

His expression was completely impassive, but she sensed that he held on to his self-control with the thinnest of threads. In that moment, Rorie felt the longing in him and knew that he recognized it in her, too.

"Oh, Clay…" she whispered, her eyes brimming with tears. The impulse to move into his arms was like a huge wave, threatening to sweep over her, and she didn't know how much longer she'd have the strength to resist.

"Don't look at me like that," Clay muttered grimly.

"I…can't help it." But he belonged to Kate and nothing was likely to change that.

He took a step toward her and stopped himself, suddenly remembering they weren't alone.

"Skip, go hold Thunder for Don. Don's trying to paste-

worm him, and he's getting dragged all over the stall."
Clay's words were low-pitched, sharp, full of demand.

"But, Clay, Rorie's about to—"

"Do it."

Mumbling something unintelligible, Skip trudged off
to the barn.

The minute his brother was out of sight, Clay caught
Rorie's shoulders, his fingers rough and urgent through
the thin cotton of her blouse. The next instant, she was
locked against him. The kiss was inevitable, Rorie knew,
but when his mouth settled over hers she wanted to weep
for the joy she found in his arms. He kissed her temple,
her cheek, her mouth, until she clung to him with hungry
abandon. They were standing in the middle of the yard
in full view of farmhands, but Clay didn't seem to care
and Rorie wasn't about to object.

"I told myself I wouldn't do this," he whispered huskily.

Rorie's heart constricted.

At the sound of a car in the distance, Clay abruptly
dropped his arms, freeing her. His fingers tangled in her
hair as if he had to touch her one last time.

"I was a fool to think I could politely shake your hand
and let you leave. We're more than casual friends and I
can't pretend otherwise—to hell with the consequences."

Tears flooded Rorie's eyes as she stared up at Clay.
Then, from behind him, she saw the cloud of dust that
announced Kate's arrival. She inhaled a deep breath in an
effort to compose herself and, wiping her damp cheeks
with the back of one hand, forced a smile.

Clay released a ragged sigh as he trailed a callused

hand down the side of her face. "Goodbye, Rorie," he whispered. With that, he turned and walked away.

Thick fog swirled around Rorie as she paused to catch her breath on the path in Golden Gate Park. She bent forward and planted her hands on her knees, driving the oxygen into her heaving lungs. Not once in the two weeks she'd been on vacation had she followed her jogging routine, and now she was paying the penalty. The muscles in her calves and thighs protested the strenuous exercise and her heart seemed about to explode. Her biggest problem was trying to keep up with Dan, who'd run ahead, unwilling to slow his pace to match hers.

"Rorie?"

"Over here." Her voice was barely more than a choked whisper. She meant to raise her hand and signal to him, but even that required more effort than she could manage. Seeing a bench in the distance, she stumbled over and collapsed into it. Leaning back, she stretched out her legs.

"You *are* out of shape," Dan teased, handing her a small towel.

Rorie wiped the perspiration from her face and smiled her appreciation. "I can't believe two weeks would make such a difference." She'd been back in San Francisco only a couple of days. Other than dropping off the MG at Dan's place, this was the first time they'd had a chance to get together.

Dan stood next to her, hardly out of breath—even after a three-mile workout.

"Two weeks *is* a long time," he said with the hint of a smile. "I suppose you didn't keep up with your vitamin program, either," he chastised gently. "Well, Rorie, it's obvious how much you need me."

She chose to ignore that comment. "I used to consider myself in top physical condition. Not anymore. Good grief, I thought my heart was going to give out two miles back."

Dan, blond and debonair, was appealingly handsome in a clean-cut boyish way. He draped the towel around his neck and grasped the ends. Rorie's eyes were drawn to his hands, with their finely manicured nails and long tapered fingers. Stockbroker fingers. Nice hands. Friendly hands.

Still, Rorie couldn't help comparing them with another pair of male hands, darkly tanned from hours in the sun and roughly callused. Gentle hands. Working hands.

"I meant what I said about you needing me," Dan murmured, watching her closely. "It's time we got serious, Rorie. Time we made some important decisions about our future."

When she least expected it, he slid closer on the bench beside her. With his so smooth fingers, he cupped her face, his thumbs stroking her flushed cheeks. "I did a lot of thinking while you were away."

She covered his fingers with her own, praying for an easier way to say what she must. They'd been seeing each other for months and she hated to hurt him, but it would be even crueller to lead him on. When they'd started dating, Dan had been looking for a casual relationship. He'd recently been divorced and wasn't ready for a new emotional commitment.

"Oh, Dan, I think I know what you're going to say. Please don't."

He paused, searching her face intently. "What do you mean?"

"I did some thinking while I was away, too, and I realized that although I'll always treasure your friendship, we can't ever be more than friends."

His dark eyes ignited with resistance. "What happened to you on this vacation, Rorie? You left, and two weeks later you returned a completely different woman."

"You're exaggerating," Rorie objected weakly. She knew she *was* different, from the inside out.

"You've hardly said a word to me about your trip," Dan complained, in a tone that suggested he felt hurt by her reticence. "All you've said is that the car broke down in the Oregon outback and you were stuck on some farm for days until a part could be delivered. You don't blame me for that, do you? I had no idea there was anything wrong with the water pump."

She laughed at his description of Nightingale as the outback.

"You completely missed the writers' conference, didn't you?"

"That couldn't be helped, but I enjoyed the rest of my vacation. Victoria was like stepping into a small piece of England," she said, in an effort to divert his attention from the time she'd spent on the Franklin farm. Victoria had been lovely, but unfortunately she hadn't been in the proper mood to appreciate its special beauty.

"You didn't so much as mail me a postcard."

"I know," she said with a twinge of guilt.

"I was lonesome without you," Dan said slowly, running his hand over her hair. "Nothing felt right with you gone."

Rorie knew it had taken a lot for him to admit that, and it made what she had to tell him all the more difficult.

"Dan, please," she said, breaking away from him and standing. "I...I don't love you."

"But we're friends."

"Of course."

He seemed both pleased and relieved by that. "Good friends?" he coaxed.

Rorie nodded, wondering where this was leading.

"Then there's really no problem, is there?" he asked, his voice gaining enthusiasm. "You went away, and I realized how much I love you, and you came back deciding you value my friendship. That, at least, is a beginning."

"Dan, honestly!"

"Well, isn't it?"

"Our relationship isn't going anywhere," she told him, desperate to clarify the issue. Dan was a good person and he deserved someone who was crazy in love with him. The way she was with Clay.

To Rorie's surprise, Dan drew her forward and kissed her. Startled, she stood placidly in his arms, feeling his warm mouth move over hers. She experienced no feeling, no excitement, nothing. Kissing Dan held all the appeal of drinking flat soda.

Frustrated, he tried to deepen the kiss.

Rorie braced her hands against his chest and tried to pull herself free. He released her immediately, then stepped back, frowning. "Okay, okay, we've got our work cut out for us. But the electricity will come, in time."

Somehow Rorie doubted that.

Dan dropped her off in front of her apartment. "Can I see you soon?" he asked, his hands clenching the steering wheel. He didn't look at her but stared straight ahead as though he feared her answer.

Rorie hesitated. "I'm not going to fall in love with you, Dan, and I don't want to take advantage of your feelings. I think it'd be best if you started seeing someone else."

He appeared to consider that for an awkward moment. "But the decision should be mine, shouldn't it?"

"Yes, but—"

"Then leave everything to me, and stop worrying. If I choose to waste my time on you, that's my problem, not yours. I think you're going to change your mind, Rorie. Because I love you enough for both of us."

"Oh, Dan." Her shoulders sagged with defeat. He hadn't believed a single word she'd said.

"Now don't look so depressed. How about a movie on Sunday? It's been a while since we've done that."

Exhausted, she shook her head. "Dan, no."

"I insist, so stop arguing."

She didn't have the energy to argue. "All right," she murmured. He'd soon learn she meant what she'd said. "All right."

"Good. I'll pick you up at six."

Rorie climbed out of the MG and closed the door, turning to give Dan a limp wave. She paused in the foyer of her apartment building to unlock her mailbox.

There was a handful of envelopes. Absently, she shuffled through a leaflet from a prominent department store, an envelope with a Kentucky postmark and an electric bill. It wasn't until she was inside her apartment that Rorie noticed the letter postmarked Nightingale, Oregon.

Thirteen

Rorie set the letter on her kitchen counter and stared at it for a moment. Her chest felt as if a dead weight were pressing against it. Her heart was pounding and her stomach churned. The post-office box number for the return address didn't tell her much. The letter could as easily be from Kate as Clay. It could even be from Mary.

Taking a deep, calming breath, Rorie reached for the envelope from Kentucky first. The return address told her nothing—she didn't know anyone who lived in that state.

The slip of paper inside confused her, too. She read it several times, not understanding. It appeared to be registration papers for Nightsong, from the National Show Horse Association. Rorie Campbell was listed as owner, with Clay's name as breeder. The date of Nightsong's birth was also recorded. Rorie slumped into a kitchen chair and battled an attack of memories and tears.

Clay was giving her Nightsong.

It was Nightsong who'd brought them together and it

was through Nightsong that they'd remain linked. Life would go on; the loss of one couple's love wouldn't alter the course of history. But now there was something—a single piece of paper—that would connect her to Clay, something that gave testimony to their sacrifice.

Rorie had needed that and Clay had apparently known it.

They'd made the right decision, Rorie told herself for the hundredth time. Clay's action confirmed it.

Clay was wide-open spaces and sleek, well-trained horses, while she thrived in the crowded city.

His strength came from his devotion to the land; hers came from the love of children and literature and the desire to create her own stories.

They were dissimilar in every way—and alike. In the most important matters, the most telling, they were actually very much alike. Neither of them was willing to claim happiness at the expense of someone else.

Tears spilled down her cheeks, and sniffling, Rorie wiped them aside. The drops dampened her fingertips as she picked up the second envelope, blurring the return address. But even before she opened it, Rorie realized the letter was from Kate. Clay wouldn't write her, and everything Mary had wanted to say she'd already said the morning Rorie left Elk Run.

Three handwritten sheets slipped easily from the envelope, with Kate's evenly slanted signature at the bottom of the last.

The letter was filled with chatty news about Nightingale and some of the people Rorie had met. There were so many, and connecting names with faces taxed her memory. Kate wrote about the county fair, telling Rorie that she'd missed a very exciting pig race. The biggest news of all was that after years of trying, Mary had finally won a blue ribbon for her apple pie—an honor long overdue in Kate's opinion.

Toward the end of the letter, Clay's fiancée casually mentioned that Clay would be in San Francisco the first week of September for a horse show. The American Saddlebreds from Elk Run were well-known throughout the Pacific coast for their fire and elegance. Clay had high hopes of repeating last year's wins in the Five Gaited and Fine Harness Championships.

Rorie's pulse shifted into overdrive and her fingers tightened on the letter. Clay was coming to San Francisco. He hadn't said anything about the show to Rorie—although he must've known about it long before she'd left Nightingale.

Kate went on to say that she'd asked Clay if he planned to look up Rorie while he was in town, but he'd claimed there wouldn't be time. Kate was sure Rorie would understand and not take offense. She closed by saying that her father might also be attending the horse show and, if he did, Kate would try to talk him into letting her tag along. Kate promised she'd phone Rorie the minute she arrived in town, if she could swing it with her father.

Not until Rorie folded the letter to return it to the envelope did she notice the postscript on the back of the last page. She turned over the sheet of pink stationery. The words seemed to jump off the page: Kate was planning an October wedding and would send Rorie an invitation. She ended with, "Write soon."

Rorie's breath caught in her lungs. An October wedding... In only a few weeks, Kate would belong to Clay. Rorie closed her eyes as her heart squeezed into a knot of pain. It wasn't that she hadn't known this was coming. Kate and Clay's wedding was inevitable, but Rorie hadn't thought Clay would go through with it quite so soon. With trembling hands, she set the letter aside.

"Rorie, love, I can't honestly believe you want to go to a horse show," Dan complained, scanning the entertainment section of the Friday-evening paper. They sat in the minuscule living room in her apartment and sipped their coffee while they tossed around ideas for something to do.

Rorie smiled blandly, praying Dan couldn't read her thoughts. He'd offered several suggestions for the night's amusement, but Rorie had rejected each one. Until she pretended to hit upon the idea of attending the horse show...

"A horse show?" he repeated. "You never told me you were interested in horses."

"It would be fun, don't you think?"

"Not particularly."

"But, Dan, it's time to broaden our horizons—we might learn something."

"Does this mean you're going to insist we attend a demolition derby next weekend?"

"Of course not. I read an article about this horse show and I just thought we'd enjoy the gaited classes and harness competitions. Apparently, lots of Saddlebreds and National Show Horses are going to be performing. Doesn't that interest you?"

"No."

Rorie shrugged, slowly releasing a sigh. "Then a movie's fine," she said, not even trying to hide her disappointment. They'd seen each other only a handful of times since Rorie's return. Rorie wouldn't be going out with him tonight if he hadn't persisted. She hoped he'd get the message and start dating other women, but that didn't seem to be happening.

"I have no idea why you'd want to see a horse show," Dan said once more.

For the past few days the newspapers had been filled with information regarding the country-wide show in which Kate had said several of Elk Run's horses would be participating. In all the years she'd lived in San Francisco, Rorie couldn't remember reading about a single equine exhibition, but then she hadn't exactly been looking for one, either.

If Dan refused to go with her, Rorie was determined to attend the event on her own. She didn't have any intention of seeking out Clay, but the opportunity to see him, even from a distance, was too tempting to let pass. It would probably be the last time she'd ever see him.

"I don't know what's got into you lately, Rorie," Dan muttered. "Just when I think our lives are on track, you throw me for a loop."

"I said a movie was fine." Her tone was testier than she meant it to be, but Dan had been harping on the same subject for weeks and she was tired of it.

If he didn't want her company, he should start dating someone else. She wasn't going to suddenly decide she was madly in love with him, as he seemed to expect.

Again and again, Dan phoned to tell her he loved her, that his love was enough for both of them. She always stopped him there, unable to imagine spending the rest of her life with him. If she couldn't have Clay—and she couldn't—then she wasn't willing to settle for anyone else.

"I'm talking about a lot more than seeing a movie." He laid the newspaper aside and seemed to carefully consider his next words.

"Really, Dan, you're making a mountain out of a mole-hill," Rorie said. "Just because I wanted to do something a little out of the ordinary..."

"Eating at an Armenian restaurant is a little out of the ordinary," he said, frowning, "but horse shows... I can't even begin to understand why you'd want to watch a bunch of animals running around in circles."

"Well, you keep insisting I've changed," she said flippantly. If she'd known Dan was going to react so strongly to her suggestion, she'd never have made it. "I guess this only goes to prove you're right."

"How much writing have you done in the past month?"

The question was completely unexpected. She answered him with a shrug, hoping he'd drop the subject, knowing he wouldn't.

"None, right? I've seen you sitting at your computer, staring into space with that sad look on your face. I remember how you used to talk about your stories. Your eyes would light up. Enthusiasm would just spill out of you." His hand reached for hers, tightly squeezing her fingers. "What happened to you, Rorie? Where's the joy? Where's the energy?"

"You're imagining things," she said, nearly leaping to

her feet in an effort to sidestep the issues he was raising. She grabbed her purse and a light sweater, eager to escape the apartment, which suddenly felt too small. "Are you going to take me to that movie, or are you going to sit here and ask questions I have no intention of answering?"

Dan stood, smiling faintly. "I don't know what happened while you were on vacation, and it's not important that I know, but whatever it was hurt you badly."

Rorie tried to deny it, but couldn't force the lie past her tongue. She swallowed and turned her head away, eyes burning.

"You won't be able to keep pretending forever. Put whatever it is behind you. If you want to talk about it, I've got a sympathetic ear and a sturdy shoulder. I'm your friend, Rorie."

"Dan, please…"

"I know you're not in love with me," he said quietly. "I suspect you met someone else while you were away, but that doesn't matter to me. Whatever happened during those two weeks is over."

"Dan…"

He took her hand, pulling her back onto the sofa, then sitting down beside her. She couldn't look at him.

"Given time, you'll learn to love me," he cajoled, holding her hand, his voice filled with kindness. "We're already good friends, and that's a lot more than some people have when they marry." He raised her fingers to his mouth and kissed them lightly. "I'm not looking for passion. I had that with my first wife. I learned the hard way that desire is a poor foundation for a solid marriage."

"We've talked about this before," Rorie protested.

"I can't marry you, Dan, not when I feel the way I do about...someone else." Her mouth trembled with the effort to suppress tears. Dan was right. As much as she hadn't wanted to face the truth, she'd been heartbroken from the moment she'd left Nightingale.

She'd tried to forget Clay, believing that was the best thing for them both, yet she cherished the memories, knowing those few brief days were all she'd ever have of this man she loved.

"You don't have to decide right now," Dan assured her.

"There isn't anything to decide," she persisted.

His fingers continued to caress hers, and when he spoke his voice was thick. "At least you've admitted there is someone else."

"Was," she corrected.

"I take it there isn't any chance the two of you—"

"None," she blurted, unwilling to discuss anything that had to do with Clay.

"I know it's painful for you right now, but all I ask is that you seriously consider my proposal. My only wish is to take care of you and make you smile again. Help you forget."

His mouth sought hers, and though his kiss wasn't unpleasant, it generated no more excitement than before, no rush of adrenaline, no urgency. She hadn't minded Dan's kisses in the past, but until she met Clay she hadn't known the warmth and magic a man's touch could create.

Dan must have read her thoughts, because he said in a soothing voice, "The passion will come in time—you shouldn't even look for it now, but it'll be there. Maybe not this month or the next, but you'll feel it eventually, I promise."

Rorie brushed the hair from her face, confused and uncertain. Clay was marrying Kate in just a few weeks. Her own life stretched before her, lonely and barren—surely she deserved some happiness, too. Beyond a doubt, Rorie knew Clay would want her to build a good life for herself. But if she married Dan, it would be an act of selfishness, and she feared she'd end up hurting him.

"Think about it," Dan urged. "That's all I ask."

"Dan..."

"Just consider it. I know the score and I'm willing to take the risk, so you don't have to worry about me. I'm a big boy." He rubbed his thumb against the inside of her wrist. "Now, promise me you'll think honestly about us getting married."

Rorie nodded, although she already knew what her answer would have to be.

Dan heaved a sigh. "Now, are you really interested in that horse show, or are we going to a movie?"

"The movie." There was no use tormenting herself with thoughts of Clay. He belonged to Kate in the same way that he belonged to the country. Rorie had no claim to either.

The film Dan chose was surprisingly good, a comedy, which was just what Rorie needed to lift her spirits. Afterward, they dined at an Italian restaurant and drank wine and discussed politics. Dan went out of his way to be the perfect companion, making no demands on her, and Rorie was grateful.

It was still relatively early when he drove her back to

her apartment, and he eagerly accepted her invitation for coffee. As he eased the MG into a narrow space in front of her building, he suddenly paused, frowning.

"Do you have new neighbors?"

"Not that I know of. Why?"

Dan nodded toward the battered blue pickup across the street. "Whoever drives that piece of junk is about to bring down the neighborhood property values."

Fourteen

"Clay." His name escaped Rorie's lips on a rush of excitement. She jerked open the car door and stepped onto the sidewalk, her legs trembling, her pulse thundering.

"Rorie?" Dan called, agitated. "Who is this man?"

She hardly heard him. A door slammed in the distance and Rorie whirled around and saw that Clay had been sitting inside his truck, apparently waiting for her to return. He'd been parked in the shadows, and she hadn't noticed him.

Dan joined her on the pavement and placed his hand possessively on her shoulder. His grip was the only thing that rooted her in reality, his hand the restraining force that prevented her from flying into Clay's arms.

"Who is this guy?" Dan asked a second time.

Rorie opened her mouth to explain and realized she couldn't, not in a few words. "A...friend," she whispered, but that seemed so inadequate.

"He's a cowboy!" Dan hissed, making it sound as

though Clay's close-fitting jeans and jacket were the garb of a man just released from jail.

Clay crossed the street and his long strides made short work of the distance separating him from Rorie.

"Hello, Rorie."

She heard the faint catch in his voice. "Clay."

A muscle moved in his cheek as he looked past her to Dan, who squared the shoulders of his Brooks Brothers suit. No one spoke, until Rorie saw that Clay was waiting for an introduction.

"Clay Franklin, this is Dan Rogers. Dan is the stockbroker I...I mentioned before. It was his sports car I was driving."

Clay nodded. "I remember now." His gaze slid away from Rorie to the man at her side.

Dan stepped around Rorie and accepted Clay's hand. She noticed that when Dan dropped his arm to his side, he flexed his fingers a couple of times, as though to restore the circulation. Rorie smiled to herself. Clay's handshake was the solid one of a man accustomed to working with his hands. When Dan shook hands, it was little more than a polite business greeting, an archaic but necessary exchange.

"Clay and his brother, Skip, were the family who helped me when the MG broke down," Rorie explained to Dan.

"Ah, yes, I remember your saying something about that now."

"I was about to make a pot of coffee," Rorie went on, unable to take her eyes off Clay. She drank in the sight of him, painfully noting the crow's feet that fanned out from the corners of his eyes. She couldn't remember their being quite so pronounced before.

"Yes, by all means join us." Dan's invitation lacked any real welcome.

Clay said nothing. He just stood there looking at her. Almost no emotion showed in his face, but she could feel the battle that raged inside him. He loved her still, and everything about him told her that.

"Please join us," she whispered.

Any lingering hope that Dan would take the hint and make his excuses faded as he slipped his arm protectively around Rorie's shoulders. "I picked up some Swiss mocha coffee beans earlier," he said, "and Rorie was going to make a pot of that."

"Swiss mocha coffee?" Clay repeated, blinking quizzically.

"Decaffeinated, naturally," Dan hurried to add.

Clay arched his brows expressively, as if to say that made all the difference in the world.

With Dan glued to her side, Rorie reluctantly led the way into her building. "Have you been here long?" she asked Clay while they stood waiting for the elevator.

"About an hour."

"Oh, Clay…" Rorie felt terrible, although it wasn't her fault; she hadn't known he intended to stop by. Perhaps he hadn't known himself and had been lured to her apartment the same way she'd been contemplating the horse show.

"You should have phoned." Dan's comment was casual, but it contained a hint of accusation. "But then, I suppose, you folks tend to drop in on each other all the time. Things are more casual in the country, aren't they?"

Rorie sent Dan a furious glare. He returned her look blankly, as if to say he had no idea what could have angered her. Rorie was grateful that the elevator arrived just then.

Clay didn't comment on Dan's observation and the three stepped inside, facing the doors as they slowly closed.

"When you weren't home, I asked the neighbors if they knew where you'd gone," Clay said.

"The neighbors?" Dan echoed, making no effort to disguise his astonishment.

"What did they tell you?" Rorie asked.

Clay smiled briefly, then sobered when he glanced at Dan. "They said they didn't know *who* lived next door, never mind where you'd gone."

"Frankly, I'm surprised they answered the door at all," Dan said conversationally. "There's a big difference between what goes on in small towns and big cities."

Dan spoke like a teacher to a grade-school pupil. Rorie wanted to kick him, but reacting in anger would only increase the embarrassment. She marveled at Clay's tolerance.

"Things are done differently here," Dan continued. "Few people have anything to do with their neighbors. People prefer to mind their own business. Getting involved leads to problems."

Clay rubbed the side of his face. "It seems to me *not* getting involved would lead to even bigger problems."

"I'm grateful Clay and Skip were there when *your* car

broke down," Rorie said to Dan, hoping to put an end to this tiresome discussion. "Otherwise I don't know what would have happened. I could still be on that road waiting for someone to stop and help me," she said, forcing the joke.

"Yes," Dan admitted, clearing his throat. "I suppose I should thank you for assisting Rorie."

"And I suppose I should accept your thanks," Clay returned.

"How's Mary?" Rorie asked, quickly changing the subject as the elevator slid to a stop at her floor.

Humor sparked in Clay's gray eyes. "Mary's strutting around proud as a peacock ever since she won a blue ribbon at the county fair."

"She had reason to be proud." Rorie could just picture her. Knowing Mary, she was probably wearing the ribbon pinned to her apron. "What about Skip?" Rorie asked next, hungry for news about each one. She took the keys from her bag and systematically began unlocking the three bolts on her apartment door.

"Fine. He started school last week—he's a senior this year."

Rorie already knew that, but she nodded.

"Kate sends you her best," Clay said next, his voice carefully nonchalant.

"Tell her I said hello, too."

"She hasn't heard from you. No one has."

"I know. I'm sorry. She wrote after I got home from Canada, but I haven't had a chance to answer." On several occasions, Rorie had tried to make herself sit down and write Kate a letter. But she couldn't. At the end of her second week back home, she'd decided it was better for everyone involved if she didn't keep in touch with Kate. When the wedding invitation came, Rorie planned to mail an appropriate gift, and that would be the end of it.

Once they were inside the apartment, Rorie hung up her sweater and purse and motioned for both men to sit down. "It'll only take a minute to put on the coffee."

"Do you need me to grind the beans?" Dan asked, obviously eager to assist her.

"No, thanks. I don't need any help." His offer was an excuse to question her about Clay, and Rorie wanted to avoid that if she could. At least for now.

Her apartment had never felt more cramped than it did when she rejoined the two men in her tiny living room. Clay rose to his feet as she entered, and the simple courtly gesture made her want to weep. He was telling her that he respected her and that…he cared for her…would always care for her.

The area was just large enough for one sofa and a coffee table. Her desk and computer stood against the other wall. Rorie pulled the chair away from the desk, turned it to face her guests and perched on the edge. Only then did Clay sit back down.

"So," Dan said with a heavy sigh. "Rorie never did tell me what it is you do in…in…"

"Nightingale," Rorie and Clay said together.

"Oh, yes, Nightingale," Dan murmured, clearing his throat. "I take it you're some kind of farmer? Do you grow soy beans or wheat?"

"Clay owns a stud farm, where he raises American Saddlebreds," Rorie said.

Dan looked as if she'd punched him in the stomach. He'd obviously made the connection between Clay and her earlier interest in attending the horse show.

"I see," he breathed, and his voice shook a little. "Horses. So you're involved with horses."

Clay glanced at him curiously.

"How's Nightsong?" Rorie asked, before Dan could say anything else. Just thinking about the foal with her wide curious eyes and long wobbly legs produced a feeling of tenderness in Rorie.

"She's a rare beauty," Clay told her softly, "showing more promise every day."

Rorie longed to tell Clay how much it had meant to her that he'd registered Nightsong in her name, how she cherished that gesture more than anything in her life. She also knew that Clay would never sell the foal, but would keep and love her all her life.

An awkward silence followed, and in an effort to smooth matters over she explained to Dan, "Clay was gone one night when Star Bright—one of the brood mares—went into labor...if that's what they call it in horses?" she asked Clay.

He nodded.

"Anyway, I couldn't wake Skip, and I didn't know where Mary was sleeping and something had to be done—quick."

Dan leaned forward, his eyes revealing his shock. "You don't mean to tell me *you* delivered the foal?"

"Not exactly." Rorie wished now that she hadn't said anything to Dan about that night. No one could possibly understand what she and Clay had shared in those few hours. Trying to convey the experience to someone else only diminished its significance.

"I'll get the coffee," Rorie said, standing. "I'm sure it's ready."

From her kitchen, she could hear Dan and Clay talking, although she couldn't make out their words. She filled three cups and placed them on a tray, together with cream and sugar, then carried it into the living room.

Once more Clay stood. He took the tray out of her hands and set it on the coffee table. Rorie handed Dan the first cup and saucer and Clay the second. He looked uncomfortable as he accepted it.

"I'm sorry, Clay, you prefer a mug, don't you?" The cup seemed frail and tiny, impractical, cradled in his strong hand.

"It doesn't matter. If I'm going to be drinking Swiss mocha coffee, I might as well do it from a china cup." He smiled into her eyes, and Rorie couldn't help reciprocating.

"Eaten any seafood fettuccine lately?" she teased.

"Can't say I have."

"It's my favorite dinner," Dan inserted, apparently feeling left out of the conversation. "We had linguini tonight, but Rorie's favorite is sushi."

Her eye caught Clay's and she saw that the corner of his mouth quirked with barely restrained humor. She could just imagine what the people of Nightingale would think of a sushi bar. Skip would probably turn up his nose, insisting that the small pieces of seaweed and raw fish looked like bait.

The coffee seemed to command everyone's attention for the next minute or so.

"I'm still reeling from the news of your adventures on this stud farm," Dan commented, laughing lightly. "You could have knocked me over with a feather when you said you'd helped deliver a foal. I would never have believed it of you, Rorie."

"I brought a picture of Nightsong," Clay said, cautiously putting down his coffee cup. He unsnapped the pocket of his wide-yoked shirt and withdrew two color photographs, which he handed to Rorie. "I meant to show these to you earlier...but I got sidetracked."

"Oh, Clay," she breathed, studying the filly with her gleaming chestnut coat. "She's grown so much in just the past month," she said, her voice full of wonder.

"I thought you'd be impressed."

Reluctantly Rorie shared the pictures with Dan, who barely glanced at them before giving them back to Clay.

"Most men carry around pictures of their wife and kids," Dan stated, his eyes darting to Clay and then Rorie.

Rorie supposed this comment was Dan's less-than-subtle attempt to find out if Clay was married. Taking a deep breath, she said, "Clay's engaged to a neighbor— Kate Logan."

"I see." Apparently he did, because he set aside his coffee cup, and got up to stand behind Rorie. Hands resting on her shoulders, he leaned forward and brushed his mouth over her cheek. "Rorie and I have been talking about getting married ourselves, haven't we, darling?"

Fifteen

No emotion revealed itself on Clay's face, but Rorie could sense the tight rein he kept on himself. Dan's words had dismayed him.

"Is that true, Rorie?" he said after a moment.

Dan's fingers tightened almost painfully on her shoulders. "Just tonight we were talking about getting married. Tell him, darling."

Her eyes refused to leave Clay's. She *had* been talking to Dan about marriage, although she had no intention of accepting his offer. Dan knew where he stood, knew she was in love with another man. But nothing would be accomplished by telling Clay that she'd always love him, especially since he was marrying Kate in a few weeks. "Yes, Dan has proposed."

"I'm crazy about Rorie and have been for months," Dan announced, squarely facing his competition. He spoke for a few more minutes, outlining his goals. Within another ten years, he planned to be financially secure and hoped to retire.

"Dan's got a bright future," Rorie echoed.

"I see." Clay replaced his coffee cup on the tray, then glanced at his watch and rose to his feet. "I suppose I should head back to the Cow Palace."

"How...how are you doing in the show?" Rorie asked, distraught, not wanting him to leave. Kate would have him the rest of their lives; surely a few more minutes with him wouldn't matter. "Kate wrote that you were going after several championships."

"I'm doing exactly as I expected." The words were clipped, as though he was impatient to get away.

Rorie knew she couldn't keep him any longer. Clay's face was stern with purpose—and resignation. "I'll see you out," she told him.

"I'll come with you," Dan said.

She whirled around and glared at him. "No, you won't."

"Good to see you again, Rorie," Clay said, standing just inside her apartment, his hand on the door. His mouth was hard and flat and he held himself rigid, eyes avoiding hers. He stepped forward and shook Dan's hand.

"It was a pleasure," Dan said in a tone that conveyed exactly the opposite.

"Same here." Clay dropped his hand.

"I'm glad you came by," Rorie told him quietly. "It was...nice seeing you." The words sounded inane, meaningless.

He nodded brusquely, opened the door and walked into the hallway.

"Clay," she said, following him out, her heart hammering so loudly it seemed to echo off the walls.

He stopped and slowly turned around.

Now that she had his attention, Rorie didn't know what to say. "Listen, I'm sorry about the way Dan was acting."

He shook off her apology. "Don't worry about it."

Her fingers tightened on the doorknob, and she wondered if this was really the end. "Will I see you again?" she asked despite herself.

"I don't think so," he answered hoarsely. He looked past her as though he could see through the apartment door and into her living room where Dan was waiting. "Do you honestly love this guy?"

"He's...he's been a good friend."

Clay took two steps toward her, then stopped. As if it was against his better judgment, he raised his hand and lightly drew his finger down the side of her face. Rorie closed her eyes at the wealth of sensation the simple action provoked.

"Be happy, Rorie. That's all I want for you."

The rain hit during the last week of September, and the dreary dark afternoons suited Rorie's mood. Normally autumn was a productive time for her, but she remained tormented with what she felt sure was a terminal case of writer's block. She sat at her desk, her computer humming merrily as she read over the accumulation of an entire weekend's work.

One measly sentence.

There'd been a time when she could write four or five pages a night after coming home from the library. Perhaps the problem was the story she'd chosen. She wanted to write about a filly named Nightsong, but every time she started, her memories of the real Nightsong invaded her thoughts, crippling her imagination.

Here it was Monday night and she sat staring at the screen, convinced nothing she wrote had any merit. The only reason she kept trying was that Dan had pressured her into it. He seemed to believe her world would right itself once Rorie was back to creating her warm, light-hearted children's stories.

The phone rang and, grateful for a reprieve, Rorie hurried into the kitchen to answer it.

"Is this Miss Rorie Campbell of San Francisco, California?"

"Yes, it is." Her heart tripped with anxiety. In a matter of two seconds, every horrible scenario of what could have happened to her parents or her brother darted through Rorie's mind.

"This is Devin Logan calling."

He paused, as though expecting her to recognize the name. Rorie didn't. "Yes?"

"Devin Logan," he repeated, "from the Nightingale, Oregon, Town Council." He paused. "I believe you're acquainted with my daughter, Kate."

"Yes, I remember Kate." If her heart continued at this pace Rorie thought she'd keel over in a dead faint. Just as her pulse had started to slow, it shot up again. "Has anything happened?"

"The council meeting adjourned about ten minutes ago. Are you referring to that?"

"No...no, I mean has anything happened to Kate?"

"Not that I'm aware of. Do you know something I don't?"

"I don't think so." This entire conversation was driving her crazy.

Devin Logan cleared his throat, and when he spoke his voice dropped to a deeper pitch. "I'm phoning in an official capacity," he said. "We voted at the Town Council meeting tonight to employ a full-time librarian."

He paused again, and, not knowing what else to say, Rorie murmured, "Congratulations. Kate mentioned that the library was currently being run by part-time volunteers."

"It was decided to offer *you* the position."

Rorie nearly dropped the receiver. "I beg your pardon?"

"My daughter managed to convince the council that we need a full-time librarian for our new building. She also persuaded us that you're the woman for the job."

"But…" Hardly able to take in what she was hearing, Rorie slumped against the kitchen wall, glad of its support. Logan's next remark was even more surprising.

"We'll match whatever the San Francisco library is paying you and throw in a house in town—rent-free."

"I…" Rorie's mind was buzzing. Kate obviously thought she was doing her a favor, when in fact being so close to Clay would be utter torment.

"Miss Campbell?"

"I'm honored," she said quickly, still reeling with astonishment, "truly honored, but I'm going to have to decline."

A moment of silence followed. "All right…I'm authorized to enhance the offer by ten percent over the amount you're currently earning, but that's our final bid. You'd be making as much money as the fire chief, and he's not about to let the Council pay a librarian more than he's bringing home."

"Mr. Logan, please, the salary isn't the reason I'm turning down your generous offer. I...I want you to know how much I appreciate your offering me the job. Thank you, and thank Kate on my behalf, but I can't accept."

Another, longer silence vibrated across the line, as though he couldn't believe what she was telling him.

"You're positive you want to refuse? Miss Campbell, we're being more than reasonable...more than generous."

"I realize that. In fact, I'm flattered by your proposal, but I can't possibly accept this position."

"Kate had the feeling you'd leap at the job."

"She was mistaken."

"I see. Well, then, it was good talking to you. I'm sorry we didn't get a chance to meet while you were in Nightingale. Perhaps next time."

"Perhaps." Only there wouldn't be a next time.

Rorie kept her hand on the receiver long after she'd hung up. Her back was pressed against the kitchen wall, her eyes closed.

She'd regained a little of her composure when the doorbell chimed. A glance at the wall clock told her it was Dan, who'd promised to drop by that evening. She straightened, forcing a smile, and slowly walked to the door.

Dan entered with a flourish, handing her a small white bag.

"What's this?" she asked.

"Frozen yogurt. Just the thing for a girl with a hot keyboard. How's the writing going?" He leaned forward to kiss her cheek.

Rorie walked into the kitchen and set the container in the freezer compartment of her refrigerator. "It's not. If you don't mind, I'll eat this later."

"Rorie." Dan caught her by her shoulders and studied her face. "You're as pale as chalk. What's wrong?"

"I…I just got off the phone. I was offered another job—as head librarian…"

"But, darling, that's wonderful!"

"…in Nightingale, Oregon."

The change in Dan's expression was almost comical. "And? What did you tell them?"

"I refused."

He gave a great sigh of relief. His eyes glowed and he hugged her impulsively. "Does this mean what I think it does? Are you finally over that cowpoke, Rorie? Will you finally consent to be my wife?"

Rorie lowered her gaze. "Oh, Dan, don't you understand? I'll never get over Clay. Not next week, not next month, not next year." Her voice was filled with pain, and with conviction. Everyone seemed to assume that, in time, she'd forget about Clay Franklin, but she wouldn't.

Dan's smile faded, and he dropped his arms to his sides. "I see." Leaning against the counter, he sighed pensively and said, "I'd do just about anything in this world for you, Rorie, but I think it's time we faced a few truths."

Rorie had wanted to confront them long before now.

"You're never going to love me the way you do that horseman. We can't go on like this. It isn't doing either of us any good to pretend your feelings are going to change."

He looked so grim and discouraged that she didn't point out that *he* was the one who'd been pretending.

"I'm so sorry to hurt you—it's the last thing I ever wanted to do," she told him sincerely.

"It isn't as if I didn't know," he admitted. "You've been honest with me from the start. I can't be less than honest with you. That country boy loves you. I knew it the minute he walked across the street without even noticing the traffic. The whole world would know," he said ruefully. "All he has to do is look at you and everything about him shouts his feelings. He may be engaged to another woman, but it's you he loves."

"I wouldn't fit into his world."

"But, Rorie, you're lost and confused in your own."

She bit her lower lip and nodded. Until Dan said it, she hadn't recognized how true that was. But it didn't change the fact that Clay belonged to Kate. And she was marrying him within the month.

"I'm sorry," Dan said, completely serious, "but the wedding's off."

She nearly laughed out loud at Dan's announcement. No wedding had ever been planned. He'd asked her to marry him at least ten times since she'd returned from her vacation, and each time she'd refused. Instead of wearing her down as he'd hoped, Dan had finally come to accept her decision. Rorie felt relieved, but she was sorry to lose her friend.

"I didn't mean to lead you on," she told him, genuinely contrite.

He shrugged. "The pain will only last for a while. I'm 'a keeper' as the girls in the office like to tell me. I guess it's time I put out the word that I'm available." He wiggled his eyebrows, striving for some humor.

"You've been such a good friend."

He cupped her face and gently kissed her. "Yes, I know. Now don't let that yogurt go to waste—you're too thin as it is."

She smiled and nodded. When she let him out of the apartment, Rorie bolted the door then leaned against it, feeling drained, but curiously calm.

Dan had been gone only a few minutes when Rorie's phone rang again. She hurried into the kitchen to answer it.

"Rorie? This is Kate Logan."

"Kate! How are you?"

"Rotten, but I didn't call to talk about me. I want to know exactly why you're refusing to be Nightingale's librarian—after everything I went through. I can't believe you, Rorie. How can you do this to Clay? Don't you love him?"

Sixteen

"Kate," Rorie demanded. "What are you talking about?"

"You and Clay," she said sharply, sounding quite unlike her usual self. "Now, do you love him or not? I've got to know."

This day had been sliding steadily downhill from the moment Rorie had climbed out of bed that morning. To admit her feelings for Clay would only hurt Kate, and Rorie had tried so hard to avoid upsetting the other woman.

"Well?" Kate said with a sob. "The least you can do is answer me!"

"Oh, Kate," Rorie said, her heart in her throat, "why are you asking me if I love Clay? He's engaged to you. It shouldn't matter one little bit if I love him or not. I'm out of your lives and I intend to stay out."

"But he loves you."

The tears in Kate's voice tore at Rorie's already battered heart. She would've given anything to spare her friend this pain. "I know," she whispered.

"Doesn't that mean anything to you?"

Only the world and everything in it. "Yes," she murmured, her voice growing stronger.

"Then how could you do this to him?"

"Do what?" Rorie didn't understand.

"Hurt him this way!"

"Kate," Rorie pleaded. "I have no idea what you're talking about—I'd never intentionally hurt Clay. If you insist on knowing, I do love him, with all my heart, but he's your fiancé. You loved him long before I even knew him."

Kate's short laugh was riddled with sarcasm. "What is this? First come, first served?"

"Of course not—"

"For your information, Clay isn't my fiancé anymore," Kate blurted, her voice trembling. "He hasn't been in weeks…since before he went to San Francisco for the horse show."

Rorie's head came up so fast she wondered whether she'd dislocated her neck. "He isn't?"

"That's…that's what I just told you."

"But I thought…I assumed…"

"I know what you assumed—that much is obvious—but it isn't like that now and it hasn't been in a long time."

"But you love Clay," Rorie muttered, feeling light-headed.

"I've loved him from the time I was in pigtails. I love him enough to want to see him happy. Why…why do you think I talked my fool head off to a bunch of hard-nosed council members? Why do you think I ranted and raved about what a fantastic librarian you are? I as good as told them you're the only person who could possibly assume full responsibility for the new library. Do you honestly think I did all that for the fun of it?"

"No, but, Kate, surely you understand why I have to refuse. I just couldn't bear to come between you and—"

Kate wouldn't allow her to finish, and when she spoke, her voice was high and almost hysterical. "Well, if you believe that, Rorie Campbell, then you've got a lot to learn about me...and even more about Clay Franklin."

"Kate, I'm sorry. Please listen to me. There's so much I don't understand. We've got to talk, because I can't make head or tail out of what you're telling me and I've got to know—"

"If you have anything to say to me, Rorie Campbell, then you can do it to my face. Now, I'm telling Dad and everyone else on the council that you've accepted the position we so generously offered you. The job starts in two weeks and you'd damn well better be here. Understand?"

Rorie's car left a dusty trail on the long, curving driveway that led to the Circle L Ranch. It'd been a week since the telephone call from Kate, and Rorie still had trouble assimilating what the other woman had told her. Their conversation repeated itself over and over in her mind, until nothing made sense. But one thing stood out: Kate was no longer engaged to Clay.

Rorie was going to him, running as fast as she could, but first she had to settle matters with his former fiancée.

The sun had begun to descend in an autumn sky when Rorie parked her car at the Logan ranch and climbed out. Rotating her neck and shoulders to relieve some of the tension there, Rorie looked around, wondering if anyone was home. She'd been on the road most of the day, so she was exhausted. And exhilarated.

Luke Rivers strolled out of the barn, and stopped when he saw Rorie. His smile deepened. It could've been Rorie's imagination, but she sensed that the hard edge was missing from his look, as though life had unexpectedly tossed him a good turn.

"So you're back," he said by way of greeting.

Rorie nodded, then reached inside the car for her purse. "Is Kate here?"

"She'll be back any minute. Usually gets home from the school around four. Come inside and I'll get you a cup of coffee."

"Thanks." At the moment, coffee sounded like nectar from the gods.

Luke opened the kitchen door for her. "I understand you're going to be Nightingale's new librarian," he said, following her into the house.

"Yes." But that wasn't the reason she'd come back, and they both knew it.

"Good." Luke took two mugs from the cupboard and filled them from a coffeepot that sat on the stove. He placed Rorie's cup on the table, then pulled out a chair for her.

"Thanks, Luke."

The sound of an approaching vehicle drew his attention. He parted the lace curtain at the kitchen window and looked out.

"That's Kate now," he said, his gaze lingering on the driveway. "Listen, if I don't get a chance to talk to you later, I want you to know I'm glad you're here. I've got a few things to thank you for. If it hadn't been for you, I might've turned into a crotchety old saddle bum."

Before Rorie could ask what he meant, he was gone.

Kate burst into the kitchen a minute later and hugged Rorie as though they were long-lost sisters. "I don't know when I've been happier to see anyone!"

Rorie's face must have shown her surprise because Kate hurried to add, "I suppose you think I'm a crazy woman after the way I talked to you on the phone last week. I don't blame you, but...well, I was upset, to put it mildly, and my thinking was a little confused." She threw her purse on the counter and reached inside the cupboard for a mug. She poured the coffee very slowly, as if she needed time to gather her thoughts.

Rorie's mind was whirling with questions she couldn't wait for Kate to answer. "Did I understand you correctly the other night? Did you tell me you and Clay are no longer engaged?"

Kate wasn't able to disguise the flash of pain that leaped into her deep blue eyes. She dropped her gaze and nodded. "We haven't been in weeks."

"But..."

Kate sat down across the table from Rorie and folded her hands around the mug. "The thing is, Rorie, I knew how you two felt about each other since the night of the Grange dance. A blind man would've known you and Clay had fallen in love, but it was so much easier for me to pretend otherwise." Her finger traced the rim of the mug. "I thought that once you went home, everything would go back to the way it was before...."

"I was hoping for the same thing. Kate, you've got to

believe me when I tell you I would've done anything in the world to spare you this. When I learned you and Clay were engaged I wanted to—"

"Die," Kate finished for her. "I know exactly how you must have felt, because that's the way I felt later. The night of the Grange dance, Clay kept looking at you. Every time you danced with a new partner, he scowled. He might have had me at his side, but his eyes followed you all over the hall."

"He loves you, too," Rorie told her. "That's what makes this all so difficult."

"No, he doesn't," Kate answered flatly, without a hint of doubt. "I accepted that a long time before you ever arrived. Oh, he respects and likes me, and to Clay's way of thinking that was enough." She hesitated, frowning. "To my way of thinking, it was, too. We probably would've married and been content. But everything changed when Clay met you. You hit him right between the eyes, Rorie—a direct hit."

"I'm sure he feels more for you than admiration...."

"No." Kate rummaged in her purse for a tissue. "He told me as much himself, but like I said, it wasn't something I didn't already know. You see, I was so crazy about Clay, I was willing to take whatever he offered me, even if it was only second-best." She swabbed at the tears that sprang so readily to her eyes and paused in an effort to gather her composure. "I'm sorry. It's still so painful. But you see, through all of this, I've learned a great deal about what it means to love someone."

Rorie's own eyes welled with involuntary tears, which

she hurriedly brushed aside. Then Kate's fingers clasped hers and squeezed tight in a gesture of reassurance.

"I learned that loving people means placing their happiness before your own. That's the way you love Clay, and it's the way he loves you." Kate squared her shoulders and inhaled a quavery breath.

"Kate, please, this isn't necessary."

"Yes, it is, because what I've got to say next is the hardest part. I need to ask your forgiveness for that terrible letter I wrote after you left Nightingale. I don't have any excuse except that I was insane with jealousy."

"Letter? You wrote me a terrible letter?" The only one Rorie had received was the chatty note that had told her about Mary's prize-winning ribbon and made mention of the upcoming wedding.

"I used a subtle form of viciousness," Kate replied, her voice filled with self-contempt.

Rorie discounted the possibility that Kate could ever be malicious. "The only letter I got from you wasn't the least bit terrible."

Kate lowered her eyes to her hands, neatly folded on the table. Her grip tightened until Rorie was sure her nails would cut her palms.

"I lied in that letter," Kate continued. "When I told you that Clay wouldn't have time for you while he was at the horse show, I was trying to imply that you didn't mean anything to him anymore. I wanted you to think you'd slipped from his mind when nothing could have been further from the truth."

"Don't feel bad about it. I'm not so sure I wouldn't have done the same thing."

"No, Rorie, you wouldn't have. That letter was an underhand attempt to hold on to Clay... I was losing him more and more each day and I thought...I hoped that if you believed we were going to be married in October, then... Oh, I don't know, my thinking was so warped and desperate."

"Your emotions were running high at the time." Rorie's had been, too; she understood Kate's pain because she'd been in so much pain herself.

"But I was pretending to be your friend when in reality I almost hated you." Kate paused, her shoulders shaking with emotion. "That was the crazy part. I couldn't help liking you and wanting to be your friend, and at the same time I was eaten alive with jealousy and selfish resentment."

"It's not in you to hate anyone, Kate."

"I...I didn't think it was, either, but I was wrong. I can be a terrible person, Rorie. Facing up to that hasn't been easy." She took a deep, shuddering breath.

"Then...a few days after I mailed that letter to you, Clay came over to the house wanting to talk. Almost immediately I realized I'd lost him. Nothing I could say or do would change the way he felt about you. I said some awful things to Clay that night.... He's forgiven me, but I need your forgiveness, too."

"Oh, Kate, of course, but it isn't necessary. I understand. I truly do."

"Thank you," she murmured, dabbing her eyes with the crumpled tissue. "Now I've got that off my chest, I feel a whole lot better."

"But if Clay had broken your engagement when he came to San Francisco, why didn't he say anything to me?"

Kate shrugged. "I don't know what happened while he was gone, but he hasn't been himself since. He never has been a talkative person, but he seemed to draw even further into himself when he came back. He's working himself into an early grave, everyone says. Mary's concerned about him—we all are. Mary said if you didn't come soon, she was going after you herself."

"Mary said that?" The housekeeper had been the very person who'd convinced Rorie she was doing the right thing by getting out of Clay's life.

"Well, are you going to him? Or are you planning to stick around here and listen to me blubber all day? If you give me any more time," she said, forcing a laugh, "I'll manage to make an even bigger fool of myself than I already have." Kate stood abruptly, pushing back the kitchen chair. Her arms were folded around her waist, her eyes bright with tears.

"Kate," Rorie murmured, "you are a dear, dear friend. I owe you more than it's possible to repay."

"The only thing you owe me is one godchild—and about fifty years of happiness with Clay Franklin. Now get out of here before I start weeping in earnest."

Kate opened the kitchen door and Rorie gave her an impulsive hug before hurrying out.

Luke Rivers was standing in the yard, apparently waiting for her. When she came out of the house he sauntered over to her car and held open the driver's door. "Did everything go all right with Kate?"

Rorie nodded.

"Well," he said soberly, "there may be more rough waters ahead for her. She doesn't know it yet, but I'm buying out the Circle L." Then he smiled, his eyes crinkling. "She's going to be fine, though. I'll make sure of that." He extended his hand, gripping hers in a firm handshake. "Let me be the first to welcome you to our community."

"Thank you."

He touched the rim of his hat in farewell, then glanced toward the house. "I think I'll go inside and see how Kate's doing."

Rorie's gaze skipped from the foreman to the house and then back again. "You do that." If Luke Rivers had anything to say about it, Kate wouldn't be suffering from a broken heart for long. Rorie had suspected Luke was in love with Kate. But, like her, he was caught in a trap, unable to reveal his feelings. Perhaps now Kate's eyes would be opened—Rorie fervently hoped so.

The drive from the Logans' place to the Franklins' took no more than a few minutes. Rorie parked her car behind the house, her heart pounding. When she climbed out, the only one there to greet her was Mary.

"About time you got here," the housekeeper complained, marching down the porch steps with a vengeance.

"Could this be the apple-pie blue-ribbon holder of Nightingale, Oregon?"

Mary actually blushed, and Rorie laughed. "I thought you'd never want to see the likes of me again," she teased.

"Fiddlesticks." The weathered face broke into a smile.

"I'm still a city girl," Rorie warned.

"That's fine, 'cause you got the heart of a country girl."

Wiping her hands dry on her apron, Mary reached for Rorie and hugged her.

After one brief, bone-crushing squeeze, she set her free. "I'm a meddling old woman, sure enough, and I suspect the good Lord intends to teach me more than one lesson in the next year or two. I'd best tell you that I never should've said those things I did about Kate being the right woman for Clay."

"Mary, you spoke out of concern. I know that."

"Clay doesn't love Kate," she continued undaunted, "but my heavens, he does love you. That boy's been pining his heart out for want of you. He hasn't been the same from the minute you drove out of here all those weeks ago."

Rorie had suffered, too, but she didn't mention that to Mary. Instead, she slipped her arm around the housekeeper's broad waist and together they strolled toward the house.

"Clay's gone for the day, but he'll be back within the hour."

"An hour," Rorie repeated. She'd waited all this time; another sixty minutes shouldn't matter.

"Dinner will be ready then, and it's not like Clay or Skip to miss a meal. Dinner's been at six every night since I've been cooking for this family, and that's a good many years now." Mary's mouth formed a lopsided grin. "Now what we'll do is this. You be in the dining room waiting for him and I'll tell him he's got company."

"But won't he notice my car?" Rorie twisted around, gesturing at her old white Toyota—her own car this time—parked within plain sight.

Debbie Macomber

Mary shook her head. "I doubt it. He's never seen your car, so far as I know, only that fancy sports car. Anyway, the boy's been working himself so hard, he'll be too tired to notice much of anything."

Mary opened the back door and Rorie stepped inside the kitchen. As she did, the house seemed to fold its arms around her in welcome. She paused, breathing in the scent of roast beef and homemade biscuits. It might not be sourdough and Golden Gate Park roses, but it felt right. More than right.

"Do you need me to do anything?" Rorie asked.

Mary frowned, then nodded. "There's just one thing I want you to do—make Clay happy."

"Oh, Mary, I intend to start doing that the second he walks through that door."

An hour later, almost to the minute, Rorie heard Skip and Clay come into the kitchen.

"What's for dinner?" Skip asked immediately.

"It's on the table. Now wash your hands."

Rorie heard the teenager grumble as he headed down the hallway to the bathroom.

"How'd the trip go?" Mary asked Clay.

He mumbled something Rorie couldn't hear.

"The new librarian stopped by to say hello. Old man Logan and Kate sent her over—thought you might like to meet her."

"I don't. I hope you got rid of her. I'm in no mood for company."

"Nope," Mary said. "Fact is, I invited her to stay for dinner. The least you can do is wipe that frown off your face and go introduce yourself."

Rorie stood just inside the dining room, her heart ready to explode. By the time Clay stepped into the room, tears had blurred her vision and she could hardly make out the tall, familiar figure that blocked the doorway.

She heard his swift intake of breath, and the next thing she knew she was crushed in Clay's loving arms.

Seventeen

Rorie was locked so securely in Clay's arms that for a moment she couldn't draw a breath. But that didn't matter. What mattered was that she was being hugged by the man she loved and he was holding on to her as though he didn't plan to ever let her go.

Clay kissed her again and again, the way a starving man took his first bites of food, initially hesitant, then eager. The palms of Rorie's hands were pressed against his chest and she felt the quick surge of his heart. His own hand was gentle on her hair, caressing it, running his fingers through it.

"Rorie...Rorie, I can't believe you're here."

Rorie felt the power of his emotions, and they were strong enough to rock her, body and soul. This man loved her. He was honest and hardworking, she knew all that, but even more, Clay Franklin was *good,* with an unselfishness and a loyalty that had touched her profoundly. In an age of ambitious, hardhearted, vain men, she had inadvertently stumbled on this rare man of character. Her life would never be the same.

Clay exhaled a deep sigh, and his hands framed her face as he pulled his head back to gaze into her eyes. The lines that marked his face seemed more deeply incised now, and she felt another pang of sorrow for the pain he'd endured.

"Mary wasn't teasing me, was she? You *are* the new librarian?"

Rorie nodded, smiling up at him, her happiness shining from her eyes. "There's no going back for me. I've moved out of my apartment, packed everything I own and quit my job with barely a week's notice."

Rorie had fallen in love with Clay, caught in the magic of one special night when a foal had been born. But her feelings stretched far beyond the events of a single evening and the few short days they'd spent together. Her love for Clay had become an essential part of her. Rorie adored him and would feel that way for as long as her heart continued to beat.

Clay's frown deepened and his features tightened briefly. "What about Dan? I thought you were going to marry him."

"I couldn't," she said, then smiled tenderly, tracing his face with her hands, loving the feel of him beneath her fingertips.

"But—"

"Clay," she interrupted, "why didn't you tell me when I saw you in San Francisco that you'd broken your engagement to Kate?" Her eyes clouded with anguish at the memory, at the anxiety they'd caused each other. It had been such senseless heartache, and they'd wasted precious time. "Couldn't you see how miserable I was?"

A grimace of pain moved across his features. "All I noticed was how right you and that stockbroker looked together. You both kept telling me what a bright future he had. I couldn't begin to offer you the things he could. And if that wasn't enough, it was all too apparent that Dan was in love with you." Gently Clay smoothed her hair away from her temple. "I could understand what it meant to love you, and, between the two of us, he seemed the better man."

Rorie lowered her face, pressing her forehead against the hollow of his shoulder. She groaned in frustration. "How could you even *think* such a thing, when I love you so much?"

Clay moved her face so he could meet her eyes. "But, Rorie…" He stopped and a muscle jerked in his jaw. "Dan can give you far more than I'll ever be able to. He's got connections, background, education. A few years down the road, he's going to be very wealthy—success is written all over him. He may have his faults, but basically he's a fine man."

"He *is* a good person and he's going to make some woman a good husband. But it won't be me."

"He could give you the kinds of things I may never be able to afford.…"

"Clay Franklin, do you love me or not?"

Clay exhaled slowly, watching her. "You know the answer to that."

"Then stop arguing with me. I don't love Dan Rogers. I love you."

Still his frown persisted. "You belong in the city."

"I belong with you," she countered.

He said nothing for a long moment. "I can't argue with that," he whispered, his voice husky with emotion. "You do belong here, because God help me, I haven't got the strength to let you walk away a second time."

Clay kissed her again, his mouth sliding over hers as though he still couldn't believe she was in his arms. She held on to him with all her strength, soaking up his love. She was at home in his arms. It was where she belonged and where she planned to stay.

The sound of someone entering the room filtered through to Rorie's consciousness, but she couldn't bring herself to move out of Clay's arms.

"Rorie!" Skip cried, his voice high and excited, "What are you doing here?"

Rorie finally released Clay and turned toward the teenager who had come to her rescue that August afternoon.

"Hello, Skip," she said softly. Clay slipped his arm around her waist and she smiled up at him, needing his touch to anchor her in the reality of their love.

"Are you back for good?" Skip wanted to know.

She nodded, but before she could answer Clay said, "Meet Nightingale's new librarian." His arm tightened around her.

The smile that lit the teenager's eyes was telling. "So you're going to stick around this time." He blew out a gusty sigh. "It's a damn good thing, because since you left, my brother's been as hard to live with as a rattle-snake."

"I'd say that was a bit of an exaggeration," Clay muttered, clearly not approving of his brother's choice of description.

"You shouldn't have gone," Skip said, sighing again. "Especially before the county fair."

Rorie laughed. "You're never going to forgive me for missing that, are you?"

"You should've been here, Rorie. It was great."

"I'll be here next summer," she promised.

"The fact is, Rorie's going to be around for a lifetime of summers," Clay informed his brother. "We're going to be married as soon we can arrange it." His eyes held hers but they were filled with questions, as if he half expected her, even now, to refuse him.

Rorie swallowed the emotion that bobbed so readily to the surface and nodded wildly, telling him with one look that she'd marry him anytime he wanted.

Skip crossed his arms over his chest and gave them a smug look. "I knew something was going on between the two of you. Every time I was around you guys it was like getting zapped with one of those stun guns."

"We were that obvious?" It still troubled Rorie that Kate had known, especially since both she and Clay had tried so hard to hide their feelings.

Skip's shrug was carefree. "I don't think so, but I don't care about love and all that."

"Give it time, little brother," Clay murmured, "because when it hits, it'll knock you for a loop."

Mary stepped into the room, carrying a platter of meat. "So the two of you are getting hitched?"

Their laughter signaled a welcome release from all the tensions of the past weeks. Clay pulled out Rorie's chair, then sat down beside her. His hand reached for hers, lacing their fingers together. "Yes," he said, still smiling, "we'll be married as soon as we can get the license and talk to the pastor."

Mary pushed the basket of biscuits closer to Skip. "Well, you don't need to fret—I'll stay for a couple more years until I can teach this child the proper way to feed a man. She may be pretty to look at, but she don't know beans about whipping up a decent meal."

"I'd appreciate that, Mary," Rorie said. "I could do with a few cooking lessons."

The housekeeper's smile broadened. "Now, go ahead and eat before the potatoes get cold and the gravy gets lumpy."

Skip didn't need any further inducement. He helped himself to the biscuits, piling three on the edge of his plate.

Mary playfully slapped his hand. "I've got apple pie for dessert, so don't go filling yourselves up on my buttermilk biscuits." Her good humor was evident as she surveyed the table, glancing at everyone's plate, then bustled back to the kitchen.

Rorie did her best to sample a little of everything. Although the meal was delicious, she was too excited to do anything as mundane as eat.

After dinner, Skip made himself scarce. Mary delivered a tray with two coffee cups to the living room, where Clay and Rorie sat close together on the couch. "You two have lots to talk about, so you might as well drink this while you're doing it."

"Thank you, Mary," Clay said, exchanging a smile with Rorie.

The older woman set the tray down, then patted the fine gray hair at the sides of her head. "I want you to know how pleased I am for you both. Have you set the date yet?"

"We're talking about that now," Clay answered. "We're going to call Rorie's family in Arizona this evening and discuss it with them."

Mary nodded. "She's not the woman I would've chosen for you, her being a city girl and all, but she'll make you happy."

Clay's hand clasped Rorie's. "I know."

"She's got a generous soul." The housekeeper looked at Rorie and her gaze softened. "Fill this house with children—and with love. It's been quiet far too long."

The phone rang in the kitchen and, with a regretful glance over her shoulder, Mary hurried to answer it. A moment later, she stuck her head around the kitchen door.

"It's for you, Clay. Long distance."

Clay's grimace was apologetic. "I'd better get it."

"You don't need to worry that I'll leave," Rorie said with a laugh. "You're stuck with me for a lot of years, Clay Franklin."

He kissed her before he stood up, then headed toward the kitchen. Rorie sighed and leaned back, cradling her mug. By chance, her gaze fell on the photograph of Clay's parents, which rested on top of the piano. Once more, Rorie felt the pull of his mother's eyes. She smiled now, understanding so many things. The day she'd planned to leave Elk Run, this same photograph had captured her attention. The moment she'd walked into this house,

Rorie had belonged to Clay and he to her. Somehow, looking at his mother's picture, she'd sensed that. She belonged to this home and this family.

Clay returned a few minutes later, with Blue trailing him. "Just a call from the owner of one of the horses I board," he said, as he sat down beside Rorie and placed his arm around her shoulder. His eyes followed hers to the photo. "Mom would have liked you."

Rorie sipped her coffee and smiled. "I know I would have loved her." Setting her cup aside, she reached up and threw both arms around Clay's neck. Gazing into his eyes, she brought his mouth down to hers.

Perhaps it was her imagination or an optical illusion— in fact, Rorie was sure of it. But she could have sworn the elegant woman in the photograph smiled.

* * * * *

The Bachelor Prince

To Anna Eberhardt,
who suggested I write a book about a Prince.

Prologue

Prince Stefano Giorgio Paolo needed a wife. A very rich one. And soon.

He couldn't put off the inevitability of marriage any longer, not if he planned to save his country from the international embarrassment of bankruptcy.

Tightly clenching the Minister of Finance's latest report, he paced the royal office, his mind racing as he trod past the series of six-foot sandstone windows adorned with heavy red draperies.

The view of the courtyard with the huge stone fountain, which dated from the seventeenth century, escaped his attention. At one time the scene below would have given him great joy. But no longer. Now it brought a heaviness to his chest. All because the courtyard was empty of tourists.

San Lorenzo, a tiny European principality, had once thrived as a fairy-tale kingdom, and drawn hordes of sightseers from all across the globe. But with the civil unrest in the Balkan states so close to its borders, the tourists stayed away.

It didn't help that San Lorenzo had no international airport of its own and the closest one was now closed to commercial traffic because of the fighting.

A knock against the heavy oak door distracted him. "Yes," Stefano blurted out impatiently. He'd left word he wasn't to be disturbed. Only a fool would dare interrupt him.

His personal secretary and traveling companion, Pietro, stepped inside the room. Stefano amended his earlier thought. Only a fool *or a friend* would dare intrude on him now.

"I thought you might need this," Pietro said, carrying in an elaborate silver tray with two glasses and a cut-crystal decanter.

"You know I don't drink during the day," Stefano chastised, but without any real censure.

"Generally that's true," Pietro agreed, "but I also know you're thinking about marriage, and the subject, as always, depresses you."

"Once again you're right, my friend." His shoulders sagging, Stefano rubbed a hand over his face and stared out the window at his small kingdom.

"Have you made your decision?" Pietro asked, lifting the stopper from the decanter and splashing two fingers into the glasses. He handed the first to Stefano, who gratefully accepted it.

"Do I have any choice, but to marry?" He felt as if he were sentencing himself to the gallows. He savored his life as a bachelor, and the freedom it offered him to sample the favors of some of the world's most beautiful women.

Frankly, he enjoyed the title of the Bachelor Prince that the tabloids had bestowed on him. The papers, if they were to be believed, claimed he was the perfect romantic prince. They touted him as tall, dark and handsome, with enough charm to sink a flotilla.

It was true he was tall—six foot two—and his skin was tanned a healthy shade of bronze from the many hours he spent out-of-doors. The handsome part, he took with a grain of salt. His features were aristocratic, he supposed. His forehead was high and his chin stately, but then his family had reined over San Lorenzo for nearly seven hundred years.

"Have you decided upon the lucky lady?" Pietro asked in that casual way of his that made Stefano's most troublesome worries appear minimal.

Frowning, Stefano thought for a moment, one hand clenched behind his back. "No." He gestured with his drink toward his friend. "I prefer to marry an American," he decided suddenly.

"Having attended Duke University, you're well acquainted with their ways. American women can be most charming."

Stefano slapped his drink down on the desk. "I don't need charm, I need money."

"Trust me, Stefano, I know that." Pietro reached inside his perfectly tailored black suit and withdrew a piece of paper. "I've taken the liberty of listing several eligible American women for your consideration."

Stefano paused and steadily regarded his friend. Oftentimes he wondered if Pietro could read his mind. "How well you know me."

Pietro bowed slightly. "It was a lucky guess."

Stefano laughed, doubting that. Pietro was much too thorough to leave anything to guesswork. In some ways his secretary knew him better than he did himself.

Like a spoiled child, Stefano had put off dealing with the unpleasantness of his situation. He sat down and rested against the back of the plush velvet chair. "Tell me what you've learned."

"There are a number of excellent young women from whom to choose," Pietro began.

For the next half hour, his secretary provided him with a list of names and the information he'd collected on each woman. There wasn't one who even mildly captured Stefano's curiosity. Perhaps Stefano was just old-fashioned enough to believe in marrying for love. When it came to choosing a wife, he would have preferred to cherish his bride with all his heart and soul, without an eye on her purse strings. But courtly ideals weren't going to save San Lorenzo.

"Well?" Pietro asked, when he'd finished.

Stefano gestured weakly with his hand. "You choose."

Pietro's eyebrows arched. "As you wish."

His companion ran his index finger down the list, pausing at one name and then another. His frown grew darker. Gauging from his reaction, Pietro was having as difficult time choosing as Stefano.

"Priscilla Rutherford," Pietro announced thoughtfully.

"Priscilla," Stefano repeated, attempting to remember

what he could about the woman. "The shipping magnate's daughter?"

"She's the one." Having made his decision, Pietro relaxed and sampled the first taste of his drink.

"Why her?"

Pietro shrugged. "I'm not sure. I've seen her picture."

"She's beautiful?"

It took Pietro a moment to respond. "Yes."

"You don't sound convinced."

One side of Pietro's mouth quirked upward. "She's not a flawless beauty, if that's what you want, but she's a gentle, kind woman all San Lorenzo will love."

"Do you have as much faith she'll fall in love with me?" Stefano asked.

"But, of course." Pietro crossed to the other side of the room and pulled open a drawer. "I've even come up with a way for the two of you to meet."

Stefano slowly shook his head. "You never cease to amaze me, my friend."

"Do you remember the letter we received last week from Ms. Marshall from Seattle?"

"Marshall, Marshall," Stefano repeated, running the name through his memory. "Wasn't she the one who wrote to invite me as her guest of honor to some kind of conference? Some group, something nonsensical...I don't recall what—only that I'd rather be shot than attend."

"She's the one, and it was a Romance Lovers' Convention."

"I sincerely hope you declined," Stefano said with an elongated sigh. "For the love of heaven, I have no time for such nonsense." Romance had no place in the life of a man who was forced to marry for money.

"Fortunately, I haven't responded one way or the other."

"Fortunately?" Stefano eyed his companion wearily.

"I have it on good authority that Priscilla Rutherford will be attending the convention. It would be the ideal way of casually meeting her."

Stefano resumed his pacing, circling his desk a number of times, his hands clasped behind his back. "You can't be serious? The Marshall woman had come up with some ridiculous idea of raffling off a date with me. Dear sweet heaven, Pietro, has it come to this?"

"This conference can help you achieve your goal."

Stefano's gaze narrowed. Surely his friend wasn't serious. He had no desire to stand on the auction block and be awarded to the highest bidder.

"The Romance Lovers' get-together offers you the perfect opportunity to meet Priscilla Rutherford," Pietro reiterated.

"You're serious?"

"Yes, Your Highness, I am."

It was the reference to his title that told him exactly how sincere Pietro was. "See to the arrangements, then," Stefano murmured. This had to be the low point of his life. He was about to become a sideshow at the circus, but if that was what it took to save his country, than Stefano would gladly sacrifice his considerable pride.

One

"The phone's for you."

Hope Jordan glanced irritably toward the wall of her minute coffee shop on Seattle's Fifth Avenue and dragged her wet hands across the white butcher's apron tied about her waist. She hurried toward the phone and reached for the receiver.

"Hello, Mom," she said, not waiting for her mother to announce herself.

"How'd you know it was me?" Doris Jordan asked, her voice revealing her surprise.

"Because no one else phones me when I'm this busy."

"I'm sorry, sweetheart," her mother said, not sounding the least bit contrite, "but you work too hard as it is."

"Mom, unless this is really important, I have to get off the phone. I've got three runners waiting for orders." Hope smiled apologetically toward the trio.

"You'll phone me back?"

"Yes…I promise. But sometime this afternoon, all right?"

"Sure. It's important, Hope. I'll give you the details later, but I want you to know that I've invested twenty-five dollars in tickets to win a date with Prince Stefano Giorgio Paolo of San Lorenzo."

Hope's head bobbed with each one of his names. She'd recently read a lengthy article about Prince Stefano, and his beautiful country. "You want to date someone young enough to be your son?"

"No," Doris said with an impatient sigh. "I bought the tickets for *you*."

"Mom…"

The line went abruptly dead. Hope stared at the phone for several seconds before replacing the receiver. Her mother was bound and determined to see her married, but buying her raffle tickets for a date was "one step over the line" of what Hope found acceptable.

Not that it would do her any good to argue. Her mother wanted her married. The wedding itself wasn't the important point. Grandchildren were. Her mother's three closest friends were all grandmothers. It had become a matter of social status for Doris to see Hope married and pregnant. In that order, of course. And if Hope needed a bit of encouragement along the way, well, Doris was more than happy to supply it. Unfortunately, her means of nudging Hope toward marital bliss bordered on meddling into her already-complicated life.

"We're ready anytime you are," Jimmy, the lovable nineteen-year-old college student, said with a mildly sarcastic smile.

"All right, all right," Hope muttered, lifting the thick paper cups holding a variety of coffees and carrying them from the counter to the waiting trays.

"The idea is to deliver them while they're hot," Jimmy reminded her.

Hope poked his ribs with the sharp end of her elbow.

"Hey," Jimmy protested, "what was that for?"

"Just a little incentive to get you to move faster," she said, grinning broadly.

"I'm outta here."

"That's the idea, Jimmy, my boy." She laughed as he rushed out the back door toward the Federal Building, where the majority of his thirsty clients waited.

When this last batch of runners was out the door, Hope brewed herself a latte and slumped into a chair. The morning rush was a killer.

Coffee Break, Incorporated, had been an idea whose time had come, if sales these past few months were any indication. Hope had started the business with a staff of three who made daily exotic coffee and latte deliveries to the office buildings around Seattle's thriving downtown area.

Soon she'd added a variety of low-fat muffins and other products to the menu and expanded to fifteen runners, who serviced a number of businesses each morning and midafternoon.

"What's wrong?" Lindy, the woman who baked the world's greatest muffins, asked as she pulled out a chair and plopped herself down next to Hope.

Hope flip-flopped her hand, too tired to complain. "My mother's up to her old tricks."

"Has she found another matchmaker?"

Hope was tempted to smile at the memory. Unfortunately, the woman at the matchmaking service hadn't completely understood that the men Doris wanted were meant for her daughter. Consequently Hope had been matched with a man sixty-three years old. Doris had been outraged and demanded her money back. But in the end, it had worked out for the best. The gentleman had taken a fancy to Doris and the two had dined together several times over the winter months.

"That was last time," Hope said.

"Did she arrange another date for you with her doctor's nephew?"

Despite her fatigue, Hope was tempted to laugh outright this time. "That mistake isn't likely to be repeated, either." Her dear, sweet, matchmaking mother had learned a lesson with that fiasco. Doris had insisted Hope meet Arnold Something-or-other. A doctor's nephew was sure to be a real catch, the perfect husband for her stubborn daughter.

Fool that she was, Hope had agreed to the blind date because her mother had been so excited. Doris had made it sound as if she'd miraculously stumbled upon the perfect man for Hope. If she agreed to just one date, then Hope would realize it herself.

Unfortunately, Arnold was a kleptomaniac and was wanted by the authorities for questioning in three different states. The date had been a nightmare from beginning to end. The moment they sat down in the restaurant, Arnold started lining his pockets with pink packages of artificial sweetener. Hope could see this man was no prince.

"Mom's on a different kick this time," Hope said, musing that her mother was determined to find her a prince, only this time it was for real.

Lindy handed her a fresh applesauce-and-raisin muffin still warm from the oven. "What's she up to now?"

"I'm not entirely sure," Hope said, lifting her tired feet from the floor and securing them in the seat of the chair across from her. "It was something ridiculous about buying raffle tickets for a date with a prince."

"Hey," Lindy said, taking notice, "I read about that. It's part of the Madeline Marshall Romance Lovers' Convention that's going on at the Convention Center next week."

"The what?" Hope brushed a stray strand of blond hair from her forehead.

"Come on, Hope, you must have heard about the conference. The newspeople have been having a heyday with this all week. It starts Thursday evening with a fancy cocktail party. Romance writers from all over the world are flying in to meet their fans. Why, it's the biggest thing to hit Seattle since the World's Fair."

"You've got to be joking."

"I'm not. Romance novels are big business. Bigger than the man on the street realizes."

"Are you telling me that you read romances?" Hope asked. Lindy? Her down-to-earth baker? It didn't gel.

"Of course I do. You mean you don't?"

"Heavens, no," Hope said, shaking her head. "I don't have time to read anything right now." The demands of her business left little time for leisure activities.

"Then you're missing out, girl. Everyone needs to kick

off their shoes and escape from the harsh realities of the world every now and again."

"But romance novels?" Her mother had been hooked on the books for years, reading them for therapy after Hope's father had passed away. Although Doris had brought several of her favorite novels to her daughter, Hope had never taken the time to read one. Most of her reading material consisted of magazine articles and nonfiction.

"Do you have something against romance novels?" the talented baker asked, standing. In her defense of the reading material, Lindy dug her fist into her hip and glared down at her employer.

It was all Hope could do not to laugh. Lindy's tall white baker's hat was askew, and her eyes flashed with righteous zeal. Apparently her friend took the subject seriously.

"I didn't mean to offend you," Hope offered as a means of keeping the peace.

"You didn't," Lindy was quick to assure her, "but having someone trash romance novels without ever having read them is a pet peeve of mine."

"I'll give one a try someday," Hope promised, but doubted that it would be anytime soon. Romance didn't interest her. Perhaps later, when Coffee Break, Incorporated, was firmly on its feet, she'd consider searching for a husband.

"I bought a raffle ticket myself," Lindy announced sheepishly. "I don't know what I'd do if I won. I swear Prince Stefano is the handsomest man alive."

Hope had seen his picture often enough in the tabloids to agree with her friend's assessment. The prince was said to be the world's most eligible bachelor. "But if you won the date with him, what would you have to talk about?"

Lindy wiggled her eyebrows suggestively. "Talk? Are you nuts? If I won the date with Prince Stefano, I wouldn't waste precious time talking."

Hope laughed, then shook her head. "Of course you'd talk. That's the point of the evening, isn't it?"

A dreamy look came over Hope's friend. "Even if we did nothing but sit across the table and stare at one another all evening, I'd be thrilled."

Not Hope. If she was going to date a prince, she'd make sure the time was well spent. Oh, good grief, she was actually contemplating what it would be like. Clearly she'd been breathing too many fumes from the espresso machine.

"You won't need to call your mother back," Lindy announced all at once.

"Why not?"

"Because I just saw her crossing the street."

Hope walked over to the picture window in front of her shop. Sure enough, her dear, sweet mother was heading straight for Coffee Break, Incorporated.

"Mom," Hope breathed when the front door opened, "what are you doing here?"

"I thought I'd come see my only child who never visits her mother anymore."

The hint of guilt hung in the air like a low-lying cloud. Hope didn't think now was the time to mention that each visit had been turned into another matchmaking opportunity. The last two trips home had been enough to keep Hope away for life.

"Mom, you know how busy I've been this summer. Besides, I talked to you no more than twenty minutes ago. Didn't you trust me to call you back?"

"I didn't want to chance it. Besides I was in the neighborhood."

Her mother avoided trips downtown like the plague. "What are you doing here?"

"Hazel and I came down to that fancy hotel on Fourth Street to make reservations for next week. Gladys and Betty, Hazel and I decided to spring for the big bucks and stay in the hotel for the conference."

"You're actually going to stay at a hotel in Seattle? We *live* in Seattle."

"We want to network. Who knows all the fun we'd miss if we had to catch the five o'clock bus back to Lake City? We decided not to chance it."

"I see," Hope said, but she wasn't entirely sure she did.

"By dividing the price of the room four ways, it costs hardly anything. You can't blame us for wanting to be where the action is, now can you?"

"Where's Hazel?"

"I left her at the hotel. She's checking out the room they're giving us. Rumor has it Prince Stefano's suite is on the nineteenth floor." She paused and Hope swore her eyes sparked with mischief. "Hazel made up a story about her blood pressure and the medication she's taking. She insisted the higher the room, the better it is for her heart." A smile dimpled each of Doris's tanned cheeks. "It worked. Our room's on the eighteenth floor."

Hope could see it all now. Four retired schoolteachers lurking in corridors waiting for a glimpse of Prince

Stefano. "So you're going to be rubbing shoulders with royalty."

"Just think of it, Hope. We might run in to the prince on the elevator."

"Indeed you might." Her mother sounded like a star-crazed teenager waiting for a glimpse of her favorite rock star.

"It's all for fun, Hope." She glanced at her daughter as if she feared Hope would say she was acting like an old lady.

"I think it's great, Mom," she said, resisting the urge to laugh. "You and your friends will have the time of your lives."

"You don't think we're a bunch of old biddies, do you?"

"Of course not."

"We're so excited."

"About meeting the prince?"

"That, too, but the opportunity to see all our favorite romance writers, and get their autographs. It's like a dream come true."

"You're going to have the time of your life."

Her mother didn't seem to hear her. All at once her face grew somber. "I always said someday your prince would come, didn't I, Hope? Now the time has come. He's going to fall head over heels in love with you, sweetheart."

Already Hope could see the wheels turning in her mother's fevered brain. It'd be best if she could root Doris in a bit of reality. "Mother, my winning the date with Prince Stefano is a long shot. I imagine they've sold a thousand chances."

"More," Doris said confidently. "It doesn't matter. You're going to win."

It wouldn't do any good to point out the mathematical odds of that happening were astronomical. Letting her mother dream wasn't going to hurt anything, Hope supposed. The whole thing was harmless. Hope had as much a chance of winning as the man in the moon.

"You'll be there for the drawing, won't you?"

"When?" Hope had no intention of attending, but she didn't want to tell her mother that.

"The lucky winner will be announced Thursday night at the cocktail party."

"I can't," she said automatically. "I'm meeting with my accountant to go over this quarter's taxes. You'll stand in for me, won't you?"

"If I must." Doris looked a bit disappointed, but Hope could see that the more her mother thought about it, the better she liked the idea. "Naturally, Hazel and the others would want to meet him."

"Naturally," Hope concurred. "I'll tell you what, Mom. If I win the date with Prince Stefano, I'll be sure that the four of you have a chance to chat with the prince, and it won't be in any elevator." It was easy to be generous when it cost her nothing.

Doris's face broke into a smile as wide as the Grand Canyon. "Wouldn't that be a kick."

Hope was convinced it would.

Prince Stefano looked out over the crowded ballroom floor and felt a cold chill race down his spine. Glasses clinked, champagne bubbled. Lights glowed and warmed the room from the huge crystal chandeliers. Stefano swore the eyes of a thousand women followed his every move.

He wasn't a man who frightened easily, but this situation was enough to try any man's soul. Stefano didn't doubt that if he were to stumble from the security of the stage, he would be stripped bare of his clothes within seconds. The crowd resembled a hungry school of piranhas.

For the first time in his lengthy history with Pietro, Stefano questioned if his secretary was friend or foe. After all, his agreeing to stand upon the auction block like a slab of fresh meat had been Pietro's doing.

Stefano's gaze scanned the crowd until he found his secretary. His companion was standing against the wall with a short young woman, wearing a revealing dress that clearly made her uncomfortable. Each time Stefano glanced her way, she was nervously smoothing the full skirt, or adjusting the spaghetti-thin straps.

So this was Priscilla Rutherford. Stefano had learned everything he could about the young woman in the past several weeks. She was the only daughter of one of America's wealthiest men. As Pietro had assured him, she was a lovely creature, comely and pleasant to the eye. Priscilla Rutherford was a gentle soul who loved animals and children. She lived with her parents in their Lake Washington estate, and volunteered her time to a number of worthy charities.

The only drawback that Stefano could see was her domineering, manipulating mother who would like nothing better than to see her daughter marry well. It was unlikely that Elizabeth Rutherford would find fault with

Stefano, but he wasn't looking forward to having a barracuda for a mother-in-law. A woman such as this could wreck havoc in his peaceful kingdom.

"I sincerely hope you're enjoying yourself, Your Highness," Madeline Marshall said as she curtsied deeply before him. She offered him her hand and Stefano bent forward at the waist and kissed her fingers.

"How can I not enjoy myself when I am with you?" he murmured. Madeline Marshall was another of life's small surprises. The woman was an eccentric, true, but she was a cagey businesswoman who knew her product. And her product was romance. Madeline had earned his grudging respect with her organizational expertise and her leverage with the media.

Pietro had reported to Stefano earlier in the day that the autographing that was scheduled for Saturday afternoon had the potential for drawing in nearly eight thousand ardent romance readers. Stefano had been amazed, and had suggested to Madeline earlier in that evening that San Lorenzo would be the perfect location for a future conference. The tourist bureau would appreciate the plug.

"We've sold over thirteen thousand tickets," Madeline whispered to him, her eyes twinkling.

"I am honored that so many beautiful women are eager to spend an evening in my company," Stefano said with a graciousness that had been drilled into him from his youth.

"From what I understand, Priscilla Rutherford bought a thousand tickets. I don't mind telling you, I purchased a fair share of them myself," Madeline said with a short, nervous laugh.

"I would be most happy if I were to draw your name, Ms. Marshall," Stefano said, inclining his head toward her.

The businesswoman broke out in a sigh and pressed her hand over her heart. "If only I were ten years younger," she whispered. "I'd give you a run for your money."

Stefano didn't doubt the truth of that.

Sighing once more, Madeline asked, "Are you ready for the drawing?"

"Of course." As ready as any man could be who was about to face a firing squad.

Madeline Marshall stepped toward the podium. An excited hush fell over the crowd as a huge plastic barrel containing the entrants' names was wheeled onto the stage. Two muscular hotel employees stood guard at each side of the barrel.

"Ladies and gentlemen," Madeline said, commanding their attention. Not that the hungry crowd needed encouragement. "The time we've all been waiting for has finally arrived. Romance lovers have snatched up over thirteen thousand tickets, all seeking the once-in-a-lifetime chance to date Prince Stefano Giorgio Paolo, the Crown Prince of San Lorenzo—the world's most eligible bachelor."

An enthusiastic chatter circled the room. It seemed to Stefano that the group was pressing closer and closer to the stage.

"As I explained earlier," Madeline Marshall continued, "the winning ticket entitles the winner to an all-expense paid evening with Prince Stefano, at the restaurant of her choice. The monies collected for this evening's event have been donated to the Literacy Councils of King, Pierce and Kitsap Counties."

Applause followed. The two burly men edged closer to the barrel and energetically stirred the hopes and dreams of thirteen thousand women. The white entries tumbled one on top of the other.

When they'd finished, Madeline Marshall opened the trapdoor and motioned for him. "Prince Stefano, would you kindly do us the honor?" she asked.

Stefano nodded, stepped toward the plastic barrel and with a sigh, inserted his gloved hand. He burrowed his fingers through the entries, grabbed several and shook his hand until only one remained. He pulled that one out.

Stepping up to the podium, he looked out over the expectant faces of the women staring up at him. Priscilla Rutherford held her arms close to her breasts, her eyes closed and her fingers crossed. He wouldn't dare to hope he would draw the name of the woman he planned to make his wife. The Fates would never make it that easy.

He swore he could have heard a pin drop in the silence. He unfolded the slip, and mentally he reviewed the name.

"Hope Jordan." He spoke into the microphone.

A scream came from the back of the room as an older, gray-haired woman raised both hands. Stefano's gaze found her and he felt his heart drop to his knees.

He was about to go out on a date with a woman old enough to be his mother.

Two

"You won!" The nearly incoherent voice shouted into Hope's ear.

Hope propped open one eye and stared at the digital dial on her clock radio. It was nearly eleven. One arm dangled over the side of the bed and the other held the telephone receiver to her ear. The side of her face was flattened against the pillow.

"Who is this?"

"It's Lindy."

"For the love of heaven, why are you calling me in the middle of the night?"

"To tell you Prince Stefano drew your name."

Both Hope's eyes flew open. Scrambling into a sitting position, she brushed the hair from her face, pressing her hand against her forehead. "Why are you calling me instead of my mother?"

"Because when your name was announced, your mother screamed, threw her arms into the air and promptly fainted."

"Oh, my goodness—" Hope bounded to her feet and paced across the top of her mattress "—is Mom all right?"

"I think so. She keeps saying something about fate and Providence and the stars all being in the right place. The paramedics don't have a clue what she's talking about."

"The paramedics?"

"That's the other reason I phoned," Lindy announced. "They need you to answer a few questions."

"I'll be there as soon as I can," Hope said, and in her rush nearly fell headfirst off her bed, forgetting where she was standing. She swore she never dressed so fast in her life, pulling on jeans and a sweatshirt. She hopped around the room on one foot like a jackrabbit in an effort to get on her tennis shoes.

Driving into town, she happened to catch a glimpse of her reflection in the rearview mirror. And cringed. She must have been sleeping hard because the mattress had creased her cheek and the hair on one side of her head resembled a ski slope. Her deep blue eyes seemed to have trouble focusing.

Hope left her car with the hotel valet and rushed around the ambulance parked by the entrance and hurried inside the lobby where Lindy was waiting for her. Hope's appearance must have taken her friend aback because Lindy reached inside her purse and handed Hope her comb.

"The prince is with your mother," she explained when Hope regarded the comb.

Hope had to stop and think what Lindy was telling her. "So?"

"I…I thought you might want to freshen up a little."

"Lindy, my mother fainted, the paramedics don't know

what's wrong. I think Prince Stefano isn't going to care if I brushed my teeth."

"All right, all right. I wasn't thinking."

If meeting Prince Stefano was enough to cause her mother to require smelling salts, frankly Hope wasn't all that keen on being introduced.

Lindy led the way to the elevator, and they rode up to the eighteenth floor. Her mother's friends, Hazel, Gladys and Betty all rushed toward Hope when she stepped off the elevator. The three were all talking at once, telling her their version of what had happened after Prince Stefano read Hope's name.

"Your mother went terribly pale," Hazel said.

"I told you she wasn't getting enough carrot juice," Betty insisted. "She isn't juicing properly."

Gladys agreed. "This is the kind of thing that happens when you let yourself get irregular."

"She asked for you," Hazel said, ignoring the others, as she gripped Hope's arm. She opened the door to the room, and with an indignant sigh, said, "Those firemen wouldn't let us in. You tell your mother we're out here waiting for her." Hope started inside the room, when Hazel stopped her. "Tell Doris she can have the Hide-A-Bed if she wants."

"I will," Hope promised.

Hope found her mother sprawled across a davenport, the back of one hand pressed against her forehead. The other hand was being held by the most incredibly good-looking man she'd ever seen. If this was Prince Stefano, then no wonder her mother had fainted.

He was dressed in some kind of deep blue uniform with

gold epaulets at the shoulders. A bright red banner crossed his chest, which was adorned with three rows of medals.

All at once Hope wished she'd heeded Lindy's suggestion about combing her hair. She looked a fright. Well, that couldn't be helped. It was too late to worry about it now.

Her mother moaned softly, and noticing Hope for the first time, Prince Stefano stood.

"Is that you, Hope?" Her mother's voice sounded as if it were coming from the bottom of a dry well. The question was followed by another low, breathy sigh-moan.

"Mom," Hope said, falling to her knees beside the sofa. "What happened?"

"I…I think I must have fainted."

"I'm wondering if you could answer a few questions?" a paramedic with a clipboard asked her.

"Of course." Hope reluctantly left her mother's side.

"There are just a few things we need to know," he said matter-of-factly.

Hope responded to a series of predictable questions, such as her mother's address, phone number, age. "As far as we can determine," the medic said when she'd finished supplying the information, "the fainting spell was caused by a sudden drop in blood pressure. Your mother seems to be doing fine for now, but she should check in with the family physician within the next week or two."

"I'll see that she does," Hope said.

The medic had her sign at the bottom of his report. "Do you have any questions?"

For one crazy moment, Hope toyed with the idea of asking if this fainting spell could be linked to a lack of carrot juice and irregularity. Fortunately, she stopped herself in the nick of time.

"Nothing, thank you," she said.

The medic tore the sheet from the top of the clipboard and handed it to her. Hope folded it in half and stuck it in the pocket of her acid-washed jeans. "Thank you for your trouble," she said, as the two paramedics gathered their equipment.

"Mom, let me take you home," Hope suggested gently, kneeling down at her mother's side.

Doris ignored the suggestion. Instead she tilted her head back so that she could get a better look at Prince Stefano. "Hope, this is Prince Stefano," Doris said, gazing at the prince as if he were a Roman god. Actually that assessment wasn't far off.

"I'm very pleased to make your acquaintance," Prince Stefano said politely.

"Me, too." She held out her hand, and then, thinking this might be considered unladylike, quickly withdrew it.

The prince offered her his own hand just as she dropped hers. He dropped his, and she raised hers. Their eyes met and Hope saw a flash of amusement dance in his deep brown eyes.

"Prince..." Doris whispered, "please excuse how my daughter's dressed. She doesn't normally look...this bad."

Hope's face filled with color hot enough to fry eggs.

"Your daughter is as beautiful as her mother."

Doris released a languished sigh.

"I understand you and I will be dining together tomorrow evening," Prince Stefano said, smiling toward Hope. He was the picture of propriety and as stiff as cardboard.

"Do you like Chinese food?" Hope asked.

"Chinese food?" Her mother propelled herself off the davenport as if she were bounding off a trampoline. "You're dining with Prince Stefano Giorgio Paolo, not Gomer Pyle. We'll start off with cocktails at Matchabelles, followed by dinner at the Space Needle.... No," Doris corrected. "You won't have a moment's privacy there. The tourists will gawk at you every moment you're there."

Hope and Prince Stefano were left speechless by her mother's miraculous recovery.

"We must plan every detail," Doris said, her voice high and enthusiastic as she started pacing. "I'll need Hazel and the others to help me with this. You two leave everything to us, understand?"

"Ah..." Hope had yet to find her tongue.

"As you wish," Prince Stefano said, ever gracious. "I'm sure you and your friends will plan a lovely evening for your daughter and me."

Doris blushed with pleasure. "I promise you Hope won't look a thing like she does now."

"Mother!"

Prince Stefano's gaze briefly skirted past Hope's, and she caught a glimmer of amusement. He reached for her mother's hand, pressed his lips to it and said, "I'm pleased to see you're feeling better, Mrs. Jordan. If you need anything further, please don't hesitate to call either me or my assistant." He reached inside his pocket and handed her a small card.

"It was a pleasure to meet you," Hope mumbled, after finding her voice.

The prince smiled warmly. "The pleasure was all mine. I'll look forward to our evening together, Miss Jordan."

"I...I will, too."

It wasn't until after he'd left the room that Hope realized it was true.

Priscilla Rutherford stood, hiding out on the balcony, sipping from a champagne glass, and feeling mildly sorry for herself. She'd counted on winning the date with Prince Stefano. It would have been a dream come true to meet His Royal Highness. Priscilla was half in love with the handsome prince. The opportunity to meet him was the reason she'd signed up for the Romance Lovers' Convention. Now that didn't seem likely, although she wasn't sure what she'd say if they did meet. She'd probably embarrass them both by staring at him, too tongue-tied to speak.

The night was lovely with stars scattered like diamond dust across a black velvet sky. The honey-colored moon was full and seemed to be smiling down on her, or so she'd like to think.

Most people assumed Priscilla lived the perfect life. She was well educated, had traveled extensively and was heir to a vast fortune. But what she sought most seemed out of reach. She longed to be a wife and mother to a man who loved her for herself and not for her father's money.

She hungered for a simple life with a husband who hurried home at night to the meals she'd cooked herself. Mostly, Priscilla longed to be a mother. How different she was from her own ambitious one. It often puzzled her that she, who was so homey, could have been born to two highly motivated, sophisticated people.

The cocktail party was winding down, but Priscilla lingered, grateful for these few moments apart from the crowd. She enjoyed people, but often felt awkward and gauche when she was in a group of strangers.

Drinking the last of the champagne, she gazed out over the midnight-dark waters of Puget Sound. A foghorn from one of the ferries sounded in the distance.

"May I join you?"

Priscilla turned around to find a tall, dignified-looking man silhouetted against the bright light spilling from the doorway. She thought he might be part of the group traveling with the prince, but she wasn't sure. During the course of the evening, she'd seen him several times. Almost always he was in close proximity to her.

He was formidable in stature, muscular and nearly as good-looking as the prince himself.

"I…I was just leaving," Priscilla said shyly.

"Please don't," he said, joining her at the railing. Resting his forearms against the wrought iron, he gazed out over the city. "It's a lovely evening, isn't it?"

Priscilla detected a hint of an accent; otherwise his English was flawless.

"Very," she whispered. It would have been far more lovely if her name had been the one drawn by Prince Stefano.

"Are you terribly disappointed?" he turned and asked her unexpectedly.

She thought for a moment to pretend she didn't know what he was talking about, then decided against it. Her disappointment was obvious. "A little."

He straightened. "Perhaps I should introduce myself.

My name is Pietro. I'm the personal secretary to Prince Stefano."

"Pietro," she said, testing the name on her tongue. "You have just one name?"

He hesitated before answering. "Yes. The prince has six, and I've decided one is less confusing."

Priscilla smiled into the balmy night. "It certainly hasn't hurt Madonna any."

"No," he agreed amiably, "it hasn't."

Their silence was a companionable one. "Do you mind if I ask you a few questions about Prince Stefano?" She hoped she wasn't being impertinent.

"It would be my pleasure."

Self-conscious, Priscilla dropped her gaze. "Is the prince as charming as you are?"

"Much more so, I believe."

Priscilla turned and braced her back against the railing in an effort to better see this handsome, mysterious man. The moonlight beamed over his shoulder, illuminating his strong facial features. Prince Stefano was world-class handsome, but Pietro was no slouch in the looks department. "What's it like working with royalty? I mean, is it continual pomp and ceremony?"

"Not at all," Pietro assured her. "Naturally, there are a number of customary obligations the prince is required to attend, but I make sure his schedule is balanced with plenty of free time. The prince loves to ride. He's an excellent swordsman, and..."

"Swordsman? But who would dare to challenge the prince?"

Once again Pietro hesitated, and Priscilla could sense

his amusement. "No one challenges the prince, Ms. Rutherford. Most often he's the one who offers the challenges."

"But whom does he fight?"

Pietro chuckled. "I'm afraid I'm his favorite opponent."

"Have you ever bested him?" Priscilla wasn't sure why she was so curious about Pietro's relationship with the prince, but the man fascinated her.

"We're evenly matched," Pietro explained.

"Then you've won?"

"On occasion."

Although everything she knew about Prince Stefano had come from gossip publications, Priscilla didn't think he'd take kindly to losing at anything. She'd only just met Pietro, but she had the unshakable impression that he wasn't a man who enjoyed losing, either.

"Have you ever *let* him win?"

"Never." His quick response assured her he was telling the truth.

"What's the prince like as a person?"

Pietro mulled over his response. "He's a gentleman. Generous to a fault. Sympathetic and sincere. He cares deeply for his country and his people."

"You make him sound like a saint."

Pietro cocked one eyebrow. "I hadn't finished yet."

"Sorry," she mumbled.

"He's not quick-tempered, but when he does become angry, it's best to find someplace to hide until he's worked out whatever is troubling him."

"My father's like that," Priscilla added thoughtfully, "but he's never angry for very long."

"Neither is Stefano."

"You're his friend, aren't you?" And just about every-thing else, Priscilla speculated.

Pietro didn't answer. Instead he surprised her with a question of his own. "Would you care to meet him?"

Her hands flew to her chest. "Is that possible? I mean, I understand he's only going to be in the area a few days and I wouldn't want to take up his time."

"Prince Stefano would deeply enjoy making your ac-quaintance." Pietro's voice was almost a monotone, crisp and businesslike, as if he were performing a necessary duty.

"I'd love to meet the prince. Every woman here would give their right arm for the opportunity." That she would actually have the chance was more than she could believe.

"He'd enjoy meeting you, as well."

"Me?"

"Why do you sound so surprised?" Pietro asked. "You're a lovely young woman."

It did her ego a world of good to hear Prince Stefano's personal secretary say such things to her. If only she weren't so clumsy and awkward.

"Tomorrow around ten for tea," Pietro suggested.

"So soon? I...I mean sure, anytime would be great."

Pietro removed a small card from inside his suit jacket along with a pen and scribbled the information down on the back. "I'll have the footman meet you in the lobby at ten. If you'll be kind enough to give him this card, he'll escort you to the prince's suites."

"Will you be there?"

It took Pietro a long time to answer. "I don't believe I will be."

"Oh," she whispered, unable to hold back her disappointment. He was about to leave when she stopped him.

"Pietro, after I show the footman the card, would it be all right if I asked for it back? I'd like to keep it as a souvenir."

"That would be fine."

"Good night, and thank you."

He squared his shoulders and bowed slightly before turning and walking back into the ballroom.

"You met her?" Stefano asked when Pietro joined him in the suite.

"Yes. Priscilla Rutherford's agreed to meet you tomorrow morning at ten for tea."

Stefano waited, and when his friend wasn't immediately forthcoming, he raised his hands imploringly. "Well, are you going to tell me about her, or keep me in suspense?"

"Her picture doesn't do her justice. She's beautiful."

Briefly Stefano wondered if they were discussing the same woman. The Priscilla Rutherford he'd seen from the stage was short and self-conscious. She looked like a timid soul who would run for cover the moment someone raised their voice at her. Not that it mattered. It wasn't her he was forced to marry, but her father's money. A bad taste filled his mouth at the thought.

"I could use a drink," he murmured.

"So could I." Pietro walked over to the wet bar, brought down two glasses, filled them with ice and poured them each a strong drink.

"How's the woman who fainted? What was her name…

Charity, or something along those lines?" Pietro inquired. Stefano had the impression his friend didn't want to talk about the heiress, but then he was just as reluctant to mention Hope.

Stefano lowered his gaze to his drink, watching the ice cubes melt. "Her name's Hope. Hope Jordan. Actually the woman who screamed and then fainted is the mother of the young lady I'll be having dinner with tomorrow evening."

"You met her?"

"Yes. Briefly."

"And the mother?"

"She's fine…a little excited, but otherwise I'd say she made a complete recovery."

"And the daughter?"

"The daughter," Stefano repeated, mentally reviewing his encounter with Hope. A smile tempted him. She had blue eyes that snapped like fire, and a look that could shuck oysters. Besides being completely incapable of disguising her feelings, the woman was downright impudent. Suggesting Chinese food… Damn, but he wished that was exactly what they could do. He'd like nothing better than to order out, then sit on the floor and use chopsticks while he learned about her life. Hope Jordan, despite her original hairstyle, interested him. Of course getting to know her beyond this one evening was impossible.

Even deep in thought Stefano could feel his secretary's scrutiny. "I'm sorry, Pietro. What was your question?" he asked.

"I asked about Hope Jordan."

"Ah, yes. We met."

"So I understand. What time's your dinner date?"

"I'm not sure," Stefano said. "Hope's mother and her friends are making the arrangements. By the way, be sure and send flowers to Doris Jordan, Hope's mother. I believe she's staying at the hotel." He paused and thought about what he wanted to say on the card. "Tell her it isn't often a beautiful woman faints at my feet."

Pietro laughed, but grew serious once more. "Could you set a time that you'll return from your dinner date?"

"Why?"

"I was just thinking you might want to make arrangements to meet Priscilla for a drink afterward."

"No," he said adamantly, surprised by his own vehemence. "Ms. Jordan won a dinner date with me, and I don't want to cheat her by abruptly ending the evening in order to meet another woman."

"You're being unnecessarily generous with your time, aren't you?"

"Perhaps," Stefano agreed, but he didn't think so. He had the feeling he was going to enjoy Hope Jordan. It might be selfish of him to want to spend time with her, but frankly, he didn't care. A lifetime of getting to know Priscilla Rutherford stretched before him like a giant vacuum.

"Tell me more about the Rutherford woman."

Pietro's hesitation captured Stefano's attention. It wasn't often his friend was at a loss for words. "You don't like her?"

"Quite the contrary. She's delightful."

"But will she make me a good wife?"

"Yes," he answered stiffly. "She'll make you an excellent bride, an asset to the royal family. The people of San Lorenzo will be crazy about her."

"Excellent."

Pietro took a long, stiff taste of his drink, and then stood. "Is that all for this evening, or do you need me for anything more?"

Stefano was disappointed. He would have preferred it if Pietro had stayed. Stefano was in the mood to talk, but he was unwilling to ask it of him.

"Go on to bed," Stefano advised.

"Will you be up much longer?"

"No," Stefano said, but he wondered exactly how long it would take him to fall asleep.

"Don't quit on me now, ladies," Doris pleaded, sitting Indian-style at the foot of the mattress. Her hair was confined to a cap and she wore a thick cotton bathrobe. "I told Hope and the prince that the four of us would make all the arrangements for their dinner date."

"Can't we do this in the morning?" Hazel asked, sounding like a whiny first grader. That was understandable, seeing that Hazel had taught first grade for nearly thirty years.

"I don't know about the rest of you, but I'm exhausted."

A chorus of agreement followed Gladys's announcement.

"I thought we were here for the Romance Lovers' Convention?" Betty muttered, her eyelids at half-mast.

Gladys lifted her head from beneath the pillow. "Just how much longer is that light going to be on anyway?"

Doris braced her hand against her ample hip. "What's wrong with the three of you?"

"I'm exhausted," Gladys repeated.

"It's barely midnight," Doris said, shocked by her friends. "How could you possibly be tired?"

Her question was answered with a chime of reasons that included a big dinner, cocktails and the excitement of meeting the prince.

"What was all this talk about renting a hotel room and being party animals?" Doris couldn't believe she was rooming with such deadbeats. "Wasn't it you, Betty, who claimed you wanted to call your son at three in the morning and tell him he had to come bail you out of jail?"

"Yes, but…I wasn't serious."

"Gladys," Doris said, eyeing her friend whose face was buried beneath a hotel pillow. "I thought you were going to stick your head out the window and serenade the prince."

The pillow elevated three inches in the direction of the ceiling. "The windows are sealed shut."

"Ladies, ladies," Doris tried once more. "We have work to do."

"We'll never agree…it's *hope*less," Hazel said. And thinking herself clever, she added, "No pun intended."

After debating for the better part of an hour, they hadn't gotten any further in planning Hope's evening with the prince than predinner drinks. From that point on, everyone had an opinion on where the couple should dine.

Hazel was partial to the restaurant where she and Hank had celebrated their fiftieth wedding anniversary. But

Betty seemed to think the prince might frown upon a steak house.

Gladys was sure Hope would be the one to object. "Would a woman who sells low-fat muffins eat red meat?"

"Can't we please decide this in the morning?"

"Oh, all right," Doris said. Her friends were a bitter disappointment to her. She reached over and turned out the light.

"Wouldn't it be something if Hope married the prince?" Betty asked with a romantic sigh into the stillness.

"It won't happen."

"Why won't it?" Doris insisted, chucking back the sheets.

"First off, men like Prince Stefano marry princesses and the like."

"Prince Rainier married Grace Kelly."

"That was in the fifties."

Silence fell over the room.

"Did Hope say anything when they met?" The question came from Betty.

"Not with words," Doris answered, "but a look came over her, like none I've ever seen. I tell you, ladies, it was like magic. I felt it. The prince felt it. It was like a bolt of electricity arced between them."

"You're not making this up, are you?"

"Either that or she's been reading too many romance novels again," Hazel inserted.

"I swear I'm not making this up," Doris insisted. "Prince Stefano didn't know what hit him."

Silence once more. Doris's eyes drifted closed. Someone sighed. Two more sighed collectively, and then…

"What about McCormick's?"

"We already decided against a steak house," Betty muttered.

"Yes, but they serve seafood, too, and I know someone there who owes me big-time. They can make sure this is an evening Prince Stefano and Hope will never forget."

The light switch was turned on, and Doris squinted.

"McCormick's," Hazel mused aloud. "Now there's a possibility."

Three

The following morning Priscilla waited in the hotel lobby. Her fingers repeatedly ran over the business card Pietro had given her the night before. The tall and stately footman arrived and read over the card without emotion when she handed it to him.

"Would it be all right if I kept it?" she asked. "I want it for my scrapbook."

He nodded briefly and returned it. Nervous, Priscilla held her breath as they approached the elevators. She'd dressed carefully for this meeting with the prince. Her mother had insisted on a white linen suit with a soft pink blouse, and a diamond brooch. It was something Elizabeth would have chosen to wear herself. If Priscilla could have had her own way, she would have picked a flower-speckled summer dress with a broad-brimmed white hat, but it would have been useless to argue. Besides, her mother paid far more attention to fashion trends than she ever did.

Both her parents were thrilled that Priscilla had been

granted an audience with Prince Stefano. Although she
was quick to assure them the invitation had come from a
staff member, not the prince himself.

Priscilla feared they were putting far too much empha-
sis on a simple invitation to tea. Apparently they expected
her to bowl the prince over with her wit and charm, and
that just wasn't possible. She so hated to disappoint them.

"Could you do something for me?" Priscilla asked the
footman as he inserted the special key into the elevator
lock that would permit them entry onto the nineteenth
floor.

"If I can," he said, looking mildly surprised.

"I need to talk to Pietro after my meeting with the
prince. Would you tell him it's important? I promise I'll
only take a few minutes of his time. I wouldn't disturb
him if it wasn't necessary. Tell him that for me, if you
would."

"I'll see to it right away."

"Thank you."

The elevator made a soft mechanical noise as it as-
cended. Priscilla's heart was close to blocking her air pas-
sage, and she worried about being able to speak normally
when introduced to the prince. Her hands felt cold and
clammy, and her knees seemed to be losing their starch.
She couldn't remember being more nervous about anything.

The elevator doors smoothly glided open and Priscilla
was escorted into a plush suite that overlooked downtown
Seattle and majestic Puget Sound. As always her gaze was
captured by the beauty of the scenery.

"Your city is beautiful," the deep, male voice said from behind her.

As if caught doing something she shouldn't, Priscilla whirled around. Finding Prince Stefano standing there, she curtsied so low, her knee touched the thick wool carpet. The prince stepped forward, gripped her hand with his own and helped her upright.

The prince was even more dashing close up, Priscilla noted, and not nearly as frightening as she'd expected. She tried to remember the things Pietro had told her about His Highness. She tamed her fear by remembering he was a gallant gentleman who deeply loved his country. If she concentrated on the things she'd learned from Pietro, she might not worry so much about making a fool of herself.

"I'm pleased to make your acquaintance, Miss Rutherford," Prince Stefano said. "Pietro spoke fondly of you."

"I am very honored and pleased to meet you, Your Highness," Priscilla said through the constriction in her throat. "I appreciate your taking the time from your busy schedule to see me. I promise not to take up much of your morning."

"Nonsense. There's always time in my schedule to meet a beautiful and charming woman, such as yourself."

Priscilla blushed.

"Please sit down." The prince gestured to the pair of white leather wing-back chairs.

"Thank you," Priscilla murmured, wondering just how long she'd be required to stay before she could speak with Pietro. "I have something for you," she said, taking the handwritten invitation from her mother and giving it to the prince.

He opened it, read the message and smiled. "I'd be honored to meet your family. Tell your parents they can expect me around three."

The prince engaged Priscilla in mundane conversation, and when there seemed to be nothing more to say, he carried the dialogue himself. He told her about the beauty of San Lorenzo, and invited her to visit his country at her earliest convenience, promising to show her the sights himself.

Forty-five minutes later, when it was time to leave, Priscilla stood gratefully and thanked him for his generous hospitality and the invitation to visit San Lorenzo.

The same footman who'd come for her earlier escorted her from the room. The minute they were out of earshot, Priscilla stopped. "Did you speak with Pietro?"

"Yes. He asked me to take you to his office."

"I hope I'm not interrupting anything important."

"He didn't say, miss." With that he led her down a wide hallway to a compact office.

"Please have a seat," he said. "Pietro will be with you momentarily." He closed the door when he left her alone. Priscilla sank into the cushioned chair, her knees giving out on her. She pressed her hand over her heart, closed her eyes and drew in a deep breath.

"Was it so terrifying meeting Prince Stefano?" Pietro asked from behind her, amusement woven through his words.

"Not exactly terrifying," she answered, straightening. "But I don't think I took a complete breath the entire time I was with him."

"What did you think?" Pietro walked around and sat down at a brightly polished desk across from her.

"Of the prince?" She hadn't had time to properly form an opinion, frightened as she was of making a mistake, or spilling her tea. "He's…a gentleman, just the way you said. He told me about San Lorenzo and invited me to visit, but I think he was just being polite."

"I'm sure he was sincere," Pietro countered.

"I've visited San Lorenzo twice before, but that was years and years ago. I didn't tell the prince that because I was far more comfortable letting him do the talking."

"You asked to see me?" Pietro asked.

"Yes." She noted that the prince's secretary was more reserved and aloof than he had been the night before. "I don't mean to make a nuisance of myself, but I thought I should explain about the invitation my parents sent." For forty-five minutes she'd sat with Prince Stefano and spoken no more than few words. Now, she couldn't seem to stop talking.

"My parents invited the prince to meet them tomorrow afternoon. I tried to explain to Mom and Dad that none of this would have happened if it hadn't been for you, but they wouldn't listen." They seemed to be under the delusion that she'd charmed the invitation from him herself.

"I'm sure Prince Stefano would enjoy meeting your family."

Dejected, Priscilla's shoulders drooped. This was exactly what she didn't want to hear.

Pietro hesitated. "Are you saying you'd prefer for the prince to decline?"

She nodded, feeling wretched.

"Is there any particular reason? Has Prince Stefano offended you?"

Her chin flew up. "Oh, no, he's wonderful. It's just that…well, if the prince comes, my parents might think he's romantically interested in me."

"If ticket sales for the date with the prince were any indication, this is what several thousand American women profess to want."

Priscilla didn't express her feelings for the prince one way or the other. She couldn't.

"If he meets my family, I'm afraid the prince might mention inviting me to San Lorenzo. You can bet my parents will jump on that."

"You don't wish to visit my country?"

"I love San Lorenzo. Who wouldn't?" This was going poorly. Every time she opened her mouth, she made matters worse.

"Then I don't understand the problem."

"No," she whispered, "you wouldn't."

"Tell me, Priscilla."

It was the first time she could remember him saying her name. Although his English was flawless, he said "Priscilla" in such a way that it sounded exotic and special. As if she were, herself.

"Are you free this afternoon?" she found herself asking all at once, the words rushing together. "It would be a shame for you to be in Seattle and not see some of the city. I could show you Pike Place Market and we could ride the monorail over to Seattle Center." Priscilla had never been so forward with a man. She couldn't believe she was doing so now.

The expensive gold pen Pietro rolled between his palms slipped from his hand and dropped to the floor. Looking flustered, he bent down and retrieved it.

When he didn't answer her right away, she knew she'd committed a terrible faux pas. A man like Pietro, Prince Stefano's personal secretary and companion, didn't have time to spend with her. By blurting out the invitation she'd placed him in an impossible position. He couldn't refuse without offending her, and he couldn't accept, either. A man in his position didn't go sightseeing, and if he did, he wouldn't necessarily want to do so with her.

"Of course you can't.... Forgive me for asking. I wasn't thinking." She was far too embarrassed to meet his gaze. She stood abruptly, gripping her purse against her stomach. "If you'll excuse me, I'll..."

"Priscilla," he said in that gentle way of his, "sit down."

She was too miserable to do anything but comply. "I'm sorry," she whispered, hanging her head in shame.

"There's no reason to apologize."

She didn't contradict him, although she didn't agree.

"First tell me why you don't wish to accept the prince's invitation to visit our country."

She swallowed tightly. "It's because of my parents. They think there's a chance Prince Stefano will become enamored with me. They don't understand that he was just being polite."

"Your parents are the reason you'd prefer the prince refused their invitation for tomorrow afternoon, as well?"

She nodded. "I shouldn't have said anything, I know. It was tactless and rude of me. I was hoping..."

"Yes," Pietro urged, when she hesitated.

"He would decline."

Pietro sighed heavily. "I'm afraid that's impossible. Prince Stefano has already asked me to accept on his behalf."

"I see." So much for that.

"I don't think you should so readily discount yourself, Priscilla. The prince was quite taken with you. He told me himself what a beautiful woman he found you to be."

Priscilla blinked several times, uncertain if what she heard could possibly be true. "He told you that?"

"Yes. Why are you so surprised?"

"I just am."

"You shouldn't be. You're a beautiful person, Priscilla Rutherford." Pietro's smile was warm and gentle, and Priscilla felt mesmerized by it.

"Thank…you," she whispered.

Pietro's gaze abruptly left her, breaking the magical spell between them. "Prince Stefano will see you tomorrow at three," he said, becoming businesslike all at once.

"Will you be joining him?" She'd feel worlds better knowing Pietro would accompany the prince.

"No."

She signed heavily, and nodded. It would have been too much to hope for.

"Now…about your invitation."

Her gaze went expectantly to his. Their eyes met and held for a long moment. Priscilla didn't bother to disguise her wishes.

Pietro reluctantly dragged his eyes from hers, and it seemed to Priscilla that he found it difficult to speak. "I must decline, but having you ask is one of the greatest compliments of my life."

She managed a wobbly smile, hoping that he understood that if he'd accepted it would have been one of the greatest compliments of her life, as well.

Hope had never had anyone fuss over her more. Her mother and her mother's three softhearted friends had driven her crazy, going over every minute detail of her hair, her nails, makeup and outfit. The dress was made of black crepe that clung to her hips and looped down her spine, revealing nearly her entire flawless back. She'd never have chosen the dress on her own, but Betty knew somebody who knew somebody who owned the perfect dress.

The high heels were leftovers from her high school prom days. A bit snug, but doable for one short evening.

She dripped diamonds—not real, of course—from her wrists, neck and ears. Between the four women, they'd come up with enough rhinestones to sink a gunboat.

The phone had been ringing since eight o'clock that morning. The *Seattle Times* asked for an exclusive interview following her date. Hope declined, but that didn't stop five other area newspapers from making a pitch.

How the media found out about her was beyond Hope. The last she'd heard, *Entertainment Tonight* had flown in a camera crew. On learning that, Hope appointed her mother as her official contact person, which kept Doris occupied most of the afternoon. It also gave her a feeling of importance to be the mother of the woman dating Prince Stefano. Doris ate up the attention.

"The limousine will be here any minute," Hazel said, checking her watch. "Are you ready?"

Hope didn't think she could be any readier. One thing was for certain, she'd never have agreed to all this priming if she hadn't personally met the prince the night before.

It wouldn't take much to improve on his first impression of her, that was sure. If the truth be known, she wanted to razzle-dazzle the man. This evening was a means of proving she didn't generally look like an escaped mental patient.

"The limo's here," Gladys shouted excitedly. She sounded like a sailor lost at sea sighting land.

Doris and the two other women rushed toward the window. Hope heard them collectively sigh. One would think Prince Stefano had come for Hope in a coach led by six perfectly matched white horses.

"Oh, my heavens," Betty breathed, gazing longingly out the window. "He's so handsome."

"I'll get the door," Doris announced, as if being Hope's mother entitled her to that honor.

"You can't be out here," Hazel insisted, taking Hope by the hand, and leading her down the hallway to one of the bedrooms. "The prince might see you."

"He's taking me to dinner, Hazel. That's the reason he's coming to the house."

"I know. We just don't want him to see you right away. It wouldn't be proper."

"You're confused," Hope said, holding in a smile. "The bride is hidden from her groom until the last moment, not on the first date."

"I know that, dear, but this is a special first date, don't you think? We want to make an impression."

Since Hope was aiming for that goal herself, she allowed herself to be ushered from the room.

The doorbell chimed and she could hear a flurry of activity taking place. What her mother and Doris's three friends were up to now, Hope could only speculate.

Hope heard the prince and was amazed at his patience with the older women. They engaged him in a lengthy conversation while they reviewed the itinerary they'd so carefully planned for the evening.

"Hope," her mother called, as if she were wondering what was taking her daughter so long.

Hearing her cue, Hope stepped into the living room where Prince Stefano stood waiting. Once more, her attention was captured by the mere presence of the man. He seemed to fill every inch of space in the room.

Holding her breath, Hope's searching gaze met his.

She wanted to impress him, wanted to be sure he didn't regret that she'd won this night with him. But she was the one who felt as if someone had knocked her alongside of the head. Her lungs froze, and it was impossible to breathe. He was the most dynamic man she'd ever encountered.

Hope didn't believe in love at first sight. That was something reserved for romantics, for women with time on their hands, not hardworking coffee-shop owners.

This whole thing with winning a date with a prince had originally amused her. She found it incredulous that a woman would actually pay for the opportunity to date any man. Personally, she couldn't understand why some-one would even want to date royalty.

All at once the answers were crystal clear, and she felt as if she were the most incredibly fortunate female alive. It was as though this evening would be the most impor-tant of her life. That this time, with this man, would for-ever change her.

Prince Stefano's eyes met hers and it felt as if every bit of oxygen from the vicinity had been sucked away. The prince was a man of the world, sophisticated and suave. He'd dated the most prominent, wealthy women on the continent, and yet when he gazed at her, he made her feel like a princess. His princess. She, in her borrowed dress, and rhinestone jewels.

"Miss Jordan, your beauty takes my breath away."

Hope's mother and her devoted friends each folded their hands as if they were praying and sighed audibly.

"Thank you," Hope murmured. It seemed such a mun-dane thing to say in light of the way seeing him affected her, but she suspected that her reaction wasn't unlike a thousand others.

"My car is waiting, if you're ready."

She reached for her evening bag, a bejeweled purse that had once belonged to Hazel's grandmother, kissed each of her fairy godmothers on the cheek and turned toward her prince.

Prince Stefano led her to the limousine. On the walk-way, Hope heard the click of cameras, although she didn't see anyone taking pictures.

"The press has gotten inventive over the years," Stefano explained. "It wouldn't surprise me to find several hiding out in the trees. The press is something I've learned to live with over the years. Everything I say and do appears to interest them. I apologize if they trouble you, but I have little or no control over what they print."

"I understand."

"They're a nuisance, but unfortunately, necessary."

"I'm not concerned," Hope assured him. "I deal with all kinds of people every day at my coffee shop. People are people. It doesn't matter if they wear a camera around their neck. There's no need to be rude or unpleasant. The press has a job to do, and so do we."

"A job?" He cocked one thick eyebrow in question.

"You and I, Prince Stefano, are about to have a most enjoyable evening."

He smiled, and Hope had the impression it had been a good long while since he'd relaxed and enjoyed himself. A good long time since he'd last thrown back his head and laughed. Really laughed. Hope wanted to see that, if only so he'd remember her. And she definitely wanted him to fondly recall their time together.

The chauffeur opened the door, and Hope and the prince climbed into the backseat. The first thing Hope noticed was a bottle of champagne on ice, and two crystal flutes.

The prince's gaze followed hers. "The champagne is compliments of Madeline Marshall."

"The conference organizer... How thoughtful of her."

"The flowers are from me," he said, handing her a bouquet of a dozen long-stemmed red roses, tied with a white ribbon.

Hope cradled the flowers in her arms and buried her

nose in their fragrance. It was the first time a man had given her a dozen roses, and she was deeply touched. "They're lovely."

"So are you." The words were whispered and it seemed to Hope that it surprised Prince Stefano to realize he'd said them aloud.

"From what I understand we'll be dining at McCormick's," Prince Stefano said next, recovering quickly.

"Yes. Hazel was the one who insisted we eat there. From what I understand, the food is delicious, but I think Mom and her friends were more interested in atmosphere." The four romantics were determined to do whatever was necessary to motivate the prince to fall in love with her, as if such a thing were possible. Hope had gone along with them because...well, because she'd met the prince by that time and was already half in love with him herself.

Once they arrived at the restaurant, the hostess greeted them warmly. Hope heard murmurs and whispers as they walked the full length of the restaurant to a private booth, separated from the other diners on three sides.

"Enjoy your dinner," the hostess said, handing them each oblong menus.

Prince Stefano set his aside. "From what I understand, our dinner has all been prearranged."

"You mean to say Mom ordered for us, as well."

"So it seems." No sooner had he spoken when a basket of warm bread was delivered to the table. The wine steward followed, bringing a bottle of chilled white wine for the prince to inspect.

Prince Stefano read over the label and approved the

choice. The steward peeled off the seal and skillfully removed the cork. He filled the two wineglasses after Prince Stefano had sampled the wine and given his consent.

"I didn't dare to hope such a beautiful woman would hold the winning ticket," he said, saluting her with his glass. "To what shall we toast?"

"Romance," she said automatically.

Her choice appeared to trouble him because he frowned. Recovering, he nodded once and said, "To romance."

They touched the rims of their glasses and then Hope brought hers back to her lips. A feeling of sadness came over her all at once. She didn't understand how it was possible. Not when she was dining with the most eligible bachelor in the world, in an exclusive restaurant.

The newspapers had touted how fortunate she was, how lucky to have won a date with the prince. It dawned on her then that this sadness, this melancholy feeling came from Stefano.

She was about to ask him about it when the sound of a violin playing a hauntingly beautiful song caught her ear. A strolling musician came into view. He nodded as he played and lingered at their table. The music was poignant and bittersweet and swirled around them like an early-morning London fog.

"That was so beautiful," Hope whispered when the minstrel drifted away. Unexplained tears gathered at the edges of her eyes. She'd never heard the tune before, but it was compellingly sorrowful.

"You know the song?" Prince Stefano asked.

"No," Hope admitted.

"It is from my country. It's a story of a princess who

fell deeply in love with a merchant's son. Her family has arranged for her to marry a nobleman and refuses to listen to her pleas. They forbid her to see the man she loves, insisting she follow through with the marriage contract."

"Don't tell me she kills herself," Hope pleaded. "I couldn't bear it."

"No," Stefano assured her softly. "The merchant's son knows that his love has only hurt his princess and so he leaves her, and travels to another country, never to return."

"What happens to the princess? Does she go through with the marriage? Oh, how could she make herself do it?"

"No, she never marries. Against her family's wishes she enters a convent and becomes the bride of the Church, forever treasuring the love she shared with the merchant's son in her heart."

"Oh, how sad."

"It is said their love for each other, however brief, was enough to carry them each through the rest of their lives."

"I...don't understand stories like that," Hope said suddenly. "They're so sad and so unnecessary. When two people love each other, truly love each other, there are no real obstacles."

The prince smiled sadly. "How naive you are, my beautiful Hope."

It seemed he was about to say something more when a plate of crab-stuffed mushrooms arrived. "I gather this is our appetizer," Stefano said, sounding grateful for the interruption.

They were enjoying their meal, a decadent assortment of meat and vegetables, when Hope first heard the rustle of voices outside their booth. She thought, for an instant, that she recognized her mother, but quickly discounted that. Doris had been adamant that Hope and the prince not be interrupted.

No sooner had the memory surfaced than Hope heard a pitch like the one used by the church choir director.

"What was that?" Prince Stefano asked.

"I'm afraid to ask."

Sure enough it was her darling mother and company, who'd come to serenade the happy couple with a rendition of Henry Mancini love songs.

Hope grimaced and gritted her back teeth as they hit a discordant note in "Moon River." Listening to them was almost painful. Hope just happened to catch the prince's eye and they both just missed breaking into hysterical laughter.

When they'd finished the song, the prince had composed himself enough to slip out of the booth and politely applaud their efforts. He personally thanked each one. Doris grinned broadly and blew Hope a kiss on her way out of the restaurant.

"I'm so sorry," Hope said when the prince rejoined her.

"Your mother and her friends are..." He struggled for the right word.

"Hopeless romantics," Hope supplied.

"And you, Hope Jordan? Are you a romantic, as well?"

She wasn't sure how to answer him. Only a few days before she would have unconditionally declared herself a realist. Romance was for...those interested in such matters. She wasn't. She hadn't the time or the inclination.

Until now.

What a fool she was. If she was going to be this strongly attracted to a man, why, oh why, couldn't it be someone other than a prince? The likelihood of her ever seeing him beyond this lone night was improbable. This was Prince Stefano Giorgio Paolo of San Lorenzo after all.

They left the restaurant and discovered the limousine had been replaced by a horse-drawn carriage. Hope laughed out loud. "I swear they thought of everything," she said, looking to Prince Stefano. "Do you mind?"

"How could I object?" he asked.

With her slinky style of dress, Hope found it to be something of a task to climb onto the carriage. Prince Stefano gripped her waist and hoisted her upward, until her shoe found the footing.

His touch was gentle, and it seemed his hands lingered several seconds longer than actually necessary. Hope's heart rate accelerated substantially as he climbed into the carriage and settled next to her, instead of across from her as she'd suspected he would.

His arm circled her shoulders and he smiled down on her. "I think it's only fair that we live up to your mother's expectations for us this evening, don't you?"

"Of course," she agreed.

Seeing that they were settled, the driver urged the horse forward. The carriage wheels clanked against the cobble road that stretched along the side streets leading to Seattle's waterfront.

The night couldn't have been more perfect.

Hope thought of a hundred things she wanted to say, and didn't voice any of them. The silence held a message of its own. For this one night, for this moment, words were unnecessary. It was as if she and the prince had known each other all their lives, as if they'd been intimate friends who knew each other's deepest secrets.

The prince brought her closer into his embrace and without her remembering exactly when or how, she found her head pressed against his shoulder.

Hope had never experienced anything like this. She closed her eyes, yearning to savor each moment, knowing they must last her a lifetime.

"How is it possible that I should find you now?" the prince breathed at the ragged end of a sigh.

Hope didn't understand his question and twisted her head back in order to meet his eyes. They were filled with a bitter kind of sadness, the same bittersweet melancholy she'd sensed in him earlier that evening.

"I don't understand," Hope answered.

"You couldn't," he said, and breathed heavily. She brought her head back to his shoulder and felt his kiss against her crown.

Hope held her palm against his heart and heard the strong, even beat. His hand folded over hers as they left the waterfront and headed toward the hotel where the limousine awaited them.

Their night would soon be over, and Hope wanted it never to end.

By the time they arrived at the hotel, a small crowd had gathered. Prince Stefano climbed down from the carriage, and then expertly aided her. The lights were bright and there seemed to be a dozen cameras trained on them.

Whereas Prince Stefano had been tolerant and patient earlier, he was no longer. He shielded Hope as best he could from the glaring lights and hurried her toward the waiting limousine.

The car sped away at the earliest possible moment. The driver, without her having to give him her address, drove directly to her small rental house.

Prince Stefano reached for Hope's hand. "I shall remember and treasure this evening always."

"So will I," she told him, forcing herself to smile.

She didn't expect him to kiss her, but when he reached for her and brought his mouth to hers, it seemed natural and perfect.

Over the years, Hope had been kissed many times, but no man's touch had affected her as profoundly as the prince's. Hope's heart seemed to swell within her chest at the surge of emotion that overtook her.

She parted her lips to him and groaned when he deepened the contact. He couldn't seem to get enough of her, or her of him. By the time he broke away, they were both panting and breathless, clinging to each other as the only solid object in a world that had suddenly been knocked off its axis.

Stefano kissed her again and again with a growing urgency and then stopped abruptly, his shoulders heaving. His hands framed her face and his large, infinitely sad eyes delved into hers.

"I apologize."

"Don't, please." She clasped her hand around his wrist and brought his palm to her lips, kissing him there.

"I had to be sure...."

"Sure?" she questioned.

Stefano shook his head, and briefly closed his eyes.

"Thank you for the most beautiful evening of my life." He paused, and she watched as his facial features tightened as if he were bracing himself for something. "Please understand and forgive me when I tell you I can never see you again."

Four

"Are you ready?"

Pietro's question interrupted Stefano's thoughts as he stood gazing out the huge picture window of the hotel suite. "Ready?" he turned and asked. He'd never felt less so.

"You're meeting with the Rutherfords in less than thirty minutes."

"Ah, yes." Dredging up some enthusiasm for this get-together with the heiress and her family was beyond him just then.

"The car is waiting."

Stefano turned away from the window. "Pietro, have you ever met someone…a woman, and known from the very moment your eyes met hers that you were going to love her?"

"Your Highness," Pietro replied with ill patience. "If you don't leave now, you'll be late for your appointment."

Frankly, Stefano couldn't dredge up the energy to care.

"Apparently you haven't experienced this phenomenon or you wouldn't be so quick to dismiss my question." Reluctantly, Stefano reached for his jacket and fastened the buttons with a decided lack of haste.

"What are the Rutherford names again?" he asked. Pietro must have told him a dozen times as it was. Stefano couldn't explain why they slipped from his memory, and then again he could.

Hope.

He hadn't been able to stop thinking about her from the moment they'd parted. In the beginning, realizing how fruitless it all was, he'd resisted, but as the night wore on and morning approached, his ability to fight his feelings for her weakened considerably.

By early afternoon, he felt as though he'd been walking around in a cloud. Certainly that was where his head was. His heart, too. Dreaming impossible dreams. Seeking what he knew could never be. And yet...and yet, he couldn't make himself stop.

"James and Elizabeth Rutherford," his secretary replied.

"Ah, yes," Stefano said, silently repeating the two names several times over in an effort to remember them once and for all.

"As I understand, they're both anxious to make your acquaintance," Pietro added, following Stefano into the next room. "Speaking of Priscilla," he added, as though in afterthought, "have you given any consideration to your next meeting with the heiress?"

"No," Stefano stated honestly. "Should I?"

"Yes." The lone word flirted dangerously with insolence. "As I understand it, marrying her is the purpose of this entire journey," he added.

Stefano turned and his eyes searched those of his friend, wondering at the other man's strange mood. "As I recall she was the bride you chose for me." ·

"Yes," Pietro said with what sounded like regret. "I was the one who believed Priscilla would make you an excellent princess."

Try as he might, Stefano couldn't picture Priscilla Rutherford as his wife. It seemed a hundred years had passed in the past twenty-four hours since he'd first met the heiress. Stefano vaguely recalled the gist of his conversation with her, although as he remembered it, he'd done the majority of the talking. Every word she'd spoken, he'd been forced to coax out of her.

Stefano found Priscilla to be a gentle and likable soul. She'd been as nervous as a rabbit, fidgeting and discreetly glancing at her watch when she didn't think he'd notice. Once they knew each other better, and she learned to relax around him, Stefano was confident they'd make a compatible couple.

"I assume you plan to ask Priscilla to accompany you to the banquet this evening," Pietro said crisply.

"Ah, yes, the banquet." The Romance Lovers' Convention was ending the festivities with a lavish dinner affair—or so the brochures promised. Stefano was scheduled to speak briefly, but he hadn't given a thought to bringing a date.

"It would be a nice touch to invite Priscilla," Pietro suggested, "don't you think?"

Stefano nodded, making a mental note to remember to

ask the heiress when he was with her later. He'd ask, because it was part and parcel of what needed to be done in order to save his country from financial ruin, but it was Hope he wanted at his side. He forced his thoughts away from Hope and made himself concentrate on Priscilla.

"Miss Rutherford's quite lovely, isn't she?" Stefano murmured more to himself than his friend.

Although a response wasn't required of his secretary, Stefano was surprised when Pietro didn't give one. He studied his companion, wondering at his friend's strange behavior of late. He might have said something, but his own conduct had been questionable.

Pietro crisply stepped across the carpet and held open the door for him. "As I explained earlier, the car's waiting."

"I want you to come with me," Stefano said, deciding all at once.

"Come with you?" Pietro repeated, as if he wasn't sure he'd heard correctly.

"Yes." Having said it, Stefano realized this was what he'd wanted from the first. "You can answer any questions Priscilla's parents might have while I talk with the young lady. I'll do as you suggest and invite her to the banquet. It might be awkward doing so in front of her family."

"I'd prefer not to go."

Stefano dismissed his companion's reluctance. "I want you with me, and be quick about it. We're going to be late."

Priscilla deeply loved her parents. She'd never understood how it happened that her gregarious parents had spawned a timid soul such as her. Personally, Priscilla would rather leap off a skyscraper than speak in public, yet her parents thrived on being the center of attention.

Priscilla also knew her parents deeply loved her, but she was realistic enough to know she was a painful disappointment to them both.

As a young girl, she'd striven to gain their approval, but as she matured, she realized she couldn't be anyone but herself. In theory it sounded quite simple, but often she felt like a salmon, fighting to swim upstream, battling the desire for their approval while struggling to be herself.

"Let me look at you, sweetheart," Elizabeth Rutherford insisted for the third time in fifteen minutes. "Now remember to square your shoulders. You don't want the prince to see you slouch."

"I'll remember." After three semesters in an exclusive charm school, Priscilla was intimately acquainted with all the ins and outs of etiquette.

"And please, Priscilla, you must smile. This is a joyous occasion." Her mother poked a finger in each of her cheeks, cocked her head to one side and grinned grotesquely. "The prince of San Lorenzo is coming to call on you."

"Mother, please. Prince Stefano is accepting your invitation. His visit has little or nothing to do with me." Priscilla didn't know why she argued. Just as she'd feared, her parents had her all but married to the prince. Little did that dear man realize what he'd done by agreeing to meet her family.

She'd tried to warn Pietro, but he hadn't listened. He didn't understand that her family viewed her meeting with the prince as something of a social coup. Nothing she said could make them believe that her time with Prince Stefano had come as a result of her meeting his secretary. Pietro had been the one who made all the arrangements.

Her parents had discounted that information from the very beginning. The prince, they told her, had sent Pietro to issue the invitation. A secretary did not make appointments without first conferring with his employer.

Their assertion seemed all but confirmed when Prince Stefano promptly accepted her family's invitation. The entire house had been in a flurry of activity ever since. The housekeeper had polished every piece of silver on the huge estate. Mrs. Daily, the cook, had been concocting delicacies for two days.

The staff had been with the family for years and this meeting with the prince gave them the opportunity to shine. And if their efforts prompted the prince to fall in love with Priscilla, then all the better. Everyone in the household glowed with pride that Priscilla had captured the attention of Prince Stefano.

At last everything was ready for the prince's arrival. Fresh flowers from the huge garden, Priscilla's first love, were beautifully arranged and graced nearly every room of the house.

Priscilla and her parents gathered in the formal living room, which was tastefully decorated in mauve and gray, and impatiently awaited the prince's arrival.

Priscilla couldn't remember ever seeing her mother this nervous. Even her unflappable father had seemed unusually tense. Every now and again, he'd smile at Priscilla and tell her how beautiful she was. In all her life, Priscilla couldn't remember her father saying such things. It seemed she'd waited all her life for a compliment from him and now that he'd given her one, she felt sick to her stomach with trepidation.

The doorbell chimed and Priscilla's parents exchanged looks as if they'd both been taken by complete surprise, and hadn't a clue as to who the visitor might be.

"I'm sure that's the prince," Priscilla said unnecessarily.

Her father cleared his throat and stood, his shoulders and back ramrod straight.

Silently Priscilla prayed that she wouldn't do anything to embarrass herself or her family. More than anything, she pleaded with the powers on high that once her parents met and talked to the prince, they'd understand that he wasn't romantically interested in her.

When she looked up, the first person she saw wasn't Prince Stefano as she suspected, but Pietro. His gaze briefly locked with hers and she knew within the space of a single breath that he didn't want to be there. She didn't share his sentiments. The moment she saw him, the room lit up with sunshine and her heart gladdened.

It would do her no good to explain to her parents that the prince's personal companion sent her pulse racing ten times faster than Prince Stefano.

Pietro diverted his attention away from her long enough for her to introduce him and the prince to her parents. After the pleasantries were exchanged, the five sat in the living room and sipped coffee and sampled a variety of delicate pastries.

Priscilla noticed that Prince Stefano and her father seemed to find a number of topics to discuss. They were deeply involved in conversation while her mother engaged Pietro in small talk. Although respectful, Pietro was clearly displeased to be thrust into this setting.

After a while, as she'd been instructed, Priscilla asked her guest if he'd enjoy seeing her garden. This was her mother's blatant effort to have the prince spend time alone with her.

To Priscilla's surprise and delight, Prince Stefano motioned toward his secretary. "Pietro's the one who appreciates gardens. I'm sure he'd be more than happy to see yours."

Priscilla cast her mother a plaintive look, when in reality it was all she could do not to leap to her feet and shout for joy.

She stood and watched as Pietro fiercely glared at the prince. Nevertheless he obediently followed her through the French doors. Once outside they walked down the winding brick walkway that curved its way through the lush, blooming flower beds.

Knowing he wasn't the least bit interested in viewing the garden, Priscilla led Pietro to the huge white gazebo that overlooked Lake Washington. A light, cool breeze came off the waters, ruffling her hair. Rainbow-colored spinnakers glided their way across the water, cutting a swatch of bright paint across the blue skyline.

"You can sit here and wait, if you prefer," she said politely.

"Wait?" he asked.

"I know you aren't interested in the garden. Why the prince insisted you come out with me, when it's so plain you had no desire to do so, I can only guess." It hurt to say it, but she braced herself and added, "I know you'd rather not spend time with me."

He was silent for a moment as though carefully weighing his words. "That's not necessarily true, Priscilla."

She loved the way he said her name, as if it were as pleasing to the tongue as the pastries they'd feasted on earlier. She closed her eyes wanting to savor the feeling.

"If you prefer, I can leave."

"Don't go," he said.

Priscilla swore those were the two most beautiful words she'd ever heard. Sitting inside the sun-dappled gazebo with Pietro at her side was a simple pleasure she hadn't anticipated in the events of this afternoon.

"I don't understand you," she said, studying Pietro. "Either you find me completely objectionable and deplore every minute you're forced to spend in my company, or..."

Pietro burst out laughing.

"Or," she said, smiling up at him, "you like me far more than you care to admit."

His laughter died as abruptly as it had erupted.

"Would you mind kissing me?" she asked him.

Pietro leapt off the bench and backed away from her as if she'd asked him to commit a heinous crime.

She laughed softly and shook her head. "Maybe kissing me would help you decide how you feel."

He paced the area in front of her like an escaped panther. His hands were buried deep inside his pockets, and he refused to look at her. "That won't be necessary."

Slowly Priscilla stood and planted herself directly in front of him. He was much taller than she was, at least six inches and she was forced to stand on the tips of her toes in order to meet his gaze. In an effort to maintain her balance, she braced her hands against his chest.

"Your pulse's pounding as hard as a freight train."

Pietro didn't comment, nor did he move away from her. His heart thudded hard and evenly beneath her palm. She watched a play of emotions work their way across his face as if he were involved in some great battle of will.

Encouraged by his lack of resistance, she closed her eyes and slid her arms upward until they were linked behind his neck. Then, with great care, she moved her lips over his.

The kiss was gentle, more of a meeting of the lips than anything deeply passionate.

When she'd finished, Priscilla blinked, lowered her arms and flattened her feet on the floor. It was then that Pietro eased her back into his arms. Holding herself perfectly still, the same way he had, she allowed him to kiss her. Only it didn't stop with a mere brushing of their lips as it had when she'd instigated the contact. Pietro's kiss intensified until a slow heat began to build in the pit of her stomach and her legs felt as if they would no longer support her.

"Does that answer your question?" Pietro whispered against her temple.

She nodded, because speaking just then was beyond her. What he didn't seem to understand was that she wasn't the one with the questions. The answers had been clear to her from that first night on the balcony.

Pietro braced his forehead against hers. Several moments passed before he spoke. "I shouldn't have kissed you."

"But why? Oh, Pietro, don't you realize it's what I've wanted from the moment we met?"

He laughed softly, but he wasn't being sarcastic.

"I like it when you kiss me." She wrapped her arms about his torso and burrowed as deep into his embrace as possible, seeking a haven for the complex emotions brewing inside her.

"Priscilla, this is all very sweet, but unfortunately, you don't seem to understand. I don't mean to hurt you, but I don't share your feelings." The change in him came on as fast as an August squall. His hands gripped her upper arms.

Hurt and stunned, Priscilla voluntarily backed away. Her cheeks flared with color so hot, it felt as if her face were on fire. She'd misread him and the situation, and embarrassed them both by throwing herself at him.

The constriction in her throat moved up and down several times before she managed to speak. "I'm…terribly sorry." Pressing her hands to her fevered face, she added in a thin, pain-filled voice, "Please…accept my apology." With that she turned and ran to the house.

By the time she arrived at the patio just outside the garden, Priscilla's heart was pounding hard and fast and she was breathless. Taking a moment to compose herself, she was standing on the other side of the French doors when her mother unexpectedly appeared.

"I was about to come and search for you. Where's Pietro?"

For the life of her, Priscilla couldn't answer. Gratefully, she wasn't required to speak because the prince's secretary rounded the corner of the garden, his steps filled with purpose. He paused when he found Priscilla with her mother.

"I hope you enjoyed your tour of our garden," Elizabeth Rutherford said.

"It's delightful," Priscilla heard him answer.

She trained her eyes away from him and called upon a reserve of composure stored deep within her. Pride wouldn't allow her to reveal how his words had crushed her. In all her life, Priscilla had never been so brazen with a man. What he must think of her didn't bear considering.

With her pulse thundering in her ears, Priscilla walked back into the living room to find her father and the prince chatting as if they were longtime friends.

Priscilla sat back down and neatly folded her hands on her lap. Her father looked approvingly at her and smiled.

It was her mother who noticed something was wrong. "Are you feeling all right, Priscilla?" Elizabeth asked. "You look flushed."

"I'm fine." It amazed her she could lie so smoothly.

"I think it must be the excitement of having the prince visit," her father supplied eagerly.

For the first time since his arrival, Prince Stefano turned his attention to Priscilla. "Did Pietro enjoy the garden?" he asked.

She opened her mouth to answer and discovered her throat had frozen shut. For an awkward moment there was silence.

"I found the gardens to be most pleasant," Pietro supplied for her. "Miss Rutherford is an engaging tour guide."

The heat in her face intensified tenfold.

"I realize this is short notice, Priscilla," the prince

said, "but I'd consider it a great honor if you'd consent to accompany me to the Romance Lovers' banquet this evening."

Once again, Priscilla found herself struck dumb. The invitation couldn't have surprised her more.

"She'd be delighted," her mother supplied, glaring at her.

"I'd be…delighted," she echoed, her heart sinking all the way to her ankles. This was exactly the thing her parents had been hoping to happen.

Priscilla found herself contemplating the prince. From the moment he'd arrived, he hadn't paid her as much as a whit of attention, and yet he sought her company. She could have sworn he was no more interested in her than the man in the moon.

Her gaze drifted involuntarily toward Pietro, and her heart clenched with an unexpected stab of regret. From the first she'd experienced an awkward fascination with the prince's companion. She'd believed he'd shared her feelings. Now she knew that not to be true.

Pietro wanted nothing to do with her.

"I can't stand this," Lindy cried after the last runner had left the coffee shop for his appointed rounds. She slumped into a chair and reached for a sugar-coated doughnut.

"Can't stand what?" Hope pried, although she was fairly certain she knew the answer.

"You've hardly said a word about your date with Prince Stefano. I asked you how it went, and you said great. Do you have a clue of how much that leaves to the imagination?"

"'Great' is a perfectly adequate description of our time together," Hope argued.

"See what I mean," Lindy cried. "You somehow manage to cleverly sidestep every other question. It just isn't fair."

"I had a fairy-tale date with a fairy-tale prince."

"Did he kiss you?"

"Lindy!" Hope flared, making busywork at the counter.

Lindy grinned from ear to ear, and wiggled her eyebrows several times. "He must have, otherwise you wouldn't look so outraged."

"It isn't any of your business."

"Did you get to talk to John Tesh from *Entertainment Tonight*?"

"Yes, briefly." This interest the media gave her had been a nuisance.

"I bet you told them more than you did me."

Hope hadn't, but she doubted Lindy would believe her.

"Are you going to see the prince again?" That appeared to be the key question on everyone's mind.

A sadness melted over Hope's heart, and she shook her head. "No."

"Why not?" Lindy was indignant. "Aren't you good enough for him? It makes me downright angry to think that after all the trouble your mother and her friends went through to make you beautiful…"

Hope couldn't help it; she laughed outright.

Her friend frowned, not understanding what Hope had found so amusing. True, getting beautiful had indeed been a chore, but Hope would have willingly gone through ten times the effort if it meant she could be with Stefano again.

But that was impossible. He'd said so himself.

"It wasn't just your mother and her friends, either," Lindy continued. "You put a good deal of effort into the evening yourself. Aren't you the least bit upset?"

"The ticket entitled the lucky winner to one date with Prince Stefano. Nothing less and nothing more. I had my one date, and it was the most beautiful night of my life. Demanding more would be greedy."

"Is he everything the tabloids claim he is?"

Hope had read the articles herself. Prince Stefano was touted as being suave, gracious and gorgeous.

"He's much more." Hope couldn't make herself regret a single minute of her time with the prince. The memory of their one night together would last her a lifetime. Someday she would hold her grandchildren on her knee and tell them the story of her one magical date with a fairytale prince from a kingdom far away. What she would hold a secret for the rest of her life was how the prince had managed to steal her heart away.

"How's your mother taking the news you won't be seeing Prince Stefano again?"

Hope closed her eyes, knowing this would be difficult. "She doesn't know yet." Her mother and company had waited up half the night for a report. The four were so exhausted from all the planning and arranging that Hope could only guess that they were still asleep.

"Mom will understand," Hope said, and knew she was being unrealistically optimistic.

"When is Prince Stefano leaving Seattle?" Lindy asked next.

"I don't know. Soon, I suspect." But not too soon, her heart pleaded.

"What are you doing this evening?" Lindy asked, between bites. She dunked her doughnut into her coffee and then carried it to her mouth, leaving a trail of coffee en route. "I don't know why I'm eating this. I think it's because I'm so jealous."

"Of what?"

"You and Prince Stefano."

"Your prince will come," Hope assured her.

"Only mine will be disguised as a frog. Life isn't fair. I would have given my eyeteeth to have bought the winning ticket, and you didn't even care. Maybe that's my problem. I've got to stop caring."

Hope realized her friend was only half-serious. She saw the irony of the situation herself. Winning the date with Prince Stefano had been a fluke, but even so, it had forever marked her life. She couldn't shake the feeling that they'd been destined to meet, destined to fall in love and destined to never have more than a single night together.

"I'm going to read a romance novel," Hope announced with a good deal of ceremony. "You asked me what I planned to do this evening, and that's it." True, it was something of a comedown after the romantic night she'd spent with the prince. But it was a way of holding on to the memories of what she'd so recently experienced.

"At last," Lindy cried triumphantly. "To think it took a date with a prince to get you interested."

They talked for several minutes more and then the

phone rang. The two women looked at each other and both knew it had to be Doris.

"At least she waited until the runners were gone this time," Lindy said, as Hope reached for the receiver.

Although her mother had heard nearly every detail of Hope's evening with the prince the night before, Hope was forced to repeat them. Naturally, there were a number of places where she skipped the more private details.

"It's all so romantic," Doris whispered.

"Yes, Mother, it was."

"You like him, don't you, Hope?"

It took Hope a moment to answer, as if she were admitting to a wrong. "Yes, Mom, I do, but then I don't know anyone who could possibly dislike him. Stefano is a…prince."

Satisfied, her mother sighed.

It had taken nearly twenty minutes for Hope to extract herself from the conversation, and afterward, she found an excuse to work in the kitchen. Her thoughts and her heart were heavy.

No matter how hard she focused on the positive, it felt as if there were a giant hole inside her. It would take a very long time to fill. A very long time to forget. That was what made it all so difficult because she wanted to remember, but remembering produced pain.

She was standing in front of the automatic dishwasher, loading cups onto the tray before sliding it inside the washer for sterilization, when Lindy joined her.

"There's a man out front who wants to talk to you."

"I'm not in the mood to deal with any salesman. Talk to him for me, would you?"

"Nope." Lindy was wearing that Cheshire cat look of hers, grinning from ear to ear. "This person insists on speaking to you himself."

"I'm busy." Stopping the washer now was a hassle she wanted to avoid. It was bad enough to be indulging in this pity party without having to deal with some slick salesman who was keen on selling her coffee filters.

"Are you coming or not?" Lindy demanded.

"Not. If someone finds it so all important to speak to me, right this instant, when I'm in the middle of this mess, then you can tell them to come back here."

Lindy frowned, and then shook her head. "I don't think that's wise, my friend." There was a singsong quality to her voice as if she were just barely able to keep herself from breaking into peals of laughter.

"Being prudent has never been my trademark," Hope muttered.

"Do you want me to get his business card for you?"

Grumbling under her breath, Hope nodded. "If you insist."

"Oh, I most certainly do."

Lindy disappeared around the kitchen door and despite her melancholy mood, Hope's gaze followed her. From the way her friend was acting, one would think... Her thoughts came to a slow, grinding halt. Prince Stefano. Was it possible?

No. It couldn't be. Stefano had told her himself anything between them was futile. She'd viewed his regret, experienced her own.

Slowly, removing one yellow rubber glove at a time,

she walked out from the kitchen, her eyes trained on the front of the coffee shop.

Her breath caught when she saw him, standing as stiff as a marble statue just inside the door.

Five

"What are you doing here?" The question was barely above a whisper. Hope was rooted to the spot, unable to do anything but gaze upon the prince in all his glory. He was even more devastatingly handsome and debonair than she remembered. Regal and noble all the way to his toes.

Prince Stefano smiled demurely and moved toward the counter. "I had an urge to sample your coffee," he said as he slipped onto a stool.

She didn't believe him for a moment, but had no choice but to pretend otherwise. "Would you like a latte?" It was difficult to keep the trembling out of her voice.

"That's the drink that's so popular in Seattle?"

Hope nodded. They'd briefly discussed her business, but she'd assumed his questions had only been polite inquiries. She hadn't realized he'd been paying such close attention.

Hope felt the sharp point of her friend's elbow in her ribs and assumed Lindy was waiting for an introduction.

Hope didn't have the heart to tell her friend that she was meeting royalty with powdered sugar coating her lips.

"It sounds very much like café au lait."

"They're similar," Hope said and, looking to Lindy with her white lips, swallowed a smile. "This is Lindy Powell. She does all the baking."

"I'm pleased to meet you, Lindy."

"I'll get you one of my muffins," Lindy offered. "It's on the house."

The minute her friend was out of earshot, Hope leaned close to the counter. "I thought you said…"

His hand covered hers. "I know." He closed his eyes, and when he opened them again she saw a flicker of pain move in and out of his expression. "I came because I couldn't stay away. Last night…I couldn't sleep for thinking of you. I shouldn't be here. I'm afraid my selfishness will only hurt you."

"Having you stay away hurts me more," she whispered.

His hand tightened over her. "Did you sleep?"

"No," she admitted reluctantly.

Her answer appeared to please him, because he broke into a wide grin. "Then you felt it, too?"

She nodded, unable to lie.

The door to the shop opened and Hope glanced up to find the windows crowded with several curious faces. Apparently the throng was hoping to catch a glimpse of Prince Stefano. Looking flustered, his bodyguard stepped inside the shop, safeguarding the door against intruders.

"We must leave, Your Highness," the beefy man said, looking concerned.

Stefano's mouth thinned, and he reluctantly nodded.

"So soon?" If anything was cruel, it would be Stefano reentering her life so briefly. All that held back the urge to beg him to stay was her pride.

"Meet me tonight," he whispered. "On the waterfront, inside the ferry terminal. You will be safe there?"

"Yes. But what time?"

"Ten...perhaps ten-thirty. I will come as soon as it is possible for me to get away."

Once more Hope's gaze was drawn to the growing multitude of onlookers, pressing against her shop window. She doubted that they'd have a moment's peace that evening once the prince was recognized.

"You'll be there?"

The wisdom of it was doubtful. She was setting herself up for a fall, but even knowing that, Hope found, she couldn't refuse him. "I'll be there," she promised.

He smiled then and it seemed the whole room brightened. He reached for her hand and gently kissed it, then abruptly turned away. The prince's bodyguard opened the door and with the aid of two footmen cleared a path to the waiting limousine. A commotion broke out once the prince appeared, and Hope heard several requests for autographs.

Within seconds Stefano was gone.

"He didn't wait for his muffin," Lindy complained, wandering to Hope's side.

"I know." Both of them stood immobilized, staring out the window as if they expected him to magically reappear. In a way that was exactly what Hope prayed would happen.

* * *

From the way Priscilla's family had reacted to the prince's dinner invitation, one would think he'd asked for her hand in marriage. The minute the prince was out the door, her parents clapped their hands with glee and hugged Priscilla.

"Mom…Dad, it's only a dinner date. Don't make more of it than there is," she pleaded on deaf ears. Her parents, however, were much too excited to listen to her protests.

"There's so much that needs to be done," her mother cried. "He'll be back to pick you up in—" she studied her diamond watch "—oh, my heavens, in less than three hours. Priscilla, come, we have a million things to do." On the way to the door, Elizabeth Rutherford barked orders to Mrs. Daily. When she realized Priscilla wasn't directly behind her, she returned to the living room and grabbed hold of Priscilla's arm.

Given no time to dissent, Priscilla was whisked off to an exclusive dress shop and forced to endure two hours of intense shopping. Her mother insisted her evening gown must be perfect, and after being subjected to at least fifty different ones, she hadn't the strength to object to the billowing chiffon creation her mother chose.

Personally, Priscilla thought she resembled Scarlett O'Hara without the nineteen-inch waist. She wasn't oblivious to her mother's choice. It was the dress that made her most resemble a princess, direct from the pages of a Grimm fairy tale.

Nothing was left to chance. By the time Prince Stefano arrived, she'd been pushed, prodded, pampered and prepared. Priscilla felt more like a French poodle than a grown woman.

The real problem was that her heart wasn't in this dinner date. If she'd had her way, she would have escaped to her room, and curled up with a good novel. Burying herself in fantasy was the only means Priscilla knew would ease the ache left in her heart after her confrontation with Pietro.

Remembering what had happened inside the gazebo was enough to turn her cheeks to a brilliant shade of red. She prayed with all her being that somehow she would escape seeing Pietro that evening. Since he was almost always with the prince, she doubted that was possible.

The prince arrived promptly at seven, dressed in full military splendor. It amused her because other than the palace guards, she was fairly certain San Lorenzo didn't have an army.

His eyes brightened when he saw her. "I didn't think it was possible to improve on perfection," he said, taking her hand, and tucking it into the curve of his elbow. "My car is outside if you're ready."

"Have a good time," Priscilla's mother crowed.

The prince seemed preoccupied on the drive into downtown Seattle. She wondered at his silence, but didn't question it since she wasn't in a talkative mood herself. All she wanted was for this evening to be over with so she could go back to own life.

This entire business had taught her a valuable lesson: to be careful what you wish for. She'd wanted so desperately to win the date with Prince Stefano. It had seemed like such a fanciful thing to meet a prince. Now that she had, everything had gone wrong.

By the time the limousine delivered them to the hotel, the banquet was about to get under way. The prince escorted Priscilla to a table at the front of the ballroom, which put him in easy reach of the stage where he'd be making his speech.

They were soon joined by Madeline Marshall, her husband, another couple—and as Priscilla had known and dreaded, Pietro. Brief introductions were made, and the necessary small talk exchanged.

To her dismay, Priscilla was positioned between the prince and Pietro.

"Good evening, Priscilla," Pietro said softly, once they were seated.

"Good evening," she said, not looking at him.

What little appetite she possessed vanished. She picked at her salad, skipped the rolls and partook in polite conversation, all the while painfully conscious of Pietro's presence.

She felt the warmth of his body so close to her own. She smelled the scent of his aftershave, a spicy rum concoction that flirted with her senses. She struggled against the memory of his arms holding her close, of his breath against her face and the whisper of his kiss over her lips.

But the beauty of that moment had been forever destroyed. She wanted to erase his words, bury them under a romantic heart and pretend. But she couldn't.

In an effort to save her from making a bigger fool of herself, Pietro had been brutally honest, brutally clear. He didn't share her feelings. Nor did he welcome her attention. The embarrassment she'd suffered then felt more acute now as she sat next to him at the banquet, wishing she could be anyplace else in the world.

"There's something wrong with your dinner?" the prince asked, when she did little more than taste the prime rib. Others were raving over the meal, while she couldn't force down another bite.

"Oh, no, it's very good," she hurried to assure him. "I guess I'm not hungry."

Stefano studied her briefly. "Are you unwell?"

"I have a bit of a headache."

"Do you wish to return home?"

"Oh, no. Please, that won't be necessary. I'll be fine."

"An aspirin perhaps? I'll send Pietro for some." He glanced in his secretary's direction and she stopped him by placing her hand on his forearm.

"Thank you, but I have some in my purse."

The prince's attention flustered her. As for his offer to take her home, it had been more than tempting, but she didn't want to explain to her parents why she was back so early in the evening. They'd never believe she had a headache. And they were right. It wasn't her head that was troubling.

It was her heart.

When the program started, the others at the table relaxed and turned their chairs around in order to get a better view of the stage.

When the prince stepped forward to speak, Priscilla stiffened, not realizing how much she counted on him as a barrier between her and Pietro.

"You're not feeling well?" Pietro asked as the prince stepped onto the stage.

"I'm fine," she whispered, focusing her attention on the prince, not daring to meet Pietro's gaze.

The silence between them was as power-packed as a minefield. Every glance his way held the potential of exploding in her face. Conversation was unthinkable; she'd never be able to manage it without revealing her pain.

The prince's speech was short and effective. He spoke of romance and love, and claimed its strength transformed lives. Love had the power to change the world. His message seemed to come straight from his heart as if he were deeply in love himself.

Priscilla noticed that she had become the focus of attention, especially when the prince joined her once more. She was momentarily blinded by the flash of cameras. Apparently the press assumed she was the woman who had captured Prince Stefano's heart. She considered that almost ludicrous, but knew her parents would be ecstatic to have the speculation printed on the society page of the *Seattle Times*.

Following the programs and the award ceremony, Prince Stefano was surrounded by a handful of admirers, seeking an autograph or a moment of his attention. Priscilla stepped aside and patiently waited.

The prince looked apologetically her way, but she assured him with a smile that she didn't mind. Indeed if circumstances had been any different she might have been one of the throng herself.

"We need to talk." It was Pietro's voice that came to her, low and sullen.

Risking everything, she forced herself to turn and meet his eyes. Pain constricted at her heart. "It isn't necessary, Pietro. I understand. Really I do. If anything needs to be said, it's that I'm so terribly sorry for placing you in such an uncomfortable situation."

"You understand nothing," he said. His jaw was clenched and a muscle leapt in the side of his face.

"Perhaps not," she agreed, "but what does it matter? You and the prince will be gone in a few days, and it's unlikely we'll meet again."

"It matters."

Priscilla was saved the necessity of an answer when the prince motioned for his friend. Pietro immediately left her side, and returned a few minutes later, frowning.

"The prince has asked me to escort you home. It seems he's going to be tied up here for some time and he doesn't wish to detain you, seeing that you're not feeling well."

Priscilla's stomach knotted with relief that this evening was finally over. And with regret that the last portion of this night was to be spent with Pietro. "That won't be necessary," she said quickly in an effort to escape. "Really... I can catch a taxi."

"Nonsense. Neither the prince nor I would hear of such a thing. You'll come with me."

His tone brooked no argument, and knowing it would be a losing battle to argue further, she obediently followed him. He guided her out of the ballroom through a back entrance. She traipsed behind him as he wove his way around the kitchen staff. Several seemed to think Pietro was the prince, and stopped and whispered in awe.

To her surprise he didn't call for the limousine, but had the valet bring a compact sports car to a side entrance.

"What's this?" she asked. She was unwilling to sit in such close proximity to Pietro. At least she could put some space between the two of them in the limousine.

"A car," Pietro answered simply, while holding open the passenger door. Only moments earlier Pietro had sought her out, and now it seemed as if he would have given anything to avoid her company. Her pride had been badly wounded by this man once already. She didn't know if her heart was up to a second round.

"I appreciate the ride, but I'd prefer a cab." She ignored his protest, and raised her hand, hoping to attract the attention of a cabdriver on the street. Naturally, when she was desperate for one, the streets were bare.

"Priscilla, don't be ridiculous."

Standing on her tiptoes, she frantically waved her arm and called out, "Taxi!"

"Prince Stefano has asked me to personally escort you home," Pietro argued.

"Do you always do as the prince asks?" she challenged, walking into the middle of the street.

"Yes," he said bitterly. "Please allow me to take you home."

The gently coaxing quality of his words was what persuaded her to do as he asked. As the prince's right-hand man, Pietro was a man accustomed to issuing orders and having them obeyed without question. Yet he was willing to plead with her.

"Please," he said again.

Defeated, Priscilla lowered her arm and walked back

to the curb. "All right," she breathed in an exercise in frustration.

"Thank you," Pietro murmured.

She walked back to the sports car and climbed into the front seat. The billowing skirt of her dress obliterated the view out the front window and she was forced to push it down. She felt like a jack-in-the-box who would spring out the minute her lid was opened.

Pietro joined her and had trouble locating the gearshift between the folds of chiffon. Priscilla pushed the fabric out of his way as best she could.

Pietro started the engine and when they stopped at a first light, he glanced at her. Priscilla felt his gaze, but couldn't see much of him because of her skirt.

She wasn't sure who started it, but soon they were both consumed with laughter. For safety's sake, Pietro pulled over to the curb. Soon their merriment died down, and there was silence.

"You are a beautiful woman," Pietro said with all sincerity, "but this dress is wrong for you."

Priscilla had known it the moment she'd tried it on. Her mother had attempted to dress her in a way that would prove to the prince she would make him an ideal wife.

"I've offended you?" he asked.

"No," she assured him.

He waited a moment and Priscilla assumed he was going to say something more, but she was wrong. When traffic cleared, he eased the car back into the flow.

More at ease with him now, Priscilla relaxed. "You... you said you wanted to talk to me," she reminded him. Now was as good a time as any.

Once again he hesitated. "Not now."

She hated that imperious way he spoke, as if everything were on his terms, on his time. "Why not?" she demanded.

"Because I'm angry."

"With me?"

"No...no." His tone gentled considerably. "Never with you, Priscilla. Never with you."

She wouldn't be so easily appeased this time. This man confused and frustrated her. "Then who?"

He waited for several seconds, then said, "Prince Stefano."

His answer surprised her. "But why?"

"You wouldn't understand."

"I might."

"No, my love. It's complicated and best left unsaid."

His love. Only that afternoon he'd pushed her out of his arms and left her reeling with shock and embarrassment. Now he was speaking to her in the tenderest of endearments.

Unwilling to be hurt again, Priscilla gathered her pride about her like a shawl and slowly drew inside herself.

Other than the hum of the engine, there was no sound. The void seemed to stretch and expand, like yeast in bread dough. She felt Pietro's gaze studying her in the dark.

"Don't be angry with me," he implored. "I can't bear that."

"Then don't call me your love," she returned heatedly. Her voice quivered, making it sound as if she were close to breaking into tears.

Her words were met with stark silence, as if she'd

shocked him. At the first opportunity, Pietro pulled off to the side of the road. He sat with his hands braced against the steering wheel, and after a moment a deep sigh rumbled through his chest.

"I'm going to kiss you, Priscilla."

She blinked, uncertain she'd heard him correctly. "Kiss me?" He made it sound as if this were the last thing he wanted. "But why…?"

"I don't think I can keep from kissing you."

"But you said earlier that…"

"Forget what I said for now." He turned off the engine and turned toward her. Their gazes met in the dim light and locked hungrily. "Forget everything I said this afternoon."

Slowly he lowered his mouth to hers.

Priscilla wanted to turn away from him, if for nothing more than to salvage her pride, but she couldn't summon even a token resistance. The moment his lips touched hers, she realized that being in Pietro's arms was more important than anything.

Hope sat with her hands buried deep in her windbreaker on the hard wooden bench inside the ferry terminal. She'd been waiting nearly twenty minutes and Stefano still hadn't shown. By all that was right she should be home and in bed asleep.

The sound of heavy footsteps echoed against the hard floor. Her heart leapt with anticipation and she looked up, and saw that it wasn't the prince. She couldn't quite believe it, but whoever it was, resembled Elvis.

Her shoulders sagged with disappointment, and she

buried her chin against her chest. She was a fool. No one else would have waited this long. No one else would have gone on hoping he'd come when it was clear he wasn't going to show.

"Hope."

Her head shot up, and she frowned. The man standing before her was Elvis and yet…

"Stefano?"

He grinned and, breathing heavily, he sat down next to her. "I fooled you?"

"Yes." She couldn't keep the amusement out of her voice or her eyes. She'd looked directly at him and hadn't realized it was Stefano. He wore a pair of rhinestone-studded white bell-bottoms and matching top, and a white scarf was draped around his neck. "What have you done to yourself?"

"I needed to escape the hotel without being noticed."

"In that outfit?"

He laughed. "Don't scoff. I paid good money for this costume."

"Where in the name of heaven did you get it?"

"From the Elvis impersonator who's performing in the cocktail lounge." He was only now catching his breath. "I can't believe you're still here. I was afraid you'd left, but I found it impossible to slip away unnoticed."

"But why?" That was by far the more curious of her questions.

The laughter drained from his eyes. "So I could be alone with you. If I came as myself, we'd be interrupted constantly. I am being selfish, but I don't wish to share this time with anyone but you."

If that was being greedy, then she was guilty, as well. "Come," he said, standing and reaching for her hand.

"Where are we going?"

The question seemed to catch him unaware. "I don't know yet. It is enough that we are together."

They walked down the ramp out of the ferry terminal and onto the sidewalk. Although it was almost eleven o'clock, the streets were filled with the continual flow of foot traffic.

Stefano slipped his arm around her waist and they strolled together. Stefano seemed unconcerned with the attention his disguise attracted. Every now and again someone would shout, "Hello, Elvis," and he'd give a friendly wave.

Finally Stefano turned off the sidewalk and led her down a long pier lined with tourist and art shops. They stopped at the end and looked out over the deep, dark waters.

The night was gorgeous and the lights from West Seattle and the smaller islands of Puget Sound glowed like rows of bright bulbs on a Christmas tree.

Stefano turned Hope into his embrace and locked his hands at the small of her back. Sighing softly, she found a peace, a serenity she couldn't explain.

Stefano kissed her cheek, her ear, her hair, before claiming her mouth. Hope experienced a deep, almost painful longing. The prince trembled and she knew he was as deeply affected by their kisses as she.

Hope pressed her head against his shoulder and closed her eyes as the warm sensations melted over her. Biting into her lower lip, she tried not to think of the impossibility of their situation.

"I was afraid of that," Stefano murmured against her hair.

"Of what?" she asked.

"Your kiss. It's even better than before." His words were sad, almost bitter, and she lifted her head, wanting to look into his eyes. He wouldn't let her.

"Please," he said gently, "let me hold you a little longer."

Hope hadn't the strength of will to resist him. Nestled in his arms, it seemed as if the world and all the troubles that plagued the universe were a million miles away.

"When I was a little girl, I used to dream of meeting a handsome prince," she told him, finding life ironic. "My mother would read me a story before I went to sleep and she'd kiss me good-night and then tell me that someday my prince would come."

"Ah, yes, your mother." Amusement laced his words. A moment passed and he chuckled softly.

Hope's head sprang upward. "What's she done now?"

"Nothing," he said, pressing her head back to his shoulder. "Don't be so concerned."

"Stefano, I know my mother. Please tell me what she's up to this time."

He chuckled softly and brushed his lips against hers. "I received a letter from her this afternoon."

"And…" Hope coaxed.

"She wanted to know what my intentions toward you were."

"No." Mortified, Hope buried her face in his chest.

"I apologize.... Oh, Stefano, forgive her. She means no harm. It's just that..." Try as she might, Hope didn't have a prayer of explaining, because she didn't have a hope of analyzing what her mother could have been thinking. "It's just that..."

"Perhaps she believes I'm the prince she told you was coming all these years."

"Mom and her friends are romantics," Hope offered as a possible explanation. "They don't understand that life isn't filled with happy endings."

It seemed his hold on her tightened briefly. "Let's not speak of the future. Not tonight. It is selfish to indulge myself with you, I know, but it is a little thing, and I hope in time you'll find it in your heart to forgive me."

Hope didn't want to think of the future, either. It went without saying she wouldn't—couldn't be—part of his life. Like Stefano, she was content to indulge her fantasies.

They didn't seem to have a lot to say. Together they sat on a bench at the end of the pier and he wrapped his arm around her shoulder. Every now and again he'd kiss her. In the beginning his kisses were gentle, but they soon took on an intensity that left Hope breathless.

He stopped abruptly and brushed a strand of hair from her cheek, and his hand lingered there. Several moments passed before he gave in to the temptation and kissed her again. She parted her lips to him and his tongue sought hers, involving her in a slow, erotic game.

Hope's breathing became heavy and shallow and when he raised his head, his gaze sought hers in the moonlight. She noted that his eyes were dark with passion and knew her own were a reflection of his.

His mouth found hers once more and when he dragged his lips away, he pressed his forehead to hers. "I can't kiss you again," he whispered.

The funny thing with greed, Hope discovered, was that she was never satisfied. At one time all she wanted was to spend time with him, then she'd be happy, she told herself. Then he kissed her, and she never wanted it to end.

"Why can't you kiss me?" she asked, spreading a series of kisses over his face, starting at his jaw and working her way over the contour of his face, teasing his lips with the tip of her tongue.

"Hope…" He trapped her face between his hands.

"Hmm?"

He directed her mouth to his and it was as if they were reuniting after a six-month absence. When he pulled away, Hope saw that his face was tight with desire.

"We must stop," he murmured, sounding very much as if he were in pain.

"I know…but I'm greedy for you."

"That's the problem," he murmured. "I am greedy for you, too. I just didn't know…"

"Didn't know what?"

"How much I need you," he whispered. "Now, please, don't tempt me anymore. You make me weak and—" he chuckled softly "—strong."

"That makes no sense."

"I know, but it's the truth." He pressed her fingers to his lips. "I want you to tell me more of your childhood."

"But, Stefano, I'm so…ordinary. Tell me of yours."

"I have no interest in hearing myself speak. Tell me everything there is to know about you."

"What about my old boyfriends? Do you want to hear about them, as well?"

"No," he said and laughed softly. "It wouldn't take very much to make me insanely jealous."

"It would only be fair," she chided. "I've been reading about your exploits for years. You aren't called the Bachelor Prince for nothing." She meant to tease him, to make light of his reputation.

He surprised her by clasping her upper arms. His eyes locked with her.

"It's true, there've been many women in my life."

"I know." She lowered her gaze, not wanting to think about all the beautiful females who had loved him. And worse. Whom he'd loved.

He lifted her chin with his index finger. "But there's only been one woman who held my heart in the palm of her hand." He reached for her hand and kissed her palm. "That woman, Hope Jordan, is you."

Six

It was the wee hours of the morning before Stefano returned to the hotel. He couldn't remember a time in his life that he'd been happier.

All his life he'd been groomed for his position as the Prince of San Lorenzo. He'd been taught the concerns of his country must come first. Duty and sacrifice were equated with honor and character. He knew he must marry Priscilla Rutherford or some other woman who was equally wealthy. There was no other option.

Now certainly wasn't the time to fall in love. Now wasn't the time to give his heart to a woman he must eventually leave.

A week, he told himself. He would give himself that time with Hope as a gift. Seven days would be ample time to fill his heart with memories. Ones that he would need to last him a lifetime.

He'd been honest with Hope from the first. She understood and accepted that there could be no future for them. And yet she'd generously opened her heart and her life to him.

By the time Stefano let himself into his suite, he realized how exhausted he was, and yet he doubted that he'd sleep. Sleep would rob him of the precious moments he had to think about Hope, to remember the taste of her kisses and how right it felt to hold her in his arms.

"Where have you been?"

Pietro's hard voice rocked Stefano. Never had anyone dared to speak to him in such a tone.

"Pietro?" His friend stood by the picture window, his hands clasped behind his back as if he'd been furiously pacing. "Is something wrong?"

"Only that you'd disappeared!" he snapped. Walking over to the phone, Pietro punched out a series of numbers and spoke brusquely to James, Stefano's bodyguard, reporting the prince's safe return.

"I apologize, my friend. I wasn't thinking."

"What is this…this ridiculous outfit?" Pietro gestured toward the Elvis costume as if he found it distasteful to look at.

"What does it look like?" Stefano was prepared to give his secretary a little slack, but Pietro was stepping dangerously close to his limit. As the crown prince, he rarely had to account for his actions, and certainly not for his choice of wardrobe.

"It looks like you've been making a fool of yourself," Pietro said heatedly.

"Pietro," Stefano barked. "I think it would be better if we saved this conversation for morning. I've already apologized for any dismay I may have caused you and the others. It's late and you're upset."

"I'm more than upset." His secretary walked over to the desk and reached for a typewritten sheet, jerking it off the top with enough energy to send several papers fluttering to the floor. He ignored the disruption and slapped the single page down on the table next to where Stefano was standing.

"This is my letter of resignation, effective immediately." Having made that announcement, Pietro stormed over to the window and stood with his back to Stefano.

The prince couldn't have been more surprised if his secretary and friend had pulled a gun on him. The betrayal was as shocking.

Stefano sank onto the sofa cushions, hardly able to believe what he was reading. Pietro had been with him for years. He was far more than his secretary and companion. Pietro was his friend. The best he'd ever had.

"Is there a reason for your resignation, other than my tardiness this evening?" he managed to ask after a strained moment.

Pietro whirled around to face him. Their gazes locked in a fierce battle of wills. It felt as if they breathed simultaneously, each harboring his own grief.

"Yes," Pietro admitted reluctantly.

"You are free to tell me what I've done to offend you." He wanted this confrontation to be man-to-man, not prince to subject, not employer to employee.

Pietro chose to sit in the chair across from him. His friend was a large man, and when he leaned forward their knees almost touched.

"I cannot. I will not," he amended heatedly, "allow you to treat Priscilla Rutherford in such an insulting manner. She is a woman worthy of being your bride."

"I fully intend to marry the woman," Stefano argued, but he could see that his reassurances did little to appease Pietro. "That's what you want, isn't it?" Stefano asked.

"Yes," he barked. "But give me one good reason she would want you after the horrible way you've treated her."

Stefano didn't have a clue what Pietro was speaking about. "Forgive me for being obtuse, but what terrible sin have I committed against the woman?"

It didn't take Pietro long to answer.

"First off, you visit her home and meet her family and completely ignore Priscilla."

Now that Pietro mentioned it, Stefano did recall becoming heavily involved in a conversation with James Rutherford. He'd been distracted, but as he remembered it, Priscilla hadn't seemed to mind.

"Nor can there be any excuse for this evening," Pietro continued.

"This evening at the banquet?" Stefano had thought he'd been attentive and thoughtful. It was apparent from the beginning that Priscilla had been ill. Rather than detain her while he dealt with the many women who sought an audience, he'd had Pietro escort her home.

"I never intended to insult her. I assumed she wasn't feeling well and thought to see to her comfort as quickly as possible."

True, he'd been eager to escape the banquet so he could meet Hope, but that had nothing to do with his time with Priscilla. "First thing in the morning, I'll send flowers and beg her indulgence," Stefano offered, hoping that would appease his secretary.

Pietro rubbed a hand down his face, and Stefano couldn't remember seeing his friend look more tired. "I've already seen to that."

"Thank you," Stefano murmured, inclining his head.

Pietro clenched his hands over his knees. "Answer me one thing."

"Of course."

"Do you care for Priscilla?"

If asked if he loved her, Stefano would have been honest. He liked Priscilla Rutherford, and was comfortable enough with her that in time he was confident he would grow to feel a deep tenderness for her. "Yes, I care for her."

"Then you intend to marry her?"

Stefano had no option. Pietro knew that better than anyone. "If she agrees to be my bride, then we will be married at the first opportunity."

Pietro lowered his gaze and after a long moment, said, "Good."

"My hope is that once we return to San Lorenzo, she will follow with her family. Once she stays at the palace and samples what her life would be like there, I'll court her seriously." He hesitated, wondering if the heiress had said something to Pietro that he should know. "Do you know what her feelings are toward me?"

"No," came the stark answer.

Stefano waited a moment more, and tore Pietro's letter of resignation in half. "Now, can we forget this nonsense? It's late and we're both tired."

Pietro studied the torn piece of paper. "I will stay with you until we return to San Lorenzo," he said, his look both troubled and thoughtful. "If you want, I'll interview the applicants for my replacement, and leave as soon as one can be trained."

Stunned, Stefano nodded. "As you wish."

Stefano woke with a heavy heart. Unfortunately, the morning didn't bring any better news. He dressed, and when his breakfast arrived, he sat alone at the table and sipped his first cup of coffee.

From habit, he reached for the morning newspaper, and scanned the headlines. As he reached for a baguette, his gaze fell upon the society page. The image of his own face smiled up to benignly greet him. It wasn't as though he were unaccustomed to finding his picture in the paper. Cameras routinely followed him.

But this photograph was different because Priscilla Rutherford was standing next to him. The lens had caught them at an opportune moment in which they happened to be gazing at each other. For all intents and purposes it looked as if they were deeply in love. The headlines gave way to speculation that an American had laid claim to Prince Stefano's heart.

The speculation in the article was even worse. The more he read, the more alarmed Stefano became. The entire piece was geared toward Stefano's attention to the heiress, and speculation as to where the romance would lead.

Stefano feared Hope would read this article and think terrible things of him. He must talk to her, assure her he wasn't playing her for a fool. But just as he reached for the telephone, Pietro brought him in some documents that required his signature.

Stefano didn't dare risk contacting Hope with Pietro in the room. As much as it was possible, he wanted to keep his relationship with Hope a secret. Later, when it became necessary for him to leave, he wanted to spare her any unnecessary attention, and/or embarrassment.

His only opportunity to speak privately with Hope was to find some errand on which to send Pietro. "I need you to do something for me at your earliest convenience," Stefano said, reaching for his gold pen and a monogrammed sheet of paper.

"Of course," Pietro replied stiffly.

Stefano wrote out a message as quickly as his hand would move the pen. He folded the note and inserted it inside an envelope. "Personally deliver this to Miss Rutherford for me," he said, "and await her response."

Pietro hesitated long enough to attract Stefano's attention. "Would you like me to leave right away?" Pietro asked.

"Please," Stefano said. He didn't know what was wrong with Pietro, but his tone implied that he'd rather walk off a gangplank than carry out this errand. If he wasn't so anxious to speak to Hope, he would have questioned his friend.

Pietro reluctantly accepted the envelope. Stefano waited until his secretary had left the room before reaching for the telephone. An eternity passed before the first ring. A second, third and a fourth followed before her answering machine clicked on.

He listened to Hope's voice and even though it came through a mechanical device, Stefano's spirits lifted just hearing her speak. She sounded upbeat and energetic, giving instructions to wait for the long beep.

"Hope, my princess..." Stefano hated machines. Now that he could speak, he didn't know what to say. "Please, my darling, don't be influenced by anything you read in the papers. You own my heart. Meet me this evening as we arranged. It's vital that we speak." With that he replaced the telephone receiver, convinced his message was grossly inadequate.

He covered his face with his hand and sighed heavily. If she hadn't already read the article, she would now. With one phone call he might have destroyed his relationship with the only woman he'd ever loved.

Priscilla endured breakfast with her parents while they touted the virtues of Prince Stefano as if he were a god. As far as either of them were concerned, the man was perfect in every way.

Neither bothered to ask about her evening. Apparently they assumed everything had been wonderful from beginning to end. But then Priscilla hadn't volunteered any information, either, and if the truth be known, she didn't know what she'd say if they asked.

The fever pitch accelerated when her mother read the morning paper and found Priscilla pictured with the prince taking up almost half of the society page.

By midmorning, the phone was ringing off the hook, and Elizabeth was in heaven delivering tidbits of speculation to her dearest friends.

As soon as she was able, Priscilla escaped with a book to the gazebo, one of her favorite hiding places. Her intention was to bury herself in the carefree world of a good story, but try as she might to concentrate, her attention repeatedly wandered from the printed page.

Instead of becoming absorbed in the novel, her thoughts countlessly reviewed the time she'd spent with Pietro. The man confused her more than anyone she'd ever known. But it didn't stop there. He intrigued her, as well. No other man had ever made her feel the way he did, as if she were a rare beauty, as if she were brilliant and utterly charming.

Priscilla discovered that all the things Pietro had told her about the prince were true for himself, as well. He was a gentle, kind and caring man.

"I wondered if I'd find you out here, miss," Mrs. Daily, the cook said, sounding winded. She wore a black dress that rounded nicely over her ample hips and a white apron. "I swear I've spent the last twenty minutes searching for you."

Disheartened, Priscilla closed the novel. She'd been found. "Is my mother looking for me?"

"No. A gentleman came to call. He gave me this card."

Priscilla examined the name and sat upright so fast she nearly toppled out of the chair. Pietro. Her heart pounded with excitement. "Has he left?"

"No. Apparently he has a letter and has been instructed to give it to you personally. He explained that he needs a reply. He's waiting in your father's den."

"Does…anyone else know he's here?"

Mrs. Daily wiped the perspiration from her brow. "Not to my knowledge."

"Thank you, Mrs. Daily," she said and impulsively kissed the older woman's flushed cheek. "You're an angel." With that, Priscilla raced across the wide expanse of groomed lawn, taking a shortcut through the garden. Breathless, she came upon the den from the outside entrance.

She stood on the other side of the double wide French doors and watched Pietro, who was standing in front of the fireplace. He seemed to be examining the carved wooden ducks her father displayed on the mantel.

Pietro turned at the sound of the door opening.

"Hello," she said, terribly conscious of her shorts and T-shirt. Her mother would most definitely disapprove, but Priscilla hadn't wanted to waste time changing clothes.

"Priscilla." She surprised him and he appeared to brace himself. At once he became stiff and businesslike. Opening his suit jacket, he withdrew an envelope.

"How are you this fine day?" she asked cheerfully.

"Very good, thank you," he returned crisply. "And yourself?"

"Great." Especially now, although it was hard to believe that the dignified man who stood before her was the same one who'd held and kissed her the night before.

"You might wish to read what's inside the envelope," he offered after a moment.

"Of course," she said, laughing inwardly at herself. It had been enough just to see him. Nothing Prince Stefano had written could rival that.

Priscilla felt his scrutiny as she read over the few scribbled lines. Either the prince had poor penmanship or he'd been in a terrible hurry. "I can't seem to make out a few lines," she said, using that as an excuse to move closer to him. "Can you?"

Pietro reluctantly read over the note. He frowned as if he were having difficulty reading the message, as well. "He apologizes for any embarrassment the article in this morning's paper has caused you."

"Did you see it?" she asked Pietro.

"No."

"Trust me, you didn't miss much. Frankly the prince is far more photogenic than I am. The article is nothing but speculation about our supposed romance, and nothing anyone with a whit of sense would take seriously. I know I'm not." She motioned toward the deep burgundy chairs that were positioned next to the fireplace. They both sat.

"Unfortunately," she confided, "that's not the case with my mother. You'd think I'd been awarded the Nobel Peace Prize from the way she's acting."

"So your parents are pleased with the attention the prince is paying you."

She wrinkled her nose and nodded. "I suppose I should let them enjoy it while they can. You see, I haven't given them that much to brag to their friends about. I'm not the least bit gifted."

His eyes snapped with disagreement. "That is most certainly not true."

If Priscilla hadn't already been in love with Pietro, she would have fallen head over heels right then. "I mean I'm not talented musically, or athletically or in some other way that parents like to brag to their friends about. With one exception," she amended, "I always achieved top grades.

For years mother wanted to test my intelligence quota so she could boast to her friends that I had a genius IQ."

"Do you?" He made it sound like a distinct possibility.

"I don't know. I refused to be tested. I mean, what does it really matter if have a high IQ or don't? Knowing my test score doesn't change who or what I am, does it?"

"Not in the least."

"I didn't think so, either. Bless her heart, my mother never understood that. And so, if she can stand in the limelight with her friends because of the attention Prince Stefano's giving me, well, I figure she's waited a long time."

Pietro's gaze found hers and she smiled at him. "What was the last part of his message? I couldn't make it out."

"He's invited you and your parents to brunch tomorrow morning at eleven."

"Oh, dear," Priscilla said with a ragged sigh. "I'd hoped the banquet might be the last of it."

Pietro frowned. "The last of it?"

"The prince's attention," Priscilla explained. "Frankly, I haven't figured out what he sees in me."

Pietro's eyes snapped the way they had earlier when she claimed she was without talent. "Can you accept Prince Stefano's invitation?" he asked brusquely.

"I'm sure we can." The truth was she'd much prefer for the prince to leave Seattle, so she could quietly return to her life. But that would mean that Pietro would be leaving, as well, so she was torn.

"Before you accept, don't you think you should speak with your parents first?"

"No," she said with frank honesty. "Because if they

have a conflict, I'm sure they'll make other arrangements. It isn't every day a father has a chance to foist his daughter off on royalty." It was a joke, but Pietro didn't laugh.

"If Prince Stefano chooses you as his bride, he will be the fortunate one. How is it your parents don't recognize the rare jewel you are?" He frowned, sincerely puzzled. His words were so genuine that Priscilla developed a lump in her throat. Several moments passed before it dissolved enough for her to speak.

"Oh, Pietro, you make me feel like a princess."

He opened his mouth as if he were about to speak, when the door to the den opened and her mother abruptly appeared.

"Priscilla, I've been looking for you for a solid hour. You've been hiding from me again," she said disapprovingly until she noticed Pietro.

He stood. "Good day, Mrs. Rutherford."

"Hello, Pietro," she greeted warmly, clasping her hands together. "I wasn't told you were here."

"Prince Stefano sent me to deliver a letter to Priscilla."

"A letter?" Elizabeth Rutherford's eyes brightened. "I was just looking to tell Priscilla a gorgeous bouquet of flowers arrived from the prince. Why, it's one of the largest arrangements I believe I've ever seen." She handed Priscilla the card and then gracefully slipped the prince's letter from Pietro's fingers.

Instead of reading the card, Priscilla watched her mother's eyes quickly scan the letter. Elizabeth seemed to have no problem deciphering Stefano's handwriting. "He's invited us to brunch," she cooed.

"Yes, Mother."

"I hope you told him we'd be most honored to accept his invitation."

"Priscilla has already accepted on your behalf."

"Very good," her mother said, and the "look" came over her as she studied Priscilla—one that Priscilla recognized all too well. The look that claimed there was nothing in three wardrobes full of clothes that was appropriate for her to wear. The look that said Priscilla was doomed to spend the entire day shopping.

"It was good to see you again, Pietro," Elizabeth said.

It demanded everything for Priscilla not to protest. She didn't want him to leave so soon. They'd barely had a chance to talk.

"Perhaps Pietro would like some refreshment, Mother," Priscilla said hurriedly.

"Of course," Elizabeth said, recovering quickly. "You must forgive my thoughtlessness. It was just that we're so very pleased to have met you and the prince. I was overcome with excitement to receive his latest invitation."

"I appreciate the offer, but I must be leaving."

"So soon?" Silently Priscilla pleaded with him to stay, but he looked away, ignoring her entreaty.

"I must return to the hotel to make our travel preparations."

Her gaze flew to his. "When…will you be leaving for San Lorenzo?" Priscilla asked, her voice hardly above a whisper. He'd casually dropped a bomb and then left her to deal with the aftermath. Not once had he mentioned returning to San Lorenzo. She knew, of course, now that the Romance Lovers' Convention was over, the prince and Pietro would be leaving, but she'd hoped it wouldn't be for a few days.

"We'll be returning to San Lorenzo as soon as I can make all the necessary arrangements," Pietro announced.

"And that will be...?" her mother pressed.

Pietro hesitated. "Two days, possibly three."

"Oh," mother and daughter murmured together in sorry disappointment.

Hope's day had been hectic. From the moment the alarm sounded that morning until this very second, she'd been on the run. There seemed to be a million errands that had accumulated in the past few weeks. Errands she'd been putting off.

This day had been perfect. Since she had a dentist appointment in the afternoon, she decided to make a day of it. To be fair, her motives weren't pure. She needed an escape to mull over and savor the evening she'd spent with Prince Stefano.

If she followed her usual schedule, she'd face countless questions. Although Hope hadn't said anything to Lindy about the prince, she suspected her friend had heard him ask her to meet him at the ferry terminal. And then there was her mother.

Hope wanted to avoid all the questions, all the curiosity, and so she'd used this day as a convenient excuse to disappear.

Since she hadn't taken time for lunch, Hope was famished when she finally arrived home. Checking her watch, she saw that she wasn't scheduled to meet Stefano for another three hours. Briefly she wondered if he was going to opt for the Elvis costume again this evening.

The phone rang just as she opened the refrigerator door. She groped inside for a carrot and then reached for the receiver. "Hello."

"Hope, sweetheart." It was her mother. "Are you all right?"

Hope frowned at the apprehension in her mother's voice. "Of course I'm all right. Why shouldn't I be?"

"Well…I just didn't know how you'd feel after dating Prince Stefano and everything. You seemed quite taken with him."

"Mother, I thought we already went over this." Hope hadn't mentioned anything to her mother and the other self-appointed fairy godmothers about seeing Stefano again.

"I know, it's just that…well, I didn't want you to be hurt."

Hope had to bite her lip to keep from commenting on the letter Doris had written the prince, asking him his intentions. But to do so would reveal that she'd been in contact with him herself.

"I'm fine, Mom."

"You're sure?"

The line beeped, indicating that she had another call. "I have to go, Mom."

"All right, sweetie. I just wanted to be sure you weren't upset."

"I'm not." The line beeped again and she picked up the second call. "Hello."

A slight pause followed her greeting. "Hope?"

"Stefano." She said his name in a rush of happiness.

"Where have you been all day? I've been trying to reach you for hours."

"I was doing a bunch of errands I've been putting off for weeks. You wouldn't believe all the red tape involved in operating a small business. Then I had a dentist appointment. You'll be pleased to know I'm cavity-free."

"When did you arrive home?"

"Just a few minutes ago." It dawned on her then that there could only be one reason for his call. He couldn't meet her as they'd arranged, and her heart sagged with disappointment. "You can't come this evening." She said it for him, because it was easier than to have him tell her.

"Nothing could keep me from seeing you again. I swear this has been the longest day of my life." His voice was low and sensual and it was almost as if she were in his arms again. Which was exactly where Hope longed to be.

"It has for me, too," she whispered.

He seemed to hesitate. "I'm scheduled to dine with the mayor and his wife this evening."

"Yes, I know. You already explained why we can't meet until later. I understand, Stefano. Don't worry."

"I've decided to have my driver deliver me to your home directly following the dinner. You'll be there?"

"Of course, but…"

"I'm sorry to be so rude, but I must go. I'm at the mayor's home now and they tell me dinner is being served. You understand, don't you?"

"Of course."

With that, the telephone line went abruptly dead, and Hope was left to wonder at the purpose of Stefano's call.

It had all been rather odd. Yes, he'd changed their plans, but she had the sinking sensation that there was far more to this than he was letting on.

Hope chewed down on the carrot as she walked back into her bedroom and sorted through her closet, reviewing her choice in outfits. She decided upon jeans and a shirt with a Southwestern pattern.

She was examining the contents of her freezer, looking for something appetizing to zap in her microwave when she remembered she hadn't checked her messages on the answering machine.

The first was from Lindy who sounded madder than hops about something. A long beep followed and Stefano's voice came on the line, claiming she shouldn't put any credence in the article in that morning's paper.

Newspaper article? She'd brought the paper in with the mail and hadn't bothered to look at it. She went through the entire front page and didn't find a single word printed about Stefano.

Not until she reached for the society page did she see it. The photograph of the prince gazing longingly at another woman seemed to slap her across the face.

For a moment, Hope actually thought she might be ill. The impact of learning the man she loved was involved with another woman quite literally made her sick to her stomach. The blood rushed out of her face so fast that she grew dizzy.

Hope slumped into the kitchen chair and waited for the nausea to subside. Three times she attempted to read the article, and each time discovered that she couldn't get past the first five paragraphs. In those few short lines she learned that it was widely believed that the heiress, Priscilla Rutherford, had captured the Bachelor Prince's heart and that a marriage proposal couldn't be far behind.

Hope didn't know how long she sat there staring into space while she attempted to calm herself.

She was such a fool. The man was known around the world as a playboy. How could she have allowed this to happen? That was what plagued Hope the most. Within the space of two days, she'd handed this man her heart. A man who collected women's hearts the way some do foreign stamps and coins.

He was good—she had to grant him that. He'd had her believing that he actually cared for her. Perhaps because she so wanted to believe it so desperately.

She didn't cry. This was a pain too deep for tears. A betrayal. The funny part of it was that she didn't actually blame Stefano. From what she saw of Priscilla Rutherford, the other woman was quite lovely. A woman Hope would like for a friend.

Hope had nothing to offer Stefano other than her heart. Unfortunately he was already in possession of that.

The doorbell chimed and she stared at the door for several moments.

"Hope, please." It was Stefano.

"Go away," she begged. "Just go away."

Seven

"I'm not leaving until we speak," Prince Stefano insisted from Hope's porch.

"I have no intention of opening this door," Hope said with equal conviction. He didn't know the meaning of the word *stubborn* until he'd crossed swords with her. "You played me for a fool!" she cried.

"All I'm asking is five minutes of your time," Stefano pleaded. "Hear me out and if you still don't want to see me, then I'll quietly leave."

It wasn't Stefano Hope didn't trust, it was herself. The prince made her vulnerable in ways no man had before. As much as she'd claimed otherwise, she'd inherited a romantic nature from her mother and her irrational heart had led her down a primrose path. What angered Hope the most was the way she'd obtusely followed. She was smarter than this. If she hadn't been so blinded by her attraction, she would have realized much sooner that a man like Prince Stefano couldn't possibly be serious about someone like her.

"Hope," he pleaded, "all I want is five minutes of your time."

"Answer me one thing," she insisted, finding herself wavering despite her earlier resolve. "Do you or do you not intend to marry Priscilla Rutherford?" The answer to that question would be all she needed to know.

The prince hesitated. "Let me explain."

"Answer the question." She trusted him to be honest. In light of what she'd learned, perhaps she was an even greater fool to believe Prince Stefano was an honorable man.

"Trust me, Priscilla has nothing to do with the way I feel about you."

"Stefano, if you want me to open this door, then you'll answer the question."

Once again he hesitated.

Fool that she was, Hope unlocked the door. Carrying on a conversation in this manner, with them both shouting to be heard through the thick oak door, was ridiculous.

The mesh screen door was solidly locked in place. She stood on one side and he on the other. The barrier was flimsy at best, but necessary.

Stefano's gaze held hers. She read the agony in his eyes, the pain of the truth.

"There are many things you don't understand," he whispered.

"I understand that you wine and dine Miss Rutherford and sneak away to meet me in a back alley. What you failed to realize, Stefano, is that I may be a nobody, but I have my pride, and frankly you've walked all over it."

By the time she finished, her voice was trembling. She stopped abruptly and swallowed in an effort to control her own pain, complicated by her considerable anger.

Stefano had made a mistake if he believed she would allow him to treat her in such a shabby manner.

Briefly Stefano closed his eyes. "I would rather die than hurt you."

Hope knew he spoke the truth, but why would he marry another woman if he cared so deeply for her? There could only be one explanation. He was ashamed of her. Her family wasn't good enough for the likes of Prince Stefano. Jordan wasn't a surname that brought instant recognition in the world of high society, whereas the Rutherford name was emblazoned across one of the finest shipping lines in the world.

"Are you going to marry Priscilla Rutherford?" she demanded, her voice strong and sure.

He hung his head and nodded. "Yes."

"That's everything I need to know," she whispered. With that she closed the door. For a moment, the pain of the truth was almost more than she could bear and she slumped against the wooden structure, letting it hold her upright.

Taking in a deep breath, she moved away from the door and looked out the window. Stefano had returned to his limousine. He sat in the backseat for several tortuous moments before giving his driver the order to leave.

The long, sleek automobile moved away from the curb. Prince Stefano was out of her life. He could have lied, she realized, could have glossed over the newspaper article as gossip. Instead he'd admitted the painful truth, unwilling to spare him or her with lies.

It seemed impossible that she could still love him, but she did.

Nestled on her sofa, Hope drew her knees up and rested her forehead there. It took her a while to sort through her emotions.

At first she was steamy with resentment. She was hurt. Angry. She looked for someone to blame. Her mother was the first person who came to mind. If Doris hadn't purchased that ridiculous ticket none of this would have happened.

Lindy was the second name on her list. If her friend hadn't fed her this line about romance, Hope might have seen through the smoke screen.

But ultimately there was no one to blame but herself. She was the one who'd been foolish enough to believe in fairy tales. She was the one who'd sat in a ferry terminal at nearly eleven o'clock at night, praying Stefano would show. She was the one who'd handed him her heart on a tarnished silver platter.

Loving Stefano had seemed so right. Hope had been foolish enough to believe she had it all figured out. Him figured out. Just as if she were reading a recipe. She'd seen the look in his eyes, tasted his kisses, held him in her arms.

For a few short days she'd believed in the impossible.

It was over now. She'd made sure he understood that. All she had left were the memories, and try as she might, she couldn't make herself regret having fallen in love with the Bachelor Prince.

An hour and a half later, Hope decided against sitting inside her home on a bright, beautiful evening and brooding over her mistakes. She needed physical activity to help her out of the doldrums. With that thought in mind, she decided to water her front yard.

A bundle of nervous energy, she changed into shorts and a sleeveless top and brought the hose around to the front of the yard. Her roses needed to be clipped, and she made a mental note to put that on her to-do list for the weekend.

A roar of a motorcycle zooming down her street caused her to turn around and glare at the rider. This was a peaceful neighborhood, and the irritation of loud noises wasn't appreciated.

The rider resembled James Dean, the legendary movie actor. He wore a white T-shirt, blue jeans and black boots, and when he saw her, he roared his bike into her driveway.

"Hope."

Not until that moment did Hope realize the rider was Stefano. Her mouth sagged open in surprise.

"I can't leave matters this way between us. Unfortunately, I fear I've been followed. Come with me. Please."

"But…"

He held his hand out to her. "I will never ask anything more of you. If you feel anything for me, you'll do as I ask without question. Hurry, please, before I'm found."

Dropping the hose, Hope leapt onto the back of the motorcycle as if she'd been born on the seat of a bike, and placed the helmet he had for her over her head. She wrapped her arms around Stefano's middle and within seconds they were off.

The prince expertly wove in and out of traffic. She saw him checking his rearview mirror several times, and when they stopped for a red light, he turned and looked over his shoulder.

"Who's after you?" Hope asked, fearing he might be in some kind of trouble.

"My bodyguard," Stefano explained.

"But don't you pay him to protect you?"

"Yes, but there are times, such as these, when I need my privacy. James doesn't appreciate that, I fear."

"How often do you come up with these disguises and the sudden need to escape?"

Stefano chuckled, but his laughter lacked any real amusement. "Only since I've met you."

"Me?"

The light changed and Stefano revved the engine, drowning out her thoughts as they continued down the busy street. Hope hadn't a clue of their destination, and she wasn't sure Stefano did, either. By the time he pulled over and parked the bike at the Ballard Locks, Hope was convinced it would take a week to clean the bugs off her teeth.

Stefano removed his helmet, helped her off the motorcycle and held her hand. They walked over to the viewing point and gazed at the long line of motorboats and sailboats awaiting their turn to travel through the locks that linked Lake Washington with Puget Sound.

"Forgive me for being so demanding," he said without

looking at her. "You had every right to refuse to come with me."

That was true. "I was under the impression that if I didn't come, you'd have kidnapped me."

"I was desperate enough to have considered that, although I'd like to think myself incapable of such a crime. After this evening, I'm no longer sure."

"This evening?"

"When you closed the door on me."

It hadn't occurred to Hope that this was probably the first time anyone had behaved so brusquely with His Highness. Generally, doors were opened for him, not slammed in his face.

"I can't bear the thought of leaving matters as they were between us," he explained. His gaze studied the deep green waters as if he dared not turn and look into her eyes.

"I don't know that there's anything left to say."

"Perhaps not, but I couldn't leave without telling you the truth. I owe you that much."

Frankly, Hope had had just about all of that she could take for one day. "I know you're going to marry Miss Rutherford. You told me that yourself."

"Yes, but you do not know why."

"I'm not stupid, Stefano. Priscilla Rutherford is far more socially acceptable than I am. I own a coffee shop, remember? Not a shipping line." Although she tried to keep the bitterness out of her voice, she feared she had little success.

Stefano turned and looked at her for the first time. He framed her face in his hands and gazed deeply into her eyes. His own narrowed with an emotion she was sure she misread...love. A love so strong, it left her shaken.

"No, my love, what you're thinking couldn't be further from the truth. I must marry Priscilla Rutherford because she's an heiress."

Hope blinked. "I don't understand. You're one of the wealthiest men in the world...or so I've read. It doesn't make any sense that you'd be forced to marry for money."

He hung his head as if deeply ashamed. "It's true. My country is on the brink of bankruptcy. For the last year I've drained my family fortune in an effort to keep the economy stable. Other than a meager trust to cover my personal expenses, I'm nearly penniless."

"Oh, Stefano."

"Falling in love now is God's joke on me. You see I never really believed in love until I met you. Isn't it ironic that I should give my heart to one woman and be forced to marry another?"

Hope blinked back the ready tears that crowded the corners of her eyes.

"I promised myself a week with you. It was selfish and thoughtless of me not to have told you the truth in the beginning. I love you, Hope. I'll always love you, but within the next couple of days I'm going to walk away from you and never look back."

A tear blazed a trail down her face and she furiously wiped it aside, hating the weakness of emotion. "This is supposed to make me feel better?"

He blinked with surprise at her anger. "I...I've hurt you again."

"You couldn't leave matters the way they were? Oh,

no, you had to be sure I knew you loved me. Well, that's just fine and dandy." More tears escaped, and she ran her forearm under her nose, and sniffled loudly. "This is just great."

Stefano looked utterly perplexed. "You'd rather not know how much I love you?"

"Of course I want to know that." The man simply didn't understand. "I love you, too. That much should be obvious. It's just that... Never mind," she cried. "Go and marry your heiress!" She walked several feet away from him and wiped the moisture from her cheeks while she attempted to compose herself.

She didn't hear him until he was directly behind her. He placed his hands on her shoulders and brought his lips close to her ear. "I cannot bear to see you cry."

"Don't worry about it," she said, and shrugged one shoulder. "I'm a big girl, I'll get over you. I mean...I fell in love with you fast enough, it shouldn't be that difficult to forget you." That wasn't true, but she was looking to salvage her pride by making light of her feelings.

His grip on her tightened. "Pietro wants to schedule our return flight to San Lorenzo for tomorrow afternoon," he whispered.

She stiffened. "So soon?"

"I'll agree to his schedule if you tell me you don't want to see me again. But if...if there's a chance you'd consider meeting me for the next two or three nights, then I'll rearrange my schedule to be sure I stay in Seattle a bit longer."

"You're asking the impossible," she cried. She couldn't bear to have him hold her, knowing there would soon be another woman in his arms. Couldn't allow him to kiss her, knowing he'd soon be kissing another.

"I know," he said in a tortured whisper. "We have so little time together. Forgive me, my love, for being self-indulgent. I should have realized I've asked the impossible."

"Stefano," she whispered, and her hands covered his.

He turned her into his arms and brought his mouth down to hers in a moist, gentle kiss. The pressure of his touch changed the moment Hope responded. He kissed her again and again with a growing desperation, an urgency that left her clinging and struggling for breath when he finished.

"I'm sorry," he whispered, "I didn't mean to frighten you."

He hadn't, but she didn't have the breath to assure him otherwise.

He kissed her once more, and his lips brushed her nose, her cheek, her ear. She heard a sigh rumble through his chest. He paused, seemed to draw upon his reserve of strength, and with some effort eased himself away from her.

"I'll take you home now," he said.

She nodded.

They rode back in silence, with none of the urgency with which they'd sped away. Sometime later, he came to a stop in her driveway. Climbing off the bike first, he helped her dismount and then escorted her to the front door.

Neither spoke. Their eyes met and he smiled weakly. "Thank you, Hope." He pressed his hand against her face and rubbed his thumb over the arch of her cheek. His eyes were filled with pain. "I don't know if I have the courage to walk away from you," he told her in a broken whisper.

"Then don't," she whimpered and flung herself into his arms. "Not yet. We'll worry about tomorrow later. For now we have each other."

Stefano dared not look at his watch again for fear the Rutherfords would think he was pressed for time. He wasn't. It was another three hours before he could see Hope again. If anything, he wanted the time to pass more quickly.

"I'm so pleased you could join me," he said, as the small group reviewed the menu selections. Personally, Stefano wasn't hungry. Hope had promised him a tour of the rain forest and a picnic. It would be a shame if brunch with the Rutherfords ruined that.

"The pleasure is all ours," Elizabeth Rutherford assured him. "Isn't that right, Priscilla?"

The woman seemed to prod her daughter at every turn. It had been a mistake to invite her parents, he realized. Stefano would have enjoyed the meal with Priscilla, but with her family present—especially her mother—the brunch was sure to be an ordeal.

"We are honored by your invitation," Priscilla said in a monotone, as if she'd been forced to rehearse the line countless times.

Stefano's gaze drifted toward Pietro who wore a deep frown. The prince didn't fully understand what was going on with his secretary. For years Pietro had accompanied him to endless state dinners, and other social functions. He often used his secretary as a buffer against the curious and meddling dowagers, keen on marrying him off to their daughters and granddaughters.

Stefano had sensed his secretary's reluctance the minute he asked Pietro to join him with the Rutherfords. He'd offered a weak excuse, which Stefano rejected, and afterward Pietro was tight-lipped and sullen.

Even now Pietro sat stiffly at the table as if he'd rather be anyplace else but with the prince and the Rutherfords. Frankly, Pietro's attitude was beginning to irritate him.

Stefano had once considered Pietro his friend. Now he was no longer sure. Although nothing more had been said between them regarding Pietro's resignation, it was understood that once they returned to San Lorenzo, Pietro would hire his replacement, train him and leave Stefano's employment.

Apparently the prince had committed some terrible crime, other than his treatment of Priscilla, which, frankly, Stefano didn't think was so bad.

He liked Priscilla, and knew the feeling would grow once he got her away from her mother's clutches. Already he had a tender spot in his heart for the heiress. It didn't compare to the fiery intensity of feeling he shared with Hope, but over time he believed Priscilla and he would be happy. As happy as any man could be who was in his situation.

"My husband and I were discussing your invitation to visit San Lorenzo," Elizabeth said, breaking into his thoughts.

Stefano focused his attention on Priscilla's mother. "Naturally I'd want you to stay at the palace."

Elizabeth exchanged appreciative looks with her husband as if she'd somehow manipulated the invitation from him.

"We certainly wouldn't want to intrude on your royal business," the elder Rutherford inserted.

"Darling, the prince wouldn't have invited us if we were going to be a nuisance, isn't that right, Prince Stefano?"

"Most certainly."

"From what I understand, San Lorenzo has some of the best hotels in all of Europe," Priscilla's father said, as if he'd be just as happy in a hotel as a guest in the palace.

"That's true." Stefano didn't mention that a good portion of those world-class hotels sat vacant and were struggling to stay afloat in the current economic slump.

"If you wish," Stefano said, glancing at his secretary, "I could have Pietro arrange rooms for you at the Empress at my expense. It is our finest hotel, and I'm sure you'd be most comfortable."

"Nonsense," Elizabeth said quickly. "We'd prefer the palace. It isn't everyone who can say they've slept there, now can they?" She laughed lightly at her own joke, but Stefano noticed no one joined in her amusement.

After an uncomfortable moment of silence, Elizabeth once more picked up the conversation, directing her comment to her daughter. "You should tell the prince about your charity work, Priscilla."

"Mother, please. If Prince Stefano wants to hear about my work at the Children's Hospital, he can ask me himself."

It pleased Stefano that the Rutherfords' daughter revealed a little pluck. He was beginning to despair.

Priscilla glared at her mother and it did Stefano's heart good to see her mother squirm just a bit. He might have lessened the older woman's discomfort by inquiring about Priscilla's charity efforts, but he decided against it.

"How long will you be in Seattle?" the elder Rutherford inquired of Pietro.

"I've arranged to depart early tomorrow morning," his secretary answered.

"Change that," Stefano said.

"Change the arrangements?" Pietro asked and glared at him.

"I've decided to remain in this beautiful city for three more days. There's some sightseeing I want to do. With my current schedule I rarely have the opportunity to become properly acquainted with an area. Seattle strikes my fancy."

If looks could kill, Stefano would be mortally wounded. Pietro all but rose from his chair. Although he did an adequate job of restraining himself, Stefano wasn't fooled.

Whatever it was that was troubling his friend had gone on far too long. At first opportunity Stefano planned on confronting his secretary. The man hadn't been the same from the moment they landed in Seattle.

As it happened, the opportunity arose soon after the meal with the Rutherfords. Stefano and Pietro rode up in the elevator to the series of suites set aside for him on the nineteenth floor.

"I'd like a word with you," Pietro said the moment they were alone.

"If you insist."

"I do." It seemed Pietro was about to explode. His jaw was set and tight, and his hands were clenched at his sides.

The elevator doors rushed open and Stefano led the way into his private quarters. "What's wrong? Something's been troubling you from the moment we arrived, and I want to know what it is."

Pietro started to pace, a habit that relieved his tension. "I'd already made the arrangements to leave Seattle tomorrow morning."

Stefano shrugged. "Change them. You've done so often enough in the past. Why does it bother you so much now?"

His friend's mouth tightened. "If you insist upon staying this additional time, then I'd like to request your permission to return to San Lorenzo on my own."

"Absolutely not." Stefano didn't need time to consider his response. Not a day passed in which Stefano didn't require his secretary's assistance. To have Pietro return ahead of him would place an unnecessary burden on Stefano.

Pietro mumbled a profanity under his breath.

"Pietro," the prince said, thoughtfully studying his friend. "Can you tell me what plagues you?"

His secretary stiffened. "No."

"I can't order you, but as your friend, I would hope you could share with me what's wrong. If I've done something to offend you, let's clear the air."

"It's nothing you've done," Pietro assured him. He slumped into a chair and buried his face in his hands. "I apologize for my behavior."

Stefano could press his friend for details, but he preferred that Pietro would offer them willingly. He didn't.

"I have an appointment this afternoon," Stefano said.

Pietro nodded, without inquiring as to the prince's plans. Generally his secretary was as conscientious as his bodyguard of his whereabouts and schedule.

"Perhaps we can talk more later," Stefano suggested.

"Perhaps," Pietro agreed.

But Stefano doubted they would. It saddened him to think he had lost the best friend he'd ever had, especially when he hadn't a clue why.

Pietro sat in his compact office, staring out of the window. The view from the nineteenth floor was spectacular. Puget Sound shone like a polished jewel in the sunlight. Ferries and an abundance of oceangoing vessels patrolled the waterways. But the beauty of the scene escaped him.

A knock sounded against his door. "Come in," he called.

A footman opened the door and approached the desk. "The front desk sent this up. It's addressed to you."

"Thank you." Pietro waited until the man had left the room before tearing open the envelope. He knew before he read a single word that the message was from Priscilla.

I'm sorry to trouble you, but it's vitally important that I speak to you at your earliest convenience. I'll wait in the lobby for your reply.

He read the note and wiped a hand down his face.

After having spent an uncomfortable hour and a half in her presence, Pietro wasn't sure he could endure much more. His restraint was stretched to the breaking point. It had demanded every ounce of self-control he possessed not to make a scene with Priscilla and her mother. Elizabeth Rutherford was a fool. Somehow he didn't think the prince would appreciate it if he'd pointed it out to him.

Knowing there was no help for it, Pietro rang for the footman and asked that Priscilla be escorted to his office.

The pair returned within five minutes. It was clear that Priscilla had returned home and changed clothes. Instead of the dove-gray suit that didn't do her beauty justice, she wore a simple sleeveless summer dress and a wide-brimmed hat.

Pietro was literally stung by her beauty. It took him a moment to recover.

"Hello, Priscilla," he offered, and gestured for her to sit down.

"Pietro." She sat and clasped her hands in her lap. "Thank you for seeing me. I imagine after the spectacle this morning, you were wishing you never had to lay eyes on me again."

Actually, quite the opposite was true. The temptation to carry her away had nearly been his undoing. He couldn't tolerate the demeaning way in which her family treated her, as if her personal value rested solely in Prince Stefano's attention.

That Prince Stefano was prepared to marry Priscilla for her fortune troubled him. But seeing that he'd been the one to handpick Priscilla Rutherford from the list of potential brides, he couldn't very well object. He, too, had discredited the woman who innocently sat across from him. Now he was left to pay the piper.

"I don't mean to be a nuisance," she said, her gaze avoiding his.

"You could never be that," he assured her, hoping to keep their conversation on a professional level, and immediately failing. It was when it swayed toward the personal that he lost control. Twice now he'd held and kissed the woman who was destined to be the princess of San Lorenzo. If Stefano had so much as a hint of his feelings for Priscilla, he'd have him banished, and with reason.

"I was wondering if you could arrange for me to meet the prince alone," Priscilla asked.

"Alone?"

"Yes. Wherever we're together, there are always a number of people around...and that makes it extremely difficult for us to speak privately."

"I see." His mind was working double-time, wondering what it was Priscilla Rutherford had to say to the prince that had to be said when they were alone.

"Since it appears we're going to be in the area a few days longer than I'd anticipated, I'll see what I can do," Pietro said. He opened a small ledger where he wrote in the prince's appointments.

He paused when he saw that there was nothing written down for the prince that afternoon. Yet he distinctly remembered Stefano mentioning an appointment.

"If you'll excuse me for a moment."

"Of course."

Pietro stepped out of the office and called for a footman. "Is James with the prince?"

"No, sir. We assumed Prince Stefano was with you."

"He isn't." Pietro didn't know what kind of childish games the prince was playing, but this was getting out of hand. "Send James up to my office right away."

"Yes, sir." The footman disappeared and he stepped back inside his office and smiled at Priscilla.

"I'll contact you later with a time," he said.

"Thank you."

She didn't leave as he expected she would. "There's something else," she said, and her shoulders rose as if it had required a good deal of courage for her to broach the subject.

"Yes?" Pietro said, looking at his watch. He didn't want to be rude, but he had a minor crisis on his hands.

"It's about—"

She was interrupted by a loud knock against the door.

"If you'll excuse me."

Defeated, she lowered her head and nodded.

"I apologize, Priscilla, but this is necessary."

"I know," she said, smiling bravely up at him.

Pietro met the bodyguard on the other side of the door and glared accusingly at the muscle-bound young man. "Where's the prince?"

"I'm...not sure."

"As I recall, this is the second time the prince has left without your protection."

"Sir, I don't mean to complain, but how was I supposed to know the man who'd dressed up like Elvis was Prince Stefano? And then last night..."

"You mean he left unescorted last night, as well?"

"Yes. I thought you knew."

Pietro ran his hand through his hair. "No. Where did he go this time?"

"I don't know. I lost him someplace in Ballard. His

motorcycle squeezed between a bus and a car, and I couldn't catch him after that."

"He was on a motorcycle?"

"Yes. From what I understand, he paid one of the hotel staff for the use of it."

Pietro splayed his fingers at his sides in an exercise in frustration. "And you don't have a clue where he is right now?"

"Not exactly."

"How about a wild guess?" Pietro was desperate. He was willing to speculate.

James shrugged his massive shoulders. "I can't rightly say."

It came to Pietro that he should fire the man on the spot, but he'd wait until later after he'd confronted Stefano. He didn't know what had gotten into the prince.

Dressing up like Elvis, riding around on a motorcycle and now this.

"I want you to report to me the minute the prince returns."

"Yes, sir," James said stiffly.

Dragging a calming breath through his lungs, Pietro opened the door and entered his office. To his surprise Priscilla was standing.

"My apologies, Priscilla. There was something you wanted to tell me."

She nodded, smiled and then casually, as if she'd been doing so for years, she looped her arms around his neck and kissed him.

Eight

Hope studied Prince Stefano's features as they stood inside the Visitor Center at Hurricane Ridge. The unobstructed view of the Olympic Mountain range with its peaks, deep valleys and ridges stretched before them, paralleling the Strait of Juan de Fuca.

Hope had never been to Europe or witnessed the splendor of the Alps, and she wondered what the prince would think of her world, so different and yet so much like his own.

"It takes my breath away," he said in awe.

"Some of those mountains remain unexplored," she told him.

"No." He raised his eyebrows dubiously. "How can that be?"

"Look at the ridges. In order to reach one mountain, you must climb a number of others. Several planes have crashed in the region, but there's no hope of ever recovering the bodies."

"How tragic. They are beautiful, these mountains of yours."

Hope smiled. "I don't exactly own them, but thank you anyway."

"You love your state?"

"Very much. Washington is quite diversified, you know. We're standing in a rain forest and in less than three hundred miles there's desert. In some areas in the eastern half of the state, the growing season is only two weeks too short for cotton."

Once more Stefano's eyebrows shifted upward. "This state of yours is amazing." His arm circled her waist. "You're amazing."

Hope smiled up at him. He hadn't worn a disguise this afternoon, at least none that required a wig. He came as himself, wearing jeans, a Western-style shirt and snake-skin cowboy boots. He looked more like a country-western star than a European prince.

"Are you hungry?" she asked.

"Famished."

She led him outside the Visitor Center. Her car was parked across the road. "There's a picnic area this way," she said, unlocking the trunk of her red Saturn.

Stefano lifted out the wicker basket and she reached for the Scottish plaid blanket. A rainbow of colorful wild-flowers brightened the slopes. They trudged uphill for several moments until they found an appropriate site for their lunch. They chose a spot that offered a maximum of privacy beneath a forest of tall conifer trees.

Spreading the blanket out beneath the shelter of a

Douglas fir, Hope and Stefano sat down. The area was sunny and warm and Hope welcomed the shade.

"What have you packed?" Stefano asked, kneeling down next to her on the blanket. He opened the basket and smiled when he viewed the contents.

"What's this?"

"Blueberry pie, fresh from the oven," she explained proudly. Now wasn't the time to let him know Lindy was the one responsible for this delectable delight.

"Ah, yes, American fruit pie," Stefano said. "I tasted it once in New York."

"You mean to say you don't have pies in San Lorenzo?"

"Not the way you do in America. You must remember fruit pies are a product of your country."

"But what about France? They're known all over the world for their pastries."

"Tarts, yes, but not pie. Generally our pies are filled with meat," he explained matter-of-factly.

Hope digested this latest bit of information. "There are more differences between our two countries than I realized."

"Many, many differences." A note of sadness entered his voice and Hope knew he was thinking about his duty to his country to marry a woman he didn't love. A woman who would save his tiny country from financial ruin.

"And what are these?" Stefano brought out the thick submarine sandwiches she'd built.

Smiling, she explained the history of the oblong sandwiches. They ate then, companionably. The sun wove its way through the limbs of the Douglas fir, leaving a lacework pattern that slowly traveled over them as it crossed the brillian, blue sky.

Afterward they went on a short hike and Hope pointed out a number of different ferns. Stefano listened politely while she spread out the leaf of a sword fern, then a bracken fern and then that of the evergreen. She found herself chatting as if it were important to relay as much information about indigenous plants as possible. If she could fill the silence with words, then she wouldn't need to think about the future and how empty it would seem without him.

"Hope?"

She closed her eyes, and he pulled her softly into his arms. There was no need for words, no need to speak what was on both of their minds.

"I knew this wouldn't work," she whispered against his shoulder. She clung to him for fear that once he released her, her arms would feel forever empty.

"I thought if I kept you to myself for two more days I would have the strength to leave you. Now I wonder." His arms tightened about her. "I have no choice, my love. The fate of my country rests on my bride."

"I know. I know." Hope did, but that didn't make it any easier, loving him like this. In thinking over Stefano's plight, she'd attempted to come up with a solution that would allow them to stay together. But she could see no way out for them.

"Come," Stefano said with some effort. "Let's not think about the future. We're together now and that's all that matters."

Hope struggled to hold back the tears.

They made their way back to the picnic area. An eagle soared overhead and Hope pointed out the magnificent bird with its huge wingspan. They stood watching the eagle making a sweeping turn over the horizon. Stefano was enthralled by the grandeur of the bird that had come to represent the United States.

Sitting back down on the blanket, Hope lowered her head, fighting back the emotion. To her surprise Stefano wandered away. He stood no more than a few feet from her, but it felt as though the Grand Canyon divided them. As she watched, it seemed his shoulders slouched forward as if the weight of his burden had increased a hundredfold.

Hope did the best she could to compose herself, and once she was relatively sure she could speak without tears leaking into her voice, she stood and moved to his side.

For a long time neither of them spoke.

"I need your forgiveness, Hope," he whispered.

"My forgiveness?"

"For being so selfish. To want you so badly, to hold on to you these few days, when my presence brings you pain."

"It brings me joy, too."

"I've been unfair to you. I see that now. It is better for us both if I left Seattle."

"No." Her cry of protest came automatically. "Not yet."

"It's impossible for us. Being with you makes it even more impossible. I've done you a grave injustice and Priscilla, too. While it's true I don't love her..."

"It would hurt her if she ever found out about me," Hope finished for him.

"Yes." The lone word was barely above a whisper.

"Then she must never know." Her words were stronger and braver than her heart. She wasn't intentionally sparing the heiress who would marry Stefano. She did it for the prince. Her prince.

"You understand why this must be the last time we meet?"

"Yes," she returned in a broken whisper.

"But we have today," he returned, gripping hold of her hand. He gestured toward the sky. "The next time you see an eagle, remember me...and that I will always love you. Hold that knowledge in your heart forever." He turned to her and cupped her face between his hands. For a long moment, he gazed into her eyes, his expression deep and troubled. "In time I fear you'll grow to hate me...that you will think me a coward," he murmured.

"I won't...I couldn't."

Briefly he closed his eyes, and shook his head. "When that happens I want you to know that leaving you has been the most difficult thing I've ever done. Please remember that, Hope, above all else. You own my heart, and always will." He paused and then gently kissed her. "As the years pass, if there's ever a time you should need me, ever a time you're in trouble—"

"No," she said, cutting him off. "It has to be over here and now, Stefano. Promise me you won't come back into my life. You must," she insisted, before he could protest, "otherwise I'll find myself waiting for you, for the opportunity for you to return. Promise me that after today I'll never see or hear from you again."

It looked as if he couldn't make himself do it.

"Above all else, I know you to be an honorable man,

Stefano. If you give me your word never to see or contact me again, then I'm free to do as you ask and treasure the days we shared. Free to take our time together and place it in the tenderest part of my heart, and cherish it. I'll be free to go on with my life."

She watched as his Adam's apple worked in his throat. "I give you my word," he whispered. "You will never see or hear from me again after this afternoon."

Hope looked away for fear he would see the tears glistening in her eyes. "Thank you," she whispered.

Priscilla knew she'd shocked Pietro by tossing her arms around him and kissing him. But she'd intended to catch him off guard. That had been part of her plan.

At first, he attempted to gently push her away, but she resisted and clung to him.

Then her hat fell on the floor and his hands were in her hair and he was slanting his mouth over hers. This must be what it would be like in heaven, Priscilla mused with a deep sigh of pleasure.

Pietro kissed her again and she gloried in his lack of control. It had happened just the way she'd planned. Once she was in his arms, he wouldn't be able to deny his feelings, wouldn't be able to brush her off with lies. He wouldn't be able to pretend.

"Oh, Pietro," she whispered, "don't stop, don't ever stop."

He stopped.

Priscilla sighed with disappointment and frustration.

They were both breathing hard, and it seemed to require several moments for Pietro to compose himself.

"That shouldn't have happened," he said, his words taut with tension.

"I kissed you, remember? You did nothing improper."

"I kissed you back." He made it sound as if he should be dragged before a firing squad.

"Don't be ridiculous, I encouraged you. I wanted you to kiss me. You might think I'm being fanciful, but I knew in the beginning that you were going to be someone special in my life."

His face tensed as if he didn't want to hear what she had to say. "Priscilla..."

"You called me your love once. Remember?"

His eyes narrowed as if to say he'd give anything never to have uttered those words. "You don't understand about such things," he said stiffly.

"I understand everything I need to," she returned with a righteous tilt of her chin. "All my life everyone else—my parents, my teachers, everyone—have seemed to think they know what's best for me. And I listened. Well, no more!" She braced her hands against her hips.

"Perhaps you should discuss this with them."

"I'm going to discuss it with you."

"Priscilla..."

"Hear me out, please," she said, and as an inducement, she stood on the tips of her toes and gently brushed her lips over his. "I know now that you were lying when you said you weren't attracted to me. I'm not sure why you'd hide the truth, but that doesn't matter any longer, because I know everything now."

"About what?" Pietro challenged.

"Your feelings for me."

A sad, intense look came over him. "I find you to be an attractive, generous young woman."

"Do you often kiss attractive, generous young women the way you do me?" she challenged. She knew he didn't.

"No," he admitted reluctantly, "but then it isn't often that one throws herself into my arms."

Although he spoke without criticism, Priscilla could feel her cheeks filling with color. "What about the time before that?" she asked. "The night of the banquet. As I recall you were the one who kissed me."

"Yes, that's true but…"

Again she sensed his reluctance, his hesitation. "But what?" she prodded.

"I'm afraid I've given you the wrong impression," he murmured. "That was the night you were feeling ill and I was attempting to comfort you."

Priscilla wasn't about to accept that excuse, either. She laughed softly and shook her head. "You're going to have to come up with a better excuse than that. I may not be as worldly and sophisticated as some women, but I know the kisses we shared were far more potent than a couple of aspirin."

As if he needed to put some distance between them, Pietro returned to his desk. Priscilla claimed the chair on the other side. He reached for a pen and rolled it between his palms.

"Hurting your feelings would greatly distress me, but I don't feel I have much—"

"Then don't." Priscilla felt on a natural high from his kisses. Little he could say or do would discourage her now that she'd discovered the truth.

"Priscilla, you're making this difficult."

"That's the reason I'm here." She beamed him a wide smile. He hesitated and looked almost grateful when the phone rang.

"If you'll excuse me a moment."

"Of course. Do you want me to leave?" she asked, thinking he might prefer privacy.

"That won't be necessary," he said, reaching for the telephone.

From her position on the other side of the table, Priscilla knew the call must be important from the way Pietro straightened his shoulders. He reached for the appointment book and flipped through the pages.

From the gist of the conversation, Priscilla could tell that he was scheduling a meeting for Prince Stefano. She couldn't be sure who was on the other end of the line, but it seemed to be some United States government official.

Pietro's look was thoughtful when he replaced the receiver. His gaze lingered there for a moment before lifting and meeting hers.

"Now, where were we?"

"We were discussing us," she said brightly.

His frowned deepened. "I didn't know there was an *us*."

"All right, I'll rephrase that. We were discussing our feelings for each other."

"I thought I'd already explained that I find you to be an attractive, likable young woman, but that I don't have any strong feelings for you one way or the other."

"I don't believe that."

He gestured weakly with his hands. "I realize that I

might have given you *some* cause to think I was romantically interested in you. If that's the case, I apologize. You're a beautiful woman and I wanted to kiss you. A kiss is a little thing, don't you think?"

Priscilla blinked, her confidence shaken. "Yes, but there was a whole lot of emotion in those kisses...for me, at any rate."

"I'm honored beyond words that you find me attractive."

Find him attractive! The man didn't seem to have a clue that she was crazy in love with him. Perhaps he did, she decided, and he wanted to extract himself from the relationship as gracefully as he could.

"But," she said it for him, rather than wait.

"But you're young and impressionable, and I fear you've placed far more credence on the few times we kissed than is warranted. I don't mean to hurt you, but it would be cruel to continue in this vein."

From force of habit, she gnawed on her lower lip. "I apologize for causing you this embarrassment," she said, her pride giving her the strength she needed.

"It's not that," he said gently. "I'm honored that anyone as lovely as you would have these feelings for me."

"Yeah, right," she murmured and stood, eager now to make her escape. She turned and paused at the door. "I have an appointment with the prince tomorrow."

"That's correct."

"I'd appreciate it if I could be alone with him." In other words, she didn't want to see Pietro again.

"I'll see to it."

Her hand tightened around the doorknob and gathering

her resolve, she pivoted around to face him. Their gazes met and held as if in a great unspoken battle of wills.

"Before I leave, I want you to know something." Her voice trembled a bit and she paused until she could be certain it would stay even and unemotional. "You're lying and I know it. I'm not exactly sure why you're sending me away.... Actually it doesn't matter. I'll walk out this door and we'll probably never see each other again. You've made it clear that's the way you want it, and I have no choice but to accept your wishes.

"You almost convinced me you don't love me," she continued and her voice wavered slightly, "but you didn't convince my heart."

She felt the tears burning for release and knew she had to leave soon. "Good-bye, Pietro," she whispered, and with nothing more to say, calmly left. The door softly clicked closed behind her.

Stefano returned to the hotel emotionally depleted. He met Pietro in the hallway outside his private quarters and their eyes clashed.

Instead of retreating to his own quarters, Stefano moved into the larger room where he'd shared tea with Priscilla Rutherford. Pietro followed.

For a long time neither spoke.

Stefano wasn't prepared for the litany of irate questions regarding his whereabouts. Not this time. He felt as if he'd been wrenched apart and was in no mood for an interrogation. Gratefully Pietro appeared to understand this.

"I see you're back." Pietro spoke first. "Will you be leaving again anytime soon?"

"No." Pain tightened the area around his heart. "I'd like for you to arrange our departure as soon as possible. Tomorrow, if we can be accommodated." If anything, this should please Pietro, who'd been eager to return to San Lorenzo for the past several days.

"You have two appointments in the morning," his secretary informed him. "The first is with Priscilla Rutherford."

"Priscilla?"

"Yes, she stopped by this afternoon to schedule the meeting."

"But I saw her earlier in the day. She didn't mention anything then."

"I was curious myself, but she gave no indication of what she wanted to discuss, although she made it clear she preferred that the two of you speak in private."

This piqued Stefano's interest. "In private?"

Pietro nodded. "The second appointment is with a representative from the American State Department. The call came in this afternoon and he requested an audience. He said it was essential that he speak to you at your earliest convenience."

"Regarding?"

"Again there was no indication."

"I see." Stefano was curious, but with other matters on his mind—mainly Hope—he didn't give the appointment much deliberation. Soon he'd be back in San Lorenzo. There he would find his peace. There he would have less difficulty accepting his duty. There he'd be surrounded by all that would remind him of his responsibilities to his country and his people.

"Would you like your dinner sent up?" Pietro asked, breaking into his thoughts.

"Dinner," Stefano repeated, then shook his head. "No, thanks, I don't seem to have much of an appetite." He walked toward the window, wanting the conversation to be over so he could escape.

"Will that be all for this evening, then?" Pietro inquired.

"Yes," Stefano said evenly.

Stefano could hear his secretary hesitate. "Are you ill?"

Yes, his heart cried. "I'm fine." More than anything, he wanted to be left alone.

"Good evening, then."

"Good evening, my friend," Stefano whispered, and rubbed a weary hand down his face. His secretary left the room and, after a few moments, Stefano sank into a chair and waited for the darkness of night to claim the room and his heart.

In the morning, the suite bustled with activity as the entourage that had arrived with him prepared for the flight to San Lorenzo that evening. Never had Stefano been more eager to be on his way. As soon as he departed Seattle, his heart was free to mend. While he remained in the city, his every thought centered upon Hope.

Pietro came to him around ten and it looked as if his friend hadn't slept all night. He wondered what could be troubling his companion. In light of their recent differences, he didn't feel he could pry.

Pietro's eyes were bloodshot. If he didn't know better, he'd think his secretary had been drinking. It happened rarely and generally when Pietro had something to celebrate. If he were happy it certainly didn't show.

"The front desk phoned," Pietro annnounced. "Apparently Doris Jordan and a few of her friends have asked to see you. Actually, it's more of a demand."

Stefano hesitated, unsure if he was up to a confrontation with that group. Generally he was amused by their antics, but it would take more than four romantics to entertain him this day.

"Should I have them sent away?"

Stefano hadn't the heart for that. "No." He would prefer to avoid a confrontation, but he found he couldn't refuse the fearsome foursome. "Send them up," he instructed reluctantly.

"I could meet with them, if you wish." Pietro checked his watch. "Priscilla Rutherford will be arriving momentarily."

The generosity of Pietro's offer to deal with Hope's mother surprised Stefano. "I'll keep the time in mind," he assured his secretary.

Within a matter of minutes four women marched into his suite as if they were looking to draw blood. Hope's mother, who'd swooned when she'd learned she held the winning ticket, looked anything but fragile. Her eyes sparkled with outrage.

"We want to know what you've done to Hope."

"Please sit down, ladies," Stefano instructed.

"We'll stand, thank you very much," Doris announced righteously.

The footman arrived just then, carrying a silver tea service. Another followed with a display of delicate pastries. Both were set on the table. The two footmen stood back and folded their hands behind their backs.

"Perhaps we have time for tea," the one Stefano remembered as Hazel said, tugging at Doris's shirtsleeve.

"Aren't those petits fours?" she asked as her voice dipped. "We might have been a bit hasty, don't you think?"

"Since the prince has clearly gone to all this trouble, I think we should stay for tea," one of the others whispered.

Stefano hadn't the heart to tell them the tea had been arranged for Priscilla Rutherford.

"First answer me one thing, young man," Doris said heatedly.

In all his life, Stefano couldn't once remember being called "young man." "Of course," he said, as formally as he could, without smiling.

"I want to know why my daughter spent the entire night in tears. She wouldn't say a word, but I know it has to do with you. What have you done to her? That poor girl's suffering with a broken heart, and nothing you say can convince me otherwise. She won't even speak to me — her own mother."

"That's not the only thing," Hazel said, wagging her finger as if she were keeping time with the music. "We aren't old fools, you know. Something's been going on between the two of you ever since the night of your date."

"I want to know about the scarf she claims she got from Elvis!" Doris demanded.

"Elvis?"

The four women broke into excited chatter all at once.

"Hope Jordan?" It was Pietro's voice that cut through

the prattle. His eyes linked with Stefano's and he watched as his secretary seemed to put everything together in his mind.

"Ladies, ladies," Pietro said, "I'm sorry to cut your visit so short, but the prince has an appointment in five minutes."

"But the tea…" Hazel cast an appreciative eye toward the plateful of delectable pastries.

"I don't think those were for us," Doris said, under her breath.

There was a chorus of disappointed sighs.

"Whatever questions you have for the prince can be directed to me," Pietro said. "If you'll come to my office, perhaps we can sort all this out."

Stefano shouldn't have been so grateful to be rescued from painful explanations, but it was a sign of how battered and spent he felt.

A short ten minutes later, Priscilla Rutherford was escorted into the suite. Clearly there was some sort of malady that had affected everyone, because he couldn't recall ever seeing anyone look more unhappy. She, too, had apparently spent the night pacing the floor. The circles around her eyes were dark, and even expertly applied cosmetics couldn't hide the sadness he sensed in her.

"Please sit down," he said gesturing toward the davenport.

She shook her head. "No, thank you. This will only take a moment."

Stefano remained standing because she did. "Have I done something to offend you?" he asked, wondering at her strange mood.

She shook her head. He noticed the nervous way she rubbed her palms together. "I've spent a good portion of the time since we had brunch yesterday speaking to my parents. I'm afraid they're rather upset with me at the moment, but they'll recover." She seemed to reach some kind of conclusion. "For that matter," she added sadly, "so will I."

"I'm afraid I don't understand."

"I don't expect you will." All at once it seemed she needed to sit down because she slowly lowered herself into a chair.

"Priscilla, are you feeling all right?"

She smiled weakly. "If you want the truth, I've never felt worse."

"Is there anything I can do?"

She looked down and shook her head. "I wish there was, but unfortunately there isn't."

He waited for several moments for her to speak, then prompted her. "You asked to see me?"

She nodded and slowly raised her eyes to his. "I think you're probably the most attractive man I've ever met."

"Thank you." He didn't like the sound of this. Generally, such compliments were followed by words he found to his disliking.

"No man has ever paid me the attention you have. On a bright note, you've made my mother a happy woman. My father thinks you're the best thing since sourdough bread and frankly, I don't know if either one of my parents intends on speaking to me ever again."

"What could you have done that's so terrible?" Stefano

pressed gently. Priscilla was as nervous as a filly, and he feared she'd burst into tears at any moment.

She folded her hands together as if she were about to pray. "I could see the handwriting on the wall," she said, studying her fingers as though the script were written out for her there. "Mom and Dad were hearing wedding bells and I'm afraid the sound of them drowned out all reason."

"How's that?"

"You see, I like you and everything and…well, if we got to know each other a little better, we'd probably become good friends, but I don't love you."

"Love is something that's nurtured," Stefano explained thoughtfully. "After the wedding, I feel we'd develop a deep friendship, in time."

Priscilla's eyes widened perceptively. "It's true, then?" she whispered as though he'd somehow shocked her.

"What's true?"

"That you were serious about…marrying me."

He nodded. "My thoughts had been running along those lines."

"My heavens." She leapt to her feet and then just as quickly sat down again. "You see, I told my parents you had no such intentions."

"All in good time, Priscilla. I didn't intend to rush you."

"But you see, I don't want to marry you."

Funny as it seemed, her reluctance to take him as a husband had never occurred to him. There could only be one reason. "There's someone else?"

Her head bent lower, before she slowly raised her eyes to meet his. He saw in her a pain he hadn't earlier, a pain that was a reflection of his own. "There was," she admitted in a choked whisper. "But he doesn't share my feelings."

"The man is a fool."

She was saved from explaining further by Pietro who abruptly stepped into the room. His gaze honed toward Priscilla as if drawn by a powerful magnet. For a breathless moment they stared at each other, and then as though by remote control, they both looked away.

"Excuse me," Pietro murmured apologetically.

"You wanted to see me?" Stefano asked.

"It can wait." He left as hastily as he'd arrived.

Stefano watched his friend and then looked to Priscilla. She'd composed herself, but in that instant he knew the man the heiress loved, the one she wanted over him, was none other than his own secretary.

Nine

Priscilla was in love with Pietro. Stefano couldn't believe that he could have been so obtuse. The evidence was all there for him to see. Poor Pietro. No wonder his secretary had been surly and short-tempered of late. Pietro had been caught between loyalty and friendship, trapped in a no-win proposition. If Stefano hadn't been so blinded by his love for Hope, he might have been able to help them both.

Priscilla studied him, and Stefano realized he was staring at the door, after his secretary. "I appreciate your honesty," he said thoughtfully, his mind working hard and fast. "Would you excuse me a moment?"

"Of course."

"Make yourself comfortable. I'll be back momentarily."

Stefano made a hasty exit and went in search of Pietro. He found his companion in his office. "You wanted to see me?" Stefano asked.

"Has Miss Rutherford left?" It seemed Pietro's gaze

bore straight through him, as if he were holding himself in tight resolve until he could be certain Priscilla had gone.

"She's waiting for me," Stefano announced and plopped himself down on the chair. "We have a problem," he announced as though the weight of this latest development were more than he could bear.

"A problem with Priscilla?"

"Yes," Stefano confirmed. "She's afraid her family is going to manipulate her into marrying me. This is the reason for her visit. She's come to explain that, although she thinks highly of me, she'd rather not be my wife. Can you believe that! The woman has no idea she's ruined our plans."

Pietro's frown deepened.

"To complicate matters, she claims she's in love with someone else—or so she says. I pried, but she wouldn't talk about him. But from what little she did tell me, she cares deeply for this other man. The cad!"

Pietro ignored the last remark. "I'm sure that in time Miss Rutherford's feelings will change. She'll grow to love you."

"We don't have the time to wait around to be sure that happens." Keeping a straight face was becoming something of a chore, but Stefano managed. "The situation is grave—you know that as well as I do."

"True." Pietro shifted uneasily in his chair.

"It's clear to me that her parents are keen on the idea of their daughter becoming my princess."

"They wouldn't object to a union between the two of you," his secretary agreed stoically.

"My thoughts precisely." Prince Stefano beamed his friend a wide grin. "That's why I believe there's only one solution to all this." He gestured with his hands, expressing his exasperation with the whole business. "We're going to need to kidnap her, and force her into marrying me."

"What!" Pietro vaulted to his feet. "You can't be serious."

"We don't have any choice. Priscilla assured me she's in love with someone else, but when I pressed her, she admitted that this other man didn't return her feelings. That being the case, we really can't allow her to throw her life away."

"Aren't you being a bit dramatic?"

"I thought that at first, but the longer we talked, the more I realized how serious she is. Priscilla's prepared to wait for this…scoundrel to come to his senses, and if he doesn't, then, well, she never intends to marry."

"She told you that?" Pietro's frown was dark and brooding.

"Why else would I be telling you this?"

His secretary wiped his hand over his eyes in a gesture of fatigue. "You can't be serious about kidnapping Priscilla."

"Desperate times call for desperate measures," the prince returned flippantly.

Pietro's fists knotted at his sides. "I won't allow it."

Stefano arched his brows in fabricated shock. "Not allow it?" he repeated slowly.

"There are laws against such matters."

"Fiddlesticks. After a month or two, Priscilla will have

forgotten about the man she thinks she loves. She'll be grateful that I had the foresight to arrange our wedding. Given the circumstances, I believe her family will fully cooperate with the idea." He paused and waited for Pietro's reaction.

"I want no part of this."

"Oh, I wasn't asking you to collaborate. I was just bouncing the idea off you."

His gaze focused away from Stefano. "This is by far the most outrageous thing you've ever suggested. Are you foolish enough to believe she'll forgive you for something so underhanded?"

"It won't matter if she forgives me or not. We both know this isn't a love match. I need her money, not her." He made his voice as frigid and calculating as possible.

Pietro's eyes narrowed to points of steel. "You're a coldhearted son of a—" He stopped himself in time to keep from swearing.

Stefano pretended to be shocked. "Why should you care? From what you claimed, your resignation will be in effect as soon as we return to San Lorenzo. You won't be around to witness any of this."

"I care," Pietro snapped.

"Apparently not enough," Stefano returned casually. He leaned back in the chair and crossed his legs.

"I was the one who chose Priscilla. You don't seriously believe I'd sit back and allow you to follow through with this preposterous idea of yours, do you?"

"Frankly, Pietro, I don't understand your objection."

"It doesn't matter if you understand it or not. I refuse to allow you to abuse Priscilla. She's warm and loving.

Heaven knows she deserves better than to be treated like an object with no feelings, no heart."

The angry words fell into the silence. This was what Stefano had been waiting to hear, what he'd been waiting for his friend to admit. "Isn't that what you were planning to do?" he asked starkly. "Abandon her to a loveless marriage?"

Pietro glared at him as if he didn't understand.

"It's you she loves, you fool, not me," Stefano said smoothly. "And, no, she didn't tell me. She didn't need to. I saw the way the two of you looked at each other just now. The woman's crazy about you, Pietro, and any fool could see you feel the same way about her."

"But—"

"I believe we've already been through this argument," Stefano cut in. "She has no intention of ever marrying me. I believe she said she'd like to consider me a friend."

Pietro said nothing for several seconds, then slowly lowered himself back into the chair. "I apologize, Stefano. When I realized Priscilla was attracted to me, I did what I could to discourage her."

"Don't apologize. It's more clear to me than ever that the two of you are far better suited than Priscilla and I would ever be. You'll make her a better husband. A woman deserves a man who deeply loves her. Don't you agree?"

It took Pietro a long time to answer. "What about you?"

Stefano laughed softly. "The only thing that's injured is my ego, and that was only dented. I'll manage, and so will San Lorenzo, at least for now."

Something would need to be done to secure his country's finances, but he didn't want to think about that. Somehow he'd find a way to manage. His country had survived seven hundred years of war and plague. A little thing like financial ruin didn't seem so daunting. He'd survive without Hope, just as his country would survive without Priscilla Rutherford's money.

Priscilla shifted her weight in the chair and glanced at her watch. Stefano had already been gone several minutes, and she wasn't keen on waiting much longer. Everything she'd come to say had already been said. She hoped she hadn't hurt the prince's feelings, and frankly she wasn't willing to argue. She wouldn't marry him, or anyone, to gain her parents' approval.

The door opened from behind her just when she'd decided the best course of action was for her to silently slip away, and hope no one noticed.

"Priscilla."

It was Pietro, and the sound of his voice, saying her name in that special way of his, was enough to cause her heart to painfully constrict.

She stood and braced herself, knowing she'd need to be strong. "Hello, Pietro. Where's the prince?"

"Please sit down."

"Is the prince coming?" She looked behind him, thinking it would be much easier to maintain her composure with Stefano in the room. Otherwise, she feared she'd do something to make an even greater fool of herself than she had already.

"No," Pietro said starkly. "The prince won't be returning."

"I...see." She didn't, but it was difficult to concentrate. Slowly she sat back down, and fiercely clenched her hands together.

He claimed the chair the prince had vacated, and leaned forward slightly. "You were correct when you said I lied," he said after a tension-filled moment.

Priscilla frowned, thinking he was about to apologize for some unconfessed sin. She looked away, not having the heart for this. "It doesn't matter, Pietro."

"That's where you're wrong. It does matter. You're right, I love you, and little in this world would make me happier than for you to be my wife."

Nothing he might have said could have shocked or outraged her more. "You love me!"

"That's what I just said." He was smiling and his eyes sparked with happiness.

"You love me and...and yet you were willing to let me walk out of your life?"

"Yes," he admitted reluctantly. "Although I swear by all that is holy, it was the most difficult thing I've ever done."

"But why? Because you believed Stefano was in love with me? That's ridiculous and we both know it."

"Priscilla," he said gently, coming off the chair. He got down on one knee before her, and captured both her hands in his. "We can argue about my foolishness for many years to come if you wish. For now, all I need is your answer to my proposal. Will you be my wife?"

It greatly perturbed Priscilla that at the most important moment of her life tears would fill her eyes and blur out Pietro's face. She wiped the moisture from her face and sniffled. "There's something you should know first."

"Yes?"

"I...I have ugly feet."

Pietro burst out laughing, which was not what she'd intended for him to do. She was serious. She didn't object, however, when his arms circled her waist and he kissed her with a hunger and longing that matched her own.

"Pietro," she whispered between kisses, "you're a fool."

"Never again, my love, never again."

Ten

Stefano found a certain solace in his homeland. One that helped ease the ache in his heart. He didn't expect the longing for Hope to fade completely, and so he savored the memories of her and the all-too-short time they'd shared. Like a young boy who buries a secret treasure, Stefano clung to the memory of Hope Jordan, the woman who'd stolen his heart.

The entire country of San Lorenzo was abloom in mid-August. Although Stefano tried not to think about Hope, he found her creeping uninvited into his dreams. She came to him a vision of warmth and beauty in his sleep, when his defenses were lowered and he hadn't the strength of will to resist.

Almost always they were at Hurricane Ridge, as they'd been the last time they were together. She'd collect a bouquet of wildflowers to bring to him, her face bright with love, her eyes filled with promises he'd never collect.

Although Stefano had vowed never to contact her

again, he'd hired a detective agency to report back to him with their findings. It was vital that he learn she was getting on with her life and that she was happy.

From what he'd learned, that was true. Hope's coffee delivery business was thriving, and the last and final report he'd received said that she was dating. Stefano had suffered the agonies of the damned, wondering about the young man she was seeing.

The prince hadn't returned to Seattle for Pietro's wedding to Priscilla Rutherford. The temptation to see Hope would have been far too strong, and he'd given her his word that he would forever stay out of her life. He'd honored his promise, but at a costly price.

Priscilla and Pietro's wedding was said to have been the social event of the year. Dignitaries from around the world had attended the festivities. From what the prince understood, the happy couple were honeymooning in Australia. Stefano wished the two every happiness.

"Your Highness." His newly hired assistant, Peter Hiat, timidly interrupted him. "Mr. Myers is here to see you."

"Ah, yes," Stefano said. "Please show him in."

Stefano stood at his desk while the other man was escorted into his private office. He'd met briefly with Steven Myers shortly before he left Seattle. Myers's purpose had to do with a proposal from the United States government regarding leasing land in San Lorenzo. Because of the emotional upheaval of those last hours in Seattle, Stefano had suggested the State Department contact him again, after he'd returned home.

When Stefano didn't hear immediately back again, he

had assumed the project was no longer of any interest to the United States.

"Prince Stefano," Steven Myers said as he walked into the office. "I appreciate your time."

"Please sit down." He gestured toward the chair.

Myers sat and lifted a briefcase onto his lap. "Thank you for seeing me."

"The pleasure is mine. What can I do for you?"

"I've come to make San Lorenzo an offer you can't refuse," Myers said with a broad smile.

Four hours later, Stefano felt as though he were walking on air. The United States, whom Myers reminded him, had always been San Lorenzo's friend, had come seeking a favor. They were looking to establish an air base in San Lorenzo. The government of the United States was offering his country more money than Stefano had ever dreamed possible. Naturally, the decision wasn't his to make alone, but the positive side of the proposal far outweighed the negative. All it would take was a simple parliamentary vote to gain approval.

His country was saved.

Once the relief hit him, Stefano's first thought was to contact Hope and ask her to be his bride. His princess. He loved and needed her.

Then he remembered his promise to stay out of her life forever. Already she'd found another. Already she had forgotten him.

"So," Lindy said, slumping into a chair, "you going out with Cliff again this evening?"

"I wish you wouldn't make it sound like he's the love

of my life. He's my cousin," Hope explained for the tenth time that day.

"I know you're related," Lindy said, biting into one of her own low-fat muffins, "but getting out again has done you a world of good. I've been worried about you lately."

This was territory Hope didn't want to traverse. Not with her friend. Especially since her own mother had been treating her as though she had a case of the measles instead of a broken heart.

Hazel and her mother's other friends were equally certain their efforts would aid Hope's recovery. They brought her jars of freshly pickled corn relish, in addition to working on a hope chest, filling it with items she'd need when she found "that special man" who would make her forget all about Prince Stefano.

As much as she loved them all, Hope felt smothered. When Cliff, a distant cousin on her father's side, arrived in town, she leapt at the opportunity to break away from the condolences being heaped upon her, and spend some time with him.

"Has Cliff found an apartment yet?" Lindy asked, carefully peeling the paper bottom off the muffin.

"I helped him move this weekend."

"Ah." Lindy's eyes avoided hers.

"What makes you ask?" Hope inquired.

Briefly, Lindy looked up and then shrugged. "No reason."

"He enjoyed the apple pie you sent over."

"He did?" Lindy's gaze widened. "Why didn't you say something sooner?"

Hope laughed and propped her feet on the seat of the

chair opposite her. "I wanted to see how long it would take you to ask."

"Hope! That's cruel."

"He asked about you, too."

"He did?"

"Yep, but I told him to look for greener pastures."

"Hope, you didn't. Tell me you didn't!"

Hope laughed. "I didn't. In fact, I gave him your phone number and he told me he'd be calling you this evening."

"He only met me the one time…." Lindy's hands nervously set aside the muffin.

"You made quite an impression on him. Then again, it might have been the apple pie," she said, giggling. It felt good to laugh again. She hadn't had much reason to laugh of late, but she was learning.

The bell above the door to the coffee shop sounded and Hope plopped her feet onto the floor. "I'll get that," she mumbled. This was the first break Lindy had taken all morning, and Hope didn't want her friend to wait on walk-in customers. Not when the kitchen demanded so much of her time.

"Hello," Hope greeted the smiling young woman. She looked vaguely familiar, but Hope couldn't place her. "Can I get you something?"

"You don't know me," the other woman said, extending her hand. "I'm Priscilla Rutherford—or rather, that was my name. I recently married Pietro. You know him as Prince Stefano's secretary."

Hope's body froze. *Not now,* she silently begged. *Please not now. Not when I'm just getting my life back together. Not when I've convinced myself I can be happy without him.*

"How can I help you?" she asked once more, stiffly this time, protecting her heart as best she could.

Priscilla smiled gently. "You can't. Pietro and I are here to help you."

Three weeks following their marriage, Pietro and Priscilla arrived home at the palace.

"Pietro," Stefano shouted when he first saw his friend. He rose from behind his desk and the two men exchanged hearty hugs. Stefano briefly kissed Priscilla's cheek. It amazed him how radiantly beautiful the heiress looked. Apparently, married life agreed with them both. Pietro had never looked better.

"I thought you two were on your honeymoon," he said, ringing for the footman, and ordering a tray of coffee to be sent up.

"We cut it short," Pietro explained. Husband and wife sat next to each other, holding hands. "We read about the agreement between San Lorenzo and the United States," Pietro explained. "It made the Australia newspapers. It's true isn't it, about the air base?"

"Yes." Stefano beamed Pietro a smile. "We're more than pleased. The parliament voted on the proposal in record time, and construction is scheduled to begin on the project after the first of the month."

"Congratulations."

"I'm grateful for the turn of events." Which was an understatement only Pietro could fully appreciate.

"What about the wedding?"

Stefano stared at his friend. "Wedding? Whose wedding?"

"Pietro," Priscilla said softly, casting a disapproving

glance toward her husband, "you're going to ruin the surprise."

"Surprise?" Stefano was beginning to feel like a parrot, repeating everything said.

"We brought you back something from our honeymoon," Pietro explained. "Would you like to see it?"

"In a minute," Stefano said. He was more eager to talk to the two. He'd deeply missed his friend. His newly hired secretary was efficient and organized, but he lacked Pietro's skill in several areas, the least of which was the sword. It'd been weeks since Stefano had been challenged. Never had he felt more alone than in the past month without Pietro at his side.

"Tell me about the wedding," Stefano instructed.

The footman delivered a silver tray with a pot of coffee and three cups. Priscilla poured, while chatting.

"First off, Mother and I had quite a discussion. She wanted a wedding that would rival something coming out of Buckingham Palace."

"It didn't help matters," Pietro said, smiling at his wife, "that you had me knighted before the wedding. Elizabeth felt that if Priscilla was going to marry a knight, she should have a wedding fit for a queen."

"Despite everything, the wedding was lovely," Priscilla assured him.

"We missed you, however," Pietro said.

"My mother was convinced you didn't attend the wedding because I'd broken your heart by choosing Pietro over you."

"That's very nearly true," Stefano returned, and shared a secret smile with his former secretary. "Now, what is it you're so eager to show me?"

"Shall we make him close his eyes?" Priscilla asked her husband.

"I don't think that's a good idea." Pietro stood and walked over to the large double door and disappeared momentarily. When he returned, Stefano was convinced he'd lost his mind—he couldn't believe what he saw.

Hope Jordan stepped into the room and smiled serenely at him.

"Hope." He rasped her name as if he were saying a prayer, pleading to the powers on high.

"Hello, Stefano."

He couldn't believe how lovely she was. Had he forgotten so much about her, so soon? It was as though she were a vision, a figment of his imagination.

"You might want to ask her to sit down," Pietro prodded.

"Of course. Forgive me."

"Pietro, don't you think we should leave these two alone for a few minutes?" The sound of Priscilla's voice drifted to Stefano but it seemed as if it were coming from a great distance.

"I suppose.... We'll be waiting in the rose garden," Pietro said as he followed his new bride out the door. Stefano barely heard his friend.

Each one of his senses was centered on Hope. "I wasn't sure I should come," she said, and for the first time he realized she was ill at ease.

"Not come?" He sat across from her.

"I wasn't sure your feelings for me hadn't changed."

"They haven't. You hold my heart in the palm of your hand. You always will."

She lowered her head and he noted the nervous way in which she nibbled at her lower lip. "You didn't contact me. Not even after you learned about the air base. I'd never have come to San Lorenzo if it hadn't been for Pietro and Priscilla."

"I'd given you my word of honor that I'd never see you again."

"But that was when you were planning to marry Priscilla Rutherford. That was when there was no future for the two of us. I thought...when I learned about the air base, what else could I think but that...well, that I'd been a passing fancy who'd amused you while you were in Seattle."

"Hope, no. Never that." He'd hurt her so much already, knowing he'd caused her additional pain brought a surge of bitter regret.

"Then why didn't you come for me?"

It wasn't easy to admit what he'd done. "I learned you were dating, and felt it was best to let you get on with your life. I'd hurt you already."

"You learned I was dating! Who told you that?" She sounded agitated, as well she should.

"I'm not proud of this...but you need to understand my state of mind. I hired a detective agency to check up on you." He drew in a deep breath and held it for fear she'd never forgive him for invading her privacy. "I had to know that you were well...I couldn't have gone on without that peace of mind."

"Oh, Stefano..."

He couldn't resist holding her a moment longer. He gathered her in his arms and absorbed the feel of her, her softness, her gentleness. Her love. For weeks Stefano had felt as if he were adrift on a wide ocean with no land in sight. He'd suffered deeply, believing Hope had found another man. He'd been torn in different directions, seeking her happiness above his own.

They kissed and it was as it had always been between them. Soon his hands were in her hair and he was drinking in the taste of her, the feel of her.

"Promise me you'll never leave me again," Hope asked.

"On one condition." He kissed her, not giving her time to respond for a long, long time.

"Anything you ask," she said with a sigh between deep, slow kisses.

"Marry me. Stand by my side the rest of my life. Be my princess."

"I'll need to think about it," she whispered. Stefano lifted his head, surprised by her response. She smiled up at him, wove her fingers into his thick hair and laughed softly, before bringing his mouth back to hers. "I thought about it."

"And?" With a great deal of restraint, he held his lips a mere inch away from hers.

"And, the answer's yes. A thousand times yes." Stefano let out a triumphant cry, wrapped his arms around Hope's waist and whirled her around. It was a fitting gesture, since she'd sent his world spinning from the first moment he'd seen her. He had a sneaking suspicion this was one joyride that was never going to end. The Bachelor Prince had met his match. His mate for a lifetime.

* * * * *

Loved this book?

Visit Debbie Macomber's fantastic website at
www.debbiemacomber.com for information
about Debbie, her latest books, news,
competitions, knitting tips, recipes,
Debbie's blog and much more…

Find even more Debbie Macomber extras at
Facebook.com/DebbieMacomberWorld

www.debbiemacomber.com

A love that lasts a lifetime…

When Julia Conrad is faced with the prospect
of losing her company or marrying Aleksandr
Berinksi, she knows there is only one option.
Marrying the Russian biochemist will keep
him in the US and it's only a marriage of
convenience…that is until love starts
to get in the way!

Make time for friends
Make time for Debbie Macomber

HARLEQUIN® MIRA®

Bringing you the best voices in fiction
@Mira_booksUK